# The
# OYSTERCATCHER
# *of* SOUTHWARK

# *The* OYSTERCATCHER *of* SOUTHWARK

ERICA COLAHAN

CHRISM
PRESS

This is a work of fiction. All characters and events portrayed in this novel are either fictitious or used fictitiously.

THE OYSTERCATCHER OF SOUTHWARK

Copyright © 2024, Erica Colahan
All rights reserved. Reproduction in part or in whole is strictly forbidden without the express written consent of the publisher.

Chrism Press, a division of
WhiteFire Publishing
13607 Bedford Rd NE
Cumberland, MD 21502

ISBN: 979-8-88709-042-9 (print)
   979-8-88709-043-6 (digital)

*For Phylis, who found us.*

*"Come away, O human child!
To the waters and the wild
With a faery, hand in hand,
For the world's more full of weeping
than you can understand."*
–William Butler Yeats, "The Stolen Child"
From *Crossways* (1889)

"The American Oystercatcher is a large, unmistakable shorebird…that solely specializes in oysters, clams, mussels, and other shellfish… Historically, the eastern population of birds was abundant until the late 1800s when they are thought to have been extirpated (made locally extinct) in much of the region as a result of over-zealous market hunting and egg collecting."
~ E. Sharron,
*Species Spotlight - American Oystercatcher,*
National Park Service

# PROLOGUE

*August 1897*
*Delaware River*
*Southwark, Philadelphia*

Mary knew fear was a living thing. It had been walking alongside her now for days, like an old friend. Looking over her shoulder for the hundredth time, she pulled her oldest child close and stuffed the red rosary into the girl's chubby hands. "In case we get separated." Mollie nodded, her solemn eyes locked on her mother's, and pocketed the trinket.

A pang of guilt ran through Mary's heart. This experience had forced her five-year-old daughter to grow up too fast, but that was the least of her worries. They had to keep moving. Her knee buckled as she labored under the weight of her baby. "Augh!"

Mollie and Sarah looked at their mother, and Mendel stirred in her arms. "Isn't the monster far behind us, *Muter*? Can't we rest awhile?"

Mary couldn't answer. People feared monsters, of course, but they didn't understand. Fear itself was the monster. It could leave you paralyzed—forcing you to stand witness to your own impending destruction—or it could propel you into fierce and reckless action.

The city's tallest buildings cast long shadows across the river as daylight drew to a close. They were getting closer to the center of town now—she could smell it. The muddy odor of the Delaware had followed Mary and the children all the way from Bristol. But now, the stench of rotting fish, sewage, and garbage rising from the city dump made Mary's nostrils flare and eyes water.

It would be dark soon. They were almost home.

The little group had kept hidden along the tree line at the river's edge for miles. The closer they got to Southwark, the more conspicuous they became against the piers and wharves that replaced the wooded riverbank. The thought of discovery made Mary's stomach churn.

It was only a matter of time until Rocco Monza caught up with her and the children. How could he not? After a long night of fitful sleep in tight quarters, they were exhausted, scared, and hungry. The groundskeeper at Andalusia had been kind, but he was no magician. Though he'd tried to make them as comfortable as possible, he couldn't pull a kosher meal out of a black hat. They hadn't eaten since the day before yesterday. Mollie's stomach growled.

"Keep walking, Mollie, dear." Mary mustered a weak smile of encouragement and pushed her daughter's grimy kerchief back over her dark curls. "We're almost there."

"My toe hurts. Where are we going, Muter?"

"Home, my dove. We're going home."

"Will Papa be waiting for us?"

"Hush, not so loud, Sarah. No, Papa went away to search for work, remember? We're going home to *my* Papa, your grandfather."

"But I don't know him. Will he know me?"

"I pray so, darling. I pray so."

Mary's steps grew labored and deliberate. Her knees ached from carrying Mendel, and the small of her back burned. But the pain wasn't what slowed Mary's pace. It was the fear that, after five long years, Papa wouldn't welcome them. What if the door to her beloved home on South Sixth Street were closed to them in their time of distress? Rocco would find them and do whatever he pleased with them.

Mary sat down hard on the sandy ground, and the girls gathered around her. She looked up at the darkening sky. *Where are you, God?*

The little ones rested in her lap as Mary turned her face to the river. Cool air touched her cheeks, and she heard a foghorn in the distance. Her exhausted mind began to wander.

She remembered a time in Italy when she'd fallen during her customary evening stroll with Papa. Her stockings had caught on a nail protruding from a post, and she had skinned her knee. Her five-year-old heart had wanted to be brave but instead she howled when she saw blood blossom on the yarn of her thick white hose. Papa had picked her up and held her close, whispering soft comforts into her ear. His firm, loving embrace had calmed her.

And now she'd traded Papa's love and protection—for what? For the passion of a man who'd left her, who'd gambled away her happiness and their children's safety.

"Jakob, how could you do this to us?" Mary shook her fist at the sky.

She'd been a fool to come back here—to Rocco's turf. *But where else could I go?*

The panic she'd fought to conquer traveled up Mary's spine, and her imagination kicked into full gear. A thick mist crept up the shore toward her and the children. Suddenly, long, thin fingers reached for her ankles from the river's depths. A darkness surrounded her, clung to her body, and seeped into her pores. The vapor swirled around her, forming shapes before her eyes—a tree, a bridge, a bird, all dancing through the haze.

She had to wake the children and get them out of there. Mary tried to jump up, but her feet seemed rooted to the ground. On her knees, she positioned herself between the mist and her sleeping offspring, stretching her arms to defend her children against the evil air.

Then she heard a voice in the darkness.

*You don't deserve your father's love and protection,* it whispered. *You forfeited that right long ago. You know of what I speak. You made the choices that brought you here. You can blame no one for your plight—not your father, Jakob, or Rocco.*

Mary put her head in her hands, tears dripping onto the sandy soil. "That's not true!"

*Yes, it is. You have no options. Rocco will find you here. He'll kill your children, you know. How easy would it be to end the pain here, in the Delaware, on your own terms?*

Mary gasped, shaking her head in defiance.

The voice continued its accusations. *You've thought of suicide before—don't deny it.*

She was so tired of running. So tired of being strong. She could finally be free of Rocco, anxiety, and pain. Mary gazed across the surface of the river. The fear she'd kept at bay sat beside her, caressing her shoulder. Her heart raced as she considered the voice's terrible, alluring proposition.

"No!" She shook herself out of the daze. "No, I could never do such a thing. There must be another way."

Mary sat up straight and took a deep breath. Her heartbeat returned to normal. The mist began to recede, then dissipated. She dug deep into her resolve, her mind calming with each second. *I must protect my children.* They were rousing now, awakened by her declaration. Mendel made a squeaking sound that reverberated against Mary's ribs. Her babies. If only for them, she had to push on.

Then she found it—her faith. It hadn't been far away.

It was night now. Mary looked away from the river toward town where lights shone like beacons in the buildings near city hall. Not too far to go. With great effort, she stood up, Mendel still snuggled in the sling. Brushing the sand off her skirt, she gave each girl an encouraging pat on the head.

Hearing the *kleep kleep* of a sea bird, Mary squinted to see a shadow closing in on a shell not two feet away from her. An oystercatcher—her namesake. She could picture the twinkle in Cenzo's eyes when he'd called her by that nickname, and her heart filled with courage. The rare bird had survived the threat of extinction, and so would she. Mary smiled.

Then a figure emerged from the darkness.

*Rocco.*

# PART ONE
*Southwark*

# CHAPTER ONE

*The Arrival*

*June 1880*
*Delaware River*
*Southwark, Philadelphia*

Homesickness washed over Sebastian Paragano as soon as he stepped off the boat. His long legs wobbled, and his heart raced with the imminent need to find food, drink, and a place to piss. He was a wild bird, pushed out of its cozy nest for the first time, destined either to fly in glory or to fall to its death in a splatter of wings and feathers on the hard, unforgiving ground. As he looked around for something familiar amid a throng of dazed men, women, and whining children, he recognized the sound of someone speaking Italian.

"*Vieni qui!* Come here!" A deep voice. "Join up with the Valero brothers right away. We'll give you a home, a job. Join up! Italians, over here!"

Sebastian turned his narrow face toward the sound, dimly aware his feet were shuffling in that direction. Someone approached and asked, "Italian?" While Sebastian nodded, the large, barrel-chested man dusted off Sebastian's jacket, clapped him on the back with a meaty hand, and steered him toward the closest taproom. He sat Sebastian down at the bar and nodded to the barman, who set two glasses of amber liquid in front of them. Grateful, Sebastian smiled, and the two raised their glasses to each other.

"*Salute.*" They both downed the spirits in one gulp.

Sebastian's eyes bulged as he gave an explosive cough, pounded his thin chest, and shook his head like a dog coming out of water. What had he swallowed? Turpentine? The stranger laughed and waved his hand. "American whiskey," he explained.

Revived by the warmth spreading through his belly, Sebastian collected himself. "Who are you, and why would you help me?"

"Ah, my name is Rocco Monza—pleased to meet you." The stranger spoke in accented English. "Welcome to the real world, man. You need a place to stay, *si*? Well, I know of a place. You need a job, *si*? Well, I can have you working tomorrow at dawn." Despite Sebastian's skeptical expression, Rocco continued. "Sounds like a dream, no? Well, this is America. It *is* a dream, man. Hahaha!"

Some men on the boat had warned Sebastian to be wary of swindlers who tricked newcomers. He'd seen a few Italian beggars wheezing a street organ on the docks, a matted monkey on their backs—a degrading spectacle. He wished he were safe at home in Perdifumo with his sweet Florentina and the children, especially his daughter Mary. His heart was sore from missing them. But no, he mustn't give into melancholy. He had to prepare a place for them to live and provide enough funds for them to make the crossing. Maybe this—Rocco?—could show him the quickest way to accomplish this.

Sebastian nodded his head. "*Bene.* Tell me what to do."

That night, in a tiny attic room above a fish market, Sebastian tucked his few pieces of clothing into the drawer next to the washbasin. He laid out his meager belongings on the top of the dresser—his comb, rosary, and pocket watch, which had once belonged to his father. They were special talismans that conjured memories of his homeland. But his most prized possession was his cameo of Florentina. He reverently brought her image to his lips, then laid the memento down in the center of his collection. Once he finished this ritual, Sebastian lay on a straw mattress, his feet dangling off the end, and studied the cracks in the ceiling. After the drudgery of the long sea passage, he was alone for the first time in months. He stretched his exhausted body across the uneven, lumpy bed and released a deep sigh that reached down to his toes.

Tomorrow, Rocco would introduce him to a man he called "The

Duke," one William Valero. The title brought to Sebastian's mind the Italian politicians and their brutal tax system that kept his family hungry back in Salerno. Sebastian had risked everything to come here, to this new land, to escape such poverty. He and his wife had placed all their hopes on the opportunities in America. Had he already fallen prey to the same corrupt system the very minute he stepped off the boat?

Rocco said Sebastian would become a part of his band of street sweepers, which didn't sound too bad. He'd be outfitted with a white uniform, given a broom and a dust cart, and join a dozen other Italian men hired to clean the streets of Southwark. At least he wouldn't be reduced to begging on the streets with an organ. No, he'd rather wear a fine uniform and work for Rocco and his Duke. He imagined himself as part of a heavenly white-winged army marching down the broad road with brooms over their arms like soldiers. *Ack! I'm deceiving myself! I know what kind of army this is. It is a dark army, not a white army. I'll be selling my soul to the devil. What am I willing to do in exchange for money?* In answer, Sebastian imagined his beautiful wife in his arms, and his heart raced at the thought. He could almost smell her—the scents of almond and geranium filled his nostrils. *Oh, Florentina! How I long for you!* With the vision of his wife in mind, Sebastian fell sound asleep.

On his first morning in America, Sebastian awakened to the bustling sounds of the fish market below. The salty scent of oysters wafted through the little glassless window above the washbasin. He splashed water on his face, made use of the chamber pot, and brushed off his suit jacket—sniffing at the armpits to make sure it didn't stink. It did, but as he had no other coat, it would have to do. When Rocco rapped on the door, Sebastian followed him down the rickety staircase and onto the street.

And what a street it was! Pushcarts and buggies crisscrossed the road in every direction. Piles of horse dung and rubbish lined the curbs. The two men stood on the corner of Queen Street and Delaware Avenue, with the wharf to their right and the markets to their left. Over the sounds of industry all around him, Sebastian could hear the calls of hucksters selling their wares.

"Fruits! Vegetables! Fresh cut flowers! Cigars! Cigars!" Everywhere cigars. The miasma of smells overwhelmed his nose. Cabbage, manure, smoke from a nearby factory, steam from the train at the railroad a few blocks away, and—beneath it all—the pervasive smell of the muddy river and dead fish. At least a dozen fishmongers sold everything from freshwater catfish to sea oysters and clams.

While passing one such stall, Sebastian heard his name. He turned, astonished to see a familiar round face beaming at him in awe.

"Cenzo! Cenzo! Is it you? Can it be you?" Sebastian called to the happy man in the language of their birth. The man, Vincenzo Carpinelli, also of Perdifumo, Italy, was the youngest brother of the late Anthony Carpinelli, who'd been Sebastian's closest childhood friend. To run into Cenzo here, on his first morning in America, struck him as a good omen.

The two men grinned at each other, shook hands, and caught each other up on gossip. Rocco stood to the side but soon glanced at his pocket watch and cleared his throat.

"Oh, allow me to introduce you." Sebastian made introductions between the two men, but they seemed to know each other already. When Sebastian mentioned Valero in his explanation of their errand, Cenzo's smile froze.

Rocco gave a curt nod to Cenzo and gestured for Sebastian to move along. Sebastien shook his old friend's hand again, then gasped when Cenzo tightened his grip and pulled him close to whisper in his ear. "Go with care, *paesano*. Don't get involved with Rocco and the Duke, Valero. They will own your soul. There are other ways to make a living in this city, but once you get into their organization, you don't get out, *capisce?*"

Stunned, Sebastian nodded and, taking a reluctant leave of Cenzo, followed his new friend through the maze of city streets.

*Sebastian Paragano*
*Southwark, Phila*
*United States of America*

*June 18, 1880*


*Florentina Paragano*
*Perdifumo, Salerno*
*Campagnia, Italy*

*Dear Wife,*
*I am safe in Philadelphia, U.S.A. I am sound in body but troubled in spirit. I arrived yesterday and have already lived a lifetime apart from you. I am writing from a small rented room above a fish market next to the Delaware River, which separates Pennsylvania from its neighboring state, New Jersey. The river teems with boats and barges of all sizes and shapes, bringing wares up the tidal waters from the sea and hundreds of poor Italian souls like me.*
*The voyage was uneventful. My seasickness lifted on the second day. You and the children will be fine. Plan to pack the largest straw mattress—rest on it during the day and rotate sleeping on it at night. Oh, and I will need you to bring my best black vest. I left it in the trunk at the foot of our bed, dear.*
*You won't believe the extraordinary events that have happened to me. My old friend Vincenzo Carpinelli popped up like a marionette when I exited this room with a new acquaintance to secure a position. Yes, the same Carpinelli from Perdifumo! He is the fishmonger whose stall lies below me. Seeing a friendly face on my first morning in America made my heart swell. I hope it is a sign that we have pursued the right path in God's eyes. Please inform Signora Carpinelli her youngest son is flourishing in the new land.*
*The acquaintance I mentioned? (Yes, Tina, I'll tell*

*you. I can hear your questioning thoughts from across the ocean.) His name is Rocco Monza. He found me on the quay, where he recruits Italian men for work. Cenzo wasn't warm with him—I will be careful. He brought me before his boss today, one William Valero, who is called "The Duke" by his associates here in Southwark. This "Duke" is the youngest of three brothers who have been successful in this city and have created jobs for many Italian men like me. You should have seen his office, Tina! A grand and beautiful place with a large marble hearth and tufted couches. Dark wood covered the walls, and the Duke sat behind a massive desk. They offered me espresso, patted me on the back, and stuffed me into a gilt chair like a sultan.*

*Signor Valero offered me a job on the spot. I will earn good money and can send for you sooner than I thought possible. I need you by my side, dear Wife—you and the children. The Duke will sponsor me here, so to speak.*

*As part of my job contract, I can reside in the little room at the river until they provide a house for us. Si, you read that right, provided for us. Once I work a certain amount of time, and recruit a few Italian men for Rocco, the Duke will grant us a house. A house, Tina! Can you imagine? I can envision our grocery market on the bottom floor. We'll be able to make our own money and get out from under this system. Finally, we'll have the freedom to live as we please.*

*The price, you ask? Well, for now, I will be a part of his street sweeper gang. Signor Valero explained how the system works, you see, and now you know why I couldn't say no. I am to join his men on the streets of Southwark, to clean the streets, yes, of course, but also to be his "eyes and ears" on the ground, capisce? He has many enemies and needs to know their thoughts and movements. He also needs help encouraging people to cast their votes for him, a Republican, and those he sponsors in the upcoming election.*

*When I opened my mouth to protest, Valero shoved in a cigar, and Rocco's big hands clamped down on my shoulders in a benediction. I am to be outfitted with a white uniform and sent out with his team of street sweepers first thing tomorrow.*

*Don't think poorly of me, my dear. I do this for you. I'd do anything for you—for the children. How else could I save enough money to bring you all here? Give my love to them, especially my little nightjar, Mary.*

*Yours,*
*Sebastian*

Sebastian put down the pen and rubbed the fingers of his right hand. As a boy, the nuns in the village school in Perdifumo had rapped their rulers across the knuckles of his left hand and forced him to write with the "correct" one, as if the left were a sinful appendage and not to be trusted with a pen. Writing to his wife was worth the pain, though.

He missed his home in Italy. Salerno was a quiet region, with simple villages scattered throughout the hills. A pretty place, but one with no future for the fourth son of a large family. He was right to come to America. Once, Sebastian had dreamed of joining the priesthood, but as soon as he met Tina, the dream had dissipated on a breath of wind. He hadn't thought of that calling in many years and found himself reminiscing about it now, with the sound of gulls calling outside his window by the Delaware River.

As a young boy, maybe about seven, he'd found a dying bird—a nightjar—floundering on the ground by the side of the road. His heart had gone out to the little bird, and he'd approached the desperate animal, crooning under his breath, until he came within range of handling it. He'd planned to pick up the nightjar and nurse it to health. His friends had sniggered behind him, teasing him and kicking at the dirt, eager to move along to their games.

"*Mingherlino,*" one boy scoffed. *Weakling.* Sebastian didn't know if the boy meant him or the bird—it didn't matter. Determined to deliver the animal from its dire plight, Sebastian reached out slowly to scoop the bird up. He'd almost touched the black feathers when the bird snapped at his fingers. It pecked and pecked, a flurry of feathers and wings that scared the life out of Sebastian. He whooped and jerked back, landing hard on his bum on the dirt road and tearing his trousers. His friends roared with laughter, but Sebastian didn't give up. He reached again, then noticed the frantic bird had hidden something. *A mama bird!* To his friends, he yelled, "Look! She's sitting on her eggs. There's no nest to protect them!"

But his friends had already moved along the road, their laughter spent. Sebastian couldn't believe a mother bird would lay eggs on the hard ground without providing a soft nest for them. She was damaged, but couldn't leave her offspring. Sebastian left the hurt, scared bird alone to fend for her vulnerable babies as best she could. Reluctantly, he turned and trotted down the road, hoping to catch up to his friends.

That night, when he explained to his mama how he'd gotten the small tear in the seat of his trousers, his heart still ached for the mother nightjar. His mama patted his hand and told him he had a kind heart. "Unlike some of your brothers, Sebastian, you'd make a fine priest." She tucked the torn pants under her arm and left him to wash.

Her words and the image of the hurt mother bird replayed in his mind many times during the next few days.

At the end of the week, seven-year-old Sebastian made up his mind. He announced his decision to the family at the supper table. "I am going to be a priest."

His mama smiled, and Papa said, "Good. Now *mangia, mangia.* Let's eat."

Twelve years later, as a third-year student, Sebastian strolled along the road, traveling home from seminary in Campobasso, when he spotted the most extraordinary sight in a field of flowers. He shielded his eyes from the midday sun. He couldn't see it clearly, but there appeared to be an enormous black bird fluttering its wings, surrounded by a kaleidoscope of wildflowers.

Sebastian remembered the injured nightjar from his childhood. Before he knew it, his legs were jumping over the fence, and his feet were sprinting across the field to assist the struggling bird.

*Silly me,* he thought as he got closer. *There is no bird as large as this!* He laughed when he discovered the bird was a young woman swooshing her long black skirts to rid herself of something.

"A bee!" she yelled as he neared her. "There is a bee in my skirts! *Aiutatemi*! Help me!"

Even in her distress, the girl was breathtaking, with long, dark hair that had come loose from her bun and whirled around her round face. Her dark eyes were large as moons and bright with anxiety, and her cheeks were rosy and dimpled. Sebastian's heart swelled as he approached who he knew must be the most beautiful woman in the world.

He closed the distance in a final leap, skidded to a halt, and knelt before her. He looked up at her face—*Do you permit me?* his expression asked. She nodded. He reached his hands into the folds of her skirts and puffed them out into the air, flouncing the fabric until he confirmed the bee was gone.

Shaky now, he stood, dusted off his trousers, and doffed his hat—wringing it in his hands. "I am Sebastian Paragano." He bowed. "Of Perdifumo."

The beautiful girl smiled at him. "Florentina Malandrino. I am forever in your debt, signor." She dimpled as she dropped a small curtsy.

"Then I will forever be at your service, *signorina*," he replied, breathless.

Sebastian shook his head from the sweet memories. He'd told Florentina then that he'd be forever at her service, and he meant it. He'd go to the ends of the earth to pick an apple for Florentina if she asked him to. And wasn't that precisely what he was doing? He was choosing an apple for his wife in America. *If working for the Duke is*

*the surest way to provide for her, then I will do it—despite the warning in my heart.* "I'll just have to be careful." Sebastian spoke to the walls. He grabbed his rosary and fingered the beads. "I'll have to keep my faith and stay strong against evil."

A rap on the door started Sebastian out of his reverie. "Who are you talking to in there, paesano?" Rocco had come to collect him for the day's work.

# CHAPTER TWO

*Lineage*

*May 2018*
*Drexel Hill, PA*

The first few weeks after her husband left, Bella existed solely on chai lattes and Skittles. Chewing the little rainbow-colored candies caused her TMJ to flare up and her migraines to start. One rainy night, her jaw got stuck closed while she slept with a night guard installed, and Bella couldn't open or close her mouth.

She woke about four in the morning to a feeling of claustrophobia and thrashed around in her now-enormous bed. In desperation, Bella grabbed the red rosary from her bedside table and stumbled downstairs in her robe. She rummaged in the freezer for an ice pack and held it to her painful cheek, hoping it was the correct remedy for such a situation.

Chilly now, Bella curled up on the sofa and worried the worn beads of her Nana's rosary. These were the times when she missed her great-grandmom, Mollie, the most. She wished Nana were alive to help her through the pain of her divorce and wondered how much Nana had known about the marriage of her own parents—Bella's great-great-grandparents. Bella had grown up hearing the family legend that Nana's mother had tried to drown her children, and her father had abandoned them. As a child, Bella had been obsessed with the story. Had Nana's mother been crazy? Had her father left her mother because of another woman? Nana had never spoken about her parents or her time in the orphanage.

Nana had been the one who taught Bella how to pray the rosary.

Bella remembered sitting on her lap in the sun, stumbling over the words. Nana had been a patient teacher. Eventually, she'd gotten it down pat. Bella tried to pray now, but the words wouldn't come. She let the smooth wood of the beads comfort her anyway as she watched the early morning sun come up, as it did every day. As it always had, as it always would. Her life would go on. Her mind knew this truth but had yet to convince her heart—the organ her husband had crushed when he walked out the door.

She was forty-three years old, alone in a big house with no husband and no child. Three years earlier, after almost two decades of false hope, months of fertility treatments, and permanent placement on the rosters of dozens of prayer lists, Nate and Bella had finally become pregnant. She was forty and considered high risk, but the miracle had occurred! Until it was suddenly over. Their baby had been born too soon.

Bella had never conceived again, and their marriage hadn't survived the heartache. Bella wondered if that'd been a blessing or a curse. Maybe raising a child would have prevented the disillusionment that had seeped into their marriage. But, more likely, a child would've propelled their disappointment to even greater heights, speeding up the inevitable separation and divorce. She'd never know.

The sun was up now, chasing clouds and the last raindrops away. Bella massaged her jaw, pushing hard under her ear until the ligament finally let go with a little *pop*. *Thank God!* She could open her mouth and take out the night guard. Before vacating her perch, she spotted a vibrant rainbow outside the window. Sunbeams reflected colorful hues of red and yellow, green and blue. She remembered her Sunday school lessons. Hadn't God created a rainbow after the flood to show his new covenant with Noah? Hadn't He sent a dove to promise life over death?

Bella hoped that promise still applied to the likes of her, but she wasn't so sure. Why did bad things happen to good people? Couldn't God have figured out a way around that by now? Or maybe He had. As she dressed and brushed her teeth, Bella wondered if she should join a local Bible study and learn more about her faith. *Do single men attend Bible studies?*

She laughed at herself in the mirror as the errant question sneaked into her reverie. With toothpaste-covered lips, she chastised herself in the mirror. "That wasn't such a holy thought, Miss Bella!" She couldn't help but smile at her reflection and marvel as her eyes sparkled with light and life, and her middle-aged wrinkles looked more like laugh lines. What a transformation a smile could make of an aging face—just like a rainbow could make of a rainy morning.

Late for work, Bella grabbed her keys from the hook, donned her hat, and swung open the front door—only to find her husband standing on the porch, looking toward the street, hands in his pockets. The rainbow had disappeared, along with her buoyant mood.

"Nate. What are you doing here?"

He turned to face her, and his eyebrows shot up.

"Nice hat. Never saw you in a cowgirl hat before."

*Is he really complimenting me right now?* "It's new. What do you want?"

Nate's eyes darted from the porch floor to the passing cars. "Um, there's something you need to know, and I wanted to be the one to tell you."

"Yeah, well, get on with it. I'm running late for work." Bella's voice came out colder and harsher than she'd intended, but her patience had run out.

Nate's shoulders slumped. "You don't have to be so mean, Bells."

Her nickname. *Ouch.* "Don't I? And don't call me that anymore." She skirted around him and started down the steps, heels clacking. She pushed the key fob to start the car.

Nate spoke to her back. "Kate's pregnant."

Bella stopped in her tracks, devoid of breath.

"I wanted you to hear it from me before the gossip mill starts."

Her eyes lost focus, and she put her hand on the car roof to steady herself. Nate was still on the porch.

"You gotta sign the papers, you know. We need to start the annulment process." Nate cleared his throat. "We're running out of time. Me and Kate want to get married before she starts to show. I'm sorry, Bells—Bella."

Bella's mind went blank. Without a word, she got into her car and slammed the door. A small part of her felt bad leaving without answering, but what could she possibly say? *Where's that promise now, God?*

Bella sat in her office at Morenstein and Foster, staring at her computer. She had a deadline, but visions of Nate holding a baby looped in her mind. What kind of father would he be? Would he end up coaching Little League or playing dress-up? She couldn't picture Nate sitting still on the floor while a little princess smeared red lipstick over his face. Tears stung Bella's eyes at the thought of him having a catch in the backyard with his future football star.

She shook her head to clear the images of the destiny she'd never enjoy. She stared at the spreadsheets on her screen but couldn't make sense of the data in front of her. Who cared about the market analysis of breakfast cereal?

*Ding!* A personal email popped up on Bella's screen. Desperate for a distraction, she opened and read the message immediately.

> From: SophieLovesDC
> Sent: Thursday, May 03, 2018, 10:35 AM
> To: bella444
> Subject: Family Tree
>
> Hello Bella,
> I found your profile on a lineage website. I am very anxious to know if you have any information about Mollie Paragano. I believe she was the sister of my dear cousin Mendel. Mendel was the son of Jakob Lichtenbaum, my great-uncle. He was very close with my family and searched for his missing sisters for decades.
> Please meet me to discuss this in person. How do you want to proceed? I live near Wash, DC. I'm 83 years old.
> Sophie

Bella sat back in her chair and released a low whistle. "Jakob

*Lichtenbaum?* Was that Nana's dad? Huh." A shiver went up Bella's spine as she remembered her morning ruminations. *I was just wondering about you, buddy.* No one in the family knew anything about Mollie's father, and the assertion that Sophie was somehow related to him piqued Bella's curiosity.

> *From: bella444*
> *Sent: Thursday, May 03, 2018, 10:41 AM*
> *To: SophieLovesDC*
> *Subject: RE: Family Tree*
>
> *Hi Sophie, it's nice to meet you. I've never heard the name Lichtenbaum before, but no one in my family knows anything about my Nana's dad except that he abandoned his wife and children. To be honest, my family has always cast him as a villain. I hope that doesn't offend you. I'm very curious to see your information.*
>
> > *Bella*

Within seconds, Bella's computer dinged with Sophie's reply.

> *From: SophieLovesDC*
> *Sent: Thursday, May 03, 2018, 10:42 AM*
> *To: bella444*
> *Subject: RE: Family Tree*
>
> *Bella,*
> *Jakob Lichtenbaum was not a villain. Meet me tomorrow at noon in the Starbucks on Maryland Ave in DC, and I will prove it.*
>
> > *Sophie*

Meeting a stranger was a crazy idea, and it could be a hoax, but getting answers about Nana's father captivated Bella and propelled her to action. Would it be reckless to drive a few hours to meet a total stranger who'd approached her online? Probably. But the shock of seeing Nate on her porch and hearing his traitorous news that morning had reverberated through Bella's heart, and she needed an excuse to leave town. Without a second thought, she flagged down her boss as he walked by her office door.

"Yeah, so, um, I know you need the reports ASAP, but I need to take off tomorrow. There was a death in my extended family, and I can't miss the funeral," she lied. How could she tell the truth? Her plans sounded ridiculous, even to her own ears.

Early the following day, Bella barreled down the highway while answering a call from her mom with one hand.

"Pull over, you idiot!" Bella blasted the horn of her VW Golf, swearing under her breath.

"Isabella Rosemarie! Are you driving?! What's going on?" Rosalie yelled through the phone on Bella's lap. Her mom could be such a worrywart.

"Sorry, Ma, I'm on 95 going down to DC, and some moron cut me off. Ugh, I can feel a migraine coming on." She rubbed the back of her neck.

"You shouldn't be on the phone while driving, Bella. Why are you heading down there anyway? Is this about Nate?"

"No, Ma, no. Why would you say that? No, I'm meeting someone. You won't believe this, but some old lady found me through a lineage website. Says she's related to us."

"Huh, you're kidding. How so?"

Bella shifted into third gear, careening past a minivan full of kids and a dog sticking its head out the window, long fur plastered against its face, revealing a blissful dog smile.

"Yeah, her name's Sophie. She says she's the great-niece of Nana's father."

"Nana's *father*? Why didn't you tell me? I would've come with you. No one knows anything about that side of the family. Nana never talked about her parents. I mean, would you? After all the rumors…"

Bella's mother fell silent, and Bella asked the question she'd wondered about a thousand times. "Ma, do you really think Nana's mother would've drowned her in the Delaware?"

"I don't know, Bella. That's what your Aunt Dorothy told me."

"Well, I've been obsessed over it since Tris and Lexi told me when I was six. They took me behind the house and whispered the story in my ear and threatened that the same would happen to me if I misbehaved. Listen, Ma, I've gotta go. I'll tell you all about it later. I hope this lady's got some intel and isn't just some loon."

Rosalie yelled, "Wait, Bella! Shouldn't you be taking care of concerns at home?" A little quieter, she continued, "I mean, Nate called. He said you haven't signed the papers yet." She paused, but when Bella didn't respond, Rosalie persisted. "He told me the news. Honey, you're gonna have to let him go."

Bella sat in the Starbucks on DC's Maryland Avenue, unsigned divorce papers burning a hole in the messenger bag slung across the back of her seat. The cafe echoed with activity as she sat by the window, fidgeting with her sapphire necklace. Nana had given her the jewel when she was a child, and she'd worn it ever since. She watched the door for the stranger's arrival, twisting the gem in her fingers with nervous energy.

Unable to sit still, Bella tidied up the table, wiping away crumbs left behind by the previous customer, somehow ending up with a spot of brown gunk on her faded Pink Floyd t-shirt. Not sure what to wear to this strange appointment, she'd picked out a favorite top for comfort, paired with jeans, a structured cream blazer, leopard print ballet flats, and a ball cap—teal corduroy with a truck and the words "Let's Just Go" splashed across the top. *Nate would hate this outfit. He would've called it trendy and accused me of trying too hard.* "Get out of my head, Nate!" A young mother glared at Bella and held her toddler close as they waited in line.

*Oh, my word! Did I say that out loud?*

Pulling the hat down further on her head, she angled away from the horrified mother and the sunlight blazing through the window, hoping to avoid another migraine. She wondered how she'd recognize this Sophie when she showed up. *I hope this meeting wasn't a total mistake.*

The only thing Bella knew for sure was that Nana had grown up in an orphanage, and her father had taken her brother away—abandoning Nana and her little sister at the institution. No one knew his name or anything else about him, and no one cared. Good riddance!

Bella removed her hat, massaged her temples to ease the tightness, and then dragged herself back into the present. *Concentrate. Don't get stuck in the past.* She sipped her now-tepid mocha and erased from her mind the horrible images of a mother drowning her children in the river and a father who turned his back on all of them.

Bella heard the bell jingle on the door and shifted to see an older woman enter the cafe.

The nose. *Nana's* nose.

Bella stood up, the legs of her chair scraping against the hard floor, all worry of a headache gone. "Sophie," she called. "Over here."

The tidy older woman wearing a sharp blue suit and short permed hairdo bustled toward her. "That door is too darn heavy," she announced to the cafe at large.

Unable to help herself, Bella chuckled.

Sophie frowned. "You must be Bella. I'm Sophie. I'm surprised you showed up today. To be frank, my family was shocked that I even asked to meet with you."

An awkward silence followed.

Bella broke it. "You have my Nana's nose."

"You're wrong." Sophie raised her chin. "Your Nana had *my* nose." The rude declaration sounded ridiculous, and the old lady must have known because her lips curled up at the edges. Bella could feel her dimples forming as she smiled. She liked this spunky lady.

"Well, I wasn't sure I would come either, so there," Bella teased. "Why did you want to meet with me, anyway?"

Sophie dragged out the chair opposite Bella and sat down. "I grew up with my cousin, Mendel Lichtenbaum, and he searched his entire life for his orphaned sisters, Mollie and Sarah. I believe you are Mollie's great-granddaughter. Am I right?"

"Yeah, that's right." Bella sat down too. "Never heard the name Lichtenbaum, but our family never knew anything about Mollie's dad except that he abandoned his family. I'd love to hear *that* story."

"Well, for starters, you shouldn't be here."

Bella winced. "Well, why did you invite me then?"

Sophie waved her hands in front of her face. "No, no, you misunderstand me. I mean, you shouldn't even *exist*." Bella's eyebrows shot up to her hairline. Sophie continued. "What I mean to say is, my family—the Lichtenbaum family—was told that your ancestor Mollie and her sister Sarah had become nuns."

"What?" Bella choked on her coffee. "*Nuns?*"

Sophie removed her coat and settled into the seat. "Yes, nuns in the Catholic Church. Why don't you buy me a cup of coffee, and I'll explain?"

A few minutes later, Bella presented Sophie with a latte, then searched her face and waited, knees bouncing up and down under the table.

Sophie took the hint. "So, here's what I know. When my great uncle Jakob went to claim his children at the orphanage, they only allowed him to bring Mendel home. The Sisters told him the girls had been baptized and taken into the Church to become nuns. They refused to release Mollie and Sarah to their father, a Jew."

The painful story sat between them while Sophie fiddled with her coffee cup.

Bella bit her nails and jiggled her foot. *This woman really believes Nana was a nun.*

"Sophie, you don't understand. My Nana most certainly did *not* become a nun. Neither did her sister, Sarah, for that matter, though Sarah died young and didn't have children of her own. They lived for five years in an orphanage because someone took them from their mother, Mary, who basically disappeared—I have no idea what happened to her. Nana married my Pop Pop, and they were together for sixty-five years. They raised six children and had nineteen grandchildren. They were even alive to welcome nine of their thirty great-grandchildren, including me."

Sophie lowered her coffee cup as Bella listed the names of daughters, sons, and cousins. "Wait a minute," she interrupted. "When exactly did Mollie die?"

"She died in 1988, when I was thirteen years old. She was ninety-six."

"Oh…" Sophie groaned. "Poor Mendel! He died in 1981, believing at least one of his sisters was out there somewhere, and longing to see her. He was right. What a waste." Sophie lowered her face and shook her head.

Bella reached across the table to squeeze Sophie's hands.

Sophie cleared her throat. "My dear, it seems the age-old institution of prejudice has wronged our two families."

"Prejudice? What do you mean?"

"Bella, you realize the Lichtenbaum family is Jewish, right?"

"Jewish?" Bella repeated. "But my Nana was Catholic. I don't understand."

"Your Nana's *mother* was Catholic, but her father was Jewish." Sophie grabbed a pen from her purse and sketched a family tree on the back of a napkin. "My great-uncle, Jakob Lichtenbaum, married your great-great-grandma, Mary Paragano. They had three children—your Nana, Mollie; Sarah; and my cousin, Mendel. What were your grandparents' names?"

"Um, Fred and Anna."

"And your folks?"

"Nicholas and Rosalie."

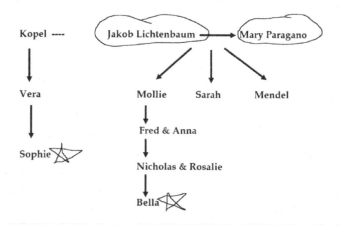

"Right." She filled in the other generations of the tree, bringing herself and Bella into the picture with a little star next to their names.

Sophie tapped the pen on the table. "Mary and Jakob were from different religious backgrounds. Right there—we need to find out how they even met. Later, something happened to separate them, but we're not sure what. The whole family got split up. The kids went to an orphanage, and the Lichtenbaums were told the girls became nuns, but they didn't.

"So, which family has the true story? Or does the truth lie somewhere in between?"

# CHAPTER THREE

*Padrone*

*July 1880*
*Southwark, Philadelphia*

In the middle of the night, three weeks into his stint with the street sweepers, a drunken man stopped Sebastian and Rocco on the corner while they were returning from an alehouse on Second Street. Obviously out of his mind with drink, the man reached out and grabbed Rocco's sleeve as they passed by. With slurred speech, he implored the two men to give him some money. The man was a Jew—they had seen him before coming and going from the local synagogue.

A Jewish man shouldn't have bothered two Italian men—and vice versa—in this neighborhood. No group of Southwark residents mixed with other nationalities except at the market. The Irish stuck with the Irish, the Blacks with the Blacks, the Jews with the Jews, and the Italians with the Italians. Whatever had made this man desperate enough to drown his sorrows, Sebastian couldn't guess, but the man was foolish to have laid a hand on an Italian, especially a brute such as Rocco.

With a stone-cold face, Rocco turned toward the beggar and said to Sebastian, "Break his arm."

Sebastian looked from Rocco to the Hebrew and back again, wishing he had misheard. "What?"

The man understood enough to remove his hand from Rocco's sleeve and back away.

"I *said*, break his arm," Rocco repeated, his voice like ice.

Realizing Rocco was serious, Sebastian drew himself up to his full height. "I will not."

Before Sebastian could say another word, Rocco grabbed the stranger's arm with surprising agility and twisted the limb behind the man's back. The poor man squirmed and begged. "Please! I meant no disrespect! A few coins is all I'm askin' for. Have pity on a rotten soul."

Sebastian looked at Rocco, raising his eyebrows in question. "Let's leave him be, don't you think?"

Still staring at Sebastian, Rocco jerked the twisted arm. The man went down on his knees with a yowl of pain. Breathless, he crumpled on the ground, clawing at his arm with his other hand, his mouth opening and closing like a fish out of water. His eyes rolled back in his head, and he slumped into the gutter, passed out from drink and shock.

Rocco spat at the beggar and stepped over his limp body. He stood eye to eye with Sebastian. "I am your *padrone*. Don't ever defy me like that again. I brought you to the Duke, and I vouched for you. It's because of *me* that you have work. It's because of *me* that you have a place to sleep at night. Do you desire your wife and children here by your side? I am the only way to make that happen. Don't ever forget it." With that, he disappeared into the night.

When Rocco was gone, Sebastian threw up in the gutter. He leaned against the nearest wall, wiped the spittle off his cheek, and looked at the drunkard passed out near his feet. The wretch rolled onto his side, moaning as he came to. Sebastian crouched before the lowly beggar and patted his back. The man searched Sebastian's face for answers, confusion creasing his brow.

"Up you go, then." Careful not to disturb the injured arm, Sebastian heaved him to his feet. He settled the drunkard's good arm over his shoulder and headed toward the Jewish Sheltering Home, hoping to find assistance for the unfortunate man.

Sebastian fell into a pattern over the next year. Roll off his pallet in the little room on Delaware Avenue at four in the morning, splash water on his face, grab a hunk of cheese and a hard piece of bread, brush off his white uniform, and head out into the streets with his pushcart and broom. He cleaned the streets before the milk carts started rolling by. Later in the morning, as vendors opened their stalls, he stopped to chat with everyone. He gathered all the gossip and noted the movements of the Italians, the Jews, the Irish, and the Blacks.

Despite this surveillance, which he reported to the Duke himself, Sebastian enjoyed getting to know the people of his new home. Although much larger and more populated, the Jewish Quarter of Southwark reminded him of the village square in Perdifumo. Like in his Italian hometown, Sebastian could count on seeing the same people in the same spots doing the same things every day. There was old Zysel with his pickle barrel on Fourth Street, singing an ancient Hebrew tune, modernized with a mix of English, Yiddish, and Polish lyrics. Peggy and John McAllister ran the boarding house in the middle of the block, proudly serving beef and ale for lunch in the dining room. He always stopped to speak with little blind Violetta, who peddled flowers from a dented tin pitcher. Sebastian purchased one every day without fail, never having the heart to tell the child that the flowers had wilted or died.

Over time, Sebastian gained respect in the neighborhood. Despite the community's disdain for Rocco and his barbaric ways, the immigrants of Southwark depended on the Duke's protection and were willing to suffer his lackey's insults in exchange.

"I prefer dealing wit' you, Sebastian, rather than that brute, Rocco." Old Henry winked his ancient wrinkled eye as he tucked a list of names into Sebastian's pocket. Sebastian marveled at the man's dark skin and asked him again where his people had come from in Africa.

"As I done told ye a hundred times, young man, my folks came here from Nigeria. Most beautiful place in the world, my Mami said." Old Henry looked over Sebastian's shoulder as if picturing the wild Nigerian sky in place of the bricks of Southwark.

"I wish I could go there someday." Sebastian patted his pocket, feeling the thick paper folded inside it.

Old Henry chuckled. "You're a strange one, Mr. Paragano. A

strange one, indeed. Though you're as dark as a guinea you'self, you considered a white man here. Now, why in heaven's name would you want to take your white self to a black country?" Henry spat a sunflower seed onto the sidewalk and shook his head. "A strange one, indeed."

Sebastian blushed and tipped his hat to Old Henry. On his walk down Sixth Street, he considered the old man's words. *I'm considered a white man here.* He'd never thought of it that way before, but that was the equivalent of a landowner in Italy. He hated being an informant to the Duke—it made him furious and impotent at the same time—but he held a certain standing in the community. And ultimately, he didn't care what he had to do as long as he could make enough money to send for Tina and the children.

A rough hand clapped him on the back, breaking his reverie. Sebastian jumped as Rocco kept pace beside him. "Why the long face, *mio amico?*"

"Ah, I didn't hear you coming. No reason." Sebastian sidestepped some rubbish on the street.

"I watched you talking with that old raisin. Why did you linger? I saw he passed you the list. There was no reason to stay."

"Oh, Old Henry? Well, I like him. He's wise and kind. Funny, too, if you get him talking. He once told me a story about…"

"Argh, I don't give a fig what the man told you. He ain't worthy to shine my shoes. C'mon, the Duke's waitin'." Rocco picked up his pace.

The cavernous lobby of Valero's office building was decked in oak paneling and marble floors. The Duke's buxom secretary, Josephine, greeted the men from behind her desk when they arrived. Rocco leaned over the surface and leered at Josephine, to her apparent discomfort. She seemed to squirm under his gaze. Sebastian hung his hat and coat on the stand, trying hard not to hear Rocco's lecherous jokes. Josephine's face went from beet red to ashen in seconds. Had Rocco threatened her?

The sound of footsteps came down the stairs—one of the Tucci brothers coming to collect them. Sebastian cleared his throat to get Rocco's attention. The Duke would not be pleased if he knew Rocco was flirting with Josephine. The poor secretary shuffled some papers on the desk and looked like she was about to lose her lunch.

"C'mon, Rocco. Up we go." Sebastian nudged Rocco and gave Josephine what he hoped was a calming smile.

Once established in the Duke's office, Sebastian presented the list he'd gleaned from Old Henry. Valero took a puff of his ubiquitous cigar and grabbed the note. He scanned the page and let out a cloud of smoke. "Ah, so that idiot Bull McBride and his Fourth Ward Irish laddies are planning to swing the vote, I see? Hmm." Valero tapped his knuckles on the desk. "Good work, Sebastian. How did you get someone to give you the names here?"

Before Sebastian could answer, Rocco laughed. "Oh, he's friendly with all the jokers in town, he is. The Irish, the Jews, the Poles—even the Blacks. Our boy has them all eatin' out of his hand. All he has to do is pretend to be interested in their pathetic lives, and they dish up all the dirt." Rocco slumped onto the tufted sofa as if he'd just given a lengthy speech and couldn't find the energy to stand any longer.

The Duke turned his gaze to Sebastian and studied him close-ly. "Is that so?" Sebastian, uncomfortable with Rocco's incorrect assessment, blushed as Valero continued. "Well, well, looks like you picked a prize on that pier last year, eh Rocco? It's been a year now, hasn't it, Sebastian?"

Sebastian didn't like Valero's condescending tone. His pulse quickened, and his palms got sweaty. He was certain the Duke was about to ask him to do violence. Ever since Rocco had broken the Jewish beggar's arm, Sebastian was anxious that he'd demand it of him next time. Sebastian had defied him then, but he wasn't sure if he could dodge the request a second time. And if the Duke himself tasked him with barbarity, how would he say no? A smooth and polished politician, the Duke never did the dirty deeds himself. But everyone knew Valero ordered violence in Philadelphia's Fourth and Fifth Wards. Knees shaking, Sebastian withered under Valero's calculating gaze. The moment passed, and Rocco heaved himself off the sofa, bidding farewell to the Duke. Sebastian followed suit, sure he'd seen a look pass between his superiors. *What do they have in mind for me now?*

Two days later, Rocco woke Sebastian by shoving his shoulder with his foot. Sebastian could smell the wine on Rocco's breath from the mattress on the floor. Sebastian shot up, wiping the sleep from his eyes. "What's amiss, Rocco?"

"Nothing's amiss, *il mio compagno*. I have something to show you. Get up, partner!"

Sebastian stumbled behind Rocco down the street, away from the river. Rocco had a swing in his step that made Sebastian nervous. "Where are we going? What is this about, Rocco?" A knot twisted in the pit of his stomach. Did Rocco plan to bring him to a scene of violence or ill repute? Sebastian prayed Rocco wouldn't put him to the test again.

Rocco stopped on the corner of Sixth and Clymer Streets, grinned at his companion, and opened his arms toward a brick corner house. "Eh?!" Rocco puffed out his chest, as proud as a peacock.

Sebastian considered the building in front of him. Three stories high, it scraped the sky. A skinny house, but wide enough to take up the corner, with a welcoming front step that spilled onto the street. Along the left side, a delivery door stood level with the curb. *The first floor of this house would be perfect for a corner market.* The two stories above had room enough for Florentina and their six children—too much to hope for.

"Rocco, why have you brought me here?"

"Well, I couldn't wait to show you. This house, you like it, *si?*" At Sebastian's nod, Rocco continued. "You see, the Duke, well, he needed to excuse a man that lived here with his family. They had to move along downriver to Wilmington. No room for them here no more. Anyway, the house stands empty, as you can see. The Duke, well, he appointed me the task of filling it. I thought of you right away, naturally." Rocco beamed.

Sebastian placed his hand on the cool bricks. "What must I *do* to get this house?"

Rocco gave a big belly laugh. He rocked back on his heels and barked a loud guffaw that echoed off the brick walls. Sebastian could hear a baby cry and the noise of children waking up. His heart melted at the sound. Oh, how he longed to reunite with his wife and children. His older girls, Clara and Gina, the babies, his precious little nightjar, Mary, and his wife, Tina—the most beautiful woman in the world. They could start their market and build a new life together here in America. His heart swelled until he almost couldn't breathe.

Yet Rocco hadn't answered the question. He waited until Rocco's mirth settled down.

"I like you, Sebastian. I really do." Rocco wiped his watering eyes with a dainty lace handkerchief tucked in his sleeve, then folded the square and put it away in his breast pocket. Patting it against his barrel chest, Rocco looked Sebastian in the eye and said with a voice like steel, "When the time comes, you will know."

Almost a year later, Sebastian stood in the center of his corner grocery store and enjoyed the sweet sensation of success. He'd done it! He had finally made enough money selling housewares and foodstuffs to his neighbors to send for his wife and children. He hopped from foot to foot, dancing a little jig and smiling like a loon. Slapping his knee, Sebastian decided to dip into his supply of pricey cigars and celebrate. As he lit up and took his first puff, he leaned against the massive countertop and offered a silent salute to the Duke. "Although I hate to admit it," he announced to the empty room, "I must thank the Duke for giving me some cash to open the business."

"Who are you talking to, fool?" Rocco had slipped into the market without its proprietor noticing.

Sebastian inhaled too deeply and let out an explosive cough. Eyes watering, he pounded his chest and tried to breathe. "Rocco! I hate when you sneak in here like that!"

"I saw you through the window dancing like an idiot and had to see what was going on. Looks like you're celebrating something, eh?"

Sebastian ignored the jab and tidied up the shop, ready to dismiss Rocco and close up for the night. Looking like he intended to linger, Rocco took off his jacket and rolled up his shirt sleeves. "Well? Out with it." He pushed past Sebastian and opened the door behind the counter where Sebastian kept his more expensive inventory.

Sebastian cringed when he heard Rocco bump into the shelves of his precious closet, rattling bottles. "If you must know my business, I am ready to send for my family."

Rocco yelled from inside the little room. "Your business *is* my business, paesano!"

He backed out of the little storage room, holding his prize. "Ahh, I say we open a bottle of this ruby-red beauty to celebrate." Before Sebastian could argue, Rocco rummaged around for a tool to open the bottle. *Pop!* Rocco didn't wait to find a glass but placed the bottle to his fat lips and slurped. Sebastian recoiled in disgust. *He takes everything!*

With a satisfied sigh, Rocco pushed the bottle into Sebastian's chest. "Your turn."

Without much choice, Sebastian tipped the bottle and took a sip, watching Rocco warily over the rim. *Be careful—he gets violent when he drinks.*

"You know, the Duke and I really did it for you, *mio amico.* Most guys have to wait years before the Duke gives them a house. You were just a natural with the job. A natural." He grabbed the bottle and took a few gulping droughts. "You have a way with the folks around here, si? They trust you for some reason." Rocco's speech became slurred. "I neva had nothin' like that. Hada work real hard fo it."

*He must have started drinking a while ago to be this far gone already.* Sebastian guided Rocco to the only chair behind the counter. "Sit down, Rocco. Take a load off." He tried to move the bottle away from his padrone, but Rocco wouldn't release his grip.

"The Duke gave you the cap...*hiccup*...capital for supplies to stock up...*hiccup*...for opening day last year. Truth? I didn't...think you'd make it. Always givin' stuff away to...*hiccup*...your wretched neighbors."

Sebastian pulled up a stool and sat down. "Well, I couldn't refuse a mother who needed food for her children or an old man who bartered roasted chestnuts for a new pair of socks. Maybe it was a rocky start, but I managed to pull it off. And now I can finally send for my family."

Sebastian thought Rocco was asleep in the chair—his head was resting on his folded arms on the countertop—one hand stubbornly holding the wine bottle. Sebastian rose quietly from his stool when he heard Rocco grunt.

"Tell me about your family, Sebastian. Tell me about the last time you saw your wife and children in Italy."

Sebastian was startled at first and resisted speaking of his precious family to Rocco. Still, his earlier exuberance returned, and he was bursting to share his excitement about sending for Tina and the children. "Well, my wife is called Florentina, and she's the most beautiful woman in the world."

Much to Sebastian's surprise, Rocco chuckled at this sentiment. "Go on."

"Yes, well, we have six children together. I'll never forget the last time I saw them—at the docks while I waved from the boat. Mary, my little nightjar, I called her, was six years old when I left. The older girls, Clara and Gina, were eight and seven—they clung to their mother's skirts. I remember they refused to look at me. Sweet Rosetta, who was four, and my son Giuseppe, who was two years old, smiled with wonder at the big boat. My wife, Tina, cried into her handkerchief. Her sister held the baby, Lizzy—I don't even know her!—and supported Tina lest she faint. It was a heartbreaking scene.

"I haven't thought about it for a long time, but I remember Mary standing stock still, observing me with piercing eyes—I can still picture her staring at me, neither smiling nor frowning. She's always been that way—intelligent and observant." Sebastian smiled. "When the coastline disappeared, I imagined Mary still standing there like a statue until the ship disappeared from her view."

Sebastian thought he heard Rocco snore, but when he stopped speaking, his padrone snorted and looked up. "Tell me more about Mary." Rocco reached for the wine and took another slug.

"Well, often, after the evening meal in Perdifumo, while Tina and the older girls cleared the supper dishes, Mary would sneak out onto the back porch to join me while I smoked my pipe. After a little while, we'd stretch our legs and amble through the field beside our home. We'd listen to the sounds of cicadas and the calls of various birds, enjoying the neighbor's vast vineyard. The rows of neat vines stretched to the horizon. It was a beautiful place."

Sebastian smiled and crossed his legs, getting more comfortable as he shared his memories.

"Mary asked me questions about everything. 'Papa, why is water wet? What does God look like? Will the sky fall on top of my head someday?' And, my favorite, 'Are the hairs coming out of Signora Corvo's chin going to turn her into a man?'"

Rocco chuckled at this.

"I had to think about that one for a moment." Sebastian reached across the table for the bottle and took a sip. "I didn't mind. Her curious mind always delighted me. During our nightly stroll, she'd tug my hand a dozen times or more, pointing at this, inquiring about that. Mary spoke of imaginary beings in the shadows, her black eyes darting from here to there. Her face alight, she'd talk about a world she had created in her young mind."

Rocco let out a huge burp. "Why the pet name?"

"The pet name?"

"You said you called her 'little nightjar.'"

Sebastian's eyebrows rose to his hairline. "I didn't think you were paying that close attention."

"I always pay close attention, Paragano."

"Well, Mary has hair black as night and dark eyes like coal. She reminds me of a little dark bird I'd once attempted to rescue as a boy. She's like an old soul housed in a girl's body."

Rocco seemed much revived and sat up straight.

Sebastian cleared his throat and took another sip of wine. "Yes, well, anyway."

"I always wanted to marry a girl like that."

Sebastian sputtered and almost dropped the bottle.

"No, really, it's true. An imaginative girl? I'm tired of these simple, empty-headed Southwark girls who can't even cook or keep house." Rocco raised his voice. "They all think they're so much better than me. Trollops, every one!" He banged his fist on the counter. "I want a wife to meet my needs at night. Who won't argue but do her duty!"

Sebastian put his stool away and cleared the cigar and wine bottle. He wiped the countertop and prayed that Rocco would shut up and go home. But Rocco wasn't done.

"And your Mary sounds like an *una bella regazza*—like she's a pretty girl."

Rocco was stone sober now and continued spouting about Mary's virtues as Sebastian's blood ran cold with dread. He kicked himself for letting his defenses down with Rocco and speaking candidly about his family. The thought of Rocco touching one of his daughters made his fists clench and his stomach sour.

Rocco continued his litany of praise for Sebastian's little nightjar as he donned his jacket and prepared to leave. "And something about the eyes dark as coal piques my interest."

Sebastian couldn't take it any longer. He kicked a box near his feet and shouted, "Mary turned eight years old on her last birthday! You are speaking about a *little girl*!"

Rocco's eyes widened like moons, and he rocked back on his heels. Silence filled the market. Sebastian stood his ground, staring at his padrone. Rocco smiled. "Oh, Sebastian, surely you know every little girl grows up someday. Don't forget, Paragano, you still owe me. *Hiccup*. And I always collect." He left Sebastian there, frozen in the middle of his grocery, where only an hour ago, he had been dancing a jig.

*What if Rocco demands one of my daughters' hands in marriage?* Sebastian ran his hands through his hair. *What choice would I have? Please, Lord, help me!*

With effort, Sebastian put the worry away. God would protect his family. He had saved enough money to send for them and couldn't wait to see his beautiful wife. To kiss her sweet lips and have her in his bed. Tomorrow, he'd leave the money at the courier's office to be taken on the next ship to Italy, to Perdifumo, to his wife. He wondered how changed the children would be. How his heart longed to see them! Especially Mary. *God, please protect them!* Desperate to erase the disgusting conversation with Rocco from his mind, he let his imagination run with images of his beloved family in Southwark.

He could picture Mary learning everything about the neighborhood within a week of her arrival. He could hear her questioning the neighbors about the best place to find bird nests in the city, where to buy the freshest cream and where it came from, and why no Irish or Blacks lived on their street. His little nightjar would ask so many questions his head would spin. He wondered how Tina had handled her during his absence these past few years. She'd never been patient with Mary and her big thoughts and dreams. Sebastian surveyed the shop, tired and ready to retire. He could picture them all here—his family—the sounds of their laughter, the smell of their hair, the sight of their smiles, the touch of his wife's hands.

# CHAPTER FOUR

*Oystercatcher*

*August 1891*
*Southwark, Philadelphia*

Sixteen-year-old Mary Paragano of South Sixth Street strained her neck to see the tops of the tall brick buildings of Southwark that reached for the sky and blotted out the sun. It was early Friday morning, but the humid summer air already stuck in her lungs, stinking of sewage. The noises of the waking neighborhood assailed her ears. Even at this hour, dogs barked, children cried, sellers hawked, old men argued, and mothers scolded. The residents of Southwark lived on top of each other.

Mary knew every street and corner of the neighborhood. Each shopkeeper, milkman, gossiping *nonna*, drunkard, and pickpocket between here and the Delaware River knew her name. From Christian up to Lombard, the streets between Sixth and Front were her kingdom, and she'd drawn every inch of it. Her sketchbook weighed heavily in the bottom of her basket—she never went without it.

Like every Friday, Mary was headed to the wharf where she bought the oysters for her family's shop. She had to hurry, for she'd lingered too long on the corner, drawing the endearing sight of a grubby child studying an ant on the pavement. Now, she would be late for her shift at Arenberg's sweatshop.

Joey Malone interrupted her thoughts, calling from his stoop, "Hey, Mary! Where's your sister?"

"Gina? She's getting ready for work, I'd wager. Like usual." The boys were always interested in her older sister Gina.

Joey winked at her, and she wished she could stop, take out her charcoals, and draw him—capture him in his relaxed pose with his insolent smile, his dark ruffled hair, and his right suspender hanging loose from his shoulder. She hurried along, though, wanting to be on time for work.

In many ways, Southwark was similar to the tiny Italian village of her birth. Perdifumo, in Salerno, was full of similar folk playing similar societal roles. Everyone knew his neighbor's business. Gone were the dirt courtyards with chickens pecking around in the hot sun. Instead, there were dirty alleys full of barefoot children chasing dogs and playing kick-the-can or jacks on the stoop. Old women with missing teeth selling cabbages from a cart on the corner had replaced the small-thinking, backward *nonnas* who "tut-tutted" at Mary when she argued with her mother in the public square.

But Mary knew in her bones that Philadelphia could offer her something Perdifumo would never allow—independence. Wasn't her neighborhood the place where the fever of freedom had first fomented? In America, she could finally follow her dreams of running her own business, like Papa and his friend Vincenzo, the fishmonger.

Mary looked forward to seeing Cenzo. He was a gentleman, not like the childish boys in the Jewish Quarter. About thirty-five years old, with a jolly round face and a little potbelly, Cenzo hailed from a strong Salerno family, and Papa trusted him. An avid reader, Cenzo was more educated than one would expect of a fishmonger. He had a head for business and politics and a quick wit with his customers. He was always jovial with Mary and had nicknamed her "Oyster-catcher"—probably because she had the job of buying oysters for her family.

Mary had never seen an oystercatcher, but Cenzo had once described them to her. "The oystercatcher is my favorite gull," he'd said, his chubby face smiling. "They look just like any old bird from the ground, *si*? White underbelly, black feathers, long spindly legs." Cenzo had winked at her. "The bird's most remarkable feature, however, is hidden from view on the ground." Cenzo had looked into the distance, his eyes losing focus as if he were watching the bird fly in the sky.

"What hidden feature, Cenzo? Tell me!"

"Well, when an oystercatcher takes flight and its wings spread wide, something magical happens. A white stripe like the cross of Christ appears across its back." Cenzo crossed himself.

Mary looked at him, incredulous. "Magic?"

"Yes, well, magic to me. There's something special about that gull, Mary. When I first came to Philadelphia, I used to see dozens of them along the banks of the river. The Delaware is tidal, *sì*? The birds used to fly here from the shoreline in Jersey to nest during the winter." Cenzo looked around the fish stall in the direction of the busy river. "Ack, there's too many boats here now. The Delaware is no place for them any longer."

Cenzo had seemed so sad about the loss of his magical oystercatchers. Mary longed to see one so she could capture its image on paper and present the drawing to Cenzo as a gift—something meaningful to him in return for his kindness.

Cenzo had also given Mary the best gift of all. He loaned her books from his extensive personal library. Most were tattered copies of novels brought from Europe that he purchased from the ships that came into port. Mary's parents never allowed her to read novels, but Cenzo didn't know that. She had almost finished Jonathan Swift's story and couldn't wait to see what would be next.

On this particular day, when Mary approached the stall, she could hear Cenzo and his assistant Tomas discussing a customer who had departed a moment before.

"What is a socialist, anyway, Signor Vincenzo, sir?" Tomas asked, their backs to her and heads bent over a newspaper being used to wrap fish. Mary spotted a large headline smudged with fish guts that read, "Socialists Publish *The People!*"

"Well, as to that, I'm not quite sure. I know they are takers. They expect everything to be handed to them. Take, take, take! They even expect the fine Italian *ragazze* of our neighborhood to meet them in back alleys. As if our Italian girls would succumb to such hanky-panky. Bah! I know they're causing trouble, and that's enough for me. It's time to speak with Officer McMurtrie at the station. Old Sully hates the socialists. His dear wife died during one of their demonstrations. Trouble, I say. Someone better wrangle them up before they deflower every young…"

At this, Cenzo noticed Mary standing within earshot, and his face turned beet red.

"Ahem…erm…well, hello there, Miss Mary. *Ciao, ciao!* And how is our little Oystercatcher on this fine summer morning?" Cenzo blushed.

Hiding her amusement, Mary bobbed a little curtsy and answered, "I'm in a superior mood today, gentlemen, thank you. The Lilliputians themselves entertained me last night. I believe I understand the allegory in Swift's novel, Cenzo. Thanks for lending it to me. Did you find these, what did you call them—socialists?—represented in the story as well?"

Cenzo coughed and waved his hands to quiet her. He stepped closer and whispered, "Be careful what you speak about on the street, Oystercatcher, or you will catch trouble instead of oysters. Some folks are calling for violence against the socialists. Steer clear of any groups of men milling about. You can be sure they are up to no good, and that's a fact." Cenzo turned back to weigh her bag of oysters. With a wink, he added a few extras.

Mary wished to continue the conversation, but Cenzo wouldn't say another word on the matter. She had been dismissed. Again. Why did men always treat her as if she had no brain? Yet Cenzo usually spoke with her about topics in their novels, including politics. He must feel strongly about these socialists to avoid the matter altogether.

She thanked Cenzo for the oysters, settled the bill with Tomas, and turned to leave. But her curiosity stirred. She wanted to know who and what the socialists were, and she was determined to find out.

The little bells above the grocery door tinkled as Mary entered the shop and found her papa reaching high on the shelf for a bag of expensive coffee while Mr. Goldman leaned against the countertop, waiting patiently. The gentlemen turned at the sound and greeted Mary with a smile.

"As I was saying, Sebastian, 'tis a terrible shame about the growing crime in the Jewish Quarter. Somebody must do something about it."

"Yes, yes, I know, Benjamin. But what can we do?"

"I don't know. Trouble has always followed my people." Mr. Goldman shook his head and sniffed the package of coffee beans. "Ahh, now there's a scent that can cheer a weary man." He counted out his bills while Sebastian tied the bag with twine.

"A good day to you then, Benjamin."

"And to you, Sebastian." Mr. Goldman tipped his hat to her papa, then gave Mary a wink as he left the store.

Mary placed the bag of oysters on the countertop. "Mr. Goldman is very kind, isn't he, Papa?"

"He is." Sebastian surveyed the catch with approval, then squinted his eyes at Mary as if wary of her next words. "What of it?"

"Well." Mary smoothed the wood of the table. "I'm just noticing that you respect other cultures, yet you do not wish for my sisters and me to associate with the young men of those cultures."

"Hmph." Sebastian straightened his apron and busied himself, packing the oysters in a barrel of expensive ice delivered from upstate. "Always so inquisitive, my little nightjar. Nothing escapes your notice."

"My most endearing quality, I'm sure, Papa." Mary hid a smile behind her hand. She lingered, hoping her papa would answer the question. Perhaps if she sat on the stool and waited a while, he would offer his opinion on the matter.

Sebastian cleared his throat. "Mary, you know I was trained in the seminary for a few years before I met your mother. I wanted to be a priest, you know."

Mary had heard this story many times and wasn't sure where her papa was going with this. "Yes, Papa, I know that."

Sebastian wiped his hands on a cloth and joined Mary at the counter. He took her hands in his. "You and your sisters are the jewels in my crown. I *do* care for others and am interested in their ways and thoughts. But nothing would ever convince me that one of my girls should *meld* with those cultures. When you marry, you will give yourself entirely to your spouse. As the Lord teaches us in the Holy Scriptures, one should not be unevenly yoked. Does this make sense to you?"

Mary wasn't sure. She knew the Scriptures her papa referred to and believed them in theory, but Southwark was such a melting pot of different faces, it was hard to deny the beauty of diversity. She didn't want to upset her father, so she brushed off these wonderings and nodded. "Yes, Papa, I understand."

"Good." Sebastian kissed her forehead. "Now, go on and get ready for your shift. I'll see you at supper."

Every evening after work, Mary kept the books for her papa—recording every purchase and sale of her family's business in her clear hand. During the past few years, she and her father had developed a deep bond as they sat at the table, dark heads bent over the large ledger books, he reciting receipts while Mary scribbled away.

That night, as Florentina mended socks by the corner wood stove with Mary's younger brother Giuseppe reading a book at her feet, Sebastian considered his daughter across the table. "I hate that this chore keeps you from other enjoyments, my nightjar. Why don't you sketch a portrait of me sitting here with my pipe, eh?"

Mary looked up, startled out of her concentration. "Papa, I'm happy to help—you know that. Besides, how else will I learn how to manage the shop?" She batted her eyes at her father.

"Mary." Sebastian sighed and slumped back in his chair. "You will never run the grocery. It's not proper for a girl. You know this."

"But Papa!"

"Let me finish, child. I know you have the ability and the desire, but this task will fall to one of your brothers." He waved his hand toward his son. "Giuseppe will be of age soon. He already shows attention to detail and the strength to labor long hours."

"That's not true, and you know it," Mary protested. "He's a child. And more of a daydreamer than I, always chasing after squirrels and birds. And see this?" Mary pointed to a line in the book. "Papa, you must stop giving Signora Malandrino lard on account—this is the third time in as many weeks."

"I believe she's somehow related to your mama, my little nightjar. Anyway, that's beside the point."

Giuseppe piped in, "Now, Father, you must admit she has a point there. We'll never profit by lending to every *nonna* in the neighborhood. And why do you insist on calling Mary that name? It is not at all complimentary. Did you know the European nightjar doesn't build a nest for its eggs? The mama bird lays the eggs directly on the ground. Can you imagine? How does she protect her offspring from the fox?"

Sebastian chuckled. "Listen to you. You sound like a fine educated American gentleman, speaking that way. How do you know this about these birds? You're too young to remember them from our homeland."

"Signor Taranto lent me a beautiful edition of Carl Linnaeus's 10th edition of *Systema Naturae*."

"Systema...what?"

As Giuseppe crossed the room to show his father the book, Mary rolled her eyes, closed the ledgers, and tidied up the table.

"See, Papa? This is exactly what I'm saying. Giuseppe is meant for studies, and I am meant to run the grocery. I can leave Arenberg's and make more money for the family here. We could get out from under Valero. In no time, I could increase our profits by settling accounts with the Duke, and..."

"Mary, that's enough." Sebastian slapped his hand on the table. "It's dangerous to speak of the Duke that way. I'm finished with this conversation and far more interested in the birds of my beloved Italy at this time." He reached for the book his son showed him. "Now, show me what you're chattering about, *figlio*."

Mary sighed, stacked the ledger books on the shelf, and excused herself from the room.

*Why is life so complicated?* Mary climbed the stairs to the bedroom she shared with her sisters on the third floor. She had a God-given talent for numbers and accounts. The family needed to improve the business, and Mary was willing to devote her life to it. But because she was a girl, the door was closed to her. *Will the status of women ever change in this world?*

At the end of the tiny upstairs hallway, she crept into the room, careful not to wake her sisters. She paused to study her eldest sister Clara's round face and saw contentment settled into her features, even in repose. Clara already had the life she dreamed of. She would marry Dominic Forte, the son of one of Papa's friends down the street. A kind-hearted fellow, keen to pursue her and provide for her upon their marriage day, Dom labored as a cobbler to save money for their future family. Clara would fulfill her dream of marriage and motherhood. It wasn't fair that Mary couldn't pursue *her* plan because it veered from the norm.

Mary slid the copy of *Gulliver's Travels* from under the dresser, lit a candle, and sank into the corner wingback chair for a few hours of bliss. This was her nightly routine—the treat she saved for herself when the household had settled. She always held her red rosary in her lap, working the beads as she read, ready with the ruse in case her parents were to open the door. Her mama and papa would never approve of her reading novels, but seeing their virtuous daughter praying fervently by candlelight would make their hearts swell.

Despite her parents' disapproval, Mary longed to escape into the many settings of her favorite tales. After reading for an hour each night, she sketched the images that had materialized from the story. The Gothic landscapes of the Brontë Sisters—England's windy moors—were her favorite places to visit. She longed for a life like her heroine, Jane Eyre, who knew the value of her mind and the contributions she could make to society.

A giggle from the bed broke Mary's reverie. "Mary, Mary, quite contrary, why are you breaking the rules?" Gina dissolved into childish laughter.

"Gina, you scared me! I thought you were asleep."

Gina glanced at Clara to ensure she was still sleeping, then rolled out of bed and joined Mary in the corner, where she perched on the arm of the chair. "What are we reading tonight, sister?"

Mary tucked the book under her skirt. "Nothing that would interest you."

Gina furrowed her brow, lowered her eyes, and sucked in her upper lip. "Humph, c'mon, Mary. Why don't you share what you were thinking about? You looked like a righteous queen sitting there with your far-away face. Spill it. You know I can't read."

"Well, if you insist." Mary shifted in the chair, considering how to explain. "I don't know, Gina. I just want to pursue an independent life as a single woman."

Gina hid a smile behind her hand.

"I know you think I'm ridiculous, but don't you ever wonder about Mama?"

"What about Mama?"

"I don't mean to be selfish, but watching her run around after so many children depresses me."

"What else would you have her do?" Gina played with the hem of her nightdress. "Mama is a simple woman and seems happy with her destiny."

"Happy? Maybe. She's perpetually pregnant, though. She runs the house with endless energy and determination, but what of her dreams? She was sixteen when she married Papa. My age."

"Yeah, so?"

"Do you think Mama desires a life she can't have because of the duties that keep her at home? Did she want to have so many children?"

"Oh, Mary. What else was she to do? She was in a tiny Italian village when she met Papa. Not like there were many choices. Not like here in America." Gina looked at Clara, sleeping soundly. "Clara's just like her, ya know? I can't believe she's gonna marry that Dom. What a bore! Not me, I'm biding my time. Gonna catch the eye of a wealthy merchant. Or maybe one of them bankers up on Market Street. I'll make him fall madly in love with me and then get me the heck out of Southwark." Gina stood and twirled around as if being led in a fancy dance. "It'll be a match made in heaven with passion and romance! Just wait, you'll see." She gave Mary a little bow and then returned to bed. "Try not to think so hard all the time, Mary—you'll drive yourself crazy. Goodnight."

"Sweet dreams, Gina."

Mary supposed there was something to be said for romance. After all, even Jane Eyre had succumbed to passion when she fell in love with Mr. Rochester. But she didn't sacrifice her mind nor deaden the private realm of her inner being when she gave in to his caresses. Rochester respected and even loved this strength in Jane. Could there be a young man like that here in Philadelphia?

She doubted it.

"Don't look now, Mary, but that brute Rocco Monza's heading our way." Gina looped her sister's arm through her own. "If he speaks to us, let me do the talking, alright? The last thing we need is you panicking in front of him."

Stung by the snide remark but thankful for her older sister's direction, Mary nodded and held tight to Gina's arm. Of all her siblings, Gina could put men in their place within a second flat. She didn't want another run-in with Rocco. He was a brute—one of Valero's thugs—acting like he ruled the neighborhood, always seeking an angle and hedging his bets. And worst of all, someone had spread a rumor that Rocco was in love with Mary. Ridiculous. But only months before, in the wintertime, she'd overheard Rocco and Papa one night while Papa swept up the shop.

When Rocco had come to the market that winter night to visit Sebastian, Mama had shooed Mary and the little ones up the stairs, pushing the children along with undue sharpness. While preparing supper, she huffed, puffed, and snapped at five-year-old Jestina, who broke a dish while setting the table.

Curious, Mary had crept along the hallway to the top of the stairs and settled a few steps down, out of sight of Mama in the kitchen above and Papa in the market below. She opened her sketchbook on her lap and feigned drawing in case someone spotted her. Her breath caught in her throat when she heard the boorish man say her name.

She pinched her arm to avoid panicking as she realized that Rocco and Papa were discussing *her*.

Mary couldn't make out the conversation, but she heard Rocco utter one word that made her skin crawl—"desire." Mary blushed and held her breath. Papa slammed his fist on the countertop, and then she heard him say, "*Giammai.*" *Never.*

Silence fell in the room downstairs. Mary imagined the two men facing each other, muscles tensed, ready to strike. But no sounds of a skirmish came. She heard Rocco laugh—a sound devoid of humor and full of spite. "I'll woo her myself then, without your blessing. By the way, the Duke sent me over to tell you the rent on this fine establishment has doubled, effective immediately." Mary didn't hear the telltale bells over the door, but Rocco must have left the market.

Mary shuddered at the memory as she watched Rocco cross the street in their direction. He walked like a lion—big and powerful, as if nothing could threaten him. He wore his greasy black hair slicked back under his hat. The cigarette hanging from his lips moved up and down as he spoke. "Good afternoon, ladies." He aimed a lewd smile at Mary.

Gina huffed and nudged Mary to the side.

"It's only a matter of time, you know." He turned to watch them walk past, and Mary swore she could feel his gaze lingering on their backs. When the sisters rounded the corner from Rocco's view, Mary released a breath she hadn't realized she was holding.

*Only a matter of time until what?*

Never before had she been so relieved to be safe at work.

Arenberg's sweatshop was sweltering. The enormous rug looms reached for the ceiling like sentries on duty along one wall. The men were already there, working the complicated machines with their sleeves rolled up and sweat dripping from their foreheads. Through the middle of the factory, rows of tables adorned with sewing machines waited for the women. The workstations were jammed next to each other, giving the ladies no room to spread out. Mary's shoulders were often tight at the end of a shift from keeping her elbows close to her sides as she worked her machine. The spools of thread spun all day as the machines whizzed through bolt after bolt of fabric. The scant light through the dirty windows illuminated a cloud of fibers billowing in the air. Every worker coughed through the entire shift, trying to dislodge the dust that tickled the backs of their throats.

Mary and her row of seamstresses worked on men's trousers. A new pile of tweed fabric waited at the end of the row. By the end of the shift, the women should have completed hundreds of pairs of pants. Heads bent, they had no time for banter, nor was it allowed in the dreary factory. The overseers walked up and down the aisles, keeping tabs on workers' productivity and correcting mistakes.

Mary bit her lip as she tried to concentrate. It was hot outside, sure, but it was a downright inferno inside Arenberg's. All afternoon, Rocco's threatening remark rang in Mary's head. *Only a matter of time until what?*

Distracted, she didn't realize someone had approached her station. Her heart fluttered. It was most unusual for a young man to approach a woman's work table. Before Mary could blink, a rakish boy—Uri, was it?—handed her a note. He winked at her as she took the folded paper, then sauntered down the line, whistling, to his place at the big looms in the men's area.

A bead of sweat ran down Mary's back. *Did the overseer notice that?* She tucked the paper into the large pocket of her apron, where she imagined it burning a hole in the thin fabric. *What could Uri want with me? What does the letter say?* She'd have to wait two more hours until the end of her shift—and then endure the walk home with nosy Gina, greet her mama and papa, finish her supper, and help clean the dishes—before she could sneak up to her room for a few precious moments of privacy. Then, she could unfold the paper and see what that insolent boy was up to. She couldn't handle the anticipation.

She didn't care for Uri. He made her nervous. He was involved with the political group that met outside the sweatshop with signs and chants; worse, he was a known libertine. Gina said she'd found Sally McAllister kissing him behind the storage shed. A scandal, but no doubt Sally was innocent—Uri, that unprincipled lecher, had taken advantage of her. *I should burn this note before even reading a word.* But, then again, Uri was always with that other boy, the one with the dimples and the beguiling eyes. Jakob.

Mary had noticed Jakob watching her before, and the notion wasn't entirely unpleasant. A scarlet blush crept up her neck, and she shook her head to clear it. *The boys are Jewish and therefore off-limits.* Her papa wouldn't stand for it, and that was the end of it.

*But the note…* Well, she'd have to wait. Mary patted her hand against the pocket of her apron and its precious contents, then returned to her sewing.

Finally, after hours of waiting on pins and needles, Mary was alone in her room. She had only moments before Gina and Clara would come storming in to claim their places in this tiny sanctuary. Mary sat in the corner chair, reached into her apron pocket, and plucked out the secret paper. She unfolded the page with trembling fingers, desperate to know if the author was Uri or Jakob.

> *Oh answer me a question, love, I pray.*
> *My heart for thee is pining day by day;*
> *Oh answer me, my dearest, answer true;*
> *hold me close as you were wont to do.*
> *Whisper once again the story old,*
> *the dearest, sweetest story ever told;*
> *Whisper once again the story old,*
> *the dearest, sweetest story ever told.*
> *Tell me, do you love me?*
> *Tell me softly, sweetly, as of old!*
> *Tell me that you love me,*
> *for that's the sweetest story ever told.*

No greeting. No salutation. Just the lyrics to a popular new song sung by Myra Mirella in theaters. Mary had seen the sheet music advertised in the 5&10 store window. The handwriting was shaky, with billowing Ts and elaborate Ws. *Whisper.* The word gave her a warm feeling. It declared intimacy. More than the words "love" or "hold me close," *whisper* implied a closeness of the soul. To share secrets with another and to whisper in the other's ear. The image captivated Mary.

*Whisper.*

But who had written these lyrics for her? Uri didn't seem the romantic type. Mary imagined his words would be saucy and forward. No, this note wasn't from Uri—he'd merely been the messenger. Could it be Jakob who had had written out these words for her? That he imagined whispering in her ear? "My heart is pining for you…" Was it true? For the first time in her life, Mary couldn't wait for morning to come so she could go to work. At the sound of her sisters' footsteps plodding down the hall, Mary folded the paper, tucked it into her novel, and hid both items under the dresser.

# CHAPTER FIVE

*The Color Purple*

*June 2018*
*Drexel Hill, PA*

Bella spent the day reliving her youth as she sorted through bins of old clothes and bright pink bedding in her mom's attic. Rosalie wanted to donate items to charity and had asked Bella to go through her college stuff. Bella laughed at photos of her roommates with their silly antics and innocent campus fun. Her semester abroad in Italy. Her sassy college roommate with the nose ring and a dolphin tattoo on her back. The Thanksgiving weekend camping trip where her gang of friends nearly froze without enough firewood. Bella spotted her tattered copy of Toni Morrison's *Beloved* under the pile of photos and stopped. Pages of notes in her scrawling handwriting stuffed the pages of the book. Discovering the novel was like bumping into an old friend at a coffee shop.

Bella sat back on her heels and thumbed through its worn pages. She'd written her senior thesis on *Beloved* at Temple University and had spent weeks immersed in the characters' lives. She remembered a time in her early thirties when she'd devoured Alice Walker's *The Color Purple* and had a million brilliant ideas about comparing and contrasting the novel with *Beloved*. She'd wanted to attend grad school to share her thoughts and discuss the themes of the two stories with other students.

The novel brought back sad memories too.

Late one night, while she'd been scribbling away by a penlight in bed, Nate had stirred and asked her what she was doing, writing in the middle of the night. "It's a weeknight, for Pete's sake! I have a meeting tomorrow."

Bella still remembered her jittery reply. "I'm discovering that the two female protagonists of these novels accepted their pasts and pushed forward into better lives. They forged new identities."

Nate had huffed and swung his arm over his eyes, blocking out the light and her very presence. "And this is important to me—why?"

Per usual, his rebuff had deflated her excitement.

The memory reached through time with a similar effect. Bella put aside the novel on the dusty attic floor with a few other treasures she wanted to keep. She stood up, brushed the dust off her jeans, stretched her arms, and twisted to release a crick in her neck. A large painting stuck behind her dad's old army chest caught her eye. She could see the top of someone's head peeking out from behind. Curious, she pulled it out and stared into the intense eyes of a striking, dark-haired woman. The lady looked at her, sad but triumphant at the same time.

Her mother's footsteps thumped up the attic steps, and Bella startled, nearly dropping the painting. "Hey, Ma. You scared me. By the way, who's this?"

Rosalie joined her at the back of the attic, peering at the solemn face over her daughter's shoulder. "I don't quite remember. My dad brought that along with Nana's things when he moved her into the nursing home years ago. It was a tough time for him, seeing his mom's decline—he was pretty emotional about her in those days, so I didn't ask. I remember it hanging over the mantle in Nana's house for decades. Lunch is ready downstairs. Egg salad, your favorite."

Rosalie started down the stairs, holding tight to the railing. "Oh, before you finish up," she called over her shoulder. "That box in the corner is full of family photos and such. I'm not interested, but you can take it today if you want."

Bella put the painting aside and spent the remainder of the day organizing the donations and packing bins and boxes into her car for the drop-off.

That evening, in her empty home, Bella sighed as she watched reruns of *The Golden Girls* while walking on a treadmill like a hamster. She was bored to tears. She and Nate used to hang out with a couple from the neighborhood every Saturday night for dinner and a movie. She'd been waiting to hear from them since Nate left. *Guess I lost them in the divorce too.* She'd filled every weekend hour with activity to distract her from the emptiness, but it had finally found her. At least she had *The Golden Girls* to keep her company. This show always made her laugh. The feisty character Sophia reminded her of her new-found cousin, and she had a strong urge to speak with her again. Bella grabbed her cell phone resting on the treadmill console and dialed Sophie's number. Thankfully, Sophie answered the phone.

"Hi, Sophie. How's your weekend going?"

"Oh, I can't complain, Bella. I'm alive and breathing. I'm watching my granddaughter this evening while her parents are at a wedding. She's doing my hair." Bella could hear Sophie admonish someone in the room with her twinkling chuckle. "No way, José, no purple."

"Oh, my word. Purple? Hey, that might look great on you." Bella had to laugh. Sophie never ceased to amaze her—her heart was so much younger than her eighty-three years. "Well, I won't keep you. I wanted you to know my mom gave me a box of old papers and photos from her attic today. I was helping her donate some stuff, and she asked me to take it."

"Anything interesting in there?"

"Well, the funny thing is, I kinda don't want to look by myself." Bella turned off the treadmill and hopped off, wiping her face with a cloth. She bit her lip and stalled. "I was wondering…"

"Wondering what? Ouch!" Sophie chastised her granddaughter, "Don't tug so hard, dear."

Bella walked over and nudged the box of old papers with her foot. She tried not to sound desperate. "Well, what would you say about meeting with me again? Maybe we could go through this box together."

"That sounds nice. I like that idea. Could you travel down here again? I don't think there'd be enough room to spread out here at my place, though, 'cause it's a tiny bungalow."

Relief washed over Bella. She hadn't realized how much it meant to her that Sophie join her in the research project. "No, no, I wouldn't want to impose. Anyway, I kinda need to get away from here and thought I might make a trip out of it. You know, see the sights in DC. I've never been to the capital museums. And, well, now that I know my family has Jewish heritage, I wanna check out the one about the Holocaust."

"The United States Holocaust Memorial Museum. I've been there, and it's hard. But, yes, you should go. *Everyone* should go. Look, if you're making the trip here, I'd like to offer some hospitality. At least let me book a hotel room for you."

"Oh, I couldn't impose, Sophie." Bella stood in her entryway, looking above the key ring next to the door. There was Nate's face, smiling at her through space and time—their wedding photo. *I gotta get out of here.*

Sophie's voice came through the line, bright and cheery. "No, it'll be fun. You do your sightseeing on Saturday afternoon, then we can dive into the box when you get to the hotel. I'll bring the folder of stuff I found about my Uncle Jakob and Mendel. I can book two rooms and make dinner reservations."

"That'd be wonderful. You're the best, Sophie." Excitement stirred in Bella's heart for the first time in weeks. "I'm happy you're doing this with me."

"Me too. I'm doing this for Mendel. He was my favorite cousin, after all. I said no purple, you stinker!" Bella could hear Sophie giggling, her granddaughter in the background in hysterics.

"Well, I better let you go. Sounds like you have your hands full. Could you send me an email with some dates? Good luck with the hair, Sophie!"

Bella ended the call, and before she could second-guess herself, snatched the wedding portrait off the wall, walked straight out the front door, and left the picture on the curb, leaning against the trash can.

# CHAPTER SIX

### *Let the Show Begin*

*August 1891*
*Southwark, Philadelphia*

"She's an angel. A complicated angel, but an angel still. She could easily bring redemption or destruction, according to her mood. My heart is hers, Uri! I wish she'd answer my letter!" Jakob cried for the dozenth time, his face in his hands.

Uri sniggered and cuffed his pal on the back. "Jakob, you're smitten. You didn't even sign the letter, you *schlemiel*, so how can she respond?"

Tired and grubby after sixteen hours at the sweatshop, they'd stopped at the taproom before returning to their pallets in the rented room they shared in Frau Levin's boardinghouse on Fourth Street—the highlight of their day. Their comrades trickled in, each exhausted and with one thought in their heads. They wanted—no, *needed*—a beer to slake their great thirst. After the first draft, they loosened up and started chatting.

They talked and talked about everything under the sun. About the neighborhood girls, the news and happenings on the streets, the show appearing at the Yiddish theater on Fifth and Gaskill, and the old drunk dying in the gutter on Seventh.

The one subject the friends never spoke of—by tacit agreement—was their homeland. No one ever spoke of the families left back *there*. No one ever acknowledged the rumor of another pogrom that had torn through their village. They were powerless to prevent such persecution, and their impotence shamed them, so they avoided the topic at all costs. In private, they might worry about their *muters*, their vulnerable *shvesters*—sisters—back home, and perhaps a childhood sweetheart left behind. But the tavern wasn't the place for those conversations.

Instead, they spoke of the Socialist Labor Party and the upcoming elections. They complained about the rent and the rising price of cabbage. Most of all, they *kvetched* and groused about their lack of prospects.

"And how, may I ask, are we to improve our circumstances with so many top hats stomping on our heads as we strive to climb the social ladder?" Ruben lamented. "The cycle's forever the same. No matter how hard we toil, comrades, we'll never get out of the boiling soup of Southwark."

Jakob's quiet and thoughtful brother Kopel asked, "Perhaps if we move along from Philadelphia? I hear there's work in Baltimore. Perhaps one could carve out a comfortable life there?"

"A life doing what, Kopel?" scoffed Ira. "I can't picture your pretty hands shucking oysters or running a fishing boat." Laughter rippled through the men along the bar.

Kopel replied, "Many banks and railroad companies in Baltimore need a strong mind such as mine. I'd miss you all, though. Especially you." He looked at Jakob. "Though I do wish you would join me."

Jakob grunted in response, hiding his face in his stein. He didn't want to face the prospect of his brother—his only family in this new country—leaving. Weeks, even days ago, perhaps, he'd have contemplated going with Kopel and quitting this unforgiving city. But then he'd seen his bewitching angel's face, and his feet were cemented in Southwark.

Uri interrupted his rumination. "I don't think he's going anywhere, Kopel. Our Jakob is in *love*." He spoke in a falsetto voice and batted his eyelashes. The group laughed.

"Who is the lucky lady, pray tell?"

"Ooh, is she pretty?"

"Does she have a sister?"

"I know, it's that dreamer, Mary—the one with the dark hair and eyes the color of charcoal." Ruben poked his fork in Jakob's direction. "You better be wary about her, Jakob. She's a smart one, you can be sure. Well-read, too, I'd gather."

"Bet she could school you on a few lessons," someone teased.

Jakob brooded into his cup and refused to answer.

Kopel came to his rescue. "Leave off, comrades. Let him be. Surely you can discern this is no joking matter to Jakob. He may be in love with this girl, and that's not something to be light about." To his brother, he whispered, "I guess you won't join me in Baltimore, eh, *Bruder*?"

Jakob shook his head. He was stuck in Southwark as long as Mary lived here. He knew in his bones that wherever she went, he'd go also.

*I must speak with her. Tomorrow. Tomorrow, I will walk up to her outside Arenberg's, reach out my hand to take hers, and declare...*

The screeching of chair legs interrupted Jakob's dramatic thoughts. Fellas in all corners of the tavern stood, hands curling into fists. Silence filled the room, and Jakob twisted to see the cause of such a disruption.

Officer Sullivan McMurtrie and his Second and Christian Street Station men had moseyed into the bar. The officer was a decent man, in Jakob's opinion; he had once seen McMurtrie assist a Jewish vendor whose pushcart had collapsed onto his leg. The large Irishman had lodged his meaty shoulder under the cart and heaved with a grunt, lifting the wagon off the Hebrew while his friends hoisted him to safety. Irish he might be, but that didn't make him a bad man. The problem with Officer McMurtrie, though—he was on the wrong side of politics. All the Irish coppers belonged to the Fourth Ward boss Bull McBride, staunch Democrats who despised the Socialist Labor Party.

"I'm searching for someone, lads," McMurtrie proclaimed in a booming voice that reached every corner of the tavern. "You may know that a fella set fire to a dumpster bin behind the station last night." His men spread out and gave menacing looks to the patrons around the tavern. "Thank the good Lord no one was damaged. I'm sure you'll be glad to know that." He smiled. "Anyone here know who did it?" He surveyed the room and was met by silent stares. "I didn't expect so. Well, my men and I will be joining you for a dram.

We'll sit here, by the door. Welcome to come chat awhile if you want."

With that, the officer and his coppers sat at the table near the exit and ordered shots of whiskey. Jakob, his brother, and their companions gave each other knowing nods over their drinks—their conversation had ended.

Solemn now, the group settled with the bartender and took their leave one by one, sidling past McMurtrie and his crew, avoiding meeting their eyes. When only a few remained, Jakob heard Uri greeted McMurtrie. "I'll share a cup with ya, Officer."

Jakob hung his head, his hand on the door frame. *Blazes! What is that idiot up to now?*

Jakob looked back at his comrade, sitting beneath the curious eyes of McMurtrie's policemen. He nodded to his pals and turned back into the tavern. One of McMurtrie's men stood to offer his chair to Jakob with a funny smile on his face. Jakob kept his wits about him as his buddy asked, "Why do you hate the SLP so much, Sully, old man?"

Sullivan placed his cup on the table, leveling his eyes on Uri. "Why do I hate the socialists, you ask? Honestly, I don't know where to start." McMurtrie shook his head with a rueful laugh. "Let's see. Life was hard enough here before that lot came traipsing into town. Every day was the same. Men—pressed for work, hungry, anxious, tired of the noise at home—getting drunk in broad daylight." Sully's voice grew louder. "The kids in the alley clamoring for their attention as the men lumbered up the steps after a long day of hard labor. The wives turning out another pot of tepid stew made from the little bits of vegetation in the back garden. The pressure boiling over and sending them right back out to the pub to while away the hours until the children were asleep on their pallets in the front room, five to a mattress."

He took a deep breath. "Look, I grew up the same way: too many kids, too little space, not enough food, and too much time. Southwark was different in those days, though. At least we had a sense of *community*. Folks *cared* about each other, ya know? We had a sense of pride—Irish pride. Then the socialists moved in back in '87, prodded everyone off Fourth Street, claimed the market neighborhood, and hawked their wares from pushcarts. Southwark was better off without the lot. Crowds of you Jewish men, smelling of pickles, picketing with signs and cat-calls. What a bunch of nonsense." McMurtrie spat on the floor.

Uri and Jakob sat in silent shock. But the big man was just getting warmed up.

"The pushing and shoving between members of the SLP and us coppers always ends in a fistfight. And in the bustle, the housewives of good Irish families…" Sully's voice wobbled as he pointed his fingers into Uri's and Jakob's faces. "Good women buying cabbage for their soup, caught in the ruckus. My Abigail!" Sully stood with such force that his chair crashed to the floor. "God, what a pitiful way to die! She deserved better than that—she and the child."

He marched up to the bar and ordered another whiskey.

Jakob and Uri turned to McMurtrie's men, eyebrows raised. "What the hell is he talking about?" Uri asked.

One of the policemen leaned across the table. "Two years ago, Sully's pregnant wife was at the market picking out wilted vegetables from a ramshackle cart when a horse broke free of the reins a block away and came bustling down the street—wagon dragged behind it, breaking apart as it came." He lowered his voice. "She had no chance to get away." The man crossed himself.

Another officer picked up the tale. "Aye. A witness informed him Abigail had been brave—defiant even—standing her ground, hands protective around her bulging belly, almost daring Death to fail in his pursuit."

"That's a sad tale, to be sure." Uri held up his glass in a silent salute to McMurtrie's dead wife. He downed his last gulp. "But what's that got to do with us?"

The first man looked behind him to ensure Sully wasn't within earshot. "Well, rumor has it an SLP member's the one that cut the reins. Payback for a fistfight the night before."

Jakob let out a low whistle.

"So, you see, Sully hates the socialists, and he's spent the last few years of his life hounding 'em—daring them to start something. I was you," the man raised his glass, eyebrows waggling, "I'd stay out of his way."

Jakob couldn't have agreed more.

A few days after sending Mary the love note, Jakob attended a matinée at the little Jewish theater on Gaskill with his brother Kopel, Uri, and a few of their friends. The afternoon was cloudy and cool for June, with the threat of a thunderstorm in the air.

Uri pinched Jakob's arm as soon as the boys were seated.

Jakob yelped. "What the heck, Uri?"

Uri flashed him a lewd smile and nodded to a pair of girls on the other side of the room. Jakob recognized Mary right away. She'd twisted her jet-black hair into a loose bun and stuffed it under a blue hat, with one rebellious strand falling across her brow. Jakob admired her serious countenance. She seemed to see beyond material things, like she knew of a secret world hidden behind a veil. *Maybe she has a vivid imagination.* Jakob didn't want Mary to catch him staring. He slumped in his seat and watched as the girls removed their jackets and adjusted their hats. Jakob smiled as Mary wrestled with the errant strand of hair, tucking it under the lip of her hat with undue force. *She's an impatient one, then.* Something about the thought made him like her even more.

Beside Jakob, the other boys laughed at something one of them said. Mary must have heard the guffaws because she swiveled in her seat, and her eyes found his like magnets.

Jakob couldn't turn away. The week before, he'd been smoking with Uri outside Arenberg's, studying her and her sister from across the street while they walked to work. She'd spotted him staring at her then too. *She must think me an idiot!*

A slow blush crept up Mary's neck, but she held his gaze.

Uri noticed him gawking and shifted to see the object of his attention. He gave Mary an insolent wink. Jakob elbowed his comrade in the ribs, mortified. Thank God, the music started, and the show began.

The crowd dispersed with laughter and good humor at the end of the performance, which had included a singing man dressed as a buxom housewife and a little boy acting as a dog doing tricks for a bone. Without warning, Gina clutched Mary's elbow and steered her to the trio of young men. "C'mon, sister, they've been staring at us during the entire show."

Mary protested, "Not on your life, Gina. Papa would be furious!" But her tone was unconvincing, even to her own ears. In truth, she wished to meet Jakob more than anything else.

They reached the young men, and Gina introduced herself and Mary. Everyone shook hands as Uri introduced the Lichtenbaum brothers, Kopel and his younger brother Jakob, new in town and now working at Arenberg's. Mary's nerves threatened to strike her dumb. She twisted her hands and dared to speak. "I've seen you at the factory, Jakob."

He gave her a dimpled smile. "And I've seen you there as well, Mary, which makes my workday something to look forward to."

Mary looked at the floor, overcome with giddiness. Since receiving the love letter, she'd also looked forward to work, like some magic trick had changed her dreary workplace into a palace and her complex tasks at the sewing machine into a lovely stroll in a fancy garden. *Is this love?* She pinched herself under the arm to keep her wits about her. She was acting like a loon!

Uri and her sister Gina were speaking behind her. Someone suggested a stroll around the neighborhood, and Kopel mentioned catching a breeze from the river. Mary let herself be swept along with the little group, her heart floating outside her body. As they crossed the Southwark streets, Jakob regaled her with his impressions of the neighborhood, the journey he and Kopel had made to Philadelphia, and the desire to own his own business someday.

Mary didn't mention her shared desire to become a businesswoman. *He'd probably be shocked out of his mind.*

After a time, Jakob reached for her hand, his eyebrows raised, requesting permission. Against her better judgment, Mary gave it. Jakob's touch sent an electric spark up her spine that left her dizzy and breathless. *This is ridiculous. I don't even know this boy!*

Before long, the group stood at the river watching the gulls sweep low over the water. A cool breeze lifted the stray hairs off Mary's neck. A storm was brewing—the clouds were growing thicker on the far side of the river, and the birds careened around them.

After a time, Kopel excused himself, glancing up at the menacing sky. "I regret that I must head uptown to arrange my move to Baltimore. I should go before the storm hits. I have much to do."

Kopel shook hands with Uri and Jakob and gave a curt little bow to Gina. However, he lingered with Mary and bowed low over her hand in an old-fashioned style, then kissed her knuckles. "I'm glad to meet you properly, Miss Mary."

Mary blushed. "How charming."

Jakob gave a slight cough under his breath. "Yes, well, I will see you this evening, Kopel. Good luck with the banker."

Mary watched him leave, sad to see him go. She liked Kopel—he was kind and good. She sensed a strong emotion between the two brothers and wanted to know them better. She noticed Jakob following his brother's departure with a brooding look. "Are you not joining your brother in Baltimore, Jakob?" She feared the answer, though it was ridiculous. So what if Jakob were to move away? She shouldn't care one way or the other.

Uri and Gina headed back to the wharf, but Jakob stood watching his brother's retreating form. "Once, there was a time I would never part with my brother. Like Ruth and Naomi, I suppose. But." Jakob paused and turned to her. "Now, I'm not so sure. I may want to stay in Southwark and see what comes."

Relief washed over Mary with a force she did not understand. "Wouldn't you miss your brother?"

Jakob hesitated. "Well, I'm not quite sure how to explain. We grew up together in Warsaw, emigrated here, and made a life for ourselves. We have no other family on this continent. To be in Philadelphia without Kopel—well, I don't know how I feel about the thought, to be honest." Jakob's face darkened like the sky overhead. "We should head back."

By the time they reached Third Street, the heavens had opened in one of those grand summer storms in which the rain fell in buckets.

A loud crack of thunder made the couple jump. They lost sight of Uri and Gina in the rain. Jakob grabbed Mary's hand with a shout and towed her down the street toward Arenberg's. He rounded the back of the building and jiggled the handle of the oversized delivery door. "The lock is broken," he shouted over the drumming raindrops. He pushed the heavy door open and swept Mary inside.

Shadow engulfed the factory. There was no light in the building, but with every flash of lightning, Mary could see the large looms and sewing machines lining the brick walls. Nighttime had transformed her familiar workplace. The shadows were alive! Every broom leaning against the wall was a slender woman in a blooming hoop skirt. Every overturned bucket was a cushioned ottoman fit for a queen. The machines resembled giant sleeping trolls, and Mary longed to capture the scene with her paper and pencils. Arenberg's was silent except for the roll of thunder and the soft hum of the boiler in the basement, which kept the water hot for the irons.

Jakob led her to the far wall where the completed rugs were stored, and they settled themselves on the pile. They were soaked to the skin. Jakob removed his jacket and draped it around Mary's shoulders. The fine wool, though wet, warmed her. Her curly black hair slowly dried, creating a cloud of unruly wisps around her face. Mary pushed her hair back and watched Jakob as he wrung his derby and shook the water out from his hair.

His face was round, with a pointed chin and defined cheekbones. His eyes were evenly set and capped with solid brown eyebrows. He had a regal look. Strong muscles showed under the wet fabric of his shirt, and Mary imagined his biceps were thicker than a tree branch! Though he was the shortest of his friends, Jakob was brawny and finely built.

He looked up and smiled. Mary nearly swooned at the sight of his dimples, deeply knit into both cheeks.

"You were the one, weren't you? You sent the song lyrics to me."

Jakob reached across the small space between them and tentatively pushed a stray wisp of hair behind her ear. "Whisper once again the story old, the dearest, sweetest story ever told." He moved ever so slightly closer, his eyes locked on hers.

Mary longed with all her soul for Jakob to kiss her, to melt away her reserve and claim her passion. But she couldn't. Theirs was an ill-fated romance, and she had to nip it in the bud. She sat up straighter, shook her head, and cleared her throat.

"Why don't you tell me about your homeland?" She broke the spell. Jakob chuckled and sat back against the wall, stretched his legs, and crossed one over the other. He wrapped his arms around his waist and tilted his head back, looking at the high ceiling. He looked every bit a man of leisure, a sultan sitting atop a pile of carpets with nowhere else to be.

"Is that really what you want to do, Mary?" he asked with a honeyed voice.

The storm had stopped. Mary wasn't exactly sure when. She and Jakob had talked for an hour, keeping a respectable distance from each other. She fiddled with the buttons on his coat, still draped over her shoulders. Hoping he wouldn't notice, she sniffed the fabric and inhaled his scent. *I think I'm falling in love.*

"We can't linger here, Jakob. We shouldn't have been alone together this long. It's not proper."

"A little too late for that, don't you think?" Jakob inched closer.

"Where have Uri and Gina gone anyway?"

Jakob's eyes lingered on her, and her resolve melted away.

As if approaching a skittish animal about to run, Jakob reached across the space between them and took her hand. He caressed her knuckles, drawing a circle on her skin. Mary shivered.

Jakob held her gaze and inched closer. He reached for her neck, focusing on the skin behind her ear. Mary released a soft groan. His face was an inch from hers, and he gazed into her eyes with a naked vulnerability she had never seen before. Mary desired to dive into those two discs of hazel brown and swim in them forever, discovering new bits of color at every turn. Jakob's eyes were a work of art. She'd never seen hazel eyes up close before, and she lost herself in them.

Then Jakob looked at her lips and leaned in.

*I must pull myself away before—*

A loud hiss escaped from one of the steam irons on the far side of the factory. Hearts pounding, Mary and Jakob separated with a little jump. They kept silent as mice for a moment, listening for the sound of footsteps in the building.

They heard no one. They smiled at each other. Mary covered her mouth with her hand, suppressing her giggles.

Jakob loved her. Of that, Mary was sure. His eyes told the truth.

Total darkness had descended outside. As reality dawned, panic rose in her mind. She blinked as if waking from a dream. "I must be getting home." She stood and removed Jakob's coat. "Heavens! Papa will be furious. What have I done? And what will he say when I show up at home, at night, *unchaperoned?*" Her voice rose an octave along with her agitation. "And where, pray tell, is Gina anyway?"

As if Mary had conjured her sister out of thin air, Gina's giggle erupted from the back door. "Mary, Mary, quite contrary, why are you in there with a boy?"

Uri chuckled behind her, "Come out, come out, wherever you are!"

Jakob smiled as if to excuse his friend's teasing behavior, but Mary was mortified. She stood up, a little unsteady, shook the rug fibers off her skirt, and shoved Jakob's jacket back at him.

Suppressing a rakish smile, he raised both hands in surrender and stood up. He gripped Mary by the waist, drew her close, and whispered into her ear, "This may be sport to Uri and your sister, but this wasn't a game for me, Mary. You've disarmed me in every sense. I am yours to do with whatever you please. You can tell me to leave you alone from this moment forward. Or you can meet me here again at the next opportunity." Then he called to Gina, "She's here. We're coming out."

He walked away, leaving Mary swaying in place behind him.

To atone for her tardiness the night before—and the lies she and Gina had told Papa to excuse it—Mary woke up extra early to retrieve the oysters from Vincenzo's stall. The neighborhood was still asleep. Following her usual route, she came around the corner of Passyunk onto Fitzwater Street to find Jakob leaning against the street lamp, smoking a cigarette. His lips smiled around the rolled paper at the sight of her, and his dimples flashed like shooting stars. Mary's heart skipped a beat, and she diverted her eyes.

He pulled a last drag, flicked the cigarette to the ground, and stomped out the ashes, letting out a long, steady stream of smoke, all the while never taking his eyes off Mary. Mary pretended she hadn't seen him, which was ridiculous, as he stood two feet away from her. Keeping her eyes toward the river, she skirted around the lamppost.

Jakob hopped in front of her, stepping backward to keep pace, and reached out his hands in mock prayer. "C'mon, Mary, don't be sore. I didn't lure you into Arenberg's to make a pass at you. I rescued you from the storm."

Mary stopped and peered at him with narrowed eyes. Jakob came to a halt in front of her, pleading for forgiveness. "I promise I'll be a perfect gentleman. Let me escort you on your errand." He reached for her market basket.

Mary bit her lip and considered her options. She enjoyed Jakob's attention and wanted to prolong it, but she hesitated to hand over her basket. In the bottom, under a cloth, was her treasured sketchbook, where she'd attempted to render Jakob's likeness several times. The dimples were easy to capture, but she had yet to master his beguiling eyes. She'd be mortified if Jakob discovered her meager attempts to capture his face.

She considered his pleading countenance, and relented. Jakob made a triumphant sound when she relinquished the basket and offered his arm. Mary couldn't help but smile. Arm in arm, they meandered in the morning light to the pier. "Today, I want to hear everything about you, Mary. Last night, I spilled my guts to you about my brother and our dreams of a new life here. Now, it's your turn. I wish to know everything that is going on behind those mysterious dark eyes of yours."

Pleased at his invitation, Mary prattled on about her family, their immigration to America, her father's prior employment with the street sweepers, their grocery, and her dreams of supervising the family market one day. She left out her reading and artwork—she wasn't quite ready to be so vulnerable.

Jakob asked her all kinds of questions. He was curious about her Catholic faith, her religion's traditions, and their kitchen customs. He wrinkled his nose when she spoke of the various seafood recipes her family enjoyed the most, including the oyster stew her mother made weekly from the catch Mary gathered at Vincenzo's stall.

"Why such a face, Jakob?"

"Oh, shellfish aren't kosher." Changing the subject, he asked, "Did you mean Vincenzo Carpinelli, the fishmonger?"

"The same. Do you know him?"

"Oh, no, not really." Jakob looked around the street. "You're headed there now, I assume?"

"Yes, I get the oysters every Friday. It's my special errand for the family. I don't mind—Cenzo is an old friend of my father's and is kind to me. He always has a new book for me to borrow..." Mary broke off, noticing that Jakob had grown distracted. "Jakob, what's the matter?"

Jakob turned and, holding the market basket to the side, grabbed Mary into a passionate, one-armed embrace, kissing her with full force on the lips. He released her as suddenly, handed the basket back into her arms, tipped his hat, and moseyed back the way they'd come.

Stunned, Mary watched him go, hands in his pockets, with a little skip in his step. She looked down at the market basket swinging from her arm and saw the words *Meet me—factory midnight* written on the first page of her sketchbook.

*How'd he manage that?* Incredulous, she turned back toward the market at the pier, careful to hide her starstruck expression, and saw Cenzo waving at her from across the street.

The room was dark, apart from a thin stream of moonlight that cast a soft glow on the bed. Mary could see Gina's grin beside her, like the smile of the Cheshire Cat floating above the ground. Clara was sound asleep, and Mary figured it was around midnight—time to go. Ignoring Gina and the mock "tsk-tsk" sounds she made, Mary crept out of the room, then closed the door behind her. She'd deal with Gina later—she had been well-bribed. A week's worth of laundry traded for her silence. This whole affair was Gina's fault anyway. If she hadn't suggested that they stroll with the boys the day before, hadn't left her and Jakob alone last night at the factory…

But in her heart, Mary knew this deception had nothing to do with her older sister. She'd move heaven and earth to be with Jakob tonight. The expectation of his touch on her skin made her breathless. She tiptoed down the stairs, her heart beating like the wings of a bird in her chest—solid, rapid beats. She hoped Papa couldn't hear her heart booming.

Mary slipped out the front door and down the alley of Clymer Street before she could say jackrabbit. At the corner of Randolf, she glanced back to ensure no one had followed her. She held back a giggle at the image of Mama chasing her down with a frying pan, wearing her nightcap and shift. The moonlight was brighter in the street—she'd have to be careful.

She giggled all the way to Arenberg's, surprised at her audacity. As she approached the back door to the factory, she started to panic. What if she was too early? Or worse, too late? Did he mean for her to enter the building? Was the door unlocked? *This was a mistake.* She was a fool to be standing here at night, alone and vulnerable. What if Rocco happened to be out, lurking around with his cronies? If he found her here, there'd be no fighting him off.

She heard a footstep behind her, and before she could twist around, his hands were on her, touching her neck and holding her head up to face him. Jakob. He looked at her with such passion that her knees became water. She melted into his embrace and kissed him long and hard. He yelped in surprise at her forwardness. She bit his lower lip. A groan rose from deep in his throat. Somehow her hair was already undone, out of its clips. His hands were running through her thick black tresses.

Jakob pulled away and, without a word, led her through the already-open door. They stumbled as if drunk, clinging to each other as they traipsed down the dark hall to the storage area and the pile of carpets. Jakob sat and pulled her onto his lap. Mary watched as he undid the top buttons of her blouse and leaned in to run his nose along her clavicle. She held her breath, dizzy with anticipation.

Mary woke with a start—Gina in bed, asleep beside her—in the humid room she shared with her sisters on the third floor of her family's home at 751 South Sixth Street. It had all been a dream; she'd never left. She'd lost something precious before she could even enjoy it, and she could do nothing about it. *Am I strong because I didn't go to meet him, or does that make me a coward?* Either way, it didn't matter. She had left him there, waiting for her. Jakob might never speak to her again.

She'd made her decision earlier that evening, while her family recited grace around the table, heads bent, petitioning for blessing over the bread and Mama's *crioli con le noci*. The dried cod cooked with chopped nuts was one of the family's favorite meals, a special delicacy reserved for celebrations—in this case, her younger sister Jestina's birthday. Before supper, Papa had given the child a new push toy. Everyone delighted in Jestina's innocent squeak of surprise, and Mary captured the moment with a quick drawing of the scene to the applause of her family. Dinner was lovely, and during the blessing prayer, Mary knew she mustn't see Jakob that night. She couldn't meet him at the factory, and she couldn't trust herself to be alone with him.

Sitting in bed now, she mourned her loss. *I may have given Jakob my heart, but I can't give my body so easily.* She'd been foolish to consider that she and Jakob could ever be together. She was a Catholic, and he was a Jew. Her papa worked for the Duke of South Philly and belonged to the political machine that ran the wards of Southwark. Jakob was a member of the Socialist Labor Party. They were as different as night and day. Papa would never agree to such a match. And Mary knew she couldn't offer herself to a man who wasn't her husband. Fate had doomed their fling from the start, like Romeo and Juliet.

Tired of being strong and fighting the tears, Mary lay back against the pillows and let them come.

Jakob paced back and forth in front of Arenberg's the following morning, watching Mary and Gina come around the corner. His nerves reverberated like harp strings, and his stomach roiled. *This is agony!*

Jakob had waited for two hours in the middle of the night, leaning against the factory wall, turning his head at every sound, his body eagerly awaiting Mary's touch. By two in the morning, he knew she wasn't coming. Oh, how his heart had sunk to his knees! Her kiss, stolen on the corner that morning, her market basket in his hands, replayed in his mind and tempted him to insanity. He wanted her. And she wasn't coming.

*She doesn't want me.*

There they were. Gina had a mischievous smile, and Mary looked like an angel of righteousness, stomping her feet in fury, closing the space between them at an alarming rate. This wasn't how Jakob had imagined their reunion. He attempted a smile as she came upon him, Gina a few paces behind her. But at the look on Mary's face, the smile died on his lips, and his shoulders slumped as if his muter had scolded him for sneaking a cooling *cebularz* from the counter.

Before Jakob could speak a word, Mary stuck her chin out and started in. "You are an insolent boy. To even suggest that I…I…" She threw her hands in the air, speechless. She gave a huff, then turned away and went into the shop.

"Wait!" Jakob reached out his arm. "Mary, wait." But Mary was already at her post. He followed her, but Gina stepped in front of him.

"Best to leave it for now. I've never seen her so upset. I wonder, what did you start?" She gave him an appraising look—one arched eyebrow high in question.

Jakob tugged on Gina's arm. "Please, implore her to meet me at the wharf after her shift. I beg you."

Gina searched his face. She looked surprised, eyes round as moons. "You love her, don't you?"

"More than my life." Jakob left Mary's sister standing there, mouth agape.

Against her better judgment, Mary went to the river to meet Jakob in the evening. Exhaustion tugged at her as she climbed down the long wooden steps to the sandy shore and saw a blanket laid for a picnic dinner. Jakob stood beside a basket, gazing at the water, silhouetted against the evening sky. As she approached, he turned to greet her. He smiled, and her heart raced, chasing the exhaustion away.

Jakob gave a little bow and offered her his hand as she settled onto the blanket. They sat for a few moments in comfortable silence. As hungry as she was, Mary couldn't even consider eating—her stomach was doing flips. She saw a fisherman in a little brown boat and smelled the salt from the marsh grasses behind them. She marveled that the tidal river brought seawater this far up the coast.

Jakob broke the silence with a little yelp of surprise. "Look, Mary!" He pointed to a few birds fighting over a closed shell on the shoreline. "That's an oystercatcher! What a remarkable sight." He shook his head in disbelief.

Mary studied the black bird with its beady eye and long orange beak. She had never seen one before. "So that's an oystercatcher. Cenzo gave me the nickname when I was ten years old, and I figured it was because I'm the one who picks up the oysters every week for the shop." She laughed. "I wonder if he was naming me after the actual bird."

"Well, it would make sense to me. After all, the oystercatcher is awfully rare." Jakob jumped up, shielding his eyes from the setting sun to get a better view of the bird. "When Kopel and I came up the river to Philadelphia, the ship's first mate regaled us about the flora and fauna of the area. We were leaning on the rail when he surprised us with a shout of joy. He pointed to an oystercatcher on the shore and said that the bird is nearly extinct now—gone from these waters."

"How wonderful. I want to draw one for Cenzo as a keepsake." Mary dug around the bottom of her basket for her pencils and book. She began right away, before the sun went down, using long strokes to sketch the bird.

Jakob settled next to her on the blanket and watched her draw. His eyes grew large as she created a nearly perfect image of the bird. "You're a rare treasure, for sure, Mary." He whistled in appreciation of her talent.

She finished the last mark with a flourish and smiled at Jakob. He withdrew the paper from her hand and placed it in the basket. He took her hands in his and spoke with an earnestness she hadn't yet heard. "A treasure that I will hold close for all my days."

Mary stared into Jakob's eyes, then at his lips. She touched his cheek.

He kissed her—long and deep. She surrendered to his kiss, to his declaration of love—to his soul. She belonged to Jakob now. She remembered her favorite line from *Wuthering Heights*. "Whatever our souls are made of, his and mine are the same." She pictured herself on the moors of England with her love and lost herself in Jakob's embrace.

# CHAPTER SEVEN

*Capisce?*

September 1891
Southwark, Philadelphia

"*Ehi*, Paragano! Over here!" Vincenzo Carpinelli waved to Sebastian and Florentina from across Fourth Street. They'd left the little ones in Gina's care and the store in Giuseppe's hands. Sebastian needed time away from the bustle of home to consider the changes he'd noticed in Mary. For the past month, his favorite daughter had hardly been home. She'd overslept that morning and almost missed her shift at Arenberg's. Mary had never acted slovenly, and he was concerned. When pressed, Gina wouldn't say a word, and Clara was too busy with her wedding plans to notice. Sebastian was relieved to see Cenzo. *Maybe he knows what's going on.*

"Cenzo, dear man! How is business?" Sebastian asked as his friend approached.

"Oh, no complaints, no complaints." Cenzo gripped Sebastian's offered hand and tipped his hat to Florentina. "I'm happy to take a break from the stall now and again. Tomas can handle affairs fine enough. In fact, he is quite possibly the best fish-seller I've ever known. My profits have doubled since he's worked behind the counter." Cenzo smiled.

Sebastian was surprised when his wife spoke. She was usually too shy. "Well, he was trained by the best, of course. A lucky boy to be taken in by you, Signor Carpinelli."

"Thank you, signora. I am also lucky to have his company. To think, ten years ago, he was a wharf orphan. And now, he has grown into a *bel giovanotto*. I am quite proud of him, I must say. He has been like a son to me." Cenzo's wide grin displayed his pride.

"Ah, yes, the blessing of children." Sebastian winked at his wife, who blushed scarlet and put a hand to her bosom. The memory of their recent lovemaking caused his heart to race. He wondered if Florentina was pregnant yet again. She dropped a small curtsy to the men and went to investigate a fabric cart.

"Speaking of children, you're an old friend, Sebastian, and I feel as if I must warn you." Cenzo peeked over his shoulder, then lowered his voice. "I have seen your Mary strolling with one of the SLP boys from Arenberg's. No good can come of this, you understand. You'll have to speak with her. She is a special person, our Oystercatcher. This is a dangerous dalliance for her, *capisce?*"

Sebastian's heart raced. His instincts were correct. An SLP boy? He couldn't believe his nightjar would get mixed up with such a person. He'd have to talk with her immediately. "Ah, yes, that is a concern for sure, Cenzo. Thank you for bringing this to my attention. I will speak with my daughter. You are good to look out for her." Sebastian clapped his companion on the back.

At the mention of their daughter, Sebastian saw Florentina shift toward them again. "What is this? What is this SLP? Who is this boy, and why is he with Mary?"

Sebastian chastised his wife. "Mind your place, Tina—we will speak in private later. Let me do business with *mio amico*."

Dismissed, Tina returned to the cart. She fingered some blue ticking fabric as she craned her neck.

He moved on a few paces with Cenzo, so the hubbub of the busy market consumed their voices. The last thing he needed was for his wife to be involved with this affair.

After departing the market, Sebastian turned with his wife toward home, their parcels tucked under his arm. After a block or two, Tina interrupted her husband's contemplative silence. "When will you explain what this is? This SLP?"

"What?" Sebastian snapped out of his reflection and turned to his wife. "Ah, the SLP. Yes. The Socialist Labor Party is the working man's party, dear, full of Marxist Germans and Russian Jews. They have a new leader now, this Daniel De Leon." Sebastian steered Tina around a puddle of muck on the sidewalk. "They're organizing themselves and even have a newspaper syndicate now. They plan to eliminate the social classes, which sounds wonderful in theory but is a vain hope that would lead to chaos and anarchy. In my humble opinion, anyway. It isn't possible for man to portion out wealth and resources fairly to the community in this sinful world. Man has his vices and can't be cured of them this side of heaven. Nothing will come of it, Tina."

"But why is this so dangerous? If nothing will come of it, why worry?"

"Well, some members of the SLP plan to use violence to seize power from the big bosses because they realize no wealthy man would willingly lay down ownership of his industry and resources." Sebastian leaned toward Florentina and lowered his voice. "The Duke and his men wouldn't hand over the keys to their castle easily, would they, Tina?"

Florentina gasped and placed her hand on her heart. "It won't come to blows, will it?"

"Now, now, don't worry, my dear. Cenzo has been in contact with an officer at the Second and Christian Street Station—a man named McMurtrie. He's a socialist-hater like our Duke and his boys. No trouble will come to our streets—of that, I'm sure. Between the Irish coppers and Rocco Monza, they'll keep this SLP in line."

Florentina looked sideways at her husband, as she always did when someone mentioned the Duke and his lackey. Sebastian knew all too well that his wife resented the control those men held over their family. Her face showed she had more questions, her mouth working back and forth as she formulated the words, but they'd rounded the corner and would be home in half a block. Sebastian put his finger to his lips. "Shh, Tina."

Speaking of such matters on the streets of Southwark was dangerous business.

After supper, Sebastian lit his pipe and eyed his daughter across the table. Mary looked eager to leave, as she often had of late. She fidgeted with her hands and looked at the door repeatedly. *What is that child up to?*

"My little nightjar, will you join me for an evening stroll?"

Mary's head snapped up, her eyebrows jumping to her hairline. "A stroll, Papa?" She cleared her throat and smoothed the fabric of her skirt.

"Like old times, child. Remember our vineyard walks in Italy?"

Mary smiled. "Yes, Papa. I remember. Yes, I will join you."

Tina cast him a suspicious glance from the sink where she and the older girls were washing the dinner dishes.

Sebastian stood and donned his hat from the stand by the door. Mary was right behind him at the bottom of the stairs. They walked through the dark grocery, careful not to bump into the barrels and boxes lining the floor. They knew every inch of the market and could navigate the room wearing blinders.

Sebastian broke the silence once on the street and well away from the Paragano home. "You were an inquisitive child, Mary. Insolent, really. Always asking questions and prodding into matters that weren't your business."

Mary grinned. "I know, Papa. I remember asking why giant Signor Gallo had a bosom like a woman."

The memory warmed Sebastian's heart. When had his nightjar grown into a woman? He had missed the transformation. He'd better start paying attention now before it was too late.

"Yes, well, it is now my turn. I have a question for you." He stopped and took her hands in his. They were such tiny, delicate hands—the fingers of an artist. "Mary, daughter, I must know. Are you giving yourself to a Jewish boy?"

Mary pulled her hands out of his, obviously shocked. It was difficult to see in the dim evening light, but Sebastian caught sight of a ruby blush creeping up his daughter's neck—a silent admission.

"Papa, I…" Mary stammered and looked at the ground.

Sebastian's face fell, and his shoulders slumped. His little girl. As he watched Mary rock back and forth from foot to foot, clearly wishing to dash away and avoid her father's judgment, his sadness turned into anger. His daughter gallivanting around with a Jewish boy? The very thought mocked him.

"*Mary!*" His voice came out harsher than he had intended. She stopped rocking and looked at him as he spat out his next question. "Is he a *socialist?*"

Mary's chin went up. Her eyes were a shade darker than Sebastian had remembered. She no longer looked like his little nightjar.

"So what if he is?"

"How dare you speak to me in such a way! Mary, the socialists are rubbish. It's bad enough that he's Jewish, and you'll ruin your reputation. But a socialist? The Duke would be furious. And Rocco! You will stop seeing this boy at once."

"I will not."

Sebastian couldn't believe his ears. "This is not a matter for discussion. You have no say in the situation, child!"

"That's just it, Papa. I am no longer a child."

"But you are *my* daughter. *Mine.*"

"No, I am no longer yours, Papa. I've given my heart to him."

Sebastian reared back as if Mary had slapped him across the face. "You will end this dalliance tomorrow, and we will never speak of this boy again."

"You don't understand, Papa. I *love* him."

"No, you don't. You will go to confession and purge this affair from your mind."

"But, Papa..."

"Mary, I forbid you to see him again. That is the end of the discussion." Before she could speak another word of defiance, Sebastian walked away and headed straight for the pub.

# CHAPTER EIGHT

*Shocker*

*June 2018*
*Washington, DC*

The wide white stone front of the National Holocaust Museum stood before Bella on a warm summer morning, its temple-like facade beckoning her to enter. She drew courage from the Washington Monument in the background, reaching toward the sky and touching the clouds.

*I can do this.*

Bella whistled under her breath as she surveyed the foyer—an impressive open space lined with light red brick walls and a high glass ceiling. At first glance, the room was bright and uplifting, with one side of the hallway hosting large archways that resembled the architecture of a synagogue she'd once visited in Philly.

But in the next moment, Bella noticed the industrial metal fixtures and cage-like railings lining the opposite side of the hallway. Rather than inspiring, the skylights oppressed the space—crisscrossed with metal beams and a walking bridge across the top. Bella imagined people watching her from above as if she'd fallen into a pit.

One wall boasted a simple line of scripture from Isaiah, chapter forty-three, verse ten. "You are my witnesses."

Bella hunched her shoulders and continued onto the elevators and the exhibit.

On the fourth floor, after passing images of Nazi propaganda and displays about the "science" of race, Bella's nerves were on edge, and she wished she hadn't come by herself. Why hadn't she brought her mom along? But then she remembered Rosalie didn't know about their Jewish heritage yet. *Why have I been too chicken to tell my mom?* It was almost like she hadn't believed it herself. Not until she'd walked the halls of this museum.

Rounding a corner, Bella ran into a stark display of violence, destruction, and chaos. *Kristallnacht*—the night of broken glass, that fateful November night in 1938 when the Nazi party let loose their unimaginable evil and set a tidal wave of violence into motion. And then she saw the name.

*Lichtenbaum.*

In one image, the storefront signage of a jeweler peeked from behind large shards of broken glass. Bella knew the jewelry store depicted in the display had been located in Germany and that Jakob's people, her people, were from Poland—but the name was the same, and the truth wounded her. Jakob's relatives had most likely suffered in the infamous Warsaw ghetto.

After the Kristallnacht display, Bella came face to face with Hitler's ungodly euthanasia program, in which hundreds of thousands of people were deemed unworthy of life and killed by gas or injection. She held her breath as she studied the photos of hospital rooms, her stomach in knots as she faced the question. *Who determines whether a person is unworthy of life?* The thought hit too close to home. Bella's dark secret fought to rise to the surface of her conscience. *No!* She hustled down the corridor, eager to leave the museum. *This was a mistake.*

At the end of the fourth-floor exhibit, she hurried into the Tower of Faces, where she came to an abrupt halt. The tower walls were covered floor to ceiling with photographs of all shapes and sizes. Jewish faces looked at Bella from every inch of the tower. All kinds of expressions greeted her—smiling, pensive, studious, laughing, loving, vivacious. The humanity overwhelmed her. All of these lovely people had been murdered. *Are the Lichtenbaums here? Am I looking into the eyes of Jakob's parents?* She knew it was unlikely—these folks were from a different part of Poland, it said so on the brochure, but she was rooted to the spot.

*I never knew.*

Unable to move, Bella stood, her hand to her mouth, her face ashen, her stomach turned sour. She'd never survive the next part of the museum about the ghettos and the concentration camps.

A pair of visitors whispered behind her. One cleared her throat. Bella didn't budge.

"First time?"

Shaking herself from her catatonic state, Bella turned to face two middle-aged women—sisters, maybe? "I never knew."

A look of compassion descended on the women's features, and the tall, stately one patted Bella's arm.

"You knew. You just didn't believe it." She offered her arm to Bella, and Bella took it, needing the borrowed courage. "C'mon. We'll go down with you to the third-floor exhibit. No one should go through there alone."

That night, Bella sat in a stiff beige armchair in the corner of the hotel room Sophie had booked for her. The box of documents and photos she'd brought from home was on the dresser. Sophie was asleep in the adjoining room.

Bella kicked her slippers into the corner, stood, and opened the lid. Her ancestors' faces looked out at her. Some she knew, some she didn't. She closed her eyes, and the Jewish faces from the museum wall stared at her through her eyelids. She'd never really understood—had never related to the sheer and utter loss of it all.

It was time to tell her mom.

Rosalie answered on the third ring. "Hi, honey, what's up?"

"Nothing. I wanted to catch you up on the research. I'm in DC with Sophie again." As an afterthought, she added, "Don't get upset."

"I'm not upset, Bella." Rosalie sighed. "Look, I understand. Maybe you needed this project to help you get through this rough patch. I don't judge. I want you to be happy. Tell me, what did you learn about Nana and her parents?"

"Thanks, Ma. Well..." Bella stalled, unsure how to tell her mother of their Jewish ancestry. "Sophie and I made progress on the family tree. She's so much like Nana—it's amazing. She has her nose, and her laugh is the same too. Sometimes when I laugh with her, I hear Nana in her voice, which almost makes me cry. God, I miss her."

"I know, Bella, me too. She was a special part of my life."

"Right? Anyway, Sophie and I endeared ourselves to the hotel staff. They're letting us use their smallest conference room to spread out. We both brought so much stuff we're taking up four tables. The banquet manager—this guy Enrique—claims to be studying his genealogy too. He says that's why he's letting us use the room, free of charge, cause he's 'in favor of our quest.' Sophie probably winked at him and passed him some cash on the sly. She's clever like that and thinks fast on her feet. You'd adore her, Ma."

"I'm sure I would, honey. Let's set up a time for us to meet."

"Yeah, that's a good idea. Turns out, Sophie is the great-niece of Nana's father, Jakob Lichtenbaum—say that five times fast. Her grandfather was Jakob's brother, Kopel. That makes us cousins of some sort, right? I'm not exactly sure. Anyway, it doesn't matter."

"Wait, hold up. Did you say Nana's father's name was Jakob Lichtenbaum? I've never heard that name before."

"That's not all, Ma. The big shocker is that Sophie and the entire Lichtenbaum family are Jewish. Jakob and his brother Kopel immigrated to the US from Warsaw in the 1880s when Jakob was sixteen years old. That means we're part Jewish too."

There was silence on the other end of the line.

"Ma? It's a bit of a shock, I know. Are you ok?" She heard a sniffle. "Ma, you're not bothered that Nana was half Jewish, are you?"

"Of course not. How could you ask such a question?" Rosalie blew her nose. "No, I'm just sad she's not here to talk about this with us. Why didn't she ever mention her father? God, were her childhood memories so horrible that she couldn't even talk about him?"

"I know. Poor Nana. Funny, for me, the weirdest part isn't being partly Jewish, but that my own husband will never know. I won't ever get the chance to tell him. Now that we're separated, we won't talk about anything anymore."

"That's a loss, Bella. Listen, I need to go. I wanna call your aunt and talk about this stuff. Is that ok?"

"Oh, yeah, of course. I'll talk to you tomorrow. Love ya."

"Goodnight, honey. Love you too."

Bella sat down on the edge of the hotel bed and tossed her phone onto the nightstand. One thought kept flowing through her mind. *I'm part Jewish, and my husband will never know.* The notion gave her an odd feeling but not an unwelcome one, like a missing piece of her identity had fallen into place. *Click.*

"Oh my word! What is this? Can this be real?" On the second day at the hotel, Bella shuffled through the box full of documents brought from her mom's attic.

"Who wrote this?" Sophie came to look at an aged and yellowed page of lined paper with a spidery script filling every inch of the margins.

Bella looked over her shoulder at Sophie, realization dawning. "My Nana wrote this." She pointed to the inscription at the top of the page: *Beginning of Mollie Lichtenbaum, 1988.* "Looks like some sort of autobiography. Check out the year—1988. That's the year she died."

*Nana!* Bella's heart squeezed tight in her chest, tears threatening to spill from her eyes. Sophie sat down in the empty chair next to her. "Can you read it out loud?"

"I think so, though it's rather hard to make out. Nana's handwriting is atrocious. She was—what, ninety-six?—when she wrote this." Straightening the wrinkled page flat on the table, Bella began to read.

*Beginning of Mollie Lichtenbaum, 1988*

*My Grandmother's maiden name was Malandrino born near Naples. Here the story my Grand Mother told of how she came to America, I was born in 1892. I don't know what the name of the boat was but I do know she came steerage with the children, my Grand Father had come to America before her, and he earned his money by sweeping the streets of Phila. I know they open a Grocery store but didn't do too well. during those years or some time in between, he dropped dead cleaning the streets. the next thing I remember being told was when the girls were very very young they went to work in what they called a sweatshop where they did men's tailoring, and that is where my Mother met my father, I do not know the details of that marriage all I know is I was born in Newark NJ. I had another Sister named Sarah and a brother named Mendel. I was the eldest.*

*My Grand Father study to be a priest and was opposed to my father. Mother eloped at age 16. The next I remember is where we lived in Newark was Polly want a cracker? Phila my Mother was going to drown us. Police picked us up—3 of us—my brother Mendel, my sister Sarah and me Mollie. They took us St Vincent's. My Father took Mendel some time later. I was there. My mother died at 26. I was ten.*

Silence filled the conference room.

*And there it is. The family legend must be true. I knew it.*

What kind of mother would try to drown her children? Bella looked at Sophie to see her reaction. Sophie sat deep in thought, with sadness in her eyes.

*My mother was going to drown us.* Bella bit her lip. She needed to defend her direct ancestor. "I'm sure it's the fuzzy notions of an aged mind. I mean, Nana wasn't quite herself when she wrote the letter, right? 'Polly want a cracker?' What's that about? Her mother wouldn't have *really* tried to drown her, right?" She fiddled with the cap of her pen. *Click. Click. Click.*

Sophie didn't reply right away, only looked at Bella with sad eyes. "Sometimes grief drives people to desperate acts." Sophie paused. "Bella, I'm wondering if maybe we should stop digging into this. Perhaps the truth will be too hard for you to face?"

"*No!*" Bella fidgeted with the papers in front of her, cleared her throat, and tried again. "I mean, no, I can handle it. I *need* this."

"Why?"

Silence. Then Bella gave a lopsided smile. "My husband left me a few weeks before I met you at that Starbucks. He was having an affair with a younger woman, and he chose her over me. Isn't that nice? I have the divorce papers in my bag, ready for my signature, and I can't face it. I threw myself into this project, avoiding my mom, my aunts, my job…" The tears came. Finally.

Sophie reached for her hand and squeezed her fingers. "That jerk. Who in their right mind would ever leave *you*?"

Bella let out a little squeak—half laugh, half sob. "That was exactly what I needed to hear, but it's hard for me to believe, ya know? I mean, what if I'm not worthy of commitment and loyalty?" A fresh wave of tears overtook her, and she choked out her more significant fear. "What if I'm not worthy of *love?* I'm the one who pushed Nate away. Right into freakin' Kate's arms." Her voice rose an octave. "You know, I was once a vibrant young thing too!"

When the tears ran out, Sophie handed Bella a hankie.

"Why, if Nate were here right now, Bella, I gotta tell you, I'd give him a lickin' like he's never known before. He'd be sniveling for his momma before I'd finished beating the living daylights out of him."

Bella's mouth dropped open, and she stared at Sophie with wide eyes. She pictured this little old lady going up against her strong, tall ex—there, she'd said it, *ex*-husband—and burst out laughing. "Oh my word, Sophie! You're a riot!" Bella laughed, and it felt wonderful, so she laughed some more. She roared so hard her stomach hurt, and she snorted through her nose—a most unfeminine sound. The laughter was contagious. Sophie chuckled, then gave a great big belly laugh.

Sophie and Bella still sat, laughing like loons, when Enrique found them in the hotel's smallest banquet room, papers scattered around the tables. He cleared his throat, and they stifled giggles. "Ladies, I do regret it, but you must pack up. The staff needs to ready this room for a wedding tonight. And before you protest—" He held up a well-manicured hand. "I'm sorry, madame, but I cannot accept another one-hundred-dollar bill to postpone your departure." He winked at Sophie before sashaying out of the room.

The women burst into laughter again.

"Oh, that was fun." Sophie dabbed at her watering eyes with a clean hankie. Where did she keep all these hankies hidden? She had a new hankie for every hour!

Bella's mirth subsided as she packed the remaining papers and photos into the old box. She placed Nana's letter into the folder in her bag alongside the divorce papers. She wasn't sure if she would ever reread the letter. The words burned into her brain—*My mother was going to drown us*—but she wanted to keep it safe. And she should probably show her mom.

# CHAPTER NINE

## *We Need to Talk*

October 1891
Southwark, Philadelphia

"No, it's fine, Cenzo. I'm fine. A little queasy this morning, that's all."

Mary collected the oysters on a crisp autumn Friday when a heat wave flowed through her belly and up her neck. A tide of nausea threatened to overtake her. She put her hand against her mouth and fought to keep the queasiness at bay. *Heavens! How embarrassing! Do not vomit in front of Cenzo. Do not vomit in front of Cenzo.* She repeated this mantra as if it could stop the inevitable. The smell of oysters had brought on this spell. But how could that be? She loved the smell of oysters.

Cenzo looked at her sideways. She could see the wheels of thought turning in his mind. She pivoted away from his gaze and threw up on her shoes. Then she threw up again. A customer in the next stall peeked over and turned away in disgust. Vincenzo came around to place a handkerchief in her hands and support her back. *What a dear friend.*

"Mary, let me assist you. Come to the back of the shop with me, where you can have some privacy." He fetched Tomas with a snap of his fingers. "Come clean this up, *per favore!*"

Cenzo escorted her to the back of the store. The smell of fish guts assaulted her. *What is wrong with me?* Cenzo steered her to a stool, placed a bucket in her lap, and left the room, giving her some privacy as she wiped her face with the kerchief. She started the process again, this time vomiting into the bucket. After a few moments, she sat with her back against the wall, straightened up, and tentatively stretched her neck. Then, in the wink of an eye, the nausea passed.

Cenzo peeked at Mary from the workbench, pretending to be busy sharpening his little shucking knife. He had an unsettling conviction that wouldn't pass. But how, how could he possibly broach the subject with Mary? Propriety demanded his silence. But Mary was his friend, and her family was like family to him. If she were—dare he even think it?—if she were with child, then she'd need his help.

As Mary gathered her wits and tidied her hair, he brought her a cup of tepid water. "Drink this, one sip at a time."

"I can't thank you enough, Cenzo." Mary accepted the cup from his hands. "I can't imagine what came over me. I feel fine now. Uncanny."

"Mary," Cenzo croaked. He cleared his throat and tried again. "Mary."

She looked up into his eyes, her brow creased in confusion. "Cenzo, I assure you, I'm alright. Something gave me a turn, that's all. Perhaps some of the oysters are bad?"

"Mary." He squatted before her, clasped her shaky hands, and squeezed. "Oystercatcher. Please forgive me, a foolish man, but dear, when was the last time you had your courses?"

Mary snatched her hands from his as if she were holding burning coals, sat straight as a rod, and tilted up her chin. She opened her mouth a few times and looked around the room. "Vincenzo Carpinelli, I will pretend you didn't ask such a question. Now, I must be on my way." She attempted to stand but plopped back down on the stool, exhausted.

Vincenzo watched as a deep scarlet blush crept up Mary's neck and bloomed over her face. He moved away to give her space. He stood against the wall opposite her and rubbed his hands over his face, wishing he were anywhere in the world but here.

"*Bene*—yes, we need a plan," Vincenzo told himself. He watched Mary pace along the river's edge. He had brought her through the fish stall's back door, down the pier's steps, and to the river. The October air seemed to refresh Mary, and her coloring returned to normal. She did seem on edge, though, after the revelation of the last hour. He couldn't blame her. Her circumstances were dire.

One, her papa... "*Dio mio*, Sebastian!" Cenzo hissed. He made the sign of the cross and shook his head up to God. Mary hadn't heard him. She beat a path back and forth at the water's edge. He could hear her muttering to herself—poor girl. Cenzo's heart squeezed at the sight of her.

*Bene, back to the plan*, Cenzo thought to himself, careful not to speak aloud this time.

One, her papa would be devastated. Understanding his precious daughter, his little nightjar, was with child out of wedlock would be painful enough. But to realize that...that good-for-nothing socialist Jew had impregnated her? Cenzo thought he'd throw up, as Mary had an hour ago. No, the truth would be a dagger to Sebastian's heart.

Two, Rocco Monza. As if hurting her papa wasn't enough, now she'd make a fool of his padrone. Everyone—*everyone*—in Southwark knew Rocco desired Mary. This truth also made Cenzo want to vomit. *Oh, what a mess!* If Rocco learned of the true father of Mary's baby—Cenzo shuddered. Rocco would do violence, for sure.

Three, and maybe this was the biggest problem of all—the baby. Shunned and ashamed its entire life, a bastard child, and a Jew to boot! No, there was no way Cenzo could let this happen to his dear Oystercatcher. Straightening his shoulders and looking up at the sky, Vincenzo Angelo Gregorio Carpinelli accepted the mantle of responsibility God Almighty had placed on his shoulders.

Now, he had to convince Mary of the plan.

"Psst, wake up, you *schlub*."

Someone pushed Jakob's shoulder. Repeatedly. He was enjoying a delicious dream about Mary and didn't wish to wake, but the shoving intensified.

"Eh? What?" He sat up, mattress squeaking beneath him, and rubbed his hands over his scruffy face. He looked around the room, disoriented. Then he saw the familiar cracked washbasin on top of the stool, under the tiny window. *I'm in my room at Frau Levin's boarding house.* Uri sat on the bed opposite him, pulling suspenders onto his shoulders in the dark. Jakob could barely see him across the narrow space.

*It's the middle of the night.*

Something was wrong. Jakob blinked his eyes to clear them, nerves on high alert.

"What happened?"

"That Italian kid, Tomas—he's at the door. Says he needs to speak with you. It can only mean one thing."

"Mary." Jakob jumped up, fully awake now, and yanked on his trousers and boots. He grabbed his hat and made for the door.

Tomas stood on the landing in the hallway, leaning on the railing and releasing a jaw-breaking yawn.

"Where is she? What's happened? Has Rocco touched her?"

Tomas didn't answer. He looked Jakob up and down and shook his head in disgust. "Come with me."

The door opened behind them, and Uri stepped out of the room. Jakob raised an eyebrow. "Figured you may need backup." Uri gave a lopsided grin, his lips already hugging a cigarette.

The group hastened down the stairs and into the night.

"She's in there, *alone?*" Jakob was incredulous. Tomas had brought them to Arenberg's. It was three in the morning.

"Si."

"We'll wait out here, Jakob, so you can have some, erm, privacy." Uri had the nerve to wink.

Jakob hurried into the factory. He knew exactly where to find her. As he rounded the corner, he saw Mary perched like a princess on the carpet pile. She seemed alright and was in one piece. His heart swelled with relief, then switched to confusion.

*What is going on?*

"Mary, are you unwell? Why did you send Tomas for me?" He placed his hands on her face, studying her in the dim light, turning her head for signs of illness or distress.

"Sit down, Jakob. We need to talk." He stopped his ministrations, and his heart sank at the sound of her voice.

*God, give me strength!* Pain strung Mary's heart as tight as a bow—one false move and she'd snap. When she saw Jakob come through the shadows, her resolve nearly melted away. She gripped the carpet folds underneath her as he touched her face. She must resist the nearness of him. He smelled of bergamot and musk and something she could never put her finger on. He smelled like *Jakob*. Her mind and body connected to his, and she reached for his hands and tilted her face up for a kiss. He delivered.

*I am making this harder for myself.* Mary jerked away, a sob catching in her throat.

"Jakob." Her voice sounded husky to her ears. He drew her close for another kiss, but she planted both hands on his chest and held him at bay. "Jakob, I can't see you anymore." She choked on the words.

"What?" Jakob's eyes went round as saucers. "Mary, what are you talking about?"

She sat up straighter and caught an errant curl, forcing the lock into the confines of her bun. She must do this for the baby—though it tore her apart, there was no other option.

"I said I can't see you anymore."

Jakob pulled back, scooting a few inches from her atop the scratchy carpet. "You're joking. Did the fellas put you up to this?" He glanced over his shoulder with a nervous laugh, perhaps expecting to see his friends hiding in the shadows of the sweatshop.

"No one put me up to this, Jakob. I was wrong to give myself to you. It isn't proper." Her body betrayed her and hungered for his touch. She was digging her own grave, and the pain would torment her for eternity.

Jakob shook his head. "No, no, I don't think so. We are one, Mary. You said so yourself—on many occasions. You can't detach from me now. We belong together. Why are you shaking your head? You know it's true." His brow creased, and his voice rose in agitation.

"We can never marry, Jakob. I love you, but we can never be together, and you know it."

"If this is about the Duke and his man…"

"It's not. It's about what is right. We can never marry, and I cannot live as your mistress."

"It's your papa. What did he say to you?"

"This is about *me*, Jakob. Don't you see? I've given a part of my identity away."

Jakob's face turned red, and his hands clenched into fists. He spat out, "Which, your *Italian* identity or your *Catholic* one?"

"That's not fair. You know I love you, no matter your race or religion."

Jakob's temper softened as quickly as it had flared. He reached for her hand. "As I love you." He pressed her palm to his cheek and held it there. "What are we supposed to do?" He sounded vulnerable— like an innocent child searching for direction—and Mary's heart broke in two. She took a deep breath and held it as if preparing to jump into a cold river. "Vincenzo has asked for my hand in marriage, and I plan to give it to him."

"*What?*" Jakob jumped up and tripped over the edge of the carpet pile, falling onto the floor with a loud thunk. "Blazes!" He couldn't believe what he'd heard from Mary's mouth. "Of all the ridiculous… what kind of game is this?" He stood up, brushing carpet fibers off his trousers.

Mary repeated her astonishing declaration. "Cenzo and I are to be married."

Jakob was a caged tiger, pacing and rubbing his hands through his hair. He needed a cigarette and reached for one in his vest pocket, only to remember he wasn't wearing his vest. He wasn't wearing his vest because he'd been woken in the night and had run out the door before donning it. The lack of cigarettes worsened matters, and he cursed a string of expletives.

Mary gasped.

He looked up at her, sitting there like a queen holding court. Even in shadow, Jakob could see the resolve plastered across her face. *I guess when Mary Paragano sets her mind to something, there's no stopping her.* Days ago, she'd succumbed to passion in his embrace, and her heart had been in his hands. He had possessed her, body and soul. *What happened to change that?* Jakob continued pacing and winced at the newly formed bruise on his hip from his fall. *What an idiot I have been.* He opened his mouth, then shut it—he had no words for Mary right now. Without a second glance, he turned and left the building.

Tomas stood leaning against the factory's outer wall, hands in his pockets. Jakob lunged at him, grabbed the collar of his shirt, and heaved the skinny teen off his feet. "And what part did you have to play in this game, eh?" he growled.

Uri yanked Jakob back, forcing him to release the startled Tomas. "Whoa, whoa, back up, loverboy. Take it easy." Uri gripped Jakob by the scruff of his neck like a puppy and gave Tomas a smirk. "You'd better get Mary back home and make yourself scarce."

Tomas disappeared into the factory.

"As for you, Romeo, we're hitting Trudy's." Uri pushed Jakob along the street. "I need a lady companion and a drink. By the looks of it, you do too."

"I don't do that anymore, you fool, you know that. Ever since I started seeing Mary…" Jakob clutched his heart as the pain of her declaration hit home again. "Oh, Mary!"

"Start talkin', ya *mensch*. What happened in there?"

"She tore my heart out and ate it for breakfast."

"That's a lovely picture. C'mon, we're nearly there."

Once established in the parlor at Trudy's, Uri handed Jakob a shot of whiskey, ordered him to wait on the couch by the fire, and then disappeared into one of the upper rooms with one of Trudy's girls. The whiskey went down smoothly, and Jakob closed his eyes. He played back the entire scene in his mind.

Mary sat like a queen, hard as stone and unwavering. No, that wasn't quite right. She was cruel, her face contorted in a malicious grin, enjoying his pain and confusion, and twisting his guts in her delicate hands. That wasn't true either, though it had appeared that way to Jakob at the time.

*Think!*

Mary's eyes were bloodshot like she'd wept before he arrived. She took deep breaths like she needed the courage to continue. She choked on her words, restraining sobs with effort. *So she isn't a heartless…wait a minute.*

She'd placed her hands over her middle when his temper flared. Her middle. As if to protect—

*Mary is pregnant.*

Jakob placed the glass on the little table by the sofa and stood. Like an automaton, he moved to the door and turned the knob. His feet shuffled along of their own accord. The sun was rising. It was dawn.

*Mary is pregnant—with my child.*

Jakob sprinted. He headed straight for her house. He had to get there before she made the biggest mistake of her life.

Mary shuffled through the grocery and up the stairs to her home at dawn. Escorted by Cenzo, she entered the family living quarters with trepidation. Tomas took up a sentry post downstairs in the market. Mary could smell the familiar scents of her beloved kitchen and the sounds of the family waking for the day. The tea kettle was rattling above the fire. The clock was ticking. Papa's pipe smoke swirled above the table. The children giggled in their rooms. Mama set the table for the morning meal while Papa sat with his ubiquitous newspaper. Papa turned to look at her from his seat, his mouth dropping open in surprise. He glanced at the stairs to the bedrooms as if he was confused as to why she wasn't coming downstairs after a good night's sleep. *He thought I was safe at home.*

Cenzo doffed his hat and wrung it as Mary's siblings came down the steps and joined the group in the tense kitchen. Everyone seemed confused. Mary's cheeks flamed red with shame. Cenzo cleared his throat as Mary looked at the floor. "Sebastian, Signora Paragano. Ahem, I'd like an audience with you, please." Cenzo looked at the Paragano children, waiting in the shadows at the bottom of the stairs. The family looked unsure whether they should enter the room or scurry back to their bedrooms. Clara looked at their mother with her eyebrows raised. When Tina nodded, Clara scooped up the little ones and ushered them up the stairs. Gina and Lizzy lingered.

Without a preamble, Cenzo started in. "Mary came to the stall and complained of stomach upset upon smelling the fish and oysters. She was sick all over the floor and then seemed to recover. It was unusual, and my mind quickly assessed the situation." He looked at Mary, but she didn't respond. "She is pregnant with my child." Cenzo winced and ran his hand through his thinning hair.

Papa drew in a sharp breath, but Mama didn't seem surprised. She placed a hand over her belly, and Mary realized Mama was also expecting. Maybe a mother knew these things before her daughters. Papa's face turned bright red as he looked between Mary and her mother. *He must be disgusted to learn that I, his favored, virtuous daughter, am with child before marriage.* Mary felt bile rise in her throat. Papa sat down hard as if their announcement had knocked the wind out of him.

"Cenzo?" He looked at Cenzo as if he'd bitten into a lemon, and his words came out in spurts. "You're my most trusted friend, Vincenzo—you're a man twenty years Mary's senior—I cannot. I cannot believe you are the father of her…baby. Outrageous." Sebastian shook his head. Mary's siblings stood stock still on the stairwell, watching.

"I will marry Mary within the month. Please give us your blessing, *mio amico.*"

Papa's mouth opened and closed and opened again. He resembled a landed fish, desperate to return to its usual environs. Mama sat at the table, reaching for the rosary in her pocket. She turned to

Papa—everyone looked at Papa—except Mary. She stood at Cenzo's side, studying the floor.

No one spoke a word. Papa cleared his throat. He drew himself up to his full height, closed his eyes, and drew a long, slow breath. Everyone waited for his next words—the words that would grant Mary his blessing in her new life as the wife of his oldest friend—or not.

Mary never knew what he'd have said, for at that moment, she heard a kerfuffle downstairs in the grocery, and Tomas yelled up the stairs, "Don't go up there, you cad!"

The door opened, and Jakob burst into the room, passion in his eyes. Everyone stood rooted to the spot. Mary's heart exploded with joy at the sight of him—the love of her life. All confusion cleared from her mind, and she gasped at the colossal mistake she'd been about to make. She belonged to Jakob, no matter what. She almost fainted in relief but was caught by Jakob, who rushed across the small room in two steps and held her in his strong embrace. Vincenzo shook his fists at Jakob with a murderous expression, his face red and his eyes bulging, ready for a fight.

Papa's face went white as a sheet as he realized his friend Cenzo wasn't the father of Mary's baby. It was, in fact, the Hebrew, a socialist Jew from Fourth Street.

The next moments were a blur. The men's hot tempers flared, and everyone yelled at once. In the end, Jakob's voice rang stronger than the others. "I lay claim to Mary." He stood with his arm around Mary, holding her up. Her head was spinning, and she couldn't think what to say. Jakob continued, "She gave herself to me willingly, and Cenzo here tried to convince her to marry him. To steal her from me!"

At this, Mary found her voice. "No! No, Jakob." She placed her hands on Jakob's chest and searched his eyes. "Cenzo was trying to protect me from shame." She turned to her father. "Papa, please forgive Cenzo! He is your stalwart friend."

Cenzo pulled out the closest chair and slumped into it. Jakob pulled away from Mary and looked at her with his eyebrows raised as if he hadn't expected her to defend the fishmonger.

Sebastian put his face in his hands, obviously unsure what to think. He turned to his wife. "Should we promise her protection in our home and have you raise the child as one of our own?" Papa seemed to be begging. But before Tina could answer, Jakob broke in.

"Never!" He placed his hands on Mary's belly. "This is my baby. Mine and Mary's!"

At this, Cenzo cursed, and Papa hurled accusations at Jakob.

Mary was sick and tired of these men fighting and making decisions for her. She loved Jakob and wanted more than anything to be with him. Why couldn't her parents allow her to marry Jakob and raise their child in peace? Why could her parents pursue such a life while they forbade her to do the same? It wasn't fair! Many Southwark couples found themselves expecting a baby before wedlock. It was an everyday occurrence. No, that wasn't the real issue here. It was because Jakob was Jewish. Papa and Cenzo could not stand the fact that Mary was carrying the baby of a Jew, and they'd go to great lengths to keep her from Jakob. Righteous indignation filled Mary's heart. She cast off shame and enrobed herself in anger.

Mary straightened her shoulders. "We've done no different than you, Papa—when you got our Mama pregnant at sixteen before marriage." Mary clapped her hands over her mouth. She hadn't meant to say such a thing. *Why can't I keep my mouth shut? I always make my situation worse!*

An electric shock ran through the room. All eyes landed on Mama and then on Clara, who had returned from settling the children upstairs. Sweet, dear Clara—Sebastian and Florentina's firstborn child—stood cradling little Anthony on the stairs, as innocent as a lamb. Mama stood up, indignation on her face. "That is a lie, Mary! How dare you besmirch my good name in such a way?"

Papa stopped her with a hand in the air. Tina sat down, sobbing, and ran her fingers over her rosary beads. Everyone else was silent.

Papa spoke one word in the silence. "*Rinnegato.*" Disowned.

Mary gasped for air. She stepped back, her hands to her heart. Jakob supported her shoulders and steered her to the door. "We're leaving." The couple stumbled down the stairs, and the sounds of the Paragano family crying and shouting followed them to the door of the market. Jakob shouldered a surprised Tomas out of the way and pushed Mary into the street. From there, he dragged her stunned form to the boarding house, where he sat her on the bed and packed his meager belongings.

Mary was in shock. She had no sense of time or space and could not make out her surroundings. She watched Jakob's hasty movements as if from a great distance and hardly noticed when someone else entered the room. Uri. Jakob was speaking with Uri. She could only make out a few words. *Train tickets.* She looked around the room. *Is this Jakob's room?*

"Mary!" Jakob's face came into view in front of her eyes. She lifted her shaking hands to his face, and he clasped them to his cheeks. "Your hands are ice." He rubbed them between his own. "It's going to be okay. We're leaving Southwark. I will take care of you. C'mon, let's go." He held out his hand, and Mary took it.

# PART TWO
*Newark*

# CHAPTER TEN

## *Norfolk Street*

Mrs. Dominic Forte
Southwark, Philadelphia

January 16, 1893

Mrs. Jakob Lichtenbaum
Newark, New Jersey

My Dearest Mary,
 Thank Jesus, you sent word to me of your well-being through Vincenzo, the dear man. Dominic will get this letter to him today. There's a packet boat that runs to Newark tomorrow morning. Vincenzo promised the boatman would be discreet and would see this missive into your hands. Rocco will never learn of it. He has no idea where you are. He's never stopped sniffing around for you, but no one will give you up. Of course, sassy Gina became his next target, but Papa married her to the first man who came knocking. A banker from Market Street, can you believe it? She always said she wanted to marry a banker! Anyway, she's safely tucked away. Papa is making plans for Rosetta and Lizzy as well, so do not fret—our sisters will be safe!
 The relief I feel at the news of your health and wellness after your child's birth is indescribable. Vincenzo reports you delivered a baby girl, who will now be about seven months old. Little Mollie, named after your husband's grandmother—what a blessing! I am

*happy to say I will soon join you on the sacred journey of motherhood, as Dominic and I expect a baby in spring. Dom is hoping for a boy, of course! But I wish for a daughter. Is your Mollie a sweet girl? Oh, how I long to hold her in my arms. And you, my dear sister.*

*You may have heard our mama also delivered a baby girl. In March, little Eta joined our family. Papa handed out free cigars from the market. He must have spent a fortune on such extravagance! Rosetta was named godmother and held our little sister with great poise and importance at the christening. We missed you.*

*My summer wedding was a beautiful affair, and I was happy to be with my husband. I am a Forte now! Mama was in her element, as well as the nonnas in Dom's family. (You can imagine the remarks old Fia made during the service, the troublemaker). Papa went through all the motions, but he was a shadow of himself. His happiness for me seemed genuine, but his heart has no joy—it died the day you left. Oh, my dear Mary, can't you find it in your heart to forgive him? I pray he will extend his hand of grace, find you, and bring you home to our family nest someday.*

*I would love to entertain you for tea. You'd love our tiny, sweet corner in Dom's mama's home, with my treasures on the mantle. I was happy to give my bed at home to Rosetta and Lizzy. There is much that has changed here. Yesterday, the most extraordinary scene happened! The new streetcar was ready to roll down the road along Sixth between Catharine and Bainbridge. The trolley made the most astounding clatter on the rails, dinging its bell up and down the street to much fanfare all day. The crowds were two people thick! It's named the Crimson and Vermillion #871 and carries the pride of us all.*

*I long for the day you come home to us, dear sister. Until then, I am faithfully yours,*

*Clara*

Mary's heart ached for her sister and home—she had been gone for more than a year. She dropped the pages of the letter onto the desk and studied the smooth, polished wood. It was a beautiful piece of furniture. "Mahogany," the landlord had bragged, nodding his approval while they'd surveyed the apartment. This place was in a prime location, and Jakob had been so proud of himself when they toured it. The rooms had come furnished on the bottom floor of a corner building. At the time, the extravagance had shocked Mary. Now, she wondered what kind of deal Jakob had made to secure such a fine place for them.

*How did I get here?*

Mary grabbed her favorite pen and a fresh piece of stationery. It was too dangerous to write anything to Southwark, but she had to get her thoughts onto paper—if only to burn them in the fireplace before Jakob returned home.

*February 10, 1893*

*My Dearest Clara,*

*Thank you for the lovely letter. Oh, how my heart warms to hear the good tidings of our baby sister and your beautiful wedding. My greatest desire is to be with you all again. So much has happened in the past year. Jakob and I survived as paupers upon our arrival in Newark, living off the generosity of others. A friend of a friend set us up in a spare room for a few months. A "halfway house," they said. It reeked of cabbage and urine, with peeling wallpaper and a leaky ceiling. You would have despised the place, dear Clara! But what could we do? We had no money. I deserved to be in such a lowly place—it was my punishment for the wrong I had done in the eyes of the Lord, the shame I had brought to our family.*

*Anyway, one day, Jakob came home triumphant, grinning from ear to ear, the dimples I hadn't seen in months deep-knit on his cheeks. He had struck a deal with a fellow in the next neighborhood and secured a good job. "The opportunity of a lifetime," he said. For weeks after that, he worked long hours and returned exhausted to our room, sometimes smelling of alcohol. He seemed happy during those weeks, so I didn't ask too many questions. He'd "struck gold," he said. When I was eight months pregnant, Jakob knelt, held my hand, and asked me to be his wife.*

*He told me he had secured a fine place for us to live on the other side of town and wanted to make an honest woman out of me. Can you imagine? What a lowly state I was in. He bought me a pretty dress—two sizes too big to accommodate my growing belly—and gave me a gold chain necklace. You have never seen such finery! Best of all, as a wedding gift, Jakob presented me with a new leather-bound sketchbook and charcoal pencils. What a joy! We rode the train into Manhattan, recited our vows in the courthouse, and enjoyed a delicious kosher luncheon at Katz's on the corner of Ludlow and East Houston. You must eat there someday, Clara! What a meal!*

*Upon our return to Newark as man and wife, Jakob steered me in a different direction than our disgusting rented room. "I have a surprise." He looked down at me with fire in his eyes. His face was luminous, and I couldn't believe I was his wife. We strolled a short distance from the train to Norfolk Street, where a gentleman waited for us with a large set of keys. The landlord showed us the rental, fully equipped. I was the most beautiful bride in the world, a large belly notwithstanding.*

Mary dropped the pen as if it were a hot coal. How far she had come from that luminous feeling. She crumpled the letter and stuffed it into her apron pocket. She couldn't risk Jakob seeing her words. She should toss the precious letter from Clara too, but couldn't bring herself to do it. Not yet. Gazing out the window onto Norfolk Street, she watched the kids play kick-the-can, lost in memories. Newark was similar to South Philadelphia. This neighborhood was full of Jews—many thriving in the textile and insurance industries—creating a warm home life for their growing families. She and Jakob were living in high style compared to her home in Southwark. They even had a cabinet with a removable board and electric iron in the kitchen! Mollie would grow up in relative comfort here. But Mollie would grow up without knowing her Italian family or her mama's Catholic faith.

*Jesus, I have denounced you. Forgive me.*

Jakob expected her to run a kosher home. One evening when they had first arrived at Norfolk Street, he brought in Mrs. Feinberg, an old *morah* from the neighborhood, who ravaged their kitchen, throwing away most of their utensils, pots, and pans. "*Neyn, neyn,*" she'd barked, pointing at this and that while Jakob carted the items away. He'd placed them into a large box and set it outside the door for the morning trash pickup.

Mary had swayed on her feet, twisting her hands and holding back tears. "We've worked so hard for these, Jakob! How can we throw away this pot because it once steamed oysters? Surely God doesn't care what it cooked before this day?"

"This is the only way for us to prosper here, Mary," Jakob hissed so he wouldn't be overheard. He guided Mary out of the kitchen, his hand tight on her elbow. "No one will take me seriously if we don't create a kosher home and keep the ways of the faith here. Why, I won't be able to sell anything if word gets out that I eat meatballs with cheese every Sunday! No, don't give me that face, girl. No crying. I insist this is how we will live and raise the baby when he is born." He turned to answer something Mrs. Feinberg asked from the kitchen doorway. "Get used to it," he added before releasing Mary's elbow and walking away.

Mary had run from the room, pulling at her hair. *Her pot* thrown herself across the bed as well as she could with belly in her way and wept into her pillow. *I want t not myself here. I'm losing myself here.* She'd wept fc like hours—days. She'd cried for her pots and pans.

herself, for Papa. She'd cried for her Mama and the babies. For Clara and Gina—oh, how she missed them! She'd longed for the river, the docks, for Cenzo and his books. She'd longed for flapjacks and oysters.

She'd sobbed until she was too exhausted to move, even to reach down to undo her laces and remove her shoes. Then, as if the baby had been crying like her mother, she hiccupped. Mary could feel the soft pulse against the skin of her belly, and the rhythm had changed everything. Baby Mollie had become her reason for living. Mary had come a long way since those early days, and could tolerate anything as long as her child was alright.

Catching her reflection in the glass, Mary saw the turmoil on her face. Tears trickled down her cheeks and onto the fabric of her dress. She saw Mrs. Ziger walk by the window and drew back, out of sight. *What would the neighbors think if they saw me standing here, blubbering?* If old lady Ziger saw her, she'd talk. Mary wiped her eyes and plumped her cheeks, and just in time—her husband came through the door, home from work.

Jakob approached her as if she were a porcelain doll, ready to break if he moved too fast. He stopped behind her, trying to hide the bruised knuckles on his hand, but she'd already caught sight of them. He'd been fighting. Again. Jakob placed his lips on the back of her neck, below her ear, and slid his good arm around her waist.

"What's wrong, wife?" he whispered. "What's amiss?"

"Nothing, nothing at all, my love. Why are you home so early in the day?"

"Mollie is asleep in her bassinet, I see. Why don't we rest awhile together…"

Mary twisted in his arms, pushing with both hands on his chest. Feigning shock, she protested, "But, sir, it's the middle of the day!"

"That's never stopped us before." Jakob smiled and traced the deep blush that darkened her cheeks.

"Jakob, I have chores to tend to." She tidied the desk.

"What's this?" Before she could tuck it under a book, Jakob reached around her, snatched the contraband letter from Clara, and scanned the pages. "From your sister?" His face went dark, and his voice grew deep. "How did this come to be here?"

"A...a...boat." The old feeling of dread blossomed—panic springing to life in her gut. *Stop*, she told her body. *Don't betray me again. Stay calm. Let me handle this.*

But Jakob had seen her flinch, and so he tried another tactic. "You don't need them anymore. I'm your family now. Me and the girl. Come rest with me while she sleeps." He slid his hand down her arm and touched the skin of her wrist. He laced her fingers in his own and led her to their bedroom.

One cold evening, while Mollie played with blocks at Mary's feet in the front room by the fire, Jakob came home with a sheepish look in his eye. As he removed his overcoat, Mary saw a flash of gold near the breast pocket of his vest. She stood, a little unsteady on her swollen feet—she was pregnant with their second child—and helped Jakob remove his woolen scarf and hat.

Mollie toddled over to wrap her arms around Jakob's legs, immobilizing him. He patted the girl's head and asked, "And how are my two turtle doves? Warm and snug in our nest on this fine evening?"

While Mary caught him up on the day's drama with the heater that needed to be bled by the landlord again, she noticed his hand returned to his vest pocket. Mollie saw as well, and reached to fish out the object of his distraction. Before he could protest, Mollie brandished an exquisite pocket watch in the air. In one deft movement, Jakob grabbed the trinket from his daughter, handed her a lollipop from his other pocket, and scooped her up to set her back on the floor with her blocks.

"Where did you get this jewel, Jakob?" Mary peered into his open hand.

"Oh, from a gentleman selling it in a hurry today, that's all. Nothing exciting. But it's a beauty, isn't it?"

Mary had to agree. "For sure. Sit by the fire and let me serve you some coffee before supper."

Jakob sat by the fire near Mollie, who enjoyed her treat. In the kitchen, preparing the cup of coffee, Mary convinced herself she'd have the courage to ask her husband about his work tonight. His occupation was a subject of mystery to her. He habitually became evasive about the details of his job at Berkheimer Insurance. He never talked about his co-workers or his manager. He kept random hours, sometimes staying late every night for two weeks straight, and other times having a few days of leisure in a row. She never knew when to expect him home. She never knew what new fancy he'd pursue with their money. She didn't know the state of their finances or where they kept their cash.

Jakob gave her an ample weekly allowance to buy the necessary goods and foodstuffs to keep a house and home. She was grateful for that, of course, but she couldn't help the anxiety of *not knowing*. Could she count on this good fortune to continue? Could she count on Jakob?

Mary scolded herself for the disloyalty of even thinking the question. Jakob loved her and provided for her and Mollie. She shouldn't doubt his methods—yet she couldn't shake this feeling of unease. She hated herself for being afraid to ask Jakob. *You are made of stronger stuff than this. Tonight is the night.* She pinched her arm to give herself courage and brought the steaming cup of coffee into the front room.

Joining her little family by the fireplace, she sat in the rocker and picked up her knitting from the basket next to the chair. She was creating a sweet set of booties for the new baby. Mollie enjoyed the treat and her game. Jakob seemed content to sip his coffee. This was the moment.

"Tell me, husband, about your work today." Mary broke the spell of contentment.

"Hmm, my sweet? What about it? I'm home with you now. Why worry about it?" He twisted the watch in his hands, head bent, studying an etching on the side.

"Yes, but I want to know what you actually do. I'm also curious to know the status of our financial situation. I mean, I used to keep the books for Papa. At the grocery, you know. I have a knack for numbers, figures, and such." She bumbled on. "Perhaps I could have a hand in keeping our family budget?"

"Oh, Mary." Jakob looked up and sighed. "There is no 'financial situation.' We don't need a budget, and we have the money we need. That's all you need to know, and there's no reason to pore over the details."

"Yes, but what do you *do* for work, Jakob? Is it sustainable for our way of living? What, exactly, do you *sell?*"

"My dear, I sell insurance. It's intangible, not something I can bring home to show you, but an agreement between men. Formed with a promise, discussed over drinks, and sealed with a handshake. It's limitless, like air, and I can sell as much as I want."

"Oh." Mary wasn't so sure. "That sounds interesting. I mean, well, hmm." Her hands shook, and the knitting needles clicked against each other.

Jakob noticed. She saw a flash of annoyance and—disgust?—race across his face.

*Why am I so nervous?* she asked herself for the hundredth time. *I have every right to ask these questions. I once dreamed of managing the grocery in Papa's place and knew what I wanted. Where did that girl go?* She knew the answer to that particular question deep in her troubled soul. That girl was gone—sold into slavery, in bondage to lust and sin. Two years ago, she had melted away with Jakob's caresses inside Arenberg's. That girl was dead.

Mary sat up straighter in her chair. *This* was her life now. She was the wife of a handsome and prosperous, if mysterious, man. Truth be told, she was enamored with him. She became undone by him—and she feared him. She knew he'd never physically hurt her or the child, but she was afraid of him nonetheless. She feared *losing* him. She feared that Jakob would one day realize his terrible mistake in loving her—that he had shackled himself to a needy woman who couldn't survive without him—and he would leave. Worse, she would *cause* him to leave. Mary knew she'd die without him. Rather, she'd *want* to die without him.

She tightened her shawl around her shoulders as Jakob got up from his chair, placed the coffee mug on the table, and retired to their bedroom to change for supper. The evil spell of doubt broken, Mary gathered her wits and challenged herself to do better—to stop searching for trouble where there was none, to let her old dreams go.

She'd find new dreams now and throw herself into her new life with all her might. She would *transform*. She'd become the Jewish wife Jakob deserved. The Jewish mother to his children that he needed. She'd try harder to embrace the Hebrew faith with every ounce of her being and keep a perfect kosher home. She noticed her daughter's face covered with sticky syrup and her hair falling out of her bun. *I'll start with Mollie, and I'll start now.* "Come, come, Mollie. Time to learn your evening prayers—there's a good girl." She wiped Mollie's face with her handkerchief and scooped her up onto her large belly.

"O, Holy Night, *hmm hmm hmm....*" Mary hummed as she helped Mollie into her little bed, tucking the blankets around her.

"Pretty, Muter," Mollie sighed, rubbing her eyes and reaching her chubby arms up to hug Mary's neck.

"I am the most blessed mother in the world, my little dove." Mary eased herself down on the edge of the bed, careful not to squish her daughter's tiny feet, hidden under the blankets. The bed groaned with her bulk—her body large with full-term pregnancy. She whispered, "Mollie, I'll tell you a secret. Can you keep a secret, even from Daddy?"

Mollie gazed at her mother with large brown eyes. "Yes."

"On this night, many, many years ago, a mother waited to give birth to her child, as I am tonight. She was close to her time. She knew the babe would come soon." Mollie's eyes closed. "The mother's name was also Mary, and she was content to be a handmaiden of God—to live her life as He saw fit—to give everything to God, her Maker." Little Mollie's breathing slowed. Mary knew she slept, but continued her story nonetheless, if only to hear herself say it. "She became the Blessed Mother of the Lord and loves each of us very much." Her voice trailed off as tears streamed down her face.

*Oh, Mother Mary, I have forsaken you and your Son. I have hidden you in the corners of my heart. I have kept you from my own child. How can you still love me? I am longing for you and my home. I'm afraid to bring this new child into the world. I feel so alone. Please forgive me, Lord Jesus! On this most holy night, please forgive me!*

Mary sat on the bed a little longer, watching her child sleep and feeling the baby within her squirm. Suddenly, the baby kicked three times in succession against her ribcage. Three huge, pounding kicks that took Mary's breath away. She waited. The kicking stopped. The baby settled down. Mary remembered a lesson she'd taught the children in Sunday school at Our Lady of Good Counsel in Southwark—the story of Saint Peter, who had denied the Lord three times before the crowd. When asked, Peter had sworn he did not know Jesus. She remembered the Gospel of Matthew, which recorded the warning Jesus gave to Peter:

"Before the rooster crows, you will disown me three times."

Saint Peter had forsaken his Savior. Like her, he had hidden Jesus in the corners of his heart and kept the Lord from others. Peter had wept bitterly.

And Jesus had forgiven him. Peter had lived his life for the Lord and become a saint in death. *Saint Peter, pray for me*, Mary implored. She continued to hum her song, remembering the candlelight at midnight Mass on Christmas. The way the light flickered across the faces of her loved ones. Her parents and siblings lined up in a row, occupying the entire pew. The little ones wiggling in their seats, anticipation of the morning gift on their precious little faces. The neighbors smiling at one another across the church. The priest raising the Eucharist high above his head.

This *was* a most holy night, and Mary knew she was not alone.

# CHAPTER ELEVEN

*Rather Hard to Believe*

*January 1894*
*Southwark, Philadelphia*

"Really, Sebastian." Rocco's booming voice filled the quiet market as cold air swirled through the door. Sebastian had been sorting boxes of buttons on the floor behind the counter and hadn't heard the bells above the door ring. Jerking up in surprise, he bumped his head on the wood countertop.

"Oh, Rocco. I didn't hear you come in." Sebastian rubbed the back of his head.

"That's because I always hold the bells above the door when I come through. I don't like to announce myself before assessing the mood of the room." He gave Sebastian a wink.

"Ah, I see. Well, the mood is calm today after the Christmas rush last week. What can I do for you?"

Rocco plucked a persimmon from the barrel by the door and tossed the fruit, catching it deftly each time it descended. "Well, paesano, maybe I miss you, that's all. It's no fun working the cold streets without you."

Sebastian was relieved. "Yes, well, those were fun times, Rocco, for sure, but I do find joy in working the market and providing for my family."

Rocco caught the persimmon and placed it on the counter before Sebastian. "Yeah, well, *I* find it hard to believe that you still have no idea of Mary's whereabouts two years after she disappeared with that socialist pig."

Sebastian coughed and squatted under the tabletop, pretending to study the buttons with rapt attention as he formulated a response to his padrone. This wasn't the first time Rocco had bothered him about Mary. His wayward daughter had damaged the brute's pride when she'd run off with the Jew. Rocco had been humiliated and disrespected. Over the past two years, Rocco had tried various tactics to rebuild his reputation. In the days after her elopement, he'd spread rumors about Mary's virtue, insinuating that the two of them had been lovers and Rocco had dismissed her when he was done with her—a thought that made Sebastian's hands ball into fists even now.

*Breathe, Sebastian! Keep your wits about you. Don't lose your temper.* Over time, Rocco had turned his attention to Gina, who was quickly packed up and married off uptown. For a while, Rocco's anger toward Sebastian seemed to cool. *Why is he picking up the thread again now?*

Rocco whistled a tune as he leaned against the workbench, as if waiting patiently for his student to answer a difficult question. Sebastian rose and squared his shoulders. "What are you trying to say, Rocco?"

"What I'm trying to say is that I heard word that your wench has recently mothered another piglet."

Sebastian's face went white. He'd heard no news of Mary for over two years. How could Rocco possibly know something about his favorite daughter that he knew nothing about? "I don't know what you're talking about."

"Congratulations, *nonno.* How many grandchildren does that make now?"

Sebastian didn't speak. His heart squeezed tight at the thought of Mary—his favorite child— his nightjar. He didn't know where she and Jakob had settled, but he wondered if perhaps Mary's sisters knew. Maybe they had been corresponding in secret despite his decree against such behavior? He'd have to get to the bottom of it, but for now, he had to get Rocco off the scent.

Sebastian cleared his throat. "Rocco, I…" But he never finished his sentence. Rocco had clasped his meaty paws around Sebastian's neck, pulling him halfway over the counter and leering into his face.

"You listen to me, you fool. I *made* you. You were just another Italian peasant when you arrived here, remember? I brought you to the Duke. I got you work. I made you successful. Everyone in Southwark knew I wanted Mary. And you let her make me a cuckold." He released his clasp on Sebastian's windpipe and patted his shoulders as if brushing crumbs off Sebastian's coat. Sebastian coughed and gasped for air.

With a rueful smile, Rocco grabbed the persimmon and turned to leave. "Find her. And tell me where she is. I'd like to extend my personal congratulations to your Mary, if you know what I mean."

Sebastian coughed again and spat on the floor. "You will never lay a hand on my daughter."

Rocco stopped before the door. Without looking at Sebastian, he laid his hand on the brick wall. "You have a nice place here, Paragano. Remember the day I showed it to you? I helped you open up the market. We should toast a bottle of wine to the success I've given you here. It's a happy home for your lady and brood upstairs, no?" He turned and met Sebastian's eye. "I'd hate to see your beautiful Tina begging on the streets. The children in rags." He shook his head. "Tut-tut. That would be a sad day."

With that, Rocco held the bells above the door and left the shop without a sound.

Sebastian doubled over as if Rocco had punched him in the gut. He leaned against the counter and sank to his knees.

# CHAPTER TWELVE

*Oysters*

*January 1894*
*Newark, New Jersey*

Mary awoke with a start from a dream of Southwark.
*That was so real.* She had been there—she'd heard the sounds of the neighborhood in the background, her younger siblings playing jacks on the corner step outside the front door. She'd smelled them—flapjacks! *Oh, it was a dream about a Friday morning.* She'd have sworn it had been real, that she had been there. She could imagine being there now, preparing to run down to the docks and buy the oysters from Cenzo.

*Oysters!*
She missed oysters the most. The salty smell and slick texture as she swallowed them whole, like a seabird. Cenzo always gave an extra handful, expecting she would sample a few of the shucked prizes on her way home, licking her fingers as she entered the grocery. Vincenzo, dear man. Mary wondered how he was faring. What would he think of her now? *He used to call me Oystercatcher.* Would he understand that she could never touch an oyster again? That they were *treif*—unkosher—and therefore not a part of her new Hebrew faith?

Would her family understand that she'd committed to raising her children in the Hebrew faith? Mollie memorized her prayers and recited *maariv* every night. The baby would learn them too. Mary knew how to keep the kitchen clean, which pot to use when cooking meat, and when and how to serve cheese. These tasks didn't bring her joy or make her feel closer to God, but she committed to them anyway. This was her lot.

She cooked their family meals in their kosher kitchen, reciting the rules in her mind on an endless loop, serving the bland food to Jakob and Mollie. She hardly ate herself—this food didn't appeal to her. She missed helping Mama craft masterpieces for Sunday supper. Mama used to roll out the pasta after returning from Mass and hang it to dry over the chair rails around the table. Within hours, they were ready for the pot. Oh, the soft, melt-in-your-mouth linguine with clams, butter, and freshly baked bread from Signor DeMarco down the street! Her mouth watered at the memory, and she groaned.

Jakob stirred. "Mary," he whispered.

She looked at him, brought out of her wistful daydreams of oyster supper.

"What are you dreaming, my dear?" He reached for her and drew her closer.

"Oh, nothing, husband."

"No, no, I saw your far-away face. No use denying it." He kissed her neck and moved his hands up and down her back.

Mary melted, and all memories of Southwark vanished. She giggled as the morning scruff around Jakob's lips tickled her ear. She could hear the baby Sarah wiggling in her bassinet. She would need milk soon. "The baby is waking, Jakob…" Mary demurred.

"The baby can wait. I want to know what my wife dreamed of." He kneaded her shoulder. "Perhaps it's something I can make a reality, hmm?" He undid the ties of her shift. "Tell me, Mary."

"Well." She hesitated. "I dreamed about oysters on Sixth Street."

"Oysters?" Jakob nudged her aside and sat up. "Of all the subjects, Mary! Why, you have no imagination whatsoever, I swear." Laughing, he settled back down to business with her shift.

"No, I mean, not *oysters*, Jakob, silly. I was remembering, well… home, actually."

Jakob's fingers stopped. "Oh." He lay back on the pillow with his hands behind his head, all amorous attention at an end. "And to think, I thought this was your home—with me and the girls."

"But Jakob." Mary reached for his hands, wishing to reengage them, but he pushed her away and got out of bed.

Careful not to wake the baby, Jakob paced back and forth along the end of the bed. Darkness descended over his features. "You know, Mary, I had to leave home too. You aren't the only one who has seen hardship. Sure," he waved his hand, "you lived in tight quarters above the market, and life was stressful at times for your family in Southwark. But you were never *hunted*. There weren't mobs of hateful Catholics *searching* for you in the alley at night. You didn't have to worry about your mother getting caught up by thugs on her return from the market."

Mary sat up straight in bed, holding the blankets to her chest. She had never heard him speak this way before. "Jakob, I…"

But Jakob didn't hear her. He paced around the room. "When I was eleven, I had to spend the last night of Chanukah huddled in our root cellar with my family. Warsaw was boiling over with riots in the streets. On December twenty-sixth, the city erupted. Sure, we knew a terrible tragedy had happened in that church on Christmas Day. We knew that. But it wasn't *our* fault. We Jews had nothing to do with *their* church. We weren't anywhere near the place! But they blamed us anyway. Blamed us for the stampede that stole almost thirty souls. It was the excuse the Russians and Poles needed to persecute my people."

Mary had no idea what Jakob was talking about but didn't dare interrupt.

"For days, we were afraid to leave home. My *mishpacha* cowered in fear. We were jewelers—had been for generations. My father was a master craftsman, and we had a beautiful shop. Now, we were living like animals. I provided for my family by sneaking into the streets to buy food and scurrying back to my parents and my brother Kopel. I was eleven years old, Mary." Jacob's voice rose and filled the room. "They treated me like a criminal. The riots were so violent. The authorities rounded up and arrested 2500 Jews for no reason. Two innocent souls died! Life was never the same afterward—we lived in fear from that day forward."

"Is that why you and Kopel came to America?" Mary whispered.

"Yes, it took a few years to make the arrangements, then my parents sent Kopel and me to America, where we'd be safe. I left home at sixteen—the same age you did. As I said, you aren't the only one who has seen hardship." Jakob slumped into the chair in the corner, his anger spent. His hands came to rest between his knees, his head bowed.

Mary barely breathed. Jakob had never spoken of his home in Warsaw. She hadn't realized he and Kopel—sweet Kopel, whom she knew as a kind-hearted and quiet young man—had lived through such horrors. She considered Jakob now, across the room—the father of her children, even more mysterious to her now than before. She reached her hand toward him, desperate to connect, to claim him as her own, to bring him back to the present and show him how grateful she was for their little family. But baby Sarah chose that moment to wake with a wet nappy and a hungry tummy.

Mary let her hand drop. Her milk came down with a rush, staining her shift. She pulled her robe over her shoulders and reached for the child in the bassinet next to her bed, deftly settling her onto the pillow and letting her nurse right away. The nappy could wait. She wasn't ready to break the silence or get up from the bed. She didn't make a move that would disrupt Jakob. He seemed troubled and dark, his brow furrowed and jaw grating back and forth as if he were grinding the memory of that tragic December into dust.

"I didn't know your family suffered so, Jakob. I never knew of these events. Can you explain what happened so I can understand?"

"Yes." Her husband looked at her with haunted eyes. "At a Christmas service in 1881, someone shouted 'Fire!' at Holy Cross Church in Warsaw. The alarm caused the congregation to rush to the doors in panic, creating a stampede that killed twenty-eight people. A disaster—a tragedy that shocked everyone in the community. But the real tragedy that day? A mob formed, claiming a Jew had raised the false alarm in the church for a diversion after being caught pickpocketing."

Jakob ran his hands down his face as if rubbing away the awful truth.

"The mob attacked Jews in their own homes. They ransacked

Jewish businesses and raped Jewish women. It was the start of pogroms that cursed my people for years. That's why so many families emigrated to the United States. That's why my parents sent Kopel and me to Philadelphia—they hoped we'd find a better life for ourselves here."

"And did you? Find a better life here?" Mary asked in a whisper, afraid to hear his honest answer.

"Oh, Mary, how can you ask such a question?" Jakob jumped up and came to the bed, wrapping her and their nursing baby into his arms. He kissed Sarah's fuzzy head at her breast and gazed into his wife's eyes. "You are my life now, Mary, for better or for worse. I have no home in Warsaw anymore. There is no home for me anywhere but beside you. I knew from the moment I first saw you." He kissed her lips hard, then her forehead with tenderness. "I will never leave your side, Mary. With you is where I belong. I swear it."

# CHAPTER THIRTEEN

*Full of Grace*

*June 2018*
*Drexel Hill, PA*

Bella woke with a scream on her lips, clutching the sheets to her chest. Heart pounding, she looked around the room and saw the cowgirl hat hanging from the hook next to the bedroom door. She'd purchased the hat the day after Nate left—her first act of rebellion. There it was, in its glory, waiting for her to don it on her way to work in the morning.

Just a dream, then.

Just a dream, but it had felt so real. The blood had cascaded down her legs, and she'd suffered the sharp electric pain coursing through her belly. She'd heard herself call for Nate, and she could see him run into the room, reaching for the phone by the bed to call 911.

"Emergency."

She could hear Nate explain that his wife was bleeding out—that she was going to faint—that she was six months pregnant with their baby.

Their baby!

A sob wrenched from Bella's throat as she relived the nightmare, unable to tear her eyes away from the film reel, replaying the worst moments of her life.

"It's my fault," she'd said then, clear and calm.

Nate had looked at her—sharp eyes taking in her words, mouth still moving as he'd barked out their address to the emergency dispatcher.

"It's my fault, Nate." She'd been adamant, tenacious almost. Convinced she was about to die with the baby, she'd wanted her last confession. To ease her conscience before leaving her crumpled body—her crumpled life—that was slipping away with each drop of blood.

"You don't know what you're saying." Nate had sat beside her on the bed. "Hush, the ambulance is on the way." He'd stroked her back. "It's not your fault."

Another stabbing pain had wracked Bella's body, and the pressure in her lower abdomen had become unbearable.

The baby was coming—alive or dead.

"I didn't want the baby, Nate. After trying for so long, I wasn't ready to be a mom." She'd sobbed then, and the stroking motion on her back had ceased.

Over her cries, she'd heard Nate whisper, "Bella, what have you done?"

Shaking her head at the memory, Bella reached for Nana's rosary nestled among her treasures on the bedside table. Working the worn, red beads, she started to pray. It was just a dream.

"Hail, Mary…"

She couldn't help but think of Mary Paragano and the terrible words she'd read in Nana's letter.

*My mother was going to drown us.*

Bella fought against the thought.

"…full of grace…"

But in her heart, Bella knew she wasn't worthy of grace.

That evening, Bella adjusted her black skirt and grabbed the cowgirl hat from its peg, leaving her bedroom with a swoop of fabric and expensive scent. She was on a mission—headed to the Station Tap for a distraction. It was five o'clock on a Friday night, so why shouldn't she head to the bar? Earlier that day, she'd played hooky from work for the second time in as many months. Unable to recover from her nightmare and the thoughts of Mary drowning her children, Bella had binge-watched reruns of *Parenthood* and eaten Cheetos all day. She hated loneliness, bad dreams, sad letters, neon-orange-stained fingers, and divorce. Maybe she was spending too much time with Sophie on this research project. She needed a break from everything.

Once settled on a stool with a martini, Bella studied the patrons filing into the restaurant behind her from the mirrored wall across the bar. It'd been a long time since she'd been here. She watched the wavy reflections of straight-haired blonds on the arms of finely dressed gentlemen or in giggling female groups out for a bit of fun. The women looked younger than she was and sounded cheerful, like they shared a secret she could never guess.

Bella noticed her empty drink and flagged down Frankie, the barkeep. He was surprised when she ordered a second. Bella and Nate used to come here on Friday nights in their thirties when she was still young and hopeful that they'd someday conceive a child. Frankie had worked here for decades. He was a good sport and always sided with her in the couples' playful arguments and trivia games. "You ain't got nothin' on her, Nate," he'd say to her husband with a wink while shaking a martini for his next customer.

Bella had believed that once—relished the thought. But now, the words brought a sour taste to her mouth. All she could hear now was, "You ain't got nothin'." And Bella knew it was true—an empty house with no children and no husband. Far worse, God had left her for dead.

Halfway through her second drink, a dark-haired man about her age left his seat at a table in the corner, approached the bar, and offered to buy her another round. Frankie waggled his eyebrows at her, but she ignored him. "Yeah, sure, that'd be nice."

The stranger pulled a stool closer to her and threw his suit jacket over the back. Rolling up his French-blue shirt sleeves, he settled with a satisfied sigh and a sip of his—what was he drinking? Ginger ale?

"Two ginger ales, please, Frankie."

Bella recognized this guy. "Hey, do you go to Saint Andrew the Apostle?"

The stranger's eyebrows went up, but he smiled. "I sure do."

"Ginger ale, huh? You mean, you're not hoping I'll get sloppy drunk and make poor choices tonight?" Bella couldn't believe her audacity—she'd never spoken like this, let alone to a strange man.

Her companion chuckled and took a sip of his fresh soda. "I most certainly am not." He offered his hand. "Tony."

She took it. "Bella. Nice to meet you." She nudged her half-finished second martini aside and took a thirsty pull on the soda straw. She leaned back in her chair with a sigh. "That's better." Tony had saved her from a demoralizing and possibly dangerous night of mistakes. He was an angel disguised as a well-dressed yet modest businessman, and a wave of gratitude washed over her.

"So, what's your story? Why are you moping around at a bar on a Friday night?" Tony challenged her with the question before she could start a benign conversation about the weather. He'd taken her off-guard, and at first, she was offended. But Bella could feel her burdens bubbling up inside her chest. She needed relief, and she needed to *vent*.

She took another sip of soda. "Tony, I don't know you. How can you possibly think I'd be willing to spill my guts to you right now?"

"I don't know. I just had a strange feeling I ought to stop here on my way home from work. I don't often hang out at bars. I walked in, weeded through the crowd of fake-happy uber-blonds, and saw you sitting alone. Looking sad. Like I was supposed to lend you an ear." Tony looked at his watch. "It's as simple as that." He settled up with Frankie, paying Bella's tab too. "And, anyway, I'm a sucker for a city chick in a cowgirl hat."

Bella smirked at him. "Ha!"

He held up his hands in surrender. "Just being honest."

Tony's joke eased the knot in her stomach, and she heard herself ask if he'd be a gentleman and walk her safely home. "If that's okay with you, Frankie?" she called over her shoulder.

Frankie blinked once or twice, scratched his chin, then nodded, touching the cross around his neck. "Yeah, he ain't got nothin' on you, Bella. You'll be alright."

Bella smiled.

Once they were out in the fresh evening air, the one-and-a-half drink buzz started to wear off, and Bella could feel her mind return to its rightful place in her body. She and Tony walked for a few blocks in amiable silence.

"My husband left me." Bella skipped around a piece of trash, careful not to let the heel of her fancy black pumps sink into a banana peel.

"Ouch." Tony helped her sidestep another piece of filth, his hand on her elbow.

"Yeah, he met a *much* younger woman and left me flat. The funny thing is, I should be furious. I mean, I should feel total righteous rage, but I don't. All I feel is shame." She shook her head. "Guilt. I don't know…"

Tony whistled low under his breath. "Why in heaven's name would you feel guilty when *he* left *you?*"

Bella stopped and threw her hands in the air. "Because I ruined everything, and it's my fault he left!"

They sat in the dark on the front steps of Saint Andrew the Apostle. Bella had talked during the entire walk from the bar, spilling the details of her twenty-something wedding, the loss of her baby, and the slow, painful death of her marriage. Tony kept quiet, interjecting the acceptable sounds of surprise and dismay at the appropriate moments in Bella's tale.

*He's a good listener.*

The sound of crickets made a comfortable backdrop during a moment of silence before Bella let drop her final confession. "In the second trimester of the pregnancy, I must have gone through some kind of hormone shift. Years of therapy and articles online have since confirmed that for me. I wasn't really in my right mind. People talk about postpartum depression nowadays, but I'd never heard of perinatal depression before." Bella looked at Tony to make sure he was following.

He sat with his arms held loosely over his knees, his hands clasped before him, his head bent. Bella bit her lip and waited for him to say something. When he didn't, she continued. "Anyway, I was obsessed with ending the pregnancy. I called a clinic a few times. Drove by. I don't know. I don't think I would have really done it, but…" A sob caught in Bella's throat. She'd come so close, so close. "I guess after we lost the baby, well, I figured God took him because of my terrible thoughts. That I didn't deserve…"

She stopped. *I can't let myself lose control.* She fought hard against the tears.

Tony turned his face to hers, his eyebrows drawn together with concern, and tears glistening in his eyes, but Bella balked and shook her head. "I can't."

Wordless, her new friend reached for her hand, never taking his eyes off hers. And that's when she lost it, succumbing to the torrent of tears. Years of built-up emotion that had no outlet or reprieve came pouring out. Tony put his arm around her and drew her head to his shoulder. The motion pushed the cowgirl hat off her head. It fell to the ground and rolled down a step. Bella clutched Tony's arm, held on for dear life, and sobbed. Underneath her heart-breaking tears, she could hear Tony praying. She could hardly discern the words, but she didn't need to. They sank into her heart, into her soul. They were the words she couldn't pray. They were the words she *needed* to pray, but still, she resisted.

"It's not your fault, Bella. God didn't take away your baby because of something you did."

She wished she could believe him. But in her heart, she didn't. Her mind read the words of Nana's dying letter. *My mother was going to drown us.* She was just as crazy as her great-great-grandmother Mary.

After a while, she wiped her eyes, reached for her hat, brushed off the dirt, and placed it securely back on her head. Tony was silent, as if waiting for her to direct their next step. She took a soothing breath and nodded at the church behind her. "I grew up in this church, ya know. We had my dad's funeral here. Ma still attends every week."

"Rosalie. Yes, I know," Tony chuckled.

Bella swatted his arm. "What? Did my mother put you up to this?"

Tony unleashed his full smile on Bella. What a nice smile. "*Noooo.*" He dragged out the word. "I wouldn't put it that way. She did mention you, though. You look like her. That's how I recognized you at the bar. I'm her accountant. She's the one who first invited me to this church a few months back."

"Ah, now I see." Bella had to smile at her mother's scheming. "That's her game plan, you know. Rosalie lures unsuspecting folks into the depths of the church, and then, to keep them coming—wait, let me guess—bribes them with her homemade—"

"Stromboli, yeah."

"Stromboli. Exactly."

# CHAPTER FOURTEEN

*Finally, a Friend*

May 1894
Newark, NJ

Mary pushed baby Sarah in the fancy pram Jakob had brought home the week before. How he had afforded it, God only knew. But it was a beautiful buggy and a fine day, and Mary was happy to be outside. They were on their way to the market. As they approached the corner house on Thirteenth Avenue—rumored to be a house of ill repute—Mary heard whispering from the doorway. She contemplated trying a different route for fear of exposing her young girls to an improper scene. But as she approached, she heard the distinctive sound of two females giggling. *Not a woman with a man, then. Well, on we go, I suppose.*

Mary straightened her jacket, gripped Mollie's hand, and picked up her pace, passing the doorway as fast as possible. Two girls came into view—they were as young, if not younger than she. *I'm not afraid of them.* She gave the girls a bland look as she passed. They erupted into laughter at her back, babbling over each other. She heard them say the word *shiksa*—Gentile. Then they said a name.

Her breath caught in her throat, and she quickened her pace. Jakob. They had said the name Jakob.

Her hands trembled. She held tighter to the pram and her daughter's hand. *Were they referring to my husband?* She squeezed Mollie's hand. *Do I want to know?* She didn't. Yet her thoughts continued to spiral. *What were they saying about him—about me—about us? Will I ever feel at home in this place? I am a stranger in a strange land. Like*

*Gulliver, I bounce from one land to another, never quite finding my place!*

"Muter, you're holding my hand too tight," Mollie whined.

Mary was surprised to find her daughter there, looking up at her with anxiety and pain on her precious little face. Mary's knuckles were white, and her strength surprised her. "My darling child, I'm so sorry." She let go and patted Mollie's head. "Muter was deciding what to buy at the market today. Shall we have roast chicken for supper tonight or lamb chops?"

Placated, Mollie replied, "Lamb chops!" and took Mary's hand anew, swinging her arm with joy.

Despite Mollie's elation for her favorite meal, distraction stole Mary's attention. She kept hearing those girls in her mind. *Jakob... Jakob...Jakob...* Their audacious, insolent voices echoed, mocking her as she went to the market. She ground her teeth. Her heart rate rose, and sweat trickled at her temples. *I must pull myself together. The whole neighborhood will see my distress.* She hurried into the busy market and went to the kosher meat section, hoping to find the chops and a vegetable or two for a stew.

*Jakob...Jakob...Jakob...* She planned to be in and out of the store before her nerves unraveled.

Mary pushed the pram before her to the register, with Mollie dawdling behind. She waited until the grocer, busy unloading a barrel of potatoes in the front window, was ready to attend to her. "Eh, hem..." She cleared her throat. He didn't hear. She stood there, pushing the pram forward and backward, keeping her eyes on Mollie, who searched for spiders in the corner. "Eh, *HEM,*" she said louder, her heart beating fast and her hands shaking.

Her panic increased when she realized she'd have to pass by the whores again on her walk home. *Jakob...Jakob...Jakob...* Calculating an alternate route, she didn't notice a second customer approach the counter to wait alongside her.

"Excuse me, are you Mrs. Jakob Lichtenbaum?" asked a female voice.

Mary whirled around, eyes bulging with misplaced anger. "And who are you, may I ask? And how do you know my husband's name?"

At the sound of her mother's angry voice, baby Sarah started to cry. Mollie dropped a nutshell she'd found on the floor and stared at her mother.

The stranger was undaunted. "Oh, I do beg your pardon, ma'am. My husband always did say as how I was an impertinent one. I didn't mean no harm in the asking. Truly, I didn't." The young woman stuck out her tiny, gloved hand for a shake.

Stunned, Mary shook her hand. The motion calmed her raw nerves.

The stranger smiled. "I'm Mrs. Efraim Danzig—Edna." She dimpled and dropped a small curtsy. "I'm pleased to meet you. My good husband works with yours at the insurance agency in town. I've seen you and your man strolling home from synagogue, and my Efraim pointed you out as fine folk to know."

Still shaking Edna's hand, Mary exhaled in a rush. The baby cried harder now. The grocer, alerted to their presence by Mary's outburst, packed her bag and asked for payment. Mollie rocked from side to side, whining for the washroom. This new woman—*Edna, was it?*—stood there looking at her expectantly. *Has she asked me a question? Am I supposed to reply?* Her mind went blank. She had escaped into a black hole and left her body standing in front of the market counter like a wooden carving.

Commanding a surprising air of authority, the diminutive Edna knelt before Mollie. "If you can wait for the potty, you will get a treat." Without a word to Mary, she picked up the baby and put her over her shoulder, patting Sarah's back to produce an elusive burp, while prodding Mary to hand the money to the grocer.

Mary followed the instructions like a child. After making her own purchase, Edna steered the little group onto the street and asked Mary to come home for tea. "I'm a few doors down, over there." She pointed down the street. "And your little one needs a wee, don'tcha, hen?" She smiled at Mollie.

Touched by the woman's kindness and seeing her daughter squirm in earnest, Mary accepted the invitation. She followed her new friend, pushing the pram as if in a trance, while Edna walked hand-in-hand with Mollie, chattering to distract her from the pressing issue of her full bladder. She made a sharp turn at a butcher shop with plucked chickens hanging from the front window. Mary followed to find herself in a dark and cramped entryway.

"We'd best leave the carriage down here, don'tcha think, hen? I don't fancy luggin' it up these steps." Edna extracted baby Sarah from the pram and left it at the bottom of the stairs. "Up we go, then," she chirped.

Desperate for relief, Mollie scampered up the steep staircase after their host. Mary followed. On the landing, Edna opened the door with a crooked number 444 sign. She handed the baby to Mary. "C'mon, little miss." Edna rushed Mollie to the bedroom to relieve herself in the chamber pot. Overcome with gratitude at Edna's pragmatic kindness, Mary sat down hard on the cushioned chair by the door, snuggling baby Sarah in her lap. The baby gazed at her wide-eyed and broke into a toothless grin. It was the first time Mary had seen her smile, and the sight warmed her to the core. The tension in her shoulders relaxed.

Edna escorted Mollie into the room. "Good girl. Now, would you enjoy a taffy to suck on?" Edna gave her a treat from her pocket and stoked the embers in the hearth. Soon, the little group gathered around a warm and inviting fire.

Edna excused herself to the kitchen, and Mary heard her preparing a pot of tea. She surveyed the room. Edna's apartment was spotless. It was also tiny. But instead of cramped, the place was homey—snug, like a bird's nest. Charming teacups perched on the table as if expecting guests. A framed portrait on the dainty mantle above the hearth showed a beaming Edna and a jolly-looking man. *That must be her husband, Efraim.*

Edna entered the room and saw Mary at the hearth, studying the portrait. "Oh, that's my good husband and me there. On our wedding day, that was. About four years ago now. He's a good'un, for sure." She poured tea. "We thought we'd be happy with a little one by now, but that hasn't happened yet. We lost the one, you see, about two years back. Nearly broke my Efraim's heart, but I told him we'd be all right. It happens, ya know?"

Edna prattled on, adding a lump of sugar to each cup without waiting for a response from Mary. "Well, the tea's laid out, and I'm right happy to have you fine ladies here this day to join me. The baby can rest on the shaggy rug by the chair with her big sister. You'll keep an eye on her, won'tcha, hen?" She grinned at Mollie. "So your momma and I can have a proper sit-down?"

Mollie's eyes went wide with the new responsibility, but she nodded and let baby Sarah suck on her braided hair. Satisfied, Edna smiled at Mary. "Please, come set yourself down." She offered a chair.

Mary felt like a princess. Here, in this tiny, modest apartment, Edna treated her with the utmost care, respect, and friendship. Edna was the most straightforward and kindest person Mary had ever met. The panic of the afternoon melted away as she swallowed a bracing sip of hot tea and listened to her hostess's twitter about her home in Pittsburgh, about traveling to the great city of Manhattan with her parents when she was young, about being orphaned when they died of typhoid soon after settling there, and how she helped to care for the babies in the orphanage where she lived until she was fourteen years old. She described the love story between her and Efraim. How he had loved her on sight and vowed to marry her and give her a good home and children.

Mary lowered her teacup, bowed her head, and sobbed.

"I thought so, hen. You're tired, you are. And weary too. Now you sit and let everything out. You can tell me what's amiss, and I will no' judge." Edna offered Mary a worn but clean hankie from her sleeve.

"Oh, Edna, you've been so kind to me—to my girls. I don't deserve it." Mary cried.

"Nonsense. Everyone deserves kindness, Mary."

"No, but you don't understand. I'm not who you think I am. I'm a fraud—a fake. I don't belong here. I don't know who I am, and I'm not sure I really know my husband either." Mary whispered so Mollie wouldn't hear.

Edna sat back in her chair, blew on her hot tea, and regarded Mary for a long minute. "No, hen, there's nothin' fake about ya, truth be told. I find you are more truthful than anyone else I've met, barring my good husband, o' course. As far as where you might belong? I don't reckon it matters, hen. You're a fighter, you are. Stronger than you think, ya know? You belong anywhere that God put you. As for your husband, well, there's a man for you. They can be strange and mysterious sometimes, can't they?" Edna nodded and took a sip of her tea.

Mary giggled. Edna seemed so sure of everything—she decided what was true and believed what she declared. She didn't seem to panic or agonize over life. Her new friend's life seemed black and white, without the muddled gray where Mary spent most of her time. In Edna's company, the knot in Mary's stomach unclenched, and her shoulders relaxed. God had blessed her with a true friend.

Sarah fussed, hungry for milk. "Edna, would you mind if I nurse the baby here before we leave?"

Edna gave her charming smile and suggested Mary rest in the armchair in the bedroom. "This is my prize possession—a most comfortable seat, perfect for nursing the baby. Please, make yourself at home." Edna hurried the soiled chamber pot out of the room, assuring Mary she'd watch over Mollie.

When the door closed behind Edna, Mary sank into the comfortable chair, and Sarah nursed contentedly at her breast. "Thank you, Lord," she prayed, "for providing a friend who is like a sister." Mary rested without the worry and guilt that usually crowded her mind and enjoyed a few quiet moments while gazing at her daughter's beloved face.

After a little while, she shifted Sarah to her other arm, tidied herself, and left the peace of the comfortable room. Edna and Mollie sat by the fire, reading from a well-worn copy of *Aesop's Fables*. Mary remembered those stories from childhood when she'd sat in her mama's lap in Italy. Edna looked up at Mary across the room and smiled her big smile. "Ya know, I believe we will be lifelong friends."

Mary nodded, hoping it was true.

"Mary!" Jakob bellowed from the bedroom. "What is *this*?"

Startled, Mary looked up from her mending to see Jakob storming out of their room, waving something in his hand. He came to stand before her, where she sat in her chair, and glared down at her.

"I *said*, what is this?" He shoved the red-beaded rosary under her nose. With all her might, Mary remained calm—thankful that their kind neighbor, Mrs. Koenig, was entertaining the girls with a tea party in her parlor next door.

She forced herself to continue sewing, watching the needle weave in and out through the thick fabric of Jakob's sock. "It's a rosary, Husband. Surely you've seen one before."

"Don't be coy with me, Wife. Of course, I know what it *is*. My question is, how did it come to be *here*?"

"I brought it with me from home." Mary raised her head and met her husband's eyes, now level with hers, as he stooped down. He curled his fingers around the rosary, encapsulating it in his fist.

"Home," he repeated in a strange voice. Jakob stretched to his full height. "Mary, I'm not a cruel man, and I won't forbid you from keeping this…this symbol of your past." He gave the beads a disdainful look. "I am, however, disappointed you hid this from me. I'm annoyed—no, that's not the word. I am *irate* that I found this bauble on our bedstand. I can't believe you'd be so brazen about displaying this in our kosher home!" He walked toward the dining table. "Today of all days, Mary?" He pounded his fist on the table. "You know I am having my comrades here to discuss the next steps with our issue in town. The men will be here soon. You were prudent enough to make plans for the girls. You tidied up the house." He pointed around the room. "You have the pot ready for tea. Yet you overlooked this little necklace, lying out for anyone to see? I don't believe it. This was intentional. You mean to discredit me before my peers—to embarrass me in front of my friends. This hurts, Mary. It's a betrayal of the worst sort."

Mary looked around the room with eyebrows raised. "And which of your so-called 'friends,' pray tell, will be traipsing into our bedroom this evening, Jakob?"

Jakob's eyebrows shot up. "I see." He gave a loud guffaw. "I see." He looked at the rosary in his hands. "So, you are now a comic, eh? That was funny, Mary. If this weren't so important, I would've laughed. As it stands, however, I don't appreciate your sense of humor. I don't appreciate your betrayal either." His voice rose. "In fact,

I believe you no longer have a use for this little bauble, and, as your husband, it is my duty to correct you of your wayward actions." He grabbed his overcoat and headed for the door, rosary in hand.

Mary stood. The sewing fell to the floor. "Jakob, no!"

He stopped.

"Please don't. You're right—I shouldn't have left that in plain view."

Jakob stilled. She approached him as if he were a firecracker ready to go off. "You're right, Jakob. I'm sorry. I'm not myself. I'm a little nervous about your friends stopping over."

He looked at Mary, seemingly unconvinced. She touched his arm. "I didn't mean to disrespect you, and you were right. I did leave the beads out on the bedstand out of spite. Please forgive me. You can forgive me, can't you?" She hated herself for begging.

Jakob squeezed his fist around the rosary beads, paused, then released them into her hands. "Yes, Mary, I suppose I can forgive you. All I ask is that you support me in my pursuits. Don't thwart my efforts to make a place for us here. I'm doing this for you. Everything I do is for you. I love you and the girls and want us to be a happy family here."

Jakob kissed her until her hands fell to her sides. His embrace left her limbless, lost in space and time. She dropped the rosary beads to the floor as Jakob bent to pick her up and carry her into the bedroom.

"We have just enough time before they arrive," he whispered, kissing her neck. "Come with me to bed."

Jakob looked at Mary dozing, curled up on the bed like the kitten she was. *I love when I make her purr like that.* He pulled on his trousers and smiled at himself in the mirror as he combed his hair. He was too high-strung to ruminate on their love-making right now, though. He laid the brush down on the dresser, careful not to wake Mary, and sneaked out of their bedroom. He snatched the rosary beads from the front room floor and stashed them in his pocket.

Jakob surveyed the room and packed the forgotten mending in

a basket by the fireplace. Everything else seemed in order. The front bay window with the mahogany desk stood across the room, facing the street. Mary had scrubbed the dining table outside the kitchen door to a shine. Through the little swaying shutter doors to his left, the kitchen was tidy, with a pot of water ready to brew the tea. The hatstand between the front door and the kitchen wasn't full—there'd be room for his comrades' coats and hats. The girls were next door, their playthings put away in their tiny room, tucked behind the washroom. He had closed the bedroom door, hiding his sleepy wife in her nest. Yes, the place looked perfect. Now, if he could tidy his thoughts, Jakob would be ready for the meeting.

But he couldn't. His appetite for Mary was so strong he almost pivoted, marched back into their bedroom, and wrapped his hands into her thick black hair if only to hear her yelp. She often undid him like this—ever since he first saw her, walking to work with her sister. That day seemed like yesterday.

Leaning against the wall of a market across the street from Arenberg's, Jakob and his buddy Uri had shared a quick cigarette. Uri, scanning the crowd for a new skirt to charm, saw them first. He nudged Jakob with his elbow and nodded at the girls, who walked together arm in arm, chatting. The sister giggled, but Mary was more serious and didn't laugh. Jakob could tell she was concentrating on something else and not paying attention to her sister. He found himself wanting more than anything to know what she thought about— to read her mind. He stared at her, cigarette forgotten. Uri grabbed it out of his hand and took a long drag.

The giggling girl looked at the boys, and Jakob blushed as she caught him ogling. The girl smiled and whispered into her sister's ear. Then Mary met Jakob's eyes across the way. Jakob was paralyzed— glued to the spot. Uri and the other girl both noticed, and both broke into peals of laughter, but Mary didn't smile. She looked away and swept past them.

"I'm going to marry that girl," Jakob said.

"Which one?" Uri chuckled, stamping out their shared cigarette.

"The one with the haunted eyes."

The memory frustrated Jakob. He had to get his head straight—

no time for romantic notions—too much to do. His comrades were about to descend on his tidy home. The Newark branch of the SLP was rallying around their man, Daniel De Leon, who'd lost his bid for governorship in '91 and planned to run again in the next election. The Newark boys had run into trouble the week before with a gang from Brooklyn who backed another candidate. A fight had broken out, and the police had arrested some of the Newark SLP members. De Leon condemned the violence in his newspaper, *The People*, but Jakob and his friends knew fisticuffs were sometimes the only way to convince folks.

The fellas had asked *him* to host this gathering. They trusted him and considered him a part of the team, accepted in the community. Everything had to be perfect.

He envisioned Mary, hair disheveled, storming out of the bedroom halfway through the gathering, a whirlwind of skirts, looking for her rosary and creating an ungodly scene. *I could lock her in there until the meeting's over. Maybe she won't wake up until the guys are gone. But I need her to serve the tea. Ahh, Mary, you frustrate me to no end! You better not have shaky hands when you pour out.*

Jakob heard footsteps in the hall and five men shuffling in from outside. Jakob didn't have time to check on Mary before they knocked. He arranged his features into a face of confident purpose and opened the door for his comrades.

# CHAPTER FIFTEEN

*In Sickness and in Health*

*December 1895*
*Newark, NJ*

In the middle of the night, Mary woke with a tight chest and a full-body sweat. Too tired to get up and change her sticky shift, she tossed and turned in the damp bedsheets. Newark had enjoyed a beautiful summer and unusually temperate autumn, but the winter was brutally cold, and many in their community suffered from severe illness. Mary shivered and shook, and her teeth clattered loud enough to wake her husband. The bright moon cast an eerie glow through the lace curtains and onto his worried face. Fear coursed through Mary's veins at his expression.

"Blazes, Mary!" Jakob touched her forehead. "Are you unwell? You look like a ghost."

She couldn't answer. When she opened her mouth, no sound came from her parched throat. She licked her cracked lips with a dry tongue, looked Jakob in the eye, and willed him into action.

"I'll get you water, sweet wife. Don't worry, I'll take care of you." Jakob kissed her cheek. She nodded and closed her eyes again.

The grippe held Mary for five days, during which time she couldn't leave her bed. Jakob ran the household with alacrity. He slept in the chair in their bedroom, fitful all night, and attended to his wife's needs. By the third day, Jakob had memorized the routine. He dressed the children in the morning and shuffled them next door to Mrs. Koenig's apartment, where she cared for them all day. Edna came each evening to check on Mary, prepare dinner, supervise the girls' baths, and get them into bed. Efraim joined her there after work and visited Jakob. The men shared a cigar and news of the day while Edna tidied the kitchen, and then Efraim escorted his wife home.

Even the SLP fellas helped. They sent a box of food from the market—lard, beef jerky, canned beans, rice, sugar, and matzah meal—delivered by a skinny boy who wore a scarf over his mouth to avoid breathing in any illness from the apartment. Tucked into the bottom of the box was a bottle of aged whiskey meant for Mary's sore throat and Jakob's raw nerves.

But it was Mrs. Feinberg who offered the most. She arrived every morning around nine and refused to leave until Edna arrived at four. She cooked, cleaned, stoked the fire, laundered Mary's bedclothes, and attended to her every need. When Mary woke from fitful dreams in the afternoons, Mrs. Feinberg held her hand and stroked her forehead until she fell asleep.

On the fourth day of Mary's fever, Jakob arrived to find Mrs. Feinberg distraught and praying over Mary as if she would die at any moment. He let out a gasp and hurried into the bedroom. Mrs. Feinberg looked at him with tears in her eyes. He had never seen the older woman become emotional before.

Her tenderness touched his heart, but he looked at her and raised his eyebrow. "Will she live?" Jakob choked on the words.

Mrs. Feinberg gave no answer but continued her incantations. She patted the bed next to Mary, inviting Jakob to join her. He sat by his wife and held her hand, bowing his head as Mrs. Feinberg murmured, *"Mi Sheberach..."*

Jakob cried.

Mary's fever broke that night.

On the fifth day, Mary was well enough to sit up in bed, propped up by a dozen pillows, her dark hair falling over them like a cascade. Jakob came home to hear Mrs. Feinberg's strong voice from the bedroom. Not wishing to disturb them, he stood in the doorway, charmed by their stern neighbor perched by Mary's bed, regaling his wife with neighborhood gossip. Mary turned to see Jakob leaning against the door frame, arms crossed over his chest. She smiled, and his heart skipped a beat.

*So, this is what it means—the vows we took—in sickness and in health.*

Despite his wife's weakness, Jakob had never been stronger.

"You don't have to continue spending every evening here, Edna. I'm well enough to care for the girls myself," Mary announced for the third time in as many days.

Edna gave her friend a frank look and cleared her throat. "It's nay trouble, Mary, and ya know it. I love spending time with your little ladies, anyhow. They're so big—there's no way you can bathe and dress them yet. Now, be a good girl and set yourself down for a cup, won'tcha? I made the willow bark tea that helps with your aching head."

Chastised, Mary obeyed and sat at the big table between the kitchen and living room, where she could see the girls playing with blocks by the hearth. She had been out of bed for a few days, but her weakness surprised her. She ached to grab her sketchbook and charcoal pencils to capture the scene before her, but she knew her limits. Even sitting at the table drained her energy. *Edna is right. It may take a few more days to return to my able-bodied self.*

She sipped the comforting tea and watched her sweet girls playing with each other. She couldn't remember life before them. A few short years ago, while toiling in the sweatshop in Southwark, she had abhorred the idea of raising babies. Perhaps because she had spent her childhood surrounded by her mama's large brood of children, incessantly needing her and tugging on her skirts. Mama had seemed the most patient of women, which Mary was not. *I suppose it's different when it's your offspring and not your siblings.*

Now, she cherished her girls and never wanted to miss spending time with them, especially after the last week of isolation. Her arms had ached to hold them, smell their hair, and feel their chubby little fingers curled in her hands. It was enough to be near them this evening—to listen to them play and watch Edna care for them. *Poor Edna, so motherly and without a child of her own.*

"Whatcha thinking about, Mary? You look so sad and forlorn." Without waiting for an answer, Edna perked up and asked the girls, "How's about we teach your muter the game we learned, doves?" She explained to Mary, "It's a learning rhyme they taught me at the orphanage. It teaches the letters of the alphabet, see? And the young'uns don't even know they're being taught nothin'," she added *sotto voce* with a wink.

"That sounds lovely." Slouching back in the chair with her tea, Mary watched as the children joined Edna on the hearthrug.

"Polly want an…apple?"

Edna nodded at Mollie, who guessed, "Polly want a…ball."

Edna clapped. "Yes, very good! Now, help your little sister, who is too young to know."

Mollie instructed Sarah to repeat after her. "Polly want a…cat."

Edna ended with, "Polly want a…dog." Then she clapped and looked at Mary. "See? They'll learn their letters in no time. They're such bright little ladies!"

Mary nodded. "What a splendid way to spend the time on cold nights, Edna. Thank you for teaching us. I miss teaching Sunday school lessons at Our Lady of Good Council in Southwark."

Mary clapped a hand over her mouth.

"Sunday school?" Edna looked confused. "You mean teaching the Torah? I didn't think the synagogue allowed women to teach."

"Oh, yes, you're right," Mary stammered, stirring her tea.

Before Edna could press her further, the girls tugged on her sleeve and begged to continue with the game.

The front door opened at ten on a Tuesday morning while Mary read her favorite Dickens novel. Taken unawares, she hid the novel under her skirts while Jakob rushed into the apartment, hung up his hat, and stubbed a cigarette into the ashtray on the table.

"Hello, dear, what are you up to?" Jakob eyed his wife with

amusement on his face. "Are the girls napping already?" He rifled through the mail on the little bench by the door.

Mary cleared her throat. Her feet were on the ottoman, and she'd folded her hands in her lap. "Yes. I'm just resting my eyes for a few moments while they sleep. What brings you home at this time of day?" She regretted the question as soon as it left her mouth. Jakob detested when she questioned his work habits, but his unusual schedule made her edgy.

"Hmm?" He folded a letter from the mail and placed it in his waistcoat pocket. Then he planted an absentminded kiss on her forehead. "What did you ask me?"

"Oh, nothing." Mary looked around, having nothing in her hands to occupy her. She was a bird in a gilded cage, watched by her curious owner, waiting for dismissal or the cage door to open. *Great Expectations* burned a hole in her skirt.

*This is ridiculous—I'm a grown woman. Don't I deserve some pleasurable pursuits now and again?*

She saw Jakob's fascination as he watched the thoughts flit across her face. "Mary, I find it hard to believe you were doing *nothing* when I walked in the door. Now, please tell me what's going on. I had a bad day at work and needed to come home for a break, not to find my wife playing the part of a bum. Have out with it."

Mary winced. She knew that tone—it was the beginning of an argument. If she hadn't hidden the book, the situation wouldn't have escalated. She was within her rights to relax for a moment's pleasure without shame in her own home! And what about Jakob? Waltzing in here during her well managed daily routine without so much as "by your leave?" Why wasn't he at the office? Why did he act so shifty when she asked about his position?

Mary brought the novel out from under her skirt and shoved it in Jakob's face.

His eyebrows shot up. "I didn't know you had this book. Where did you get it?"

Mary sat up straight and raised her chin. She looked down her nose at her husband. "From the butcher's wife, Lorraine. She and I got to chatting while I waited for the chops. Lorraine offered to lend me some books. She has a fine library..."

Jakob flung his hands in the air. "Mary, it's not that I mind you reading, but going around discussing books with every vendor in town? What will people think of us? That I'm a stooge, bossed around by my wife, who has enough leisure to read for pleasure? That I run around caring for the house chores and wiping the girls' faces while you lie around enjoying novels? It's bad enough that my wife is an artist! They know we don't have the money for a maid or kitchen help, so either that makes me slovenly, or I'm bewitched by a...a... domineering, overbearing, controlling..."

"Jakob, stop." Mary stood up. "What is going on here? Are you angry that I am reading this book? Or is something else the matter?"

Jakob gaped at his wife, his hands clenched at his sides. "I don't see why you must reveal us to everyone in town, Mary. Can't you just be a *balabusta* and avoid outside interests?"

"What on Earth is a *balabusta*?"

"It's a Jewish homemaker, a capable housewife. Not a woman who messes up every kosher meal she tries to cook! Not a wife who spends her day drawing, reading books, and announcing it to the entire neighborhood. Mary, your indiscretion makes us vulnerable."

"Indiscretion? Vulnerable? How can borrowing a book from a kind woman I see once a week while purchasing meat for your table be considered indiscreet?"

"*My* table? As if I don't provide for you in every way! I work my tail off out there, day in, day out, humbling myself to the world, bringing home money without fail. You are free to purchase whatever you see fit to run this home. I never question. I never argue. All I ask is that you do your part."

Mary stomped her foot. "Do my part? All I do is provide a clean and tidy home for you and our children. I shop at the market, launder the clothes, and school the girls. I have learned to keep a *kosher* kitchen—all for you, Jakob! Can't you see how hard it is sometimes? How much I have *sacrificed*?"

It was the wrong thing to say, but Mary couldn't have stopped herself had she tried. She never could resist shooting the last arrow.

Jakob reached his hand out for the book. She handed it to him without a word. He looked at the fine binding, fingered the leather strip that kept her page, and surveyed a few sentences of the chapter. Mary clenched her jaw, terrified he'd toss the book into the fireplace and ruin her new friend's property. She waited and held her breath.

He returned the book to her, turned on his heel, and strode to the door. "*Great Expectations,* indeed." He smirked and shook his head. "And how, pray tell, does your pursuit of this pleasure contribute to our situation?" He slammed the door behind him, waking the girls from their nap.

"And then Cassie slapped Howard's face while everyone on the floor watched from their doorways!" Edna's face wrinkled with mirth.

Mary wiped her watering eyes. "Poor Howard, he must have been mortified."

"Well, he's gonna have to return home to his parents, tail between his legs, that's for sure." Mary and Edna enjoyed a rare moment of grown-up time, gossiping about the neighborhood while the girls played with their dolls. But Mary's buoyant mood shifted when Edna mentioned returning home. Edna must have noticed her expression change, for she held her hand across the table as a tear slid down Mary's cheek.

"What's amiss, Mary?"

"Oh, Edna, I miss my sisters in Southwark terribly. They would have loved this conversation—laughing about old Howard. Clara would be gracious, but I imagine Gina would have a few choice remarks!" Mary dabbed at her eyes with her sleeve. "Every morning, I imagine them going about their daily routine—Mama toiling at the stove, the little ones at her feet, and the boys chasing each other down the street. I picture the girls heading to work without me. And Papa with his pipe. Oh, Papa!" She dissolved into tears while Edna held her hands across the table.

The little girls looked at their mother with concern, and Mary didn't notice Jakob's arrival. He stood inside the doorway, head tilted to the side. *Oh no! He must have overheard our conversation.*

"You think you're the only one who misses a loved one?" Jakob asked with a roll of his eyes. Mary knew that voice—sarcasm was one of Jakob's strong suits. "What about me, Mary, deprived of my brother Kopel—the only family I have on this *continent*?"

Edna cleared her throat and busied herself with the tea tray, and the girls turned back to their dolls. They'd heard it all before. Better to acquiesce and give Jakob what he wanted so it would be over faster.

As Edna carried the tea tray into the kitchen, Mary approached her husband with her head down. "Jakob, you're right." She placed her hands on his chest and looked into his eyes. "It was selfish of me to complain so."

Jakob smoothed a wrinkle from his vest. "Yes, well, I need to prepare for the meeting tonight. The boys want to discuss our plans for the next election. I will wash up and change, then head to the pub after supper." He glanced at the kitchen. "What's cooking? You're not mixing the meat with your cheese again, are you?"

As soon as Jakob left the room, the friends let out a collective breath and sat in silence for a few moments, letting his anger dissipate from the air. Mary's cheeks burned red in shame. She had abased herself again to keep the peace in front of her friend and spare her daughters another scene.

"Why do you make yourself so small for him?" Edna whispered, studying her face.

When Mary didn't answer, Edna changed tactics.

"Wanna play a hand of cards to pass the time until supper is ready?"

"Good idea." Mary walked to the desk by the big bay window and plucked a deck of cards from the top drawer. Before she closed it, she saw a handwritten note scrunched into a ball and shoved towards the back, behind the detritus of junk captured there. She unraveled the paper, revealing a sprawl of ugly words across the crumpled page. The words jumped off the page and went straight to her heart.

"Mary? Are you alright?" Edna joined her at the desk. "What in the name of all that's holy is that?"

Edna reached for the paper and grabbed it out of Mary's hands.

> *We know who you are backing. Your cause will fail. You owe us money. Pay it and go back to Warsaw, or else.*

Mary snatched the offensive note, went to the hearth, and threw it into the fire, where it disintegrated in seconds. She wiped her hands and shrugged. "Let's play double solitaire."

"You're losing your mind, Mary. It's been a long year, I know, but I swear you are crazy," Jakob hissed at her from across the room. They'd had a knock-out argument upon Jakob's return from the tavern. Efraim had asked him about his courtship with Mary in Southwark. He'd explained Edna's concern for Mary—that losing her family had been a terrible blow, and she still suffered. Efraim had hinted that Jakob had jumped into bed with Mary and dragged her away from her family, destroying the possibility of a match with a well-respected fishmonger in town.

"That's not what happened that night, Mary," Jakob yelled. "Don't you realize what you're doing? You're twisting the story in your favor. To cast yourself as the damsel in distress from one of your beloved novels. You've written me into your story as the villain—the perpetrator of your plight. I won't have it! I am your husband. And I can't trust you anymore." He pounded his fist on the table. "I forbid you to visit with Edna on your own again. You may see her when we are together as a family. From now on, I must attend during your conversations with her."

Mary threw herself into the chair, pulling at her hair while rocking back and forth. He'd taken it too far, but there was nothing for it now. He'd made a decree and couldn't back down for fear of losing respect. Mary had been wrong to speak of their intimate relationship to another woman—the wife of one of his friends and co-workers, no less!

How could he face Efraim tomorrow after the man had pulled him aside to inquire about his marriage? The audacity of that buffoon! Efraim was an idiot. He was jolly and fun to drink with but soft-hearted to a fault. He allowed his tiny yet big-mouthed woman to boss him around. And the fool didn't seem to mind one bit. He had even seen fit to follow Edna's suggestion to speak with him—something other men would never do.

The idea that Mary had spoken poorly of him to her friend made his heart feel fit to burst. He needed to punch something—repeatedly. But Jakob hadn't intended to be so harsh with her or end Mary's friendship with the woman. Edna had been kind, especially during Mary's recent illness. It was a loss, but he could do nothing about it. This wouldn't have happened if Mary had minded her place and hadn't gossiped about their life.

Mary made a low moaning sound, looking at the floor and rocking back and forth in her chair as if mad. His blood ran cold. Had his wife gone crazy? "Mary." He stepped closer to her, hesitant to touch her. "Mary, after all…"

Her body went still. She stopped rocking, stared at the floor, and fell as silent as if she were dead.

Jakob put on his coat and left the flat. What else could he do?

When she heard the door click, Mary focused her eyes on the wood floor, scrubbed to a shine, below her feet. She studied the details of the wood grain, a stain of coffee in the rough edges on the side of one of the floorboards. *Little Sarah could get a splinter there. I must sand the wood down smooth tomorrow.*

Mary took a deep breath—filled her lungs—then let it out again. She looked at her hands, closed into fists in her lap, and loosened her grip, watching each finger uncurl. She counted to twenty, rolled her head from side to side, and heard the pop of her spine. The tension in her shoulders eased. *It's not true. I didn't betray him. I'm allowed to have my own thoughts and to speak to a close friend when I'm troubled.*

Mary wasn't ready to consider dear Edna yet. She clamped down on the idea of losing her friendship before the anguish could engulf her.

She continued to take inventory of her body. She had a pulsing headache behind her eyes. She was heart-sore and exhausted by Jakob's accusations, suspicions, constant criticisms, and questions. She had opened up to Edna about their courtship, the family fight, and their dramatic elopement to Newark. Nothing in her story made Jakob out to be an evil man, yet he accused her of painting a poor picture of him. Mary sat staring at the floor, lamenting the loss of the only real friend she had ever had besides her sisters.

*I can't live like this anymore! The real issue is Jakob's pride.* Mary snorted. The sound shook her out of her frozen and submissive state. She sat up straighter.

She was like a butterfly specimen, nailed into place and kept under glass to be regarded by future specialists who would discuss her attributes even after she was dead and dried up. She may have once been beautiful and carefree, but then, in one moment—that exact moment when he'd pinned her to the felt board—she'd become forever stuck, forbidden to move forward, incapable of going back. Jakob kept her affixed by guilt she didn't claim. She hadn't done anything wrong. She loved him, the man who'd swept her off her feet. She'd married him and borne his children. Why did he treat her as his enemy? Why did he always blame her for his unhappiness? She was his beautiful, dead butterfly, stuck in time and space. Mary looked at the ceiling and moaned. *I have no way out.* She imagined herself floating away in the swift current of a river, the water taking her far away from her difficult reality. *My only option is—no, no, I could never. But I'm not strong enough to continue like this, Lord! Will I ever feel free?*

In answer, she experienced the undeniable sensation of a baby's kick in her womb.

# CHAPTER SIXTEEN

### *The Tide Is Turning*

*June, 1896*
*Newark, NJ*

"Mary, wake up." Someone tapped her cheek. Mary smelled incense and heard the murmurs of a small gathering in the next room. She lay on her bed atop the coverlet.

"What happened?"

"You went white as a sheet, and then your eyes rolled right up into your head." A familiar voice suppressed a giggle. "You went down like a tree felled in the forest!" A snort—Edna. Mary recognized her best friend's voice, and a wave of relief swept over her. Then she heard baby Mendel's cry from the other room, and the memories flooded her brain, piecing together like a jigsaw puzzle.

"Heavens! The *bris*! The baby's circumcision is today."

Edna patted Mary's knee. "It's alright now, Mary, dont'cha worry one bit. You aren't the first momma, Jewish or not, to faint at her little man's bris. Lucky for you, Efraim stood as *sandek*. He held onto that baby like a king would clutch his crown. He didn't even notice when you went down, so intent he was on his honored purpose of keeping the baby still."

"Ugh, Jakob must be mortified. I've shamed him." Mary put her face in her hands.

"No, no, my girl. Don'tcha go worrying after the man and his pride." Edna was still perturbed by Jakob's erratic behavior over the last year. Why, last winter, he'd *forbidden* Edna to speak with Mary—of all the hogwash she had ever heard. Efraim had confronted his friend and demanded he fix things between their wives. At first, it was a shaky truce. The two couples had spent nearly a year in an awkward dance.

But when Mary gave birth to a son, Jakob's demeanor had shifted. He'd shown up at their little apartment one night, drunk as a skunk, and waved a cigar in Efraim's face by way of apology. Efraim, good soul that he was, forgave his friend, clasped his hand, and enveloped him in a brotherly embrace.

Serving tea to the men at their little table, Edna had watched as Jakob asked her husband to have the honored position of *sandek* at the baby's bris, meaning he'd hold Mendel during the ceremony. It was more than an olive branch—it was a great homage to their friendship. Efraim had accepted, nodded once, and swallowed a slug of tea to hide his tear-filled eyes.

Jakob had risen from his chair, revived by the strong brew, and approached Edna with his hands clasped in supplication. "Miss Edna, wife of my dear friend, can you find it in your heart to forgive a stupid man?" He'd unleashed the full power of his handsome, dimpled smile, then gripped her hand in his and bowed over it. "I'm sorry I forbade you to speak with Mary. I trust you with her life." He'd straightened and looked her in the eyes. "As a token of my good faith, I'm entreating you to please stand as *kvatterin* to Mendel and deliver him into the sure arms of your husband for his circumcision."

How could Edna hold a grudge against the man after *that* performance? She'd been touched and aware that the honor bestowed on her in being named kvatterin—godmother—was a hopeful blessing from God that she and Efraim would finally have a child. She'd smiled and tittered. "Sit down, you lout, and finish your tea."

"Ha! You'll do it, then?" Jakob had kissed her on both cheeks before returning to his seat.

Edna remembered beaming at her husband across the table, who'd favored her with a warm smile. Maybe with the birth of his son, Jakob would pull his act together and stop being involved in dirty politics, drinking, and gambling so much. But Edna also remembered seeing Jakob pull a silver flask from his vest pocket and sneak a dollop of amber liquid into his tea.

Edna shook her head, and the warm feeling in her belly went cold. She took Mary's clammy hand, urging her to rise.

"Up you go, Mary." Edna pulled her friend to her feet. "A bracing cup of tea will right you, sure enough. You tidy your hair, and I'll sneak to the kitchen to pour you a cup."

Mary nodded and gave Edna a tentative smile. "You're a saint, Edna. I've hardly survived without you all these months. You're a sister to me. I'm so glad Jakob has finally righted the wrongs between our families. Oh, he must be mortified by my fainting spell." Mary's eyes filled with tears.

"Now, don't go crying on me. C'mon, we've got to get you back in there to your baby. Put yourself together. And don't you worry about Jakob anymore. Believe it or not, the world doesn't revolve around the man."

Jakob Lichtenbaum restrained himself with great effort. If he punched Harris in the face, he'd lose his job *and* be locked up in the jailhouse overnight. He'd narrowly escaped that fate a week ago when he cheated at cards and started a fistfight with the Grove Street boys. No, he had to calm himself. He counted to five, then opened his eyes and stared at Harris across his obnoxious desk. The man was a buffoon and didn't know how to run an agency. He was a fool not to take Jakob's advice on the life insurance policy for Mr. Carter. It would've brought in enough revenue to run the agency for a year. So what that it wasn't entirely accurate? Who would even know?

But Harris knew, and he didn't like it. He'd called Jakob into his office first thing in the morning and made his decree. Jakob was to clear out his desk immediately and excuse himself from the office without notice and without trouble. From the corner of his eye, Jakob saw Efraim Danzig standing at his desk and craning his neck to look through the little window of Harris's office door.

Efraim, the big lug, would probably agree with Harris, which made Jakob's blood boil even more. He was a good pal—loyal—but righteous to a fault. Efraim reminded Jakob of his brother Kopel, and he couldn't handle the sight of Efraim's pitying eyes right now. He turned his back on the office window and clenched his hands into fists. One, two, three. A deep breath. Jakob plastered a dimpled smile on his face and, his voice dripping with sarcasm, bowed and thanked Harris for the pleasure of his company these past few years.

Within minutes, Jakob had cleared his desk and exited the building, Efraim hot on his heels. They headed straight to their favorite tavern. Once established at the bar with Efraim, Jakob released the breath he'd been holding since hearing Harris's words of dismissal. Now that reality was hitting his brain, he needed a drink, and fast. The barman presented two shots of whiskey, and Jakob reached for both. His old pal shook his head, smiled ruefully, and ordered another for himself.

"What are you gonna do now, Jakob?"

"I haven't the slightest idea. And what is Mary going to say when she finds out? She just had the baby a few weeks ago, and she'll go into a full-fledged panic, I know it." He downed the whiskey in one fiery gulp. "Don't look at me that way, Danzig. I don't want your pity."

Efraim looked away and took a dainty sip of his spirit. Jakob had already finished his second and waved his hand for another. With a sigh, Efraim settled the bill and recommended they head home. "It's the middle of the day, after all. And you've gotta figure out what you're gonna do."

"Well, I certainly don't need you to keep reminding me." Jakob winced as the third shot burned its way down his gullet. "Efraim." Jakob clapped his big friend on the shoulder. "I'm thinking I can make a go at it with the cards. I've got a strong poker face. If I can steer clear of the Grove Street boys, I could probably keep at it for a while, save up the cash, and coast for a bit until I figure this out."

The friends left the bar, and Efraim steered Jakob toward home. After a few blocks, the big oaf said the most surprising thing. "Jakob, have you ever thought of maybe starting your own business? Maybe you and I could join up and open an agency together?"

Jakob was touched. That his friend would believe in him enough to take a chance on him made his heart swell. He missed his brother Kopel more than words could express, but having Efraim beside him made him feel like he was with family.

Efraim stopped him, draped his arm around Jakob's shoulders, and pointed at the sky, writing letters in the air. "Can't you picture it? 'Danzig and Lichtenbaum, Insurance Brokers?'"

Jakob let out a guffaw. "Ha! You mean 'Lichtenbaum and Danzig' of course."

"You have a deal." Efraim held out his meaty hand for a shake, but Jakob let out a whoop, legged a jig, and pulled his friend in for a bear hug.

A few months later, as Jakob rounded the corner of Central and First, he ran smack into Simon, Danny, and Billy—the Brooklyn SLP boys. Jakob had known this day would come, but he wasn't ready for it. He ducked to his right, narrowly missing a punch to the face, only to catch it in the gut from big Danny, the largest man in the gang. Jakob's breath came out in a ragged huff. Now that they had his attention, the boys pushed Jakob against the wall and held him there. Simon reached into Jakob's vest pocket and retrieved his expensive watch.

"Not the timepiece, Simon." Jakob could hardly speak. "I'm particularly fond of it."

Simon looked up. "Ha! You're in no place to comment, Lichtenbaum. You owe our boss money, and we're here to collect, so pony up. This is a simple exchange. A man of business like yourself must surely understand." He gave Danny a nod, and Jakob's kidney exploded under the force of another hit.

"So, where were we?" Simon looked him up and down. "Grab his cash."

Jakob was promptly relieved of the wad of bills in his pocket. "Be a friend and leave a few bucks for supper," he panted. "The wife planned to make beef stew this evening."

At this, Simon tossed the pocket watch and then caught it. He paced back and forth in front of Jakob, pinned against the wall, squirming to get out from under the sweaty weight of his attackers. Jakob didn't like the look on his face.

"Ah, yes, the wife." Simon whistled. "A pretty thing, your Mary." He considered Jakob, eyebrow raised. "Perhaps we can make a different kind of arrangement. I like this watch, sure, but there are other ways to pay off a man's debt."

Jakob thrashed and kicked at Danny and Billy, fury flowing through his veins. He spat on the ground in front of Simon. "Touch my wife, and I'll kill you."

"Tsk, tsk, tsk. You're in no position to make threats, Lichtenbaum. Besides, pretty Mary will be willing. After all, we're gonna have the leverage we need when you're knocked out cold and the boys have their blades to your little ones' throats. She may even enjoy…"

Simon never finished his sentence. An otherworldly strength overtook Jakob, and he pulled himself out of the men's grasp, advancing on Simon with the force of an enraged father. Simon didn't see Jakob's fist coming and went down like a flour sack. Shocked, the other men were slow to react. Then a copper's whistle blew across the street. The men snatched their leader off the ground and stumbled into the shadow of the alley as Jakob ran full tilt in the opposite direction, clutching his abdomen.

The next week, a tentative knock came to the door as Mary helped Mollie tie her fraying shoelaces, preparing to take a stroll with the children before supper. Late afternoon was an unusual time to receive the post. It must be bad news. She opened the door to see an unfamiliar delivery boy, who seemed to know precisely who she was. Mary accepted the letter like it was a bomb about to explode. She gave the messenger a penny. He tipped his hat, bowed, and lingered in the hallway as if he had no intention of departing, which made Mary nervous. Unsure what to do, Mary went inside and closed the door behind her.

The children were restless, so Mary distracted them with a gumdrop from her secret stash on top of the icebox. She opened the letter and recognized her sister Clara's beautiful script. A handful of bills clipped together in a wad fell to the floor with a thunk. Mary snatched the money and pocketed it. Then she read—and sucked in her breath at the first words.

*Mrs. Clara Forte*
*Southwark, Philadelphia*

*June 10, 1897*

*My Dearest Mary,*
*I write to you in all haste, hoping you will join us in prayer for our dear friend Vincenzo. The other day, Tomas came to find Mama and Papa with news that Cenzo had fallen at his fish stall. He was half-conscious when found and not able to walk. His friends on Delaware Avenue assisted him to his room above the store and sent for medical attention. He has slurred speech, and one arm lies limp at his side. The doctor doesn't know if dear Cenzo will walk again.*
*Mama went to his aid, along with Giuseppe and Rosetta. Papa refused to go. He hasn't found it in his heart to forgive Cenzo for his complicity in your plans. Pray that Papa will forgive! Oh, Mary, you must come to Cenzo. He will be revived if he sees you—I know it. He has been your faithful servant these past few years, arranging secret messages between you and me and keeping your whereabouts a secret. He loves you so.*
*As you see, enclosed in this missive is enough money to buy yourself a round-trip fare to Phila and back. No, don't fret, dear! Dom and I insist you use these funds for this journey. Tomas's friend, who has delivered this to you, can secure you the ticket on the day of your choice. He will wait for your direction. I'm sure your good husband will understand your errand and arrange care for the children in your absence. Come home, Mary!*
*Cenzo is in God's hands. But here on earth, his*

*friends will care for him. Mama will continue to send meals to nourish him. My dear Dom will inquire of the landlord what is to be done regarding the rent and will try to sort Cenzo's affairs. We appealed to an officer at the 2nd and Christian Station, one Sullivan McMurtrie. He and Cenzo have become friends in recent years. The officer has promised to look in on him every week.*

*And Tomas, sweet boy, won't leave the man's side except to run the fish stall. He reads to him every night from one of the many books that pile around the room. What a devoted friend! He is an orphan, you know. Vincenzo found him wandering the docks as a child and took him under his wing. What a beautiful idea that familial love and devotion can be found in the most painful of circumstances. I don't know of any fate as terrible as an orphan's, but it seems one needn't be a relation to become a family.*

*Come home to us, dear sister.*

*Yours,*
*Clara*

"I must go home to Southwark, Jakob." Mary didn't realize she'd been holding her breath until after she spoke. She let it out now in an extended release of air. She clasped the letter in her hands behind her back. She sought courage from the smooth pages of Clara's beautiful stationery—a wedding gift, no doubt.

Jakob, sitting with his back to her at the mahogany desk, head bent over a newspaper, looked at her as if out of a daze. "What are you talking about, Mary?"

"I must go home to Southwark for the day. Mrs. Koenig can care for the children next door while I'm gone."

"What's happened? Is it your mother?" Jakob hopped out of the chair and reached for Mary's hand, leading her to sit. They both knew that fear of Rocco and despair about her falling out with Papa were enough reasons to keep Mary away from Philadelphia. The fact that she sought to return could mean only one thing—someone lay dying or dead.

"It's Vincenzo. He's had an apoplexy." Mary held out the letter from Clara.

"Vincenzo?" Jakob scoffed. His nostrils flared and his face turned red. "Are you seeking my permission to leave our children, put yourself in harm's way, and travel alone to your family home—where you are no longer welcome—all for the sake of your past *suitor*? You must think I'm either a saint or an idiot. How could you even ask this of me?"

"Jakob, don't be daft. You know very well that Cenzo was never my suitor. He is a stalwart friend, who was willing to sacrifice so much to care for me and the baby. It was a valiant act he offered to do for me."

She shouldn't have said that. Jakob sucked in his breath and bit his lip. His eyes bulged, and he drew himself to his full height, jerked his vest tight, and headed for the door, ignoring Mary.

"No, Jakob! Don't skip out on this conversation!" Mary spoke to his back. "You always leave when we argue. Don't be a coward. I'm asking for a simple favor—an important favor—I'm asking to see a dying friend."

Jakob stood silent, eyebrows raised.

"You won't even have to pay a penny. My sister Clara has sent some money, see?" Joining Jakob by the door, Mary held out the letter and the bills folded into the envelope.

This seemed to make matters worse—she shouldn't have mentioned money. She knew Jakob and Efraim were trying to get their insurance agency off the ground, and she sensed that things weren't going as well as planned. Bringing up the cost only hurt her husband's pride.

"Oh, I see, you have it all figured out, is that so, Wife? Well, not so fast. I'm not allowing you to go. I will *not* have my wife gallivanting about, leaving me with the children while she goes out of state to visit another man. The answer is a firm *no*. Now, if you'll excuse me, I believe some of my comrades are expecting me at the pub."

"The pub? Is that where you've been spending your evenings? I thought you and Efraim were working hard on the new business. Edna says Efraim is working overtime every week. Aren't you helping him?" She'd really started it now, and why not? It was time to hold her husband to task. Mary had a sneaking suspicion that Jakob was gambling away the meager earnings he brought in. He'd already instructed her to cut back on purchasing beef and tea—expensive items that were part of their daily meals.

Jakob rounded on her with fire in his eyes. "How dare you question my methods? Have I ever failed to provide for you and the children? Have you ever gone hungry?"

Mary winced. It was true. They'd never starved. But…

As if he could see the uncertainty on her face, Jakob hung his head and left the apartment without another word. There was nothing to say. Mary stood alone in the front room, an envelope of cash weighing heavy in her hand, the news in the letter weighing heavy on her heart.

Sometime around midnight, Jakob stumbled into the bedroom, reeking of whiskey, and tossed his jacket on the dresser. Mary was awake—had been awake all night. Despite her anger toward Jakob, Mary's body relaxed, knowing her husband was safe at home. Although she was hurt by Jakob's earlier outburst, worried about her good friend Cenzo, and confused about what to do, her body responded to the nearness of her husband, who slid under the coverlet and reached for her hips in the darkness.

It was always this way with them. This push-pull. They fought. She sometimes stood her ground, but more often, she relented with apologies. Jakob left, he came home, and then they found each other, without words, in each other's arms. They were magnets, often repelling each other, then joining together with such force that they become one, melding and molding together in the night.

*Is this what love is supposed to be?* Mary's body shivered as Jakob's tongue traced the delicate line of her clavicle, his whiskers tickling her skin and his large hands wandering down her spine. "Jakob." She fought through the distraction. "I need to go to Southwark."

Jakob's mouth found hers and kissed her with such passion that she melted into his embrace, unable to continue her plea.

Sometime later, in the deep stillness of the night, Mary came to consciousness, aware of her husband's body curled around hers, with his arms around her waist in a protective embrace. She knew he was awake—could tell by the sound of his breathing, light and quick—could almost hear the thoughts in his head. About the dangers of her proposed journey? Or his jealousy about the reason she wanted to go? The moon was high in the sky, and the window behind their bed let in enough glow for Mary to see her husband's worried face.

"Mary, you must know." Jakob cleared his throat, thick with the aftereffects of too much whiskey and lovemaking. He tried again. "You must know I cherish you above all. The prospect of losing you makes me sometimes act like a…a…."

Mary put her finger on his lips. She already knew. "Jakob, you won't lose me. I'm your wife. 'Till death do us part,' remember?" She kissed him and put her forehead against his, so they were eye to eye. *Yes, this is what love is supposed to be.* Mary sighed, ready to fall back asleep.

The crash of broken glass hit her ears a half second after a rock bounced off her leg and onto the floor. Shards of glass rained over their faces and stuck in Mary's hair. *What's happening?*

Jakob jumped, grabbed the window pane, and leaned halfway out. "Get out of here! Are you crazy?!"

Then he looked at his wife. "Mary, are you hurt?" Jakob brushed broken glass off Mary with his shirt sleeve and checked for blood. The thick quilt had softened the blow, and she was unharmed.

"I'm all right. I'm all right!" She spotted something on the floor. "Jakob, there is a paper tied to the stone." With trembling hands, Mary pointed to the rock as if it were a viper ready to strike.

"Mary, go check on the children. Watch your step—don't cut your feet. I'll clean up this mess."

Once Mary left the room, Jakob picked up the rock, untied the string, and opened the paper. It was as he feared—the threat was real.

*Pack your bags, Jakob. We're riding you out of town on a rail.* He'd need to skip town. After all this time, he had finally, undeniably, irrevocably run out of luck. He slumped into the chair and ran his hands through his hair. An errant piece of glass cut his finger. "Ouch!" He put his finger in his mouth, but the coppery taste of blood upset him even more. "Blazes!" Jakob shook his head to settle his nerves. *Think!* He'd need to run. Mary and the children would be safer if he were gone. *It's me they want. Surely, they'll leave them alone if I'm gone.*

Jakob looked up and saw Mary standing in the doorframe of their bedroom, her black hair in total disarray, her shift swaying in the breeze that came through the broken window. She communicated everything to her husband with her haunted, dark eyes—her fear, her worry, her *disappointment*. There was nothing for it now. He'd have to confess.

"Get dressed. You and the children will go to Efraim and Edna's flat. Stay there for a few days while I clear out. I'll lay low for a few weeks, then return for you. Hurry, now, Mary! It's safer for you if we're apart!"

Mary tiptoed around the broken glass on the floor and approached him, seated there, defeated. He desperately needed her to embrace him—hold him close as if he were a child—and tell him everything would be alright. That she forgave him, loved him. His body anticipated the contact as she drew nearer, and he experienced a longing he had never known. At the final step that would close the distance and give him redemption, Mary reached around him, opened the little drawer of his bedside table where he kept his most valuable items, and rummaged around until she found what she wanted.

With eyes blazing like fire, his wife waved her fist before his face. Red rosary beads dangled down her delicate wrist.

She left the room without a backward glance.

A knock on the door roused Efraim and Edna awake. Efraim jumped to his feet, grabbed his housecoat from the door peg, and slipped his feet into slippers. Edna used to hop out of bed like that, but dizziness and nausea prevented her from stirring quickly these days. They heard a muffled voice at the front door.

"It's me, Mary."

Edna's heart filled with alarm, and she prodded Efraim along. "Hurry up, you old bear! Something's amiss!"

Efraim tied his robe around his waist and nodded. He crossed the apartment in two steps and opened the front door to find Mary Lichtenbaum clutching baby Mendel to her shoulder and Mollie behind her, clinging to little Sarah at the top of the stairs.

"I had nowhere else to go."

Efraim ushered them inside and looked at Edna for guidance, his eyebrows raised to his hairline. Edna emerged from her cocoon, where she languished most mornings in a nauseous haze, and took charge, barking instructions to Efraim about brewing tea. She led the children to the rug by the fire while handing them nursery rhyme books and a bag of jacks, then led Mary to the chair at the table.

Crisis seemed to push her fragile being into another body altogether, one that was hearty and hale and—if she had a moment to think about it—blooming the way she always pictured herself to be when carrying a child. Despite the seriousness of the scene unfolding around her, Edna's heart swelled in her chest as she watched Efraim put on the pot for tea in their tiny kitchen. Yes, today marked the day her pregnancy had passed the point of their prior losses. Memories of that moment suffered a few years ago when she'd clasped her hands to her middle, doubled over in agony, and sent Efraim out for the midwife, were too traumatic to dwell on. She shook her head to clear the memory and concentrated on her best friend, Mary.

Jakob must have left. *What the devil did that boy do now?* Efraim was Jakob's loyal friend to a fault. Edna knew her husband loved spending time with his buddy after a long day, enjoying a pint at the local before his walk home, but sometimes Jakob drank too much. Edna didn't resent him even for that. The problem with Jakob was he went too far. Efraim told her Jakob was overly generous with his money, lavishing gifts on his friends at the bar, offering to cover this one's tab one night and pay for that one's drinks the next. He sometimes bet his entire bank account on a strong hand.

Edna could overlook these inadequacies. She chalked up these habits to Jakob's intense need to be liked. To feel as though he fit in, was one of the comrades. What Edna couldn't abide, however, was Jakob's infidelity. Her husband suspected Jakob slept with one of the whores on Thirteenth Avenue. He'd spied Jakob exiting the whorehouse in the middle of the night a few weeks back, shirt untucked and lipstick smeared on his neck. Edna had vomited when he told her that.

Efraim returned to the living room with the tray of tea things as Edna decided what to do. Once Efraim had poured the tea and settled at the table with the women, Edna glanced over her shoulder at the children, then leveled her gaze on her friend. "Out with it, then."

"You poor dear!" Edna clucked her tongue and shook her head. "Who'd do such a thing?" She looked at her husband, wearing nothing but his robe. Efraim looked ridiculous but charming, and Edna's heart was fit to burst. *He is such a dear man,* she thought for the thousandth time. *And a better provider than that cad Jakob has ever been!* Jakob was gone—and her friend was left alone to care for the children. Alone and afraid. Efraim and Edna listened to Mary's tale, hearts sinking with each new revelation.

"And then he lost a wager. He owes money to the Brooklyn SLP boss. I imagine it's a lot of money—he wouldn't say. Word got out, and well, the gang found out where we live. They won't stop until they find him. Jakob swears they'll leave me and the kids alone—that they just want him. But I fear they'll ransack the apartment! I don't know what they're capable of. I…I can't return there." Mary shook her head, looked at the children sleeping in a cozy pile of arms and legs on the sofa, and cried.

In the end, after they got the entire story out of Mary, it amounted to this—the Brooklyn boss had tracked down Jakob for payment, and Jakob had gone on the lam. His absence would affect the Danzigs too, of course. Jakob had abandoned his wife and left the heavy lift of starting a business for Efraim to handle alone. The two of them would have to care for Mary and the children. *Just when I need my husband most. Oh, I could strangle Jakob!*

Exhausted, the couple tucked Mary and the three children into their bed and settled themselves on the davenport, where they tried to doze.

The morning dawned bright and warm, a beautiful summer day, but Edna's heart was heavy for her dear friend. Mary's life would never be the same. Efraim was snoring in her ear. She nudged him and rose from the couch slowly, testing the waters. The nausea wasn't too bad this morning. Efraim snorted as he woke to see Edna's worried face hovering over him. "They'll have to stay here for a while, you realize?" she said.

This got Efraim's attention. He sat upright and rubbed his eyes. "Of course. I'll go over to the apartment later. Pack up a few of their things. Fix the broken window. Jakob—I could strangle him."

The Danzigs did everything they could to make Mary and the children feel welcome and safe, but the tiny apartment grew increasingly cramped as the days turned into weeks. Their hospitality was running as thin as their bankroll as Edna's belly started to grow.

They received no word from Jakob. Mary and the little ones could not return to Norfolk Street. And they could no longer stay here.

# CHAPTER SEVENTEEN

## *The Demon*

*June 1897*
*Southwark, Philadelphia*

"Mary!" Sebastian sat bolt upright in bed, scaring Florentina and the little ones who slept between them. A cold sweat broke out on his brow as the demon chased him into consciousness.

Tina flinched and gasped. She made the sign of the cross and murmured a prayer under her breath.

"Just a dream. It was just a dream, Tina," Sebastian panted. "Go back to sleep now, everyone." But Sebastian couldn't stay in bed. While Tina soothed the little ones back to sleep, he flung his legs over the side of the mattress and rubbed his hands over his face as if he could wipe the image away.

He donned his nightrobe and slippers, gave a frightened glance at the bedroom window, and trod downstairs to the giant kitchen table. He lit his pipe and settled into his favorite chair, but the demon had followed him. A shudder ran across his shoulders. If only he could draw it like Mary could. Perhaps he could exorcise it by revealing its visage to the world. But he wasn't an artist, and he couldn't draw. He couldn't even describe the beast to Tina—she'd think him a lunatic.

No, no, the only thing Sebastian could do was push it aside, tuck it far away into the back of his brain. He was an educated man—he had gone to seminary, after all! He knew demons existed and stalked the Earth. He also knew his imagination was strong and riddled with guilt, a potent emotion.

Sebastien pulled on his pipe and examined his conscience. He wished with all his soul that he hadn't run into Vincenzo's assistant, Tomas, yesterday and overheard Tomas speaking with an errand boy about his delivery to Mary in Newark. He wished his brain could refuse the information. He wished he didn't have a choice to make. What could he do? Mary had forced his hand. When she'd come home pregnant a few years ago, he had not been able to abide her insolence and still maintain respect as the head of his household. As a father, he had to uphold discipline so that the older girls could model correct behavior to the little ones, or else he'd be running a whorehouse! "Ugh!" Nausea rose in Sebastian's gullet. Not only that, but Mary had chosen a Jew and a socialist to boot! He'd feared the Duke's wrath and had been forced to send her away. And then Rocco...*Rocco!* His padrone was still furious that Sebastian refused to give him Mary's hand in marriage and wanted revenge. Rocco would turn them out if Sebastian didn't tell him what he knew.

"I may as well face the demon," he said to no one. Sebastian looked at his pocket watch—one in the morning. Sid would be at the tavern, for sure. He needed some companionship and a great deal of courage, so he headed to the pub on Fourth Street. After a few shots of whiskey, he'd be brave enough to face his dreams. His dream followed him to the bar and wouldn't leave his mind. He kept seeing the enormous black bird swooping over the roof of his house, calling with its ghoulish voice, *"Mary! Mary!"* and scratching at the window with its sharp orange beak. Its twisted talons grabbed onto the window ledge, and its black, beady eyes—Rocco Monza's eyes—bored through the glass, into the room, into his eyes, into his soul.

Sebastian pounded his whiskey glass on the bar, patted Sid's back, and mumbled goodbye. Like a man walking to his death, he left the tavern and walked to the brothel on Bainbridge. He knocked on the door like an automaton. The madam's eyes went round as moons at the sight of Sebastian. Everyone in Southwark knew of his devotion to the beautiful Florentina. He'd never been a customer here. With bloodshot eyes, Sebastian nodded at the painted lady and pushed through the door. "I need to see him. Get Rocco."

# PART THREE
*Return to Philadelphia*

# CHAPTER EIGHTEEN

*Dirty Laundry*

*June 2018*
*Drexel Hill, PA*

The words of Nana's letter—tucked in the messenger bag slung over Bella's shoulder—played like a broken record in her mind as she balanced the full laundry basket on her hip and fit the key into her mother's front door. *My mother was going to drown us.*

"Ma?" Bella yelled down the hall as she bustled through the kitchen to the laundry room by the back door. "Ma! I'm stopping to do some laundry. Sorry, but Nate's packing his college stuff in the attic at the house, and I need something to wear to church tomorrow."

Rosalie appeared and leaned against the laundry room doorway in a sweater, yoga pants, and slippers. Her hair was piled high on her head in a neat chignon, and she held a cup of coffee between her manicured hands. "Not even a 'hello, how you doing?'"

"Sorry, Ma." Bella leaned in to kiss her mom on the cheek. "I hate to do this, but thank you in advance for the use of your washing machine."

"It's okay, Bella. This is your home—as long as I'm alive, anyway." Rosalie moved to the dryer, placed her mug on top, and pulled out a load of warm towels to fold on the table behind her. "I do, however, have a visitor stopping by soon." She gave Bella a pointed look. "Are you going to wear that?"

Bella loaded the last of her jeans into the washer and looked down at her mismatched clothes. Her shirt was a faded gray baseball tee with yellow floral sleeves, and her pajama pants were a bright green and red plaid overlaid with oversized Christmas tree lights. In her haste to get out of the house before Nate arrived, she'd grabbed them out of the bottom drawer.

"Well, obviously, I'm low on clean clothes, hence the need to borrow your washer." Bella chuckled and shook her head. "What, you trying to set me up with someone else now, Ma?"

Rosalie went stock still.

"I met a guy named Tony last night." Bella glanced at Rosalie to see her reaction. She almost missed the slight hitch in her mom's breath.

Rosalie smoothed her hands over the tower of clean linens. "Oh yeah?"

That confirmed it—she was too nonchalant. "Ma! You told your accountant about me, didn't you? Oh, my word. How embarrassing!"

Bella watched in fascination as Rosalie's face turned a deep shade of red. "I hardly did anything! He found you on his own, didn't he?" She turned the full force of her smile on her daughter and added, "He's cute, isn't he?"

Bella had to laugh. "Yeah, he's cute, Ma. More importantly, he's kind. But you shouldn't try to be a matchmaker for me. I'm a grown woman! And, besides, the divorce papers aren't signed yet."

"You're right. I know. It's just he's such a great guy. I know he'll be a good friend to you during this difficult time. I promise not to meddle. But for now, I implore you to grab some of those jeans out of the washer and change into them. They're not that dirty. You do *not* want him to see you in those ridiculous Christmas pajamas."

"Him who?"

Rosalie didn't answer. She picked up the towels and headed into the kitchen, abandoning the mug on the dryer. Bella fiddled with the buttons on the washer, trying to stop the cycle so she could grab a pair of pants.

"He should be here any minute," Rosalie called over her shoulder.

"Who exactly is coming for an appointment, Ma?"

"Well, it's funny, really, but I needed some financial advice and maybe enticed my accountant to visit on a Saturday morning—with the promise of homemade cinnamon rolls, of course."

Bella hopped around the laundry room on one foot and almost fell over, one leg stuffed halfway down the leg of her tightest jeans. "Tony? You mean *Tony* is your visitor? Oh, my word. Oh, my word."

Rosalie pulled the pastries out of the oven, and the smell of warm cinnamon-childhood-goodness wafted into the hallway as Bella rounded the corner into the kitchen. Her heart was in her mouth.

"Pull yourself together, Bella. Go comb your hair, for heaven's sake."

"Okay, okay, Ma!" Bella ran up to her old bedroom, taking the stairs two at a time. *Easy, Bells,* she chastised herself. *There's no reason to get excited.*

But there was. Bella couldn't deny the thrill coursing through her veins as she brushed her hair. She looked critically at herself in the pink wicker mirror over her childhood dresser. She hadn't been this giddy about a man since she'd met Nate all those years ago. She hadn't thought she was capable of ever feeling this way again. It was intoxicating. And also terrifying.

Then she heard the front door open and Rosalie's chuckle as she greeted Tony and invited him into her home. "You'll never believe who arrived just before you." She heard Rosalie explain her presence.

*Well, there's nothing for it now. Not like I can hide up here all day in my teenage girl cave.* With a silent salute to Simon Le Bon, smiling at her from the 1985 Duran Duran poster on the wall, she gathered her courage and prepared to enter her mother's web.

Bella need not have worried. Tony was pleasantly surprised to see her—that was clear—but his behavior gave no indication that she had bared her soul to this stranger a mere ten hours ago. He was a perfect gentleman, never alluding to her deepest, darkest secrets that she'd confided to him the night before on the church steps. Only once did he wink at her over the kitchen table as they consumed Rosalie's delicious baked goods and coffee. She remembered their joke about her mom luring people in with her delectable cooking and detected a blush blooming up her neck. Tony cleared his throat and looked away.

*He really is handsome. And kind.*

Rosalie broke into her thoughts. "So, Tony. Did Bella tell you that she's researching a family mystery with our new-found long-lost relative?"

Tony leaned forward, eyebrows raised. "She did not."

Rosalie topped off his coffee and turned to Bella. "Well, why don't you catch us up."

An hour later, with the coffee cold in the cups and the cinnamon buns gone, Bella wrapped up the story. "So, yeah, Sophie is really neat. I feel like I've known her forever. And she's a diligent researcher. We're lucky she found us."

Rosalie slapped her hand to her forehead. "Found us. My goodness, I'm so forgetful! I completely forgot to tell you. A distant cousin contacted me the other day after visiting with my Uncle Don. Says Don mentioned our interest in Nana's childhood and that he has some information." Rosalie retrieved her laptop from the living room and pulled up an email from a man named Henry Cassia.

"You're kidding, Ma. It's like these relatives are popping out of the woodwork. What is his relation?"

"Says he grew up with Mollie. Apparently, his Grandma Lizzy adopted her. Henry said Lizzy wrote some memoirs detailing events in Mary's life. He said he'd send them to us if we want them."

Tony interrupted. "Adopted her? So, your Nana ended up as an orphan? I wonder what happened to her parents?"

Bella trusted Tony but couldn't repeat the horrible words that had been floating in her head since she'd read Nana's troubled letter.

*My mother was going to drown us.*

"Ma, can you ask him to send the memoir, please? And since we're sharing info, I have something to show you. It's pretty sad, and I avoided showing you, but, well."

Bella rummaged in her messenger bag and pulled out Nana's tattered letter. She smoothed it on the table, fiddled with her sapphire necklace, and then pushed it over for her mom to see.

Rosalie put on her glasses and started to read. Bella watched her mother's expression change as she read the haunting words.

*My mother was going to drown us.*

"That was quite an interesting visit." Tony fumbled in his pocket for his car keys. "I like spending time with you and your mom. You have a funny way together." He leaned his back against the car door, seemingly in no hurry to leave.

Bella crammed her hands into the pockets of her tight jeans and rolled back and forth on her toes, feeling awkward.

Tony continued, "It was nice to be in a family setting for a while. I miss my parents. They moved to Arizona a few years ago. And my son, well, he's a freshman at Penn State." Tony waved his hands to the left as if his son's dorm room was at the end of the block.

Bella swallowed and asked the question she'd been wondering since she met Tony at the bar. "And your son's mom…?"

"Tracey. Yeah, we split up when my son was little. It was a rough time for all of us. Not what I expected to happen in life, but the Lord got me through it." Tony cleared his throat. "You know, the annulment was a healing process for me."

Bella's eyebrows shot up. "Really? How so?"

"Well, it forced me to take an inventory of my life—my faults, my dreams, my false hopes. In the end, I realized I'd been relying on my wife for happiness instead of on God. I found the truth during the process. Listen, your Nana's story is sad, but I'm glad you're searching for the truth about her folks. Maybe it'll bring you some sort of healing."

"Yeah, well, remind me when this is all over. Sometimes, I don't know if I want to find the truth."

Tony tilted his head to the side. "Why not?"

Bella looked at the ground, forming the words carefully in her mind. She watched a woman walking a dog down the street. When she finally spoke, her words came out as a croak. "What if Mary *was* crazy? What if she really did try to kill her kids?" She looked Tony in the eye and dropped her voice to a whisper. "What if it runs in the family?"

"*No!*" Tony cleared his throat. "I mean, no way. You are the sanest woman I've ever met. You're brave and strong, honest and kind. Most of all, you are *good*." He reached out his hand as if to take hers, then let it fall to his side. They stood face to face, like embarrassed teenagers, until Tony gave her a nod and got into his car. Bella waited on the curb as he started the engine and rolled down the window.

"I'd like to see you again, Bella. I mean, it may be too soon for you. I can wait. We can take our time. I'm not going to push you. I'm babbling."

Bella shook with suppressed laughter. She could feel her dimples popping out, deep in her cheeks. "I'd like that too, Tony. It's *almost* the right time. Just don't eat too many of Ma's baked goods while you wait for me."

"Deal." Tony flashed her a sweet smile as he drove away.

# CHAPTER NINETEEN

*All Aboard!*

*July 1897*
*Newark, NJ*

"This ain't enough for all of ya to get to Philly, ma'am." The clerk at the Newark train station spoke with kindness, handed the money back through the ticket booth window, and looked at the children below. "It's only enough for one ticket on the *Pennsylvania Limited*."

A few minutes before, Mary and the children had bustled into the station, calling attention to themselves in a flurry of nervous energy. The man at the counter had watched them as they approached the booth, a deep crease forming across his forehead. The girls stopped before his desk like tiny women, brave and strong, looking up at him with solemn faces.

"I'll tell you what." He scratched the stubble on his chin. "You've enough for tickets to Princeton. If you're eager to begin your journey, you can start there, right?" He lowered his voice and leaned closer to the window. "I know a feller in Princeton that can help ya catch a freighter from the yards. It would be safe enough if you and the babies were to hop into the rear-most car. It's a common practice Jimmy'd look after ya, make sure ya got on alright." He waggled his eyebrows at her, prompting her to answer.

Mendel tugged at the buttons on Mary's shirtwaist, ready to nurse. The girls stood like statues at her sides, waiting for her direction. What were her options? It wasn't as though they could walk all the way to Philadelphia. Mary replied, "Princeton, yes, that should be fine." She looked back at the man. "That should be fine," she repeated.

With a nod, he wrote out the tickets for Princeton and jotted down an introduction to Jimmy and instructions on how to find him. "Good luck to ya, ma'am. You and the little ones."

Mary nodded her thanks, grabbed the tickets, pocketed the paper, and went to the platform with her children in tow, Newark at their backs.

The connection with Jimmy in Princeton never happened. No one at the train station could tell Mary where he lived, but one man said Jimmy had had a fever a few days before and was recovering at home. No one was as kind as the ticket man in Newark. No one in Princeton understood Mary's plight without her saying a word. She wandered around the Princeton train station for an hour, dragging her children to and fro, deciding what to do next.

She had no money, connections, or friends in this town, and a steward paced the station, watching her and the children. *Soon, he'll approach and ask what we're doing here. He'll know I'm a runaway and try to send me home. But where is my home? Oh, Jakob! Where are you?*

Mollie tugged on her arm. "Sarah is wandering off to look for spiders, Muter." Mary hadn't noticed that Sarah no longer held her skirt. She looked up and scanned the room for her three-year-old daughter. The panic rose—she could feel bile at the back of her throat. *Pull yourself together, Mary!* She pinched herself. *Stay calm.* Maybe playing the little word game with Mollie would help settle both their minds.

"Polly want an…ant." She nodded at Mollie in encouragement.

Mollie looked up at her mother, trust in her eyes. "Polly want a… button."

"Polly want a…cracker. Oh, I see her! Sarah!" Dragging Mollie along, Mary carried Mendel to a bench on the far side of the station, where Sarah sat prattling to an old man.

"And Papa went away to find work in another town," Sarah explained in her sweet little voice.

"Sarah!" Mary grabbed Sarah by the arm. "So sorry to bother

you, sir. She's just a little child. Please don't bother with anything she may have told you." She gathered her wayward daughter in her other arm and lugged her off the bench.

The old man smiled a sad smile and waved.

In a full-fledged panic, Mary dragged the children out of the station. The steward watched them leave with a beady eye. Outside, she found a bench by the tracks, put the baby down, and placed the girls on either side of him. "Don't move a muscle." She paced back and forth in front of the bench, her hands on either side of her head. *Pull yourself together and figure out what to do next.* They'd have to hop on the rear-most car of the next freight train without help from the missing Jimmy.

In the end, a man named Angus lent a hand to Mary and the little children. He was already riding in the boxcar, one leg hanging out the side door as if he were on holiday. He reached for Mary and the children as the train rumbled through the station, the moon high in the middle of the night. Mary had been ready, as the freighter was long—traveling south from Albany, full of timber for the southern states. When the last car came, Mary and the children were poised to hop onto the back of the train. Angus, quick and decisive, lifted the three little ones and Mary into the car.

If she weren't so upset, the experience might have been exhilarating. Mollie hooted in joy when Angus whisked her into the car. He laughed along with Mollie as he helped get the children settled into the boxcar.

"Welcome to da train!" Angus grinned, showing a mouth full of missing teeth, as he sat at the other end of the car, allowing Mary and her children some space. "This here's the finest ride this side of the Appalachians, and that's a fact. I'm headin' back out west'er here, back to da coal mines In West Virginny, meself. Where y'all headed, ma'am?"

"Home." After a pause, Mary added, "We're headed home—to Southwark."

"Well, why don'tcha take a rest there, ma'am? I'll keep watch o'er y'all. I don't sleep much anyways."

Sometime later, when the children stopped their chattering and fell into exhausted sleep nestled around her in the boxcar, a tangle of legs and arms, Mary allowed herself to close her eyes for a few minutes.

*Home.*

Soon, she'd see her papa. For five years, she'd mourned her family as if they were dead. And now—now, out of desperation, she'd return home to beg for mercy at Papa's feet.

For her babies' sakes, she would prostrate herself before Papa on the front doorstep, face to the ground, and beg him to extend grace for the sake of his grandchildren. Mary hoped they'd arrive after Mama had provided Papa with a good meal for supper so he wouldn't be cranky. That the house was in good order, and the little ones were on their best behavior. *He used to call me his nightjar.* She rocked with the rattle of the train. *He used to love me.* Mary drifted to sleep with her papa's face set in her mind.

She woke with a start, sensing something was wrong. Adrenaline shot through her system, and she sat bolt upright, nudging the children. "Wake up!" She hissed at her eldest daughter. "Mollie, get the baby. Sarah, wake up!"

The train had stopped.

Mary saw Angus through the dim light of the box car, wide-eyed, a finger to his lips. *Stay quiet,* his eyes implored. *Danger.* She felt it in her bones—someone was coming. Mendel whimpered. She snatched him from Mollie and placed her finger in his mouth to suck. They heard the voices of two men outside the car. The strangers laughed as they went behind the caboose to relieve themselves in the woods beside the tracks. One of them said, "Yeah, we'll take a look in there next."

Mary raised her eyebrows at Angus in supplication. *What should we do?*

Angus nodded to the side door. He slid it open enough to let them pass, then hopped out and reached for the children. He placed the girls on the ground and handed baby Mendel to Mollie. Then he settled his hands on Mary's hips and whisked her out of the boxcar.

The little group ran into the thick copse of trees in the opposite direction of the men.

Once they were well away, Angus turned to Mary and chortled.

Laughter escaped through her own clenched teeth. She clasped her hand over her mouth in surprise, giggling in earnest. The two adults doubled over with contagious mirth, hands on their knees.

Mollie stared at her mother as if she thought she was mad as a hatter. Mary shook off the last giggles, sat in the leaves, grabbed Mendel, and held him close to her chest. The baby needed nursing and nosed around her shirt like a truffle pig on the scent of its treat.

Angus looked away and coughed. "And this is where's I leave ya, ma'am. I'm away, headin' west'er here, as I done told ya." He tipped his hat to her.

Mary stared around at the unknown woods, panic rising as her breath came in shallow gasps. "But where are we?"

"Oh, I'd guess we're somewheres a bit north o' Trenton." Her guide extracted a dented compass out of his jacket pocket. "If ya follow the tracks long 'nuff, you'll find yer way to the bridge over the big river and inta PA. Ya can't miss it—a marvel it is! After ya cross the Delaware, juss keep goin' south, an you'll git to Phila soon 'nuff. 'Bout 33 mile," he guessed. "Well, good luck to ya, ma'am." He gave a little bow in her direction and waved to the girls. "Little ladies, gidday."

Mendel rooted in earnest now, tugging at Mary's blouse. Mary tucked him into nursing while she watched Angus go off whistling through the woods. The girls watched until he was gone. Then they joined their mother, who sat cross-legged in the grass, dark curls wild about her head, and their brother nursing in her arms.

*What now?* Their little faces seemed to ask.

Mary patted the ground beside her with her free hand. "Come rest with me awhile, my little doves." She gave them a tentative smile. The girls complied, snuggling on each side of Mary. The quiet soothed them. Soon, Mendel fell asleep. Mary put him on her shoulder and elicited a contented burp. Then she leaned against the nearby tree and relaxed into a momentary calm.

"Did I ever tell you how oysters changed my life?" Mary gave her daughters a lopsided smile.

"Oysters?" Mollie looked confused. "What do you mean, Muter?"

"No matter, darling, no matter. That's a story for another day."

After they had rested awhile and relieved themselves in the bushes, Mary brushed the leaves off her grimy dress and sorted through their meager belongings. She cut the remaining loaf of bread into portions and tucked them away for later. She divided a hunk of cheese and handed each girl a piece. *Oh, how I wish we could eat salami with it! Salami travels well and pairs nicely with cheese.* Mary understood, not for the first time, the limits of her options since she had committed her household to kosher ways. She gave Mendel a piece of apple to suck on. Mary ate little, not knowing what the journey ahead would entail. Once the children were satiated and growing restless, she announced it was time to depart.

Mollie and Sarah bounced up and down as if they anticipated another fun ride on the train. When their mother hoisted the baby onto her shoulder and headed toward the tracks, Mollie asked her if they'd have proper seats on the train this time. "No, dear. I'm afraid we'll have to hike from here, little doves. We'd best get started so we make it to Southwark before nightfall. Mr. Angus told us the bridge is that way." Mary pointed over her shoulder. "So, let's get on with it. To the river!" Without another word, she headed out, her girls following behind her like little ducks in a row.

Mary kept a stiff smile on her face for miles, appearing cheerful for the sake of her exhausted daughters. At three years old, Sarah couldn't keep walking much longer. Mollie's shoe had lost part of its sole, and Mary could see her brave five-year-old limping. Her feet were sore, too, but nothing compared to the aching in her back—her shoulders were on fire. Mendel was a heavy little boy—when he fell asleep, he became a dead weight in her arms.

They had traveled about three or four miles in the woods, near the tracks, when the trees opened up, and they came to a hill overlooking the river, with an enormous bridge spanning its banks. The view stole Mary's breath. The Delaware River lay below, down a sloping bank full of gray boulders. The land on the other side was far— Mary could make out the rooftops of a little town peeking through the treetops. There was a ferry, navigating its way through the middle of the current, headed away from her. She could see tiny passengers leaning against the sides of the little boat, watching the birds.

*Oh, how nice it would be to ride with those people in safety and comfort! I wish I had the funds to purchase some tickets.* But she didn't. They'd have to walk across the bridge over the river. Terror seized Mary's heart. She squeezed Mendel tight to avoid fainting. To distract herself before the daunting journey, Mary sat the children down in the shelter of a large gray boulder covered with moss. She dared not cross the bridge at night, in the dark—that was out of the question—but she didn't want someone to discover them. She decided to wait until evening, when the ferry had stopped operating and most people would be retiring to the local pub or home for supper.

In the meantime, she needed to prepare. Mary surveyed the bridge while the children snacked on the last of their food. Five enormous wooden arches rested on wide brick piers some fifty feet above the water. From her vantage point, Mary could see a few lanes running through the center of the bridge—one for the train, one for carriages, and two on each outer side for people. Mary placed her hands on her forehead, shielding her eyes from the sun. She could just make out the form of a man walking across the bridge. Mary swallowed a lump in her throat. She'd never walked across a bridge before, and had never been at such a height. She'd lived next to the waters of this river for years but had never seen it from above. Mary wiped her sweaty palms on her skirt.

Terrified she'd drop Mendel during the crossing—and realizing she'd need to hold tight to both of her daughters' hands—Mary fastened a carrier with her jacket. She tied it around her shoulders and then around her waist, using the buttons to secure a little pocket for Mendel. She tested the weight and found it sturdy. Perfect.

Now, to prepare her mind. She looked at the children, resting with their backs against the warm stone, and her heart flooded with love and determination. There was no turning back from this point. They were crossing into their future, whatever that might be. Mary explained to the girls that they were about to have a fantastic adventure climbing across the bridge. Then she sat and dozed.

She woke to the sound of a foghorn a few miles north of them and judged by the light that it was around five o'clock—time to go. Mary picked up Mendel, kissed his head, and placed him in the makeshift carrier. His chubby legs stuck out of the sleeves on each side of her slim waist. The girls giggled. Mary prayed it was secure enough to hold his weight while they crossed.

They approached the bridge. The opening looked like an elaborate mansion with arched doorways over the footwalks and roadways, and a cedar-shingled roof covered the entire expanse of the bridge. The family stepped through the little door and found themselves on a four-and-a-half-inch wooden floor suspended from the ceiling by iron rods fastened in the wood above. Mary swore she felt the floor move in the breeze and wished she could shut her eyes, but the thrill seemed to embolden the girls. They clung to the single handrail that ran along the footpath and peered over the side, pulling Mary and Mendel along with them. Mary stopped dead, sure she would faint. "Girls!" She tugged them away from the edge and was surprised to hear them squealing in delight at the gulls flying underneath their feet, close to the water's surface. Mary took two deep breaths and imagined oystercatchers in flight to keep her mind off her surreal circumstances. One false step, and they'd tumble to their deaths in the churning water below. Baby Mendel squeezed his legs so hard around her waist, she almost lost her footing.

"Look, Muter, the moon." Mollie stopped and stared in awe upriver, where the moon rose over the trees.

"Mollie, keep moving. Please don't stop again." Mary recited a prayer. "Hail Mary, full of grace…"

Somehow, they made it across. Once their feet hit solid ground, Mary sank to her knees and kissed the dirt. Mendel peeked out of his little nest, confused by this more than anything else that had happened so far.

On the other side of the river, the group entered a small settlement of homes and shops, where they found a well and pump with drinking water. Mary splashed some cold water on her face, which refreshed her enough to carry on.

They continued walking, but they couldn't reach Southwark by nightfall. That terrifying fact flooded Mary's thoughts. When it came before her eyes, she swatted it back into the recesses of her mind. What else could she do? She had no money, no food, no protection, and no transport. They traveled for miles in a southward direction in hopes of—what? Strolling straight into her parents' home and tucking the children into her old bed? Her life there had ended that night five years ago when she and Jakob had eloped against her papa's wishes.

*Oh, Jakob! How could you leave me? Me and the babies?*

Her papa had been right. Vincenzo, the dear soul, had been right. Her sisters had been right. Even little Giuseppe had been right. Jakob wasn't reliable, and he couldn't provide for her. He had robbed her of her security and her family. She had squandered it all for lust and love.

*Was it worth it?* She asked herself for the hundredth time. How could she think otherwise when she looked into the innocent faces of her offspring? Her precious children? The little ones wouldn't be here if she hadn't gone with Jakob. Well, maybe Mollie would be with her. Maybe her father would have allowed her to marry Cenzo, and he'd have helped to raise the child.

Mary's imagination took flight. Right now, Mollie would be playing at Mary's feet before a warm fire, the smell of fish wafting through the open window at the wharf, while Mary read to her from one of the dozens of novels lining the walls of Cenzo's flat. So what if she'd have been a fishmonger's wife? At least she'd have been cared for and respected.

"Ah," Mary moaned, tormented by visions of what could have been and distressed that she had given in to such dreams. She'd never give up two of her babies for such a life.

"Muter!" Mollie called. "Muter, Sarah has twisted her foot."

Shaking herself out of a daze, Mary heard Sarah's muffled voice crying. "Oh, my darling dove, I shouldn't have thought such evil thoughts! I'm so sorry, love! Will you ever forgive me?" She knelt beside her daughters and laid their brother down on the grass so that she could take hold of Sarah's foot. Sarah yelped at the touch, clearly in pain.

*Now what?*

Mary sat on her heels and wrenched her hair. She wanted to give up and stay in the middle of the woods forever. She was exhausted, body and mind. They had been roaming all day, and in a few hours, it would be dark. "What am I going to do?" she yelled at the sky. "Jesus, where have you gone? Don't forsake me, as I have forsaken you!"

Mollie and Mendel joined their sister and started to cry. A few minutes later, two strangers appeared from behind the bushes near the river. A tall, lanky young man with a peach-fuzz mustache, a fishing rod laden with fish over his shoulder and a tackle box dangling from his hand, stood back a few paces while a lovely teenage blond girl slowly approached the crying group.

"My name's Bridget Oliver." She flashed the children a pretty smile and nodded to Mary. "That there is my brother, Ryan." She glanced back at the young man, eyebrows raised. "We live near here and are happy to help you."

Ryan put his fish and tackle down and squatted beside Sarah, lifting her swollen ankle. While Mary dried her eyes, Bridget picked up Mendel and cradled him in her arms. "And who is this little man?"

Mary brushed leaves off her dress and sat up straight while gathering Mollie into her arms. "That's my baby brother, Mendel," Mollie said.

Mary smiled. "Yes, and this is Mollie. And Sarah, who sprained her foot."

Ryan furnished a piece of cloth from his tackle box and wound it around Sarah's ankle while the little girl looked up at him in awe. "Well, lucky for you, Bridget and I were just heading back from our jaunt to the river. Just over there is our favorite rock, where the water runs deep. Bridget loves to swim, and I fish for the restaurant. Our momma's restaurant, more like."

"We live at Delaware House." Bridget lifted her chin with pride. "Our mother is the proprietor."

Mary listened to the teens as she tidied her hair and prepared to embark. Ryan carried little Sarah on his back and led the group off the trail and onto the street at the edge of a little town. "This is the town of Bristol." He pointed to a wide, cream-colored building with dark maroon shutters that took up the entire block. "And that there is Delaware House."

Mary held tight to Mollie's hand as the little group walked down the street toward the inn. "Your mother *owns* this hotel?" Mary couldn't believe it.

"Yep. Momma purchased the inn in '92 after Papa died. It was called The Fountain House back then. She got it from an old man who was ready to retire." Ryan adjusted his hold on Sarah, who was watching Ryan speak with rapt attention. "Momma changed the name to Delaware House in hopes of luring more city folks to see the commanding view of the river. You know, back in Revolutionary times, the place was called The King George and had famous guests like the Marquis de Lafayette and John Adams."

Mary was impressed. A woman owning an inn? It was amazing. She wished she weren't forced to meet such a woman in such humble circumstances. But there was nothing for it. Sarah's foot needed medical attention, and they were desperate.

"Well, young man, I certainly appreciate your coming to our rescue and will accept any help your momma may offer."

As they entered the servants' door in the back, Bridget sprinted through the kitchen, alerting the copper-haired housekeeper, who sat at the big oak desk in the corner.

"Mrs. McLaughlin!" Bridget came up short in front of the busy woman, breathless. "We need a room for our new friends. Ryan and I found them by the river along the tracks. They've journeyed all day, and the little one has sprained her ankle. Shall we call for the doctor?"

Mrs. Oliver accommodated her children's unexpected guests.

Once she heard the tale of the Lichtenbaum family's trials, she pronounced orders to Ryan, Bridget, and the staff with calm and definite authority. Ryan ran for the doctor across town. Mrs. McLaughlin bathed the children and then drew a fresh bath for Mary. Bridget went to secure clean, if moth-eaten, clothing from the rag bag in the attic, which contained all sorts of apparel left behind by patrons over the years. One of the housemaids prepared the farthest room at the end of the servants' hall with fresh sheets, a clean chamber pot, and a water pitcher.

As soon as the little group arrived, Grannie Boone—the inn's cook, a full-figured, buxom woman—tried to stuff the children with meat pasties that had been cooling on the rack by the hearth.

"Children, do not take a bite of that food!" Mary ordered.

Grannie Boone looked startled, her eyes round as saucers on her large face.

"My apologies, Grannie Boone, but we are Jewish and must adhere to a kosher diet or risk breaking God's commandment."

"Well, I never. I don't understand a thing about Jews or kosher food and whatnot, but I know plenty about God's commandments." She asked Mrs. Oliver, "Shall we send for Old Leah Baumbach from down the street?"

"That's a grand idea, Grannie Boone." Mrs. Oliver explained to Mary, "Mrs. Baumbach is a Jewish widow, famous in the neighborhood for her delicious latkes and kugel. I know she will be happy to help."

An hour later, Old Leah bustled into the little bedroom where the family rested. She spoon-fed the children with chicken broth and handed them matzah made in her kosher home. The girls giggled about eating on their beds and looked to their mother for permission. Once assured they were allowed, they tucked into the meal with alacrity.

"I'm so relieved to see my girls eat their fill." Tears ran down Mary's cheeks. "How can I ever thank you?"

"Tsk, tsk," was all Leah said in reply.

Mrs. Oliver lingered in the doorway, touched to see baby Mendel nursing at his mother's breast, and Mary eased of a burden too enormous to bear alone.

Mrs. Oliver knew what it meant to be a widow. Mary's husband must be dead and buried, for why else would a young woman walk from town to town with her three young children? Her husband must have died, and she planned to return home to her family. Not every woman was as resourceful as she—to invest money, purchase a property under a false male name, and then run the place like a ship at sea. It made her feel good to help this unfortunate young girl and her offspring.

The doctor shuffled down the hall. Mrs. Oliver cleared her throat and waved at Mary to cover up before allowing the doctor to examine the little girl. When he advised that Sarah keep off the foot for at least a week, Mrs. Oliver formulated a plan.

"You will stay here for the week, Miss Mary," she commanded. "Delaware House will be your home. After you rest tomorrow and regain strength, Bridget can mind the children while you assist downstairs in the dining room. You can serve the meals and help clean up the dishes." At Mary's look of shock, Mrs. Oliver put up her hand to stop any blubbering. "No, I won't have any discussion on the matter. This is the plan. All will be well if we stick to it, I assure you. Now, we will leave your family in peace to rest and see you in the morning for breakfast. Goodnight, Miss Mary. Goodnight, children. Sleep well." She closed the door, shepherding Bridget and the doctor into the hall.

The next day, while Mary made up the beds and opened the calico curtains of their little room, she heard a knock on the door. Mary jumped at the sound but took a deep breath and reminded herself they were safe at Delaware House. She pinched her cheeks to make them rosy and put on a smile. "Come in!"

Mrs. Oliver opened the door and peeked into the room. "I've come to check on my guests." Without invitation, she sat on the bed beside Sarah and touched the girl's cheek. "My husband was a Quaker, God rest his soul. He was read out of Meeting when he married me, poor man. I always felt a bit guilty about that, but he was sure he wanted me as his bride. We had a good life together. We were a team. He's probably rolled over in his grave knowing I sell liquor here at Delaware House. I never made false promises, though. He knew that and loved me anyway. Although I never adopted his Plain Speech or agreed with all of the Quaker faith, I respect the basic principles. I abhor violence and cruelty and accept folks as God made them. All are welcome at my hearth. I don't know much about the Hebrew religion, but I understand the importance of pursuing one's beliefs.

"Madame Baumbach will help you sort out the meals for yourself and your children. If that means you must prepare meals in her home, I'm sure she will be happy to have you. Leah has been lonely these last few years after her son died of consumption. She was widowed decades ago, and I don't believe she has broken bread with a fellow Jew since her son passed. You will be doing her a kindness by sharing her kitchen. As for the little ones, they will be in Bridget's care." She smiled at Mollie and Sarah. "You'll have great fun, dears."

Mary held back tears of gratitude. "I can't thank you enough, Mrs. Oliver." She spread out her hands, encompassing the whole room. "For everything."

"Nonsense. We have plenty of hands to help. Bridget is thirteen and capable. Ryan will watch over them when he can, between his chores and errands. Mrs. Elspeth McLaughlin, my stalwart housekeeper whom you met last night, will show you the tasks you'll attend to. Rest up for the day, and we'll get you to work tomorrow. I'm a busy woman, but I wish you to visit me in my office in two nights' time." Mrs. Oliver stood up to leave and glanced back from the door. "You will be safe here."

Mary cleared her throat. "Safe? Yes, yes, I believe so."

With a nod, Mrs. Oliver left Mary to her thoughts. As the children dressed for the day, Mary found peace in their morning ablutions. She hadn't realized how much she missed a simple routine. Gone were her dreams of being an independent woman. After the trials of the past few weeks with Jakob gone, she only wanted to live a quiet life as the mother of her darling children. It didn't matter if they lived in a fancy apartment or above a market in Southwark. Mary wasn't ready to face a future without Jakob, but she must. Her heart wrenched at the thought that he had abandoned her and the children, but it was true. Why else hadn't he contacted them?

"I took the liberty of airing out your bag, Miss Mary," Mrs. McLaughlin announced later that morning after the doctor had been to check on Sarah, who slept in the bed. Bridget had taken the other children for a tour of the hotel, and Mrs. McLaughlin lingered in the bedroom to tidy up. At Mary's alarmed expression, she continued, "Well, the satchel was wet and muddy. I assumed the clothes inside would get musty. Anyhoo, I found some beautiful drawings—did you draw those?—and this wee bawbee." She held out the red rosary to Mary with a hesitant smile.

Mary's face went white as snow. The rosary was her most prized possession, but she was Jewish now and shouldn't be seen with such an item.

"Oh, dinna fash, *m'eudail*, your secret's safe with me. See, I'm a Papist too." She plucked out a set of worn wooden beads from her apron pocket. "'Tis nothing to be sorry aboot. As Mrs. Oliver explained, she welcomes all kinds here at Delaware House. What got my mind wondering, though, is why do you keep this hidden away and go aboot cooking kosher food for your wee bairns? I dinna ken your story, but I'm here to listen if you need an ear."

Mary considered Mrs. McLaughlin as she plumped the pillows on the bed, taking in her copper hair with gray streaks drawn into a tidy bun on top of her head, rosy cheeks, and bright blue eyes. She was big-boned and stocky, with wide hips and short legs. She had a motherly way about her, and Mary wanted to trust her. "I wasn't always Jewish," she blurted.

Mrs. McLaughlin hid a smile as she shook out the curtains. "Ye don't say, lass?"

Mary took a soothing breath. She sensed a kindred spirit in the housekeeper and let down her guard a little. "I am Catholic. I fell in love with a Jewish boy. Jakob." Her voice caught on his name, and she held back tears.

"Oh, aye." Mrs. McLaughlin sat on the bed beside Mary. "But surely you know that once you're baptized in Christ, He leaves an indelible mark on your soul. It canna be erased. No matter what you do, you're still His."

Mary wept at this, and poor Mrs. McLaughlin couldn't console her. She patted Mary's shoulder, humming small noises and saying nonsensical words in her native Gaelic. Mary couldn't understand, but the intent was clear. Everything would be alright—God cared, and she wasn't alone.

When Mary's tears dried up, Mrs. McLaughlin gave her a clean hankie from the sleeve of her sweater. Mary blew her nose and wiped her eyes as a weight fell from her shoulders. She'd forgotten how healing a good confession could be. Now that she thought of it, she longed for the rite of confession with her whole soul. She needed reconciliation more than she needed air. But this had been a start. She glanced at Sarah to be sure the girl still slept, then smiled at her new confidant. "I don't know how to thank you, Mrs. McLaughlin."

"Elspeth. Call me Elspeth, *m'eudail.*"

"May-tall? What does that mean?"

"Och, where I come from, it means 'dear.' My people hail from the Highlands of Scotland, ye see. My parents settled here when I was thirteen."

"Oh, I see. Well, Elspeth, I am somewhat undone—boneless, almost. I believe I've cried all the tears in the ocean."

"Well, you certainly made a go of it." Elspeth chuckled.

Mary smiled. "I've been living this lie for so long that I don't know who I am anymore. First, love drove me away from home, but now fear holds me away."

"Fear?" Elspeth gave her a sharp look. "Dinna tell me yer man abused you?"

"No, no, it's not that. Jakob and I married against my papa's wishes. You see, the fact that Jakob is a Hebrew, and I am—was—a Catholic would be enough reason for Papa to disown me, but he's not a cruel man. Papa loves me…well, at least, he loved me before. I know he did. But Papa worked for a powerful man when he arrived in Philadelphia ahead of Mama, my siblings, and me to establish our home. And you see, no one says 'no' to the Duke of South Philly or his men—not when you owe him everything."

Elspeth leaned closer. "And what did your papa say 'no' to?"

"My hand in marriage." Mary looked at her hands, twisted in her lap. She took a deep breath and continued her story. "One of the Duke's men, Rocco Monza, asked Papa for my hand, and Papa refused him outright. I listened in the stairwell. I remember hearing Rocco say he desired me—*wanted* me. Ugh." A wave of nausea swept over her at the idea of sharing Rocco's bed. "He is a brute of a man."

"Aye, I ken what yer saying, Miss Mary." Mrs. McLaughlin patted Mary's knee and nodded. "Your papa was right to turn the man away. But what of the consequences?"

"Well, for a time, Rocco would follow and harass me at every opportunity. He often grabbed my skirt when I passed by. Once, he found me alone in the sweatshop and forced me into his embrace. I'm ashamed to say this—I've never spoken a word to anyone about this before." Mary wrung her hands in her lap.

"Go on, m'eudail," Elspeth encouraged.

"Well, he…he tried to kiss me. I turned away, but his breath was hot on my neck, and his whiskers rasped my chin. He had his arm like a vise around my waist, and with his other hand, he…reached down my bodice. I managed to slap him across the face. I guess it excited him, and it, well, it made his advances even more ardent."

She avoided Elspeth's eye, her face as red as a beet, and closed her mouth. But Mrs. McLaughlin persisted. With a kind voice, she asked, "And then what happened? You may as well get it all 'oot in the open."

Mary cleared her throat. "Well…as I said, he seemed to find the struggle some kind of sport, and he, ahem, he backed me up against the wall and pressed himself into me." Mary squirmed, unable to look at Elspeth. "I could feel his body respond to my nearness. I was terrified of being violated. And then he said the most disgusting thing." Mary assumed a low, grumbling voice. "'You know you want it from me and not from that Russian dog of yours.'

"I brought my knee up hard into his groin and pushed his chest in one motion. He moaned and fell backward." Mary smiled a shaky smile at the memory. She had never felt such power before that moment. "I straightened my dress and smoothed down my hair, watching him wriggle on the floor. I stood up tall and looked down my nose at him. I should have walked away right then, but I have a habit of needing the last word. I stared at him until he faced me. And then, I said…"

"What?" Elspeth stared at her in anticipation. "What did you say, Miss Mary?"

Mary gave a rueful smile. "I told him, 'He's not Russian, he's a Warsaw Jew. And I'd rather give *it* to the entire Russian army than to the likes of you, you worthless pile of horse manure.'"

"Baha!" Elspeth hooted, slapping a hand to her chest and glancing behind her to ensure she hadn't woken Sarah. "Well, now, that's the spirit, lass! I'd pay a price to have seen the look on the scabby goon's face, and that's a fact."

Mary laughed along with her new friend. But, deep inside, the usual unease crept into her heart as it did whenever she remembered that day. She could still see Rocco's visceral reaction to her remark, as if she had spat at him. He had stumbled to his feet, hand grabbing his groin, and faced her with hatred burning in his eyes. "This isn't over, Mary Paragano." He'd brushed off his hat and placed it on his head. "Your papa owes me—you will be mine." He'd left Mary then, standing against the wall, hands balled into fists behind her back, ready to defend herself again. When he was gone, the air had rushed out of her lungs, and she'd doubled over with dry heaves, panic roaring through her body.

Mary forced the memories away. Surrounded by the strong women of Delaware House, she sat in a safe and sunny room, her sweet daughter sleeping in the bed by the window and her new friend chuckling as she tidied the room. Mary hadn't felt this way—like she belonged—since she had dreamed of managing her family's grocery as a girl.

*Can I make a home for my family here?*

She wouldn't allow memories of Rocco Monza to ruin this peaceful place.

Mary smoothed white linens on the tables in the dining room in preparation for the lunchtime rush. She had about an hour before the hungry patrons would arrive. The children were outside, enjoying the cool air from the river, playing fetch with a little dog on the dirt road. Ryan carried Sarah down to sit on the porch so she could watch the fun. She smiled at her little brother Mendel, who toddled around, holding tight to Bridget's hands, taking tentative steps. Mollie laughed as the dog caught the ball and repeatedly dropped it at her feet.

Mary watched them from the window, her heart filled with joy at seeing her children happy and healthy, apart from Sarah's foot. She smiled, clasped her hands together, and brought them to her heart. She memorized the scene before her to capture with her charcoal pencils later.

"Ahem." A voice in the room behind her startled her out of her reverie. She turned to see a large man with soft features wearing overalls, a white collared shirt, and the most enormous boots she had ever seen. He was young—mid-twenties—and looked simple-minded, but he seemed kind and tender despite his vast size. He carried himself in a childlike way, with an open expression and straightforward demeanor. *Not a threat, then.* The man doffed his cap and made a little bow before her.

"And who might you be?" Mary put out her hand to shake the hand of the gentle giant before her.

"I'm Pauly—Pauly Holmes. And I'm pleased to meet you, ma'am." He cleared his throat, then shook the proffered hand with a sweaty palm. Pauly reminded Mary of a gigantic bear she had seen as a child at the carnival down by the river. She remembered being sad that the animal sat behind bars, unable to run free.

She shook the memory away as she considered her new acquaintance. Usually, such a large man would threaten her, but this person appeared simple and sweet, and he enchanted her.

THE OYSTERCATCHER OF SOUTHWARK

Pauly followed her gaze out the window toward the children playing. "Yours?"

"Three of them, yes." Mary pointed at her offspring one by one. "That's my baby Mendel and little Sarah on the porch. She twisted her ankle. And there, that's my big girl, Mollie." Her eyes teared up with pride.

Pauly nodded as if she had asked him a question. He lumbered across the room and went behind the big mahogany bar, then grabbed tall glasses from the shelf. "Sarsaparilla—for them." He wiped each glass with a clean rag and set them along the bar, one next to the other, then poured a bubbly amber drink into each.

Mary joined him at the tall counter. "Ahhh, you must be the barkeep, then. That's nice of you. Shall I call them in for the treat before the lunch rush?"

Pauly nodded his big head and smiled the sweetest smile Mary had ever seen.

She smiled back at her new friend, then went out the front door to collect her children.

# CHAPTER TWENTY

### *Mrs. Oliver's Twist*

*August 1897*
*Delaware House*
*Bristol, PA*

After the last of the inn's patrons had retired to their rooms and Mary had turned down the kitchen lights, she tucked the baby into bed between his sleeping sisters and went to Mrs. Oliver's study. She tapped on the door, not sure what to expect.

"Come in."

To her astonishment, Mary opened the door to find her benefactor relaxing in an overstuffed armchair with her feet up on a stool, smoking a cigar as big as a banana and reading a newspaper.

At her look of wide-eyed wonder, Mrs. Oliver blew out the smoke in a long, steady stream, winked, and waved Mary into her inner sanctum. Mary had never in her life encountered such a woman. An enormous oak desk split the office into two sections. Papers, books, and ledgers covered the desk. Mary smelled leather bindings and the sharp scent of ink under the fug of tobacco smoke. She scanned the book titles and saw some well-worn Dickens, *Uncle Tom's Cabin*, and a shocking title, *The Woman's Bible*. The shiny book sat front and center on the desk—a new acquisition?—prized by Mrs. Oliver. The other side of the room resembled a cozy parlor, with a cheery fireplace stacked with books and two chairs arranged around a small table with an elaborate tea tray.

"Welcome, Miss Mary. Please, do sit down. I asked Mrs. McLaughlin to arrange some refreshments for us—a leftover piece of rum cake and a pot of tea. Please, help yourself. I practice elevating my feet every evening for an hour to ward off the bulging veins that lurk behind my knees."

As Mary poured herself a cup of tea and settled across from Mrs. Oliver on the settee, her eyes returned to the cigar. She had never seen a woman enjoy such a manly pursuit. It gave Mrs. Oliver an air of authority, as if she could conquer the world and boss President McKinley around.

Mrs. Oliver laughed at Mary's fascination. "Do you smoke?"

Mary shook her head. "I've heard of a women's smoking room in Manhattan, but I've never seen a female smoking before. I'm sorry for staring. It surprised me. I fear it would be a downright scandal back in Southwark. I wonder, what does it feel like?"

Mrs. Oliver smiled. "Why don't you try a puff?" She leaned forward and handed the stogie to Mary, who reached for it as if it were an explosive device about to go off. She sniffed it, twisted it this way and that, then settled herself to the task.

Her first drag ended in an explosive cough. Eyes watering, she handed the vile contrivance back to Mrs. Oliver, who chuckled.

"Have you read about this astonishing woman, Nellie Bly?" Mrs. Oliver waved the newspaper at her. "What a person! I never tire of discovering her words. This is an old copy of the *New York World* from a few years ago. I have kept every piece of her printed thoughts. Did you know she feigned insanity and got herself committed to the asylum on Blackwell Island so she could report from the *inside?*"

Mary shook her head in astonishment.

"It's true. She exposed the horrid conditions of the city's insane house from *inside* its walls. The bravery, to endure such hardship for ten days, all in the name of journalism. Astounding."

Mary couldn't imagine such an experience. She'd never be brave enough to go through such a harrowing adventure.

Mrs. Oliver folded the paper and changed the subject. "Well, Mrs. McLaughlin and Granny Boone both report that you are providing strong work in the dining room. They say you are quite adept at remembering patrons' names and helping them feel welcome.

You're quick on your feet and thoroughly clean the kitchen after it closes. I'm happy to have you here."

Mary beamed with pride and melted into the settee. The tobacco had relaxed her nerves. "Well, Mrs. Oliver, I'm happy to repay your kindness however I can. You, your staff, and your children have saved us from a dire situation, and I can never thank you enough."

"About that dire situation." Mrs. Oliver gave her a pointed look. "I don't mean to pry, but I want to understand why you and your children were wandering along the tracks so late in the day. Bridget told me that Mollie mentioned you are from Newark and are traveling home to your family in South Philadelphia?"

"That is correct." Mary clamped her lips shut in a tight line.

"Hmm." Mrs. Oliver nodded as if deciding something. "Well, I didn't come this far in life without a great dose of discretion. If you don't want to explain your circumstances, keep them to yourself. No matter. In you, I see a strong-willed, hard-working young woman who would go to great lengths to provide for and protect her children. I am a great judge of character. Whatever forces brought you to Delaware House, I am thankful to them."

Mary brought her hand to her heart in delight. "Oh, thank you, Mrs. Oliver." She had never heard such praise from another person. So often in her life, she'd been belittled, confused, and dismissed. Jakob had made her feel so valued and prized when they first met. But that esteem had vanished after they established themselves in their flat on Norfolk Street.

From the day he'd demanded that she keep a perfect kosher home, Mary had never been able to catch up—constantly striving and failing, falling short. She had stepped out of her skin into a character's costume in a play. Her life had no longer been her own, no longer authentic. And because she'd tried so hard to become someone else, to please her husband above all else, she had failed.

And now, here she sat, across from an older woman, a widow and mother who had taken destiny into her own hands and had built a life out of thin air. Mrs. Oliver had outsmarted and outwitted the world by somehow purchasing property for herself—which wasn't even legal—and creating a source of income to care for her children and see her family thrive. Mary coveted Mrs. Oliver's freedom more than anything else.

Could such a life be possible for her? All she desired was a safe place for her children to grow up, surrounded by caring and hard-working people, whether they were blood relatives or not. Couldn't these people become family to her? She'd grown comfortable with these strong women: Granny Boone, Elspeth McLaughlin, Mrs. Baumbach, and Mrs. Oliver had banded together to create a community at Delaware House.

To Mary's surprise, Mrs. Oliver said, "I'd like you to stay."

"Stay?" Mary choked on her tea, sputtering and pounding on her chest.

"Well, yes. I can see you have great potential for operating a business. You are smart, Mary, and a hard worker. I won't live forever, you know, and I would feel easier as I age if I had a protégé, so to speak—someone to learn the ways of Delaware House so she can run it after I retire."

"But wouldn't you leave the running of the inn to your children? Wouldn't Ryan protest? He is the man of the house, after all."

"Bah! Man of the house? Ryan is only sixteen! He thinks he's a man, but he's but a boy. A sweet, kind boy, but a boy nonetheless." She shook her head. "He couldn't run a tea party, let alone a great establishment such as this."

Mary protested, "Yes, but I'm sure you will have many more years—decades—to teach him the business."

Mrs. Oliver cut her off. "I am dying, Mary."

Mary placed her teacup back on the tray, a sense of dread filling her heart. "Heavens! I'm so very sorry. I had no idea. You seem so hardy."

Mrs. Oliver plowed on. "The doctor says I have a year, maybe two." She waved her hand as if the details were unimportant. "A cancer of the lungs, you see." Mrs. Oliver shrugged, took another drag, and returned her attention to her companion. "The children don't yet know, and I need it to remain that way."

"Yes, of course." Mary cast her eyes down at her hands in her lap. She didn't know what to say. To think this incredible force of a woman, on whom so many depended, would be cut short in the prime of her life! It wasn't fair. But then...

*Could I take Mrs. Oliver's place as the proprietor here?*

Mary's old dream of running a business floated before her eyes. It would be a challenge but a welcome one. She could use her talents—her gift with figures and numbers, her creative spirit, and her knack for business. And she'd be an independent woman. Mary's heart felt fit to burst. The reason for the necessity would make it a bittersweet enterprise. It was a distressing picture: Mrs. Oliver languishing in the upstairs bedroom, living out her last painful days while Mary ran the business. *I'd be doing her a kindness, though, affording her peace before death, assurance that her children and staff were safe.*

Mary saw Mrs. Oliver watching her as she pondered these affairs. She steadied her face to hide her thoughts, and Mrs. Oliver broke into her reverie. "I don't require your decision tonight, Miss Mary. I have laid a great opportunity in your lap. One you must consider from all angles before you give me your answer. And, for now, I'm tired and ready to retire."

Mary fussed with the tea set, folding napkins and placing a lid on the rum cake.

"Please, leave the tea tray. Mrs. McLaughlin will see that a chambermaid comes in to tidy up my den." Mrs. Oliver rose and gave Mary a nod. Mary placed the teacup on the tray and gave her hostess a curtsy as if she were a queen, then left the room without giving any indication of her decision.

After a night full of colorful dreams in which Mary and the children played kick-the-can through the hallways of Delaware House and painted the patrons' faces with rouge while smoking cigars, Mary woke with the sun and giggled at the fading memory of her strange visions. She lay in bed listening to the gentle breathing of her precious family, and her heart filled with love at the sound. She'd do anything for them, and she marveled at the adventure they had been through in the past few days. She thought of Mrs. Oliver's extraordinary offer to her the night before.

*The proprietor of a successful inn?* Mary couldn't believe it. *Can you imagine?* She smiled. *Yes, yes, I can.*

Mary was more at home at Delaware House than she had been with Jakob in their apartment in Newark. The children were happier than she had ever seen them, Sarah's sore ankle notwithstanding. Mollie adored Bridget and the little dog that followed her everywhere. Sarah was enamored with Ryan. Mary was ashamed to admit it, but being the wife of Jakob Lichtenbaum now paled before the life of an independent business owner, a dream she had nurtured since arriving in America as a naïve girl.

She loved Jakob, of course, but his dimpled smile had caused her more heartache than she could stand. He'd lured her away from the security of her home and family with his sweet words and passionate kisses. The more she thought of it, the more she understood that her home with Mama and Papa was gone—wholly and irrevocably gone. She had chosen Jakob over them and had broken her papa's heart. She was foolish to think she could return, and besides, there was still the menacing Rocco Monza to deal with in the old neighborhood.

She got out of bed, tidied the room, and dressed while considering her options. Jakob was gone, smile or not. She had yet to learn where he was or if he'd return. She'd had no word from him. Mary clenched her fists, a wave of righteous anger swelling in her heart.

Why wouldn't she accept the offer of this magnanimous woman? Mrs. Oliver believed in her and was willing to take a chance on her. Yet one thought kept tugging at her heart.

*Cenzo.*

Clara believed Mary could bring life back to the dying man, but that was foolishness. Mary could no more heal Cenzo than she could squeeze water from a stone. It pained her heart to consider it, but her friendship with dear Cenzo was gone too.

Best she faced the facts—her old life was over. Mary had decided by the time the children woke up, stretching their skinny limbs and yawning enormous yawns.

She couldn't wait to tell them.

"What I don't understand, Miss Mary, is why a kosher Jew can't eat something with yeast?" Granny Boone kneaded bread dough, her massive hands covered in flour and pounding back and forth with surprising dexterity. Mary enjoyed a moment's respite after the dinner rush and sat in the cozy kitchen on a large stool at Granny Boone's counter, sipping tea. They'd need her in the dining room soon to assist with dessert and coffee, but she could afford a few moments of rest. She planned to tell Granny Boone and Elspeth of Mrs. Oliver's incredible offer and her decision to stay at the inn.

Granny Boone got the next morning's bread dough ready to rise overnight. The little tin pans full of rising dough covered with muslin cloth would stay on the radiators around the edge of the kitchen for their overnight transformation. Mary could already smell the telltale scent of fermentation, and her mouth began to water.

"Well, technically, Jews can eat leavened bread outside Passover," Mary answered. "It's because of the Old Testament passage which spells out…"

A crash and the sound of shattering glass came from the bar in the dining room. The two women jumped in surprise, and Granny Boone grabbed her ample bosom with a floured hand, leaving behind a perfect handprint on her apron. An argument had broken out. Mary could hear the distinct sound of an Italian man swearing. The voice sounded familiar. With his bumbling mannerisms, she heard Pauly Holmes attempt to placate a furious customer. He must have dropped the man's glass.

"What in the name of all that's holy is going on in there?" Granny Boone pounded the bread dough with undue force.

Mary put her teacup down and stood to go find out.

"I'll go, Miss Mary." Mrs. McLaughlin came bustling into the kitchen with a basket of clean towels from the laundry. Mary began to protest, but she waved her hands. "No, no! Dinna fash, dearie. You go on and finish your tea. I'll see to the kerfuffle." Elspeth put the basket on the counter and hastened into the dining room. "Now, boys, you best be behavin,' or you'll get a lickin'!"

As the dining hall returned to its usual hum of evening activity, Mary enjoyed her last sip of tea and prepared to return to her duties.

She'd announce the exciting news after supper ended and the diners retired to their rooms.

Elspeth returned to the kitchen. "Some burly Italian a'stoppin' through on his way to Newark on party business, he says. Not to worry, Pauly gave him a dram on the hoose to settle him down."

Newark? Mary felt the hairs on the back of her neck stand up. The description of a "burly Italian man" brought images of Rocco Monza to mind. But no, Rocco wouldn't be this far north. He was miles and miles away in Southwark and no threat to her here. "Thank you for the tea, Granny Boone. I'll be getting back to it then."

Elspeth kept talking as she washed her hands in the large sink by the back door. "Oh, Mary! Bridget has your bairn in the hall for him to get his goodnight kiss. Our Italian stranger was quite taken with little Mendel when Bridget brought him down the stairs."

Every instinct in Mary told her to run to Mendel. She pushed through the kitchen door and rushed into the dining hall. Sure enough, Rocco Monza stood across the room, speaking with Bridget and squeezing Mendel's chubby hand. Bridget was noticeably uncomfortable, feigning interest in the conversation while casting desperate eyes at Pauly, who stood behind the bar, oblivious to the scene. Rocco eyed Bridget as if she were a meal.

Mary heard him ask if the baby belonged to her. "You can't be old enough to have such a child." His eyes ran over her breast and lingered there. Mendel started to cry. The baby squirmed in Bridget's arms and caught sight of his mother at the kitchen door.

"Mama!" Mendel reached his arms for her. All eyes locked on Mary.

At the sight of her, Rocco's face went white with shock in one instant and then red with anger in the next. "What are you doing here, *puttana*? I thought you were in Newark!" He spat on the floor. Rocco looked between her and the baby, and realization dawned across his meaty face. "So *this* is the bastard baby of your Jewish dog of a husband?" Bridget strained as far away from the brute as she could.

When jumping into a passing train, Mary had needed a strong dose of bravery. She'd drawn strength from some otherworldly source when she'd had to shepherd her children across a dangerous bridge.

But not this time. Without thought, without fear—as if she did this every day—she planted her hands on the bar counter and catapulted herself over it. She scratched at the huge man and pushed Bridget and the baby behind her in one fluid motion.

But Rocco was ready for her. He rushed at Mary, grabbing a fistful of her hair and pulling her toward him. Mary twisted out of his grip, hair pulling out of her bun, and threw herself backward, hitting her head against the bar. Bridget screamed, and everyone in the kitchen flooded into the dining room. The few remaining patrons were on their feet, unsure what to do.

Ryan Oliver—God bless him—burst in from the front porch, where he'd been smoking his evening cigar. He ran at Rocco full tilt, jumped on the beast's back, and gouged at his eyes. Rocco growled and clawed at the boy behind him. Mary came to, slumped against the bar, and shook her head to clear the ringing in her ears. She heard Mrs. Oliver say from the stairway, in a voice as cool as a cucumber and strong as steel, "Pauly, take him out."

Pauly nodded once, walked around the bar, planted himself in front of Rocco—who seemed to shrink before the gentle giant—and plunked his enormous fist on top of Rocco's head. One stroke, and Rocco went down like a sack of potatoes. Ryan rolled off onto his knees. Rocco lay still, out like a light.

Everyone let out a collective breath. Mendel whimpered. Mollie and Sarah, thank God, were nowhere in sight. Mary clutched the baby from Bridget. "The girls?"

Bridget quivered. "Upstairs, they're upstairs."

"Thank Jesus," Mary proclaimed, crossing herself for the first time in five years. "Saint Michael, preserve us," she added for good measure.

Mrs. Oliver knelt on the ground next to Rocco and checked his pulse. Once assured of his wellbeing, she stood and addressed the room. "I do not hold with violence, and as you all witnessed, this was self-defense." She looked at Mary. "But as soon as he comes to, we'll have to let him go."

From behind her, Mrs. McLaughlin declared, "There's nothing for it, *m'eudail*—you'll have to run."

"There's bread and nuts in the satchel. Bridget! Bring the girls along—hurry now!" Elspeth McLaughlin was in her element. Born and raised in the Scottish Highlands, she knew something of running from danger. Her people had been persecuted and tormented for generations, and it was in her blood to be prepared for a quick exit.

Mary experienced a strange calm. "Where will you go?" Mrs. Oliver asked, putting her hand on Mary's shoulder.

"I have no choice. I'll go home to Southwark. I have a friend there—Cenzo. He's dying, but he will know what to do. Lord, please let him still be alive!" Mary put the bag over her shoulder, tied her jacket into a baby carrier as she had when they'd crossed the bridge, and secured Mendel inside. He was snug as a bug and sound asleep.

"Ah, here are the girls." Mrs. Oliver knelt and looked into their sleepy eyes. "Little women, you will need to be brave and strong. Mind your mother, and above all, hold to hope." Then she spoke to Mary. "Ryan will go with you as far as the Neshaminy Creek crossing. He can help you navigate the canals and inlets along the river here. Stay close to him. It is growing dark. Once you cross the Neshaminy, it's a straight path. Follow along the Delaware for an hour or two until you come to Andalusia House. You can't miss it—there is a large, formal garden. You will think you have wandered into a dream."

Granny Boone enveloped Mary in a teary-eyed embrace, smelling of salt and yeast and everything warm and good. She strapped a little travel pack onto Mollie's back. Brusque and full of haste, Elspeth shook Mary's hand, pulled her in for a pat on the back, and then kissed the top of Mendel's head.

"You're a right braw lass, Miss Mary, and that's a fact. Go canny, aye? That devil will be after ya as quick as a wink. Off you go then, *m'eudail.*"

Mrs. Oliver continued her instructions as the little group moved through the back door. "Andalusia House is the Biddle home. They are a large and venerated family whose people were Quakers when they arrived in this country. I wouldn't deem myself a peer of Letitia Biddle, but she is an acquaintance and a kind soul. She is head of the garden club of which I am a member. She knows me. Tell her I sent you. Mary…" She touched Mary's cheek with tenderness, and Mary broke into tears. The women looked into each other's eyes in silent recognition of the fragility of life and the uncertain futures they both faced. "Do not be afraid." With that, Mrs. Oliver ushered them through the kitchen and out the door.

Ryan met them outside, his walking stick in hand. He nodded at Mary. "I'm ready." To his mother, he whispered, "He started coming around, but Pauly forced a dram of whiskey down his gullet, and the brute fell back into a stupor. We don't have much time." He gave his sister a quick hug. "I'll be alright, sis. I'm gonna follow our trail to the fishing hole by Otter Creek. Be back before you know it."

Bridget nodded and bent down to kiss the girls. "I'll miss you, little poppets."

Mrs. Oliver gave the group a final farewell. "Off you go, friends! May you know that God is with you."

"It's not possible, Muter. See!" Mollie pointed to a life-size hedge shaped like a stallion charging at full speed. "A horse made of *bushes*?"

Despite her fatigue and anxiety, Mary chuckled at her daughter's amazement. "That's called a hedge, which a careful gardener can sculpt into any shape. Look around. There's a rabbit, and there," she pointed toward the river, "a pirate ship with what appears to be *Il gatto con gli stivali*—Puss in Boots—as captain."

Sarah's face was full of wonder, and little Mendel peeked out of the baby sling, eyes round as moons. The deep blue sky of early evening cast an eerie glow on the lawn sloping down to the Delaware River. The garden at Andalusia indeed seemed like a scene out of a dream. The grounds boasted a hedge maze of tall yew bushes, with benches along the outer wall and topiaries as tall as giants guarding the exit points.

Mollie whispered, "I can't believe it."

Mary patted Mollie's head. "As Alice declared, 'There's no use trying…one can't believe impossible things.'"

"I don't understand, Muter," Mollie said. "I see the hedges are real plants, but how were they shaped that way?"

They heard a dog bark across the large lawn and saw a light flickering.

"Guess we'll ask him." Mary pointed to the man hurrying toward them, a dog trotting at his heels.

"Ho there!" He came upon them, a little breathless, the lantern swinging back and forth at his side. To the dog, he commanded, "Sit, Pilot!" The dog sat at his master's feet.

"Pilot? Like Mr. Rochester's faithful mutt in *Jane Eyre*."

"The same, miss." The man's eyes widened in surprise. "Welcome to Andalusia House." He gave a sharp nod of the head. "I'm the groundskeeper, Mr. Grady. May I be of assistance to you? Why are you and the little ones wandering about? Night is upon us, after all." Mr. Grady raised his eyebrows.

Mary gathered her courage and asked Mr. Grady for a place to rest. "I can explain everything once we're safe."

At the word *safe*, Mr. Grady looked around the dark property as if a pirate would emerge from behind one of the hedges at any moment, brandishing his sword. "Follow me."

They rested on a horsehair blanket on the dirt floor of a greenhouse, the air moist with condensation and pungent with the fecund scent of potted plants. Mary touched the sore bump on the back of her head and winced as Sarah and Mendel dozed at their mother's feet. Like a little lady, Mollie sat up straight next to Mary, alert and attentive to the adult conversation.

"I can't have you stay in Andalusia House, miss, as much as I'd like to extend the hospitality."

Mary glanced down at her grimy dress, muddy shoes, and the dirty faces of her children. She blushed, ashamed.

Mr. Grady hastened to clarify. "You misunderstand me. Under normal circumstances, all are welcome at Andalusia House, but the family is in Europe, and I'm in charge of keeping everything in order. I'm not to have strangers in the house, you see."

"Oh, I thought…yes, of course, Mr. Grady, I wouldn't have you in a tight spot on our account." Mary considered the cozy greenhouse. "This is a perfect hideaway."

Mr. Grady seemed surprised at her choice of words and waited for an explanation. When Mary didn't offer one, he cleared his throat and suggested he bring some food from the kitchen for them.

The children were starving. In their hasty departure from Delaware House, there had been no time to pack Mrs. Baumbach's kosher food. The bread, apples, and nuts that Elspeth McLaughlin had packed were long gone. Mr. Grady's offer was kind, but Mary doubted the staff at Andalusia were Hebrew and, therefore, able to provide kosher food. Mary would not, *could* not, allow Mollie, Sarah, and Mendel to eat unclean food. After everything she and Jakob had put these precious children through, Mary wouldn't allow them to break a commandment. So, hungry as they were, she had to refuse the offered meal. Mary shook her head and tried to explain. "Thank you kindly, Mr. Grady, but my children are Jewish and cannot eat food prepared by unclean hands."

Mr. Grady reared at this comment, looking at the soot and dirt on his hands.

"No, no, Mr. Grady, I don't mean your hands are *dirty*. Heavens! No, how can I explain? Well, the children would be breaking a commandment if they ate food that was not kosher—prepared in a certain way according to our religion."

"Ah, I see." With another glance at the soil under his fingernails, Mr. Grady changed the subject. "Perhaps you can explain your unusual and dramatic circumstances. What brought you to Andalusia in such a state?"

"Well, we're traveling to Southwark to visit family, and we've run out of money. You've done us a great kindness, and I'll be forever grateful if the children and I can sleep here tonight—without too many questions." Mary leaned forward in emphasis.

Mr. Grady nodded his assent. "Of course, miss. Sleep well. Pilot will stay outside the greenhouse door until morning and alert you if anyone approaches. I'm traveling to the market at first light, so I'll take my leave of you now." To Mollie, he gave a little bow. "Little lady, sweet dreams." With that, he got up, brushed off his trousers, and left them, taking the lantern. Mary heard him say, "Stay!" to Pilot, who whined once or twice but obeyed his master and settled on the ground before the door. Mary watched the lantern light flicker through the greenhouse window, casting an unearthly glow in the night as Mr. Grady strode back to the house.

Tomorrow, she and the children would walk home.

The morning sun dawned bright and hot. Mary and the children greeted Pilot on the threshold of the greenhouse with a little pat on the head. Thus dismissed, the hound trotted toward the river to hunt for breakfast. Andalusia House stood empty; Mr. Grady had gone to the market before sunrise.

Time to go.

Through the night, Mary had kept vigil over her family with a shard of broken glass from one of the greenhouse windowpanes in her lap. Besides Pilot, it was her only form of defense. She heard noises from every direction, and her imagination ran wild with each new sound. She was dizzy with a pounding headache from the blow to the back of her head. The memory of Rocco grabbing her played over in her mind like a nightmare. He was a brute. Had he followed them? Was he out there somewhere right now, searching for them? She couldn't be sure.

Rocco had thought she would be in Newark. How did he know that? Had he been on his way to find her? Was he on an errand for the Duke? One did not dismiss the Duke's orders on a whim, so maybe he continued on his way. He'd seemed surprised to see her at the inn. Was it pure coincidence, or had he been tipped off? Mary shook her head to clear it. One thing she knew. Rocco hated her. Why?

Ridiculous to think he was jealous. Jealous of what? Jakob was gone and had left her with the care of three young children. Not quite what you'd call a "catch." Mary was sure Rocco didn't love her—he was incapable of love. Mary didn't believe it was lust either. There were plenty of Southwark girls prettier than she. No, Rocco hated her—and, by extension, her children—because Papa's refusal of her hand in marriage had affronted him.

No one had ever denied Rocco before, Mary was sure of that. She had never considered the risk Papa took when he rebuffed Rocco and, by extension, the Duke. They could've turned the Paragano family out of their home and forbidden anyone else to help them. *Blacklisted.* That's what they called it, and it happened too often to ignore. What did Papa have to do to protect the family from that fate? There was only one way to find out. She and the children had to return to Southwark and beg forgiveness from her papa.

"Off we go, little ones." She forced a smile.

Mary hoisted Mendel into her arms, secured him in the sling, gave the girls a little pat, and walked down the lawn to the river. She led them south toward Philadelphia, surprised that they offered no complaint. *They're too tired to object.*

Mr. Grady had told her it would be about a six-hour journey to the docks of Southwark. But after one hour, they had to stop and seek shelter under a small bridge, as Mary feared Sarah would collapse. The poor child's ankle was still weak, and she couldn't take another step.

The little ones were asleep when Mary heard men's voices in the distance toward the main road. She sat bolt upright. *Is it Rocco? Did he follow us after all?* Mary was tempted to pop out of her hiding place like a marionette, wave the strangers down, and give up. She didn't want to run anymore. At least one of the men must be reasonable. How could they all be crazy like Rocco? But no, she dared not risk it. She huddled closer to her offspring, waiting for the voices to disappear down the road. Their hideaway smelled of mud and rotten fish. Mary was hollow from hunger and fear.

*I must keep my wits about me.*

A few hours later, she roused the children and started them on the journey again. They plodded along, one foot after the other, for miles. Finally, when evening came, Mary saw the tall buildings of Philadelphia rise in the distance. *Keep going.*

When they were close enough to Southwark that she could smell it, Mary became overrun by doubt. While the children rested, she battled her demons and banished fear from her side.

*You have no place in my heart.*

Night had fallen. They were in the final stretch of their journey. Not long now.

"Come on, doves. It's time to go."

"I'm afraid, Muter," said Mollie.

Mary was afraid too, but she wanted to give her daughter courage. How could she assure her child that all would be well? She looked over the river and wished they could swim across and hide from Rocco in New Jersey, where he'd never find them. Here, on the riverbank, they were vulnerable. "We need a miracle, God," she prayed.

Mary imagined a glorious, bright angel carrying them over the wide Delaware. His presence overwhelmed her, but Mary wasn't afraid of him. He enveloped her in warm light and hope. As the imagined angel carried her family over the water, Mary caught a glimpse of herself on the surface. How beautiful she looked.

*Is this how God sees me?*

"I know you're scared, Mollie. I know. But consider this." She pulled her daughter to her feet. Helped Sarah adjust her shoe. Centered Mendel on her chest. "Look out over the water, darlings. See how far the other bank is?"

The girls nodded their heads in unison.

"Well," their mother continued, "God will carry us across the chasm and place our feet securely on the other side of this trial. I know it."

Mollie and Sarah gazed at the river, and Mary turned toward town, only to see Rocco Monza sauntering toward them as if on a holiday stroll. Her heart froze in her chest.

Rocco took a long drag of a cigarette, then flicked the stub onto the sand, releasing a steady cloud of smoke through his lips. "Ah, there she is. Our Jewish whore and her little piglets."

Rocco approached her, step by step, his eyes blazing under his Jeff cap like two burning coals in the night sky. Behind him, a few nameless, faceless men fanned out, lurking, leering.

Mary should have been terrified. She wasn't. She had already banished that demon. Fear was no companion of hers. She'd been foolish to let him linger so long, to let him direct her decisions and hound her every move. No, fear was gone, and panic with him. She was a child of God, and her children needed her to be brave.

"Get *back*. All of you." Mary wished she had a broom or a stick or, better yet, a knife. All she had was the shard of glass she had found on the floor of Andalusia's greenhouse. A meager weapon, but it would have to do. She produced it from the large pocket of her apron, where it had rested below her sleeping baby.

She brandished the glass like a sword, pushing the girls behind her body with her other hand. Mendel squirmed in the sling at her chest, twisting to see what the commotion was about. He wiggled out of the carrier in a swoosh and almost fell face-first into the sandy soil. Mary grabbed him but dropped her weapon at the same time.

Rocco nodded toward his men. They closed in. Step by step, the thugs corralled the little family closer to the water's edge. Mary heard gulls screaming above her as if in sympathy for her plight.

"Leave us be. They're children, for heaven's sake!"

"Oh, not for long. The girls will bring a good price. I know a dealer over in Jersey."

Bile rose in Mary's throat. *God, help us! My girls!*

"It's the boy I want—the little Jewish git. I can't have him growing up under Sebastian's roof in this town. His very life mocks mine. No, his little light will go out—tonight."

*Never.*

In the same instant that Rocco lunged, Mary channeled the rage of every woman and child on earth who had ever been harassed. She borrowed the fury and hidden strength of every marginalized, patronized, used, neglected, abandoned, beaten, and broken woman. Its force flowed through her veins as she released a thunderous shriek—a primitive sound from the dawn of time.

The men froze, their mouths agape.

But not Rocco. With terrible force, Rocco grabbed Mendel out of his mother's arms. The momentum pushed Mary to the ground, where she scrabbled to get back on her feet. Mollie and Sarah held onto each other and screamed. Mary clawed at Rocco's legs, and then she saw his face.

*He's going to drown Mendel in the river! Saint Michael, protect us!*

Before he could reach the water, Rocco and his gang turned at the sound of men yelling from the docks—the police. The coppers ran full tilt toward the struggling group, their lanterns swinging with each step and casting frantic streams of light across the scene. Mary used the distraction to her advantage and pounced on Rocco. She snatched Mendel from his grasp and clutched him to her chest. She twisted away from the thug and raced to the water's edge. There was nowhere else to go.

Mollie saw her mother running with the baby to the water and screamed, "Muter! Don't drown us!" Then Mollie fainted to the ground, and Sarah shrieked as she fell.

Mary continued toward the policeman she'd spotted at the river's edge. She thrust Mendel into his arms before her knees gave out, and she sank into the sand. The other officers chased Rocco and his thugs, blowing whistles and yelling after them into the night.

Mary crawled over to her daughter, lying still, and put her head against Mollie's chest. Once assured Mollie was breathing, she reached for Sarah, who clung to her waist. Mary held her girls close, wrapped her arms around them—one on each side—and cherished their solid weight. She smelled the scent of their hair and soothed Sarah's sobs with her kisses.

"It's alright, my doves. It's alright. God is with us. He was always with us."

They were safe. It was the only thing that mattered. That, and the knowledge that she'd have killed for them—would have died for them.

Mary closed her eyes and knew no more.

# CHAPTER TWENTY-ONE

From the Desk of Elisabetta Paragano-Cassia
Norfolk, Virginia

December 18, 1965

Today, they named me Catholic Mother of the Year in our parish. There was a crowded luncheon in the fellowship hall after the ceremony. They served roast pork with new potatoes and carrots, but the meat was dry. The Ladies' Auxiliary prepared and served the meal. I think Betty supervised—her meat is always dry. She gets too distracted babbling away with the other gals and should use a good meat thermometer.

Anyhow, it was a nice ceremony, and my children were there. Mollie too, dear girl—she's not a girl anymore, but a grown woman and a grandmother to boot—with her husband, Frank. They pinned a beautiful corsage on my lapel with a lily in it. I'm an old woman. They should have given this honor to a younger mother, but I will admit, my heart swelled when they announced my name.

Now that I'm home, ensconced in my favorite armchair, a cup of bracing English breakfast on the little table next to me, I feel deflated by the attention. Being honored for something I had to do—it doesn't feel authentic. No one knows this, of course. At least, those who know it don't speak of it. My adopted son John urges me to write it all down. He says it will be cathartic—cleansing. He, of all people, would be thankful for the turn of events in my family's life, which helped to shape and form my being. Maybe he wouldn't be *grateful*, but he would understand the significance. But he doesn't know. He doesn't know how he has benefited—how we all have. Must I expose it now?

Father Marin's speech at the ceremony today highlighted my devotion to children. He named the twenty-five foster children my husband and I cared for throughout our lives. Since I was twenty-one, I have raised orphans and cared for children. Dear John, my devoted son, the one refilling my tea now as I write this memoir, has stayed with me since he was eleven. He was a foster child from a broken home. Father spoke about the sacrifices I made to care for so many children. At this, Mollie looked at me with tears in her eyes. You see, she knows the "why" better than anyone else. I took her in, after all—Mollie and her sister, Sarah. I got them from the orphanage and raised them until Mollie married and Sarah was dead and buried.

To tell the truth, I don't deserve the Catholic Mother of the Year award because of my work with orphans and wayward children. I love all of them fiercely, of course. But I'm not remarkable or noteworthy—or good. I had no choice but to adopt Mollie, *capisce?* I *had* to make amends, even if it took a lifetime. See, I was there that fateful night—I was there, and I did nothing.

It was hot that summer, I remember that. It was 1897, and Southwark had suffered a heat wave for weeks. The humidity could make folks crazy back then, living so close together in city row homes. There was no fresh air or breeze except down by the river. (A shudder runs through me even now, thinking of the river.) My sister, Mary, had been gone for five years, living in Newark with her husband, Jakob, and her three little children. Mollie was five years old by this time, Sarah was three, and little Mendel must have been ten or eleven months old and still at the breast.

My elder sisters had smuggled letters to Mary for years with the assistance of our family friend Cenzo and his stalwart assistant Tomas. Those fine fellas had a network of friends along the river, up to Manhattan and down to Maryland. Word would get back to us— how Mary fared, how old the children were, and what was to-do up in Newark. We coveted those whispered messages and kept them quiet in our hearts. Papa had forbidden any communication with Mary, period.

The knowledge that his daughter Mary had married a socialist Jew from the Fourth Street sweatshops was a stain on our family name. The Duke had a long-standing vendetta against the socialists. It was bad enough that Mary had become pregnant before wedlock, but the parish priest could have smoothed over such an affair—it was a common occurrence. No, it was Mary and Jakob's elopement that caused a strain on Papa's relationship with the boss. A socialist Jew as a son-in-law? Unacceptable. Allowing her to marry Jakob after refusing her hand to his padrone, Rocco? Unforgivable. Mama, my sisters, and I waited for years to see what Rocco would do in revenge against our family. But nothing ever happened. Had Papa worked out a deal with Rocco?

I've come to understand Mary had no choice but to run. I know she changed her name every time she signed an official document. Why, even on her wedding certificate, she listed her name as Mary Bichler. She was scared. For all intents and purposes, Mary had wiped away all mention of her Paragano family or her association with Philadelphia. She reinvented herself upon arrival in Newark with her new husband.

*Was it worth it, Mary?*

Maybe sometime soon, I will be able to ask her face-to-face. For now, as I still toil among the living, I must put the question aside. I have other questions as well. What went so terribly wrong in Newark? Did Jakob lose his position at the insurance agency? Make a lousy investment? Run into trouble with the law? Or did the Valero brothers find him—up there, in his new community? I know from Cenzo that Jakob was still involved with the socialist party, backing a new candidate who ran against the Manhattan machine. Dangerous business, that.

For what it's worth, I don't think Mary even knew what happened. She was caught up in an ill-fated romance, one that was doomed from the start. Mary was in over her head when she met Jakob. That was clear to everyone. In the end, all I have are unanswered questions, fading memories of Mary, and painful realities of what happened next.

"Get on with it," my beloved husband would say with a wink if he were here. And so, I shall.

It was a hot night, as I said before. I sat in the upstairs window of our home in Southwark, hoping to catch a breeze. Impossible in the city. I longed to be at the river, but dusk would soon fall, and I couldn't walk alone at night. I was fifteen years old. Desperate for relief, I convinced my younger brothers, Manny and Michael, to escort me to the river to look for oyster shells. The gulls brought them all the way up from the sea, following the tidal Delaware River, to their nests along the city's wharf. I bribed the boys with the promise of taffy upon our return. Papa nodded his assent, distracted while poring over his ledgers from the day's market sales.

Our excursion began with joyful energy. The prospect of collecting shells excited the boys. Manny was about twelve years old—on the verge of manhood but still a boy at heart. They were dear boys. We skipped down "Little Fitz" Street, and the river revealed itself across the way. Oh, the river! The busy street was all buttoned up from the day, the shops and stalls closed for the night. The working men had gone to the local pub for an hour or two before returning home to their crowded flats. The wharf was deserted.

The sun descended behind us, casting long shadows on the water before us. Gulls were diving low along the water, screeching in competition for the prizes along the shoreline. I glanced at Cenzo's room, nestled above his fish stall. The window flickered with candlelight. *Tomas must be there, caring for the poor man.* I'd prayed for Cenzo every day since the apoplexy had rendered half of his body useless. Tomas said he couldn't understand Cenzo's slurred speech and had to help him use the chamber pot. Dear Tomas—such a devoted friend. He was devoted to us all.

The boys and I enjoyed the fresh air. I was watching our shadows make grotesque figures upon the swift current when I heard a muffled cry off to our left, upriver. I strained my eyes to see, but the shadows played tricks in the evening light. Michael turned his head in that direction and asked, "What was that? I heard a baby's cry."

Manny scoffed. "It's the gulls, *fratellino*. C'mon, I bet you can't catch me."

He ran off, slapping Michael on the back as he passed, and our little brother followed close on his heels. I continued to scan the riverbank to the left. The light was fading. One moment, it was dusk, and the next, it was dark. There were shapes on the river's edge in the distance, but I couldn't see well. The breeze shifted toward me and brought the sound of screaming children. The cries made my feet turn to lead. I was rooted to the spot. Then I heard a sound like no other—a haunted cry that struck my heart and shook me out of my trance. It was the sound of a woman keening—a wild, hysterical sound—one that still haunts me to this day.

Until that moment, I didn't know I could be brave. I ran toward the sound. As I came closer, human shapes morphed out of the shadows. I saw two tiny little girls clasping each other and screaming. I saw a woman on the ground next to the girls, clutching a little body close to her chest, her feet scrabbling at the loose soil, trying to get purchase in the sand. They were at the water's edge. Before I could blink, I saw a large man grabbing the baby. The woman clawed at his face, hysterical now. I saw two other men racing from the docks, lanterns swinging from their hands, casting eerie, shifting light onto the scene. Someone yelled, "Don't drown us!"

In one flash of light, I saw the face of the angry man grabbing the babe—it was Rocco Monza. He had the baby and glanced at the water, an evil look in his eyes. The lantern swung away and threw the scene into complete darkness. I started to scream when a hand clasped over my mouth from behind.

Dazed, I didn't protest as someone yanked me into the shadows and dragged me downriver. My assailant released me and spoke to my younger brothers, who had appeared out of nowhere. My mind whirled, and I thought I would faint. Why were my brothers speaking in such normal tones to my abductor? Why weren't we upriver helping the hysterical mother and screaming children? Was Rocco saving the baby, or was he about to drown him in the river? Who was this man who had pulled me away?

It was Tomas. He gave the boys urgent instructions.

"We can't allow that man to drown a baby, Tomas!" I yelled. "We have to go back and help them!"

"Lizzy, stay calm. I saw one of the cops holding the baby. It'll be alright, the police are there. I don't know what's happening, but we need more help. Let's go!" He moved off toward the pier. Manny took my hand and towed me along behind Tomas. Michael trotted close beside me. I followed the boys like an automaton, unsure what had happened.

Our little group climbed the stairs of the docks and followed Tomas into a door next to Cenzo's fish stall. We went up a rickety, narrow staircase to the rooms above the shop. At the top, Tomas put his finger to his lips. He went into the room and spoke with urgency to Cenzo. My brothers and I came into the apartment to see Cenzo propped up on pillows, his brow furrowed and his twisted mouth contorted into a frown. Tomas described the scene by the river. Cenzo's crooked face showed alarm. Then I heard Tomas speak a word that struck me to the core.

"Oystercatcher."

My breath caught, and my hand went to my heart.

"Mary?" I cried. "Was it Mary and her children at the river's edge?"

Cenzo spoke, but we couldn't understand him. "Find...Murtrie," he managed to choke out.

With that, Tomas jumped up, grabbed my hand, and led us down the stairs and back onto the street. He ordered my brothers to escort me home with haste. He impressed upon us the necessity to keep the scene at the river a secret from Papa. Tomas ran for help. My brothers and I hurried home, hand in hand, and Tomas vanished into the night.

My arthritic fingers are acting up. This account has taken me the better part of the evening to write. I'm exhausted from the day's events and the memories that flood my mind. My sweet John is urging me to rest. But I can't—I can't! I must finish the story now. I may burst if I don't continue. Why does my generation keep secrets for so long? What if I were to die in my sleep tonight? No one would know. No one would tell the story. Mary and her daughter, my dear Mollie, deserve better than that.

The boys and I walked home, as I said. We entered the house as if nothing strange had happened, remembering Tomas's admonishment to keep the events a secret from Papa. Perhaps I should have spoken right then and there to give Papa time to figure out a plan. Did my silence put the nail in Mary's coffin? Did I betray my sister? I will never know.

My brothers went to their room on the third floor to play cards before bed. I helped Mama tidy the kitchen so she could rest her aching back, with the little ones reading their primers at her feet by the hearth. Papa sat in his usual chair at the table, reviewing the *Philadelphia Evening Item*. All was peaceful in our home. Who could have known what would happen next and how this night would affect our lives forever?

A loud pounding resounded on the front door downstairs. Rocco Monza yelled up to the open windows. He sounded furious. My heart caught in my throat. Mama and Papa looked at each other across the room. Their sharp and wordless exchange was almost imperceptible to the children, but I had seen it. I was about to warn Papa right then about the dramatic scene at the river's edge—that Mary was here, in Southwark, with her three tiny children. The words were on the tip of my tongue. My hands were wrung around the dishcloth, almost cutting off circulation to my fingers.

At that moment, Rocco bellowed, "Come down here, Sebastian, and speak to me face to face, man to man, about the insult your *puttana* has caused me!"

Papa leaped from his seat, knocking the chair backward onto the floor. Little Angelo cried, hiding in Mama's skirts. In two steps, Papa went across the room and down the stairs. The words of warning died on my tongue. There was nothing to do now but wait to see what would happen.

Nothing to do but wait—and pray.

# CHAPTER TWENTY-TWO

### It is Done

*August 1897*
*Second and Christian Street Station*
*Southwark, Philadelphia*

Mendel whimpered again because his nappy was wet. Mollie smelled pee. They were in a room with a checkerboard floor—Mollie, Mendel, and Sarah. A desk stood in the center, and a hat tree in the corner loomed like a tall, skinny man. The room was quiet except for the sound of their mother crying in the next room. The men were talking to her and asking her questions. At the end of each sentence, their voices went up and then fell silent. Their mother did not answer.

Mollie waited, unmoving, and studied the checkerboard floor. She counted the black squares and held Sarah's hand, afraid if she let go, her little sister would wander off to search for spiders in the corner of the room. She didn't remember how they'd gotten here. Someone had tucked baby Mendel into his blanket on a bench behind her.

He whimpered again. Who would change him? Sarah's tummy grumbled. Mollie was hungry too. Sarah tugged on her arm. "Mollie...Mollie..." she fussed.

Mollie started their favorite rhyme. "Polly want a cracker?"

"Polly want *Muter*," Sarah answered. Mollie wanted her mother too.

The man said, "She's unhinged."

Mollie was tired, and her legs ached from walking all night. She had a sore toe that pulsed and sandy soil in her stockings. She sat down hard on the checkerboard floor with her back against the bench, where Mendel whimpered. Sarah sat too. They waited on the ground for Muter to open the door, scoop them up, and lift them into the air like little birds.

Muter said one word. "Jewish."

Mollie fell asleep, slumped against the bench, Sarah leaning on her shoulder. When she woke, Muter was gone.

---

Telephone Connection 2913
The Pennsylvania Society to Protect Children from Cruelty
Incorporated March 10th, 1877
Twenty-First Annual Report
Covering the Operations for the Year 1897
Office of the Society,
No. 217 South Broad Street, Philadelphia

Details of Cases, Page 51
  No. 16,431 Neglect and No Home.

Lieut. Gillingham reported the above case, with the statement that the woman and children had been on the street in this district and without a home for two or three weeks, her husband having deserted her. She is an Italian and appears to be weak-minded. The father of the children is a Hebrew. The woman claims that she has embraced the Hebrew faith, giving this as an excuse for not allowing the children to eat food given them. The woman's parents will not permit her to come to their home.

She was given a hearing before a magistrate who, after hearing the evidence, committed her to the House of Correction, and the children to the care of the Society.

---

"But this isn't true—not a word of it!" Sully slammed the society report down on the secretary's desk. The secretary had typed it up while Sully chased after Rocco Monza for questioning. The man from the society, a gentle soul named Watson, winced at the force and looked anxious to get moving with the children.

"Gillingham's orders," replied the station secretary as he wiped off his smudged spectacles. It had been a long night.

"That's hogwash!" Sully had been roused during his supper by Cenzo's assistant Tomas, entreating him to help. Mary Paragano had returned to Southwark with her three little children in tow, and Rocco had threatened to drown the baby in the Delaware River if Mary didn't agree to marry him. The situation was dangerous—not much an officer like Sully could do against one of the Duke's men. Fortunately, two boys from the Fourth Ward had arrived in time to break up the fray. They told Rocco to leave the scene and held Mary and the children until McMurtrie arrived. Someone had stabbed one of his men. A glancing blow, nothing serious, but the evidence pointed to Rocco.

"I outrank you, McMurtrie." Gillingham appeared out of nowhere and approached the desk. "Is there a problem here, *Officer* McMurtrie?"

"Sir!" Sully stood at attention and clicked his heels for emphasis. He clenched his jaw and chose his words with care. "Sir, I know this woman, this family. She ain't mad, and she ain't been begging in the neighborhood for weeks. For God's sake, she only arrived in our jurisdiction last night! And you and I both know her parents didn't even have a chance to welcome her back—she never made it home."

"So what?"

"So, this report is full of lies. Mary Paragano didn't do anything wrong, and I brought her in to protect her. He was attacking her, and her children were terrified by that lout, *Roc...*"

Quick as a rabbit and ten times as strong, Gillingham grabbed McMurtrie by the collar and leaned in so close, Sully could smell the sour scent of decaying teeth. "Don't. Get. Involved." The men stood toe to toe, glaring into each other's eyes.

Sully blinked. It was enough to break the standoff.

The lieutenant let go and patted Sully's shoulders as if brushing crumbs away. "If I were you, I'd stay out of this. You don't wanna have to speak with the Duke *directly*, do you?"

Sully took a deep breath. "No, of course not. But, out of curiosity, sir, why? Why do you even care about this girl and her little children?"

"Why? Because her father refused her hand in marriage to his padrone, that's why! He let her run off and marry a socialist pig instead! We can't let this kind of affront go unpunished. She's made her bed—now she can lie in it. She's shipping off to corrections, departing in ten minutes." Gillingham glanced at his watch. "And, in my opinion, she *is* crazy. She was mad enough to marry that Marxist. The offspring? We'll order the society to send them to the Young Women's Union. Let the Jewish *bubbes* take care of 'em."

"No!" At his superior officer's sharp look, Sully continued, "With all due respect, sir, have a heart. They ain't Jewish, no matter who their father is. The children are Catholics and belong to Christ, whom we both serve above all. Send them to Saint Vincent's. Please, I beg you."

Gillingham looked him up and down, as if measuring him against some internal yardstick. "Fine." He nodded to the man from the society. "See that the children find their way to a Catholic orphanage."

"And what about Rocco, sir? He stabbed one of my men."

"A shame, that. But your cop's gonna live, and I didn't hear anything about it."

The lieutenant turned to leave and noticed a reporter at the door scribbling in his notebook. "And somebody get this keyhole journalist out of here!" He stomped out the door and slammed it shut behind him. The men still in the room could hear him muttering down the hallway. "And now we have hacks snooping around the station digging for a scoop. Nothing's sacred…"

⁓⟨ ❋ ⟩⁓

"Bless me, Father, for I have sinned." Sebastian kissed the crucifix on his rosary. "It's been two months since my last confession, and these are my sins." The dark confessional box closed in around him. The thin veil across the screen fluttered as the priest breathed a steady sigh.

"I'm wracked with guilt and haunted by dreams. It's a demon,

Father. It chases me. A large, hellish, hideous bird—it attacks my home and threatens my family. It's been after Mary all these years. It came because I am no longer a free man. I've sold my soul to the devil. Rocco and the Duke *own* me. If it weren't for their hold on me, I wouldn't have…I wouldn't have…" He couldn't breathe. *I'm going to suffocate in here!*

The priest waited in silence.

"Father, Rocco came to the market a few weeks ago and demanded I reveal Mary's whereabouts. I didn't know where she was! But he told me to find her. And I did. I did, Father! I betrayed my own daughter." Sebastian took a staggering breath. "Tonight, Rocco came to the house and pounded on the door. He called me out to answer for insulting him. Said I betrayed him when I withheld Mary's hand in marriage, and now, look what she's done, whore that she is. I couldn't stand there listening to him disparage my daughter. I advanced on him, fist raised. And then, he smiled. That slow, evil smile of his. He put his hands in his pockets and rocked back on his heels, tilted his head and considered me like I was a calf for slaughter.

"I stopped in my tracks. I knew the meaning of that expression. He's threatened me like that before. He spat on my doorstep, walked around me, and placed his hands on the bricks of my home. 'Remember that day, all those years ago, Sebastian?' he asked. I knew what he meant. Father!" Sebastian's voice rose above a whisper, desperate for absolution. "They would've turned us out—blacklisted us. Tina, the babies." Sebastian put his face in his hands. "There was nothing I could do! The police took her, and I did nothing to prevent them from dragging her and the children away. What could I do?" His body crumpled, defeated, and his chest heaved with sobs.

The priest waited as Sebastian mourned. After Sebastian collected himself, the priest spoke. "There is always something you could do. I wonder, son, if you should examine your justification."

Silence enveloped the small space. *What have I done? My little nightjar!* Sebastian resisted the pain he knew would come if he were to admit —*No! It wasn't my pride that did this to Mary. I didn't push her away. No, I cannot live with that. She made her choice. This is all Mary's fault.*

Sebastian took a deep, shuddering breath. "Father, there was nothing I could do."

Another sigh. "And now, your daughter and her children are gone."

"Yes, Father. And now they are gone—along with my heart."

A pause. "Then that is penance enough, my son."

# PART FOUR
*Blockley*

# CHAPTER TWENTY-THREE

## *The Article*

*July 2018*
*South Philadelphia*

Sophie's number came up on Bella's phone screen. She put aside her work project and answered.

"I found her." Sophie's voice was tinny.

"Where are you, Sophie? It sounds like you're in a cave."

Sophie laughed. "I'm calling from the National Archives in DC. It *is* rather cavernous here. It's huge. I can hear my echo. Wish you were here with me. Ever since we read Mollie's letter, I couldn't stop thinking of her mother, Mary. I mean, did she *really* try to drown her children? I figured if that happened, there'd have to be some police report or newspaper article or something, right? So I dug around in the archives. It's amazing here. You'd love it. I have a wonderful archivist helping me—Ken—he's amazing. And, well, I found something. You're gonna flip out. Are you sitting down, Bella?"

"No…I'm heading back to my office from the ladies' room."

"Well, you might wanna find a seat. I found an actual newspaper article in *The Philadelphia Evening Item* from Tuesday, August 3, 1897, which relays the story of the police picking up Mary and the children in South Philadelphia."

"You're kidding me." Bella sat down at her desk.

"I'm not. Here, stand by. I'll send you a snapshot." Bella could hear Sophie fumbling with the phone, a sound like a rustling of leaves. Sophie mumbled in the background, "I can never get this darn thing to…oh! Here we go, yes, okay. I snapped a photo. Headed your way, Bella! Wait till you see this. You're gonna flip. I think we hit the motherload."

Waiting as the photo loaded on her smartphone, a thrill ran through Bella's veins.

*This is really happening.*

"I see it, Sophie!" Bella read the headline aloud. "'Her Pitiful Story. Homeless with Three Young Children. Picked up by Police. The Youngsters Provided for by the SPCC.' Oh, Sophie, this is it! This must be it!"

"I know, it's crazy. What a stroke of luck. Can you read it okay?

The newspaper itself must be a mess, it's so old. I'm looking at it through microfiche."

"Yeah, I can read it. What the heck is the SPCC? Reminds me of the SPCA, but that's for pets. How horrible."

"It must be something like that but for children," Sophie replied. "We can figure it out later. Let me read the rest of the article to you."

*A pitiful case, in which, motherly love showed itself as the predominating feature, was brought to the attention of the police last night, when Officer McMurtrie of the Second and Christian Street Station, arrested Mrs. Mary Lichtenbaum and her three children and took them to the station house.*

*It was close on to midnight when the officer saw the woman, with one of her babes in her arms, another holding her by the skirt and with the hand of the third grasped tightly in her own walking about the streets.*

*She was crying pitifully, and as she told the officer that her husband had gone away several weeks ago to look for work, leaving her and the three children penniless, the officer's heart—hardened to such scenes— was touched.*

*He tenderly took one of the children from its mother, and then had all of them taken to the station house where they received proper treatment.*

*Agent Watson, of the Society for the Protection of Cruelty to Children, was summoned and he, with Magistrate Smith, learned a pitiful tale from the mother.*

*She said that she was an Italian by birth and up to about five years ago lived with her parents.*

*Then she met the man to whom she was married. A child was born them and their married life began happily. Her husband was of the Jewish faith and she embraced his religion. Her child, Mollie, was brought up in the Jewish faith and when two years later, another was born, it too, was brought up in the same way.*

*All this time her husband was working and they lived in fairly good style. About a year ago a little son was born to them, and shortly afterward her husband lost his position. He wandered around now working at this place, now working at another, but all the while supporting his family.*

*Then work grew duller and positions fewer and fewer. Times grew hard with them and about two weeks ago when her husband went away to see if he would secure work, the rent was unpaid and she was in sore straits indeed.*

*Friends of her husband were appealed to, and they responded nobly. They took the unfortunate woman, and her offspring in, and besides housing them, fed them, too.*

*This could not last long, and she was compelled to go from door-to-door begging.*

*As to herself she would eat anything that was placed before her, but her children—they had been brought up in the religion of their father, and his faith had to be respected. She would allow them to eat nothing that had not been prepared by Jewish hands and according to the Jewish customs.*

*When the children were brought into the station house, the matron, as she bathed them procured some slices of nice bread and butter, but hungry as the children were, their mother would not allow them to partake of the food. She cried and raved all night and when the Magistrate questioned her to-day, her eyes were red and swollen from her grief.*

*Agent Watson said that he thought the children—Mollie, aged five years, and Sarah, aged three years, and Mendel—who is only eleven months old—should be placed under the care of his society.*

*The Magistrate accordingly placed the children under the care of the Society and Mrs. Lichtenbaum was taken to the House of correction, from whence she will be transported to the Almshouse.*

Silence filled the line when Sophie finished reading the account. Both women were quiet as they contemplated the horrible fate of Mary and her children.

*My mother was going to drown us.*

"Sophie, the article doesn't mention anything about Mary and the children at the river. We're missing something."

Sophie cleared her throat, about to speak, but someone knocked on the door to Bella's office before she could. "Sophie, I've gotta go. I'm at work." She hung up before Sophie could reply.

Bella swiveled in her chair and saw her boss looking through the open doorway, eyebrows raised. "I'm gonna need that report by three today, okay?"

Bella nodded.

Her boss joked, "You all right? You look like you've just seen a ghost." He left without waiting for a response.

"Yeah, I think I did," Bella whispered to no one.

After work, Bella rode the train down to South Philly. She wanted to walk the path Mary had walked all those years ago, to place her hands on the bricks of Mary's home—where she had lived when she met Jakob in 1891, and her life turned upside down. *Were relationships much different back then?* Bella was tired of running from her own upside-down life.

Nate had loved her once. When had that changed? Bella watched the neighborhoods fly by in a blur as the train rolled down the line. They had moved from South Philly to the suburbs when they first married. She missed living in the neighborhood that used to be called Southwark, with its churches and synagogues, restaurants, and shops. The area probably hadn't changed much since the day a police officer found Mary struggling with three crying children in tow. The article hadn't mentioned the river, but Bella knew it had a part to play in this story.

She got off the train at Second Street and ambled toward the Delaware. Amazing to think that if the officer hadn't intervened that night, Bella wouldn't even exist. She marveled at the thought. When

Bella had first explained that she was looking into Nana's history, her mom had asked, "Why dredge up the painful past? You may not like what you find, Bella." Bella wouldn't admit that she needed to know if her ancestor was crazy. That she was worried if Mary had tried to murder her children, maybe that evil had seeped through the generations and affected her somehow. No, she couldn't tell Rosalie that. Bella allowed her mother to believe that she was seeking a diversion from the painful circumstances of her divorce. It was true enough, anyway.

The day before, she'd run into Nate's thirty-year-old, pregnant girlfriend in the Hallmark store. She'd seen the young tramp once before but managed to avoid eye contact. This time, there was no such luck. She had hurried into the store on her way to the office in a frantic daze, hoping to grab a card for her co-worker whose dog had died, and come face to face with the woman who had destroyed her marriage. Kate. The home wrecker. The young, perky, and pregnant home wrecker. Nate and Kate. Ugh, how cutesy. He was too old for her, and he was making a fool of himself.

Kate's eyes widened, and her mouth opened into a perfect little "O." She nearly dropped her bag in surprise. Bella held her ground and didn't budge. Kate had to walk around her to get to the exit— precisely what she did. Though it was hard for Bella to admit, she gave the girl credit for pulling herself together, standing up straight, and wordlessly skirting around the wife of her boyfriend. Took some guts. Bella had watched her walk to her car with a Hallmark bag overflowing with baby blankets and stuffed animals.

The wind from the river whipped Bella's hair as she dismissed the memory with great effort. She never wanted to relive that again. Seeing Kate had paralyzed her, made her feel weak and bereft. She looked over the water of the Delaware River across to New Jersey. *Is this where my Nana almost drowned as a child? Where her mother, Mary, lost her mind, her family, and her freedom all in one night?* She thought of the tragic story and wondered if even God could redeem it. Tony seemed to think so.

The thought of Tony gave her heart a warm glow.

She inhaled a few deep breaths and smelled the tangy air of the city at her back. Gulls screeched, skimming the shore for shells. The foghorn of a barge echoed downriver, and a light breeze off the water caressed her cheek. *I'm not avoiding anything. I'm searching for something—more than a story from 125 years ago.* Had Mary really been crazy? Why had she tried to kill her children? What kind of mother would do such a thing? *What if Tony is wrong? What if I'm just like her?*

With one last glance at the water, Bella turned her back to the river and walked to South Sixth Street, where she sat on the stoop of Mary's house and asked God to show her the answers.

# CHAPTER TWENTY-FOUR

## *You Ain't Goin' to No Bellevue*

*August 1897*
*Southwark, Philadelphia*

Over her shoulder, Mary could see the tiny forms of her children at the receding station house. The society man led them to the wagon, one after the other. The girls held hands, faces solemn. A woman she didn't know held her baby boy in her arms. An old brown horse shuffled its feet in anticipation.

Mary's heart shattered as her plight became crystal clear—she had lost her beloved children. They didn't even let her say goodbye, and now she was being carted away in a paddy wagon to the House of Correction. Prison! For what? She hadn't done anything wrong. A deep moan came from her chest, like someone had torn her soul in two.

Mary had no memory of being taken into the prison building, of being questioned all night by authorities about the scene by the river, of being processed into their system. She vaguely remembered a light bulb flash as a man took her photograph with his giant brown box. She sobbed and moaned, incapable of speech, overcome with grief and confusion. Her breasts were hard as rocks from the extra milk baby Mendel would never receive. She was fevered and delirious. Sometime near dawn, the warden called an ambulance and had Mary removed from the prison.

The driver's eyes looked at her through a little mirror in front of the wagon. She sat in the back of an ambulance on the way to God-knew-where, and somewhere deep in her bones, she knew she would never return.

She'd never been in an ambulance before. She sat on the edge of the cushioned bench in the back, nerves tight as wires. It was an imposing wagon made of dark maple and pulled by a large black horse. She sat in a little cage-like box behind the driver's seat. A series of bars ran across the space in front of her, as if the ambulance driver and his assistant feared she would reach across and strangle them. If she weren't so exhausted, she might have done just that. But she couldn't. She was a captive, and she could do nothing about it. Even if she were to scream, the men wouldn't care—they'd probably heard it all before. Worse, even.

"Where are you taking me?" Her voice came out raspy.

There was no answer.

"Where am I going?"

"Well, you ain't goin' to no Bellevue." The assistant chuckled.

"Blockley?" Mary gasped.

"Knock it off, Joe." The driver stole another glance at Mary in the mirror, then darted his eyes away. Mary held onto the seat cushion, white-knuckled and desperate. Everyone knew to avoid 'Old Blockley' Almshouse at all costs. A part of Philadelphia Hospital, supposedly a good hospital that treated severe injuries and ailments, Blockley was best known for its poor house and—insane asylum.

*Oh, God, they think I'm crazy!*

Mary couldn't breathe. She took heaving gulps of air, but her brain wasn't communicating with her nervous system. The air wouldn't get to her lungs. She put her face down, studied the wooden floor of the ambulance, and counted to twenty. *Oh, God. Oh, God, please help me.* She had to keep her wits about her to reason with the authorities and get out of Blockley as soon as she arrived.

They traveled in silence down Market Street while the city roused from its slumber. Shop doors opened, and merchants emerged. Milkmen delivered milk. Newsies called the headlines from each corner. The usual comings and goings of commerce awakened all around her as the ambulance carried her to her death. Blockley was her tomb, and this was her funeral procession.

Mary concentrated on the sights around her to keep the panic at bay. She couldn't help but watch in fascination as the blocks of West Philadelphia went by. She'd never been to this part of the city before. The people and houses looked different. There were stone-fronted buildings with sturdy porches where housewives beat rugs with brooms and gossiped with neighbors. Soon, the houses gave way to fields on the city's outskirts. Then they crossed a wide river. Mary shuddered at the sight of the dark, swirling water, the memory of the struggle with Rocco by the water's edge threatening to overtake her mind. But, no, this wasn't the Delaware.

*This must be the Schuylkill.* Over a bridge they went—clop, clop, clop—and Mary craned her neck to see out of the front of the vehicle. An impressive stone building with an imposing Greek-columned portico loomed above. She hadn't imagined Blockley to look so regal. A sliver of hope blossomed in her heart. *This place seems respectable, and I'll be able to reason with the administrators, I'm sure.*

But the driver pulled past the beautiful porch and stopped the horse next to an enormous arched gateway adorned with a white sign that boasted striking black letters. *Philadelphia Hospital.* A guard opened the gate, and the ambulance glided through it, crunching gravel beneath the wheels. The guard secured the gate behind them.

The driver parked before a long, three-storied, dull gray building with a low, sloping roof. Mary winced when she heard her captors climb down from their perch. This was it! She released the breath she hadn't realized she'd been holding. Her eyes were puffy from sobbing all night, and she was heart-sore. She wanted her children, her mama, her home, and Jakob.

The driver opened the cage door, and each man took an elbow to escort Mary into the gloomy hall of her new home.

Mary yelped as freezing water cascaded over her head. She was sitting naked in a dirty metal tub, a line of other miserable women waiting their turn at the door. A large, red-headed woman hoisted

Mary to her feet, rivulets of cold water running down her body, and forcibly spun her around. Shocked that so many eyes were watching her, Mary struggled to cover her nakedness. A petite, dark-haired nurse pulled Mary's hands away from her private areas and lifted her arms. The redhead patted a strong-smelling powder into Mary's body hair and onto her head.

The two women twisted and turned her until satisfied she was— what?—clean? Indeed not, as the water was filthy. At Mary's look of confusion, the dark-haired woman said, "Pyrethrum powder. To kill the lice." She patted Mary on the back. "Off ye go then. Nurse C will give ye clothes. Next!" The nurse motioned for another unfortunate soul to enter the tub.

Thus, Mary was escorted from the bathing room, dripping, un-clothed, freezing, and humiliated, by a girl she assumed was "Nurse C." This nurse was surprisingly pleasant and chatted to Mary as they walked down the hall. Mary couldn't believe her surreal circumstanc-es. Surely, she'd walked straight into a Dickens novel. She was in Do-theboys Hall and half-expected to see Nicholas Nickleby leading a charge of boys down the dark, narrow hallway. She would join them, naked or not, and run for her life during the coup. To freedom.

"I don't belong here," she squeaked, but the chatty nurse didn't acknowledge her. She pulled Mary into a closet and held up various garments, gauging their size compared to Mary's diminutive frame, talking all the while. Satisfied with a dull dress the color of dung, Nurse C clucked her tongue and draped the fabric over Mary's head. Mary allowed herself to be dressed like a child, holding her arms out for the scratchy sleeves.

Next came the shoes, if such items could be called shoes. Nurse C strapped bits of leather around Mary's feet and tied them with string. Mary looked down at herself in her lowly state and repeated, "I don't belong here." Her heart raced, and bile rose up her throat. She grabbed Nurse C by the arm and searched her eyes. But the girl did not react to the touch. She gave no recognition whatsoever that Mary had spoken.

Finally, Mary noticed Nurse C hadn't said anything coherent, and she was speaking nonsense in a happy, sing-song voice.

*She's mad as a hatter. What kind of place is this, where the loon is leading the sane into a madhouse?*

Nurse C led Mary into a large room with tiny windows placed high in the walls, toward the ceiling, and cots arranged around the room, spaced with two feet between them. One electric bulb hung from the center of the room, casting a dismal amount of light into the cavernous space. The windows were open a crack, but they were so small that air couldn't flow through. The room was stifling and smelled of human sweat and dead mice. Mary gagged with dry heaves. She hadn't eaten for two days, so there was nothing to bring up.

Women in various states of awareness occupied every square inch of the ward. Old women, young women, and some girls no more than sixteen. At the sound of Nurse C's prattle, they turned as one, looking at Mary and assessing her. A pretty blond woman peered out from behind a screen in the far corner. They'd tucked her mattress into the tiny space next to a bed stand with a photo of an old couple on top. Her clothes were of better quality than her roommates'—just a tad, but still.

After a silent assessment, Mary's fellow inmates returned to their activity. Some pulled on worn-out shoes with toe holes and paper-thin soles. Others combed through their filthy hair with their fingers. A few women were still in bed, moaning or mumbling to themselves with vacant eyes that stared at the ceiling.

Mary resisted Nurse C's effort to pull her into the dismal scene. She tugged back against the girl with such force that she fell on her bottom, much to the enjoyment of her new associates. Nurse C didn't seem to notice, but continued babbling nonsense. The other women chuckled and shook their heads at Mary, who sat on the filthy floor.

Mary put her face in her hands and sobbed.

The blond emerged from her den and hauled Mary to her feet. She brushed her off and held her hand. "What's your name, doll?"

Mary couldn't speak. Exhaustion pulled at every fiber of her body, and her mind was numb with distress. All Mary wanted now was the sweet oblivion of sleep.

"Well, I'm Dorothy, but the gals call me Dot. C'mon, you can rest in my room." She led Mary to her corner and sat her in the tiny chair between the bed and the screen. This simple kindness was Mary's undoing, and she commenced sobbing. Dot didn't seem to mind and went about her business, using a shiny tortoiseshell hairbrush to smooth her long blond hair, stroke after careful stroke.

Sometime later, Mary woke from a deep sleep with her head leaning against the wall. She was so disoriented as she looked around the small space that she nearly fell off the little wooden chair. When her brain caught up with what her eyes were seeing, memories from the morning came crashing into her mind.

*Mollie! The babies. Oh, God, this is real.*

The pain of losing her children threatened to break her. Mary bit her fist to keep from crying out in grief. She peeked around the screen. Most of the women from the ward were gone. One or two women remained abed. The moaner and the mumbler were there, moaning and mumbling. Dot had left. Mary had no idea what time it was. The windows didn't let much light in, and it was impossible to see the sky. Judging by her hunger pains, it was probably noon. She was ravenous. Sleep had been a mercy. Being awake was torture.

She got up, stretched her aching neck, and looked for a chamber pot under the bed. As dehydrated as she must be, her body still needed relief. Once that was accomplished, she ventured from behind the screen into the large dormitory. She walked past dozens of cots made with a single threadbare blanket. No pillows. Mary surveyed the room and considered approaching the moaner and the mumbler, but thought better of it. The others must be at the midday meal. She'd have to figure this out on her own.

Once in the hallway, Mary followed the click-clack sound of utensils and pottery. Her stomach turned over in a nauseous wave—a mix of hunger pains and disgust at the foul stench. The dining hall was about thirty yards to her left, and as she approached, the distinct smell of rotten eggs and curdled milk grew stronger. When she arrived at the cafeteria doorway, she tiptoed into the room, hoping not to bring attention to herself.

No such luck. Nurse C stood up from her bench at the sight of Mary, clapped her hands, and gave a little shriek of pleasure. A buxom matron swooped down on her and slapped her back with a stick. Nurse C sat down and didn't make another sound, though her simple smile remained.

Mary felt a pang of guilt that the girl had received a beating because of her. Holding back tears, she spotted Dot and saw her flick her head to the left. Mary saw an empty seat on the bench next to Dot's table. She approached and sat between two waifs with limp hair and decaying teeth. They were twins—astonishing. Was Mary to believe that they were both insane? They nodded to the empty seat and allowed Mary to sit between them.

Their breath smelled of rotten fish, but they had kind eyes and nudged some of their food in front of Mary. If it could be called food. The girl to her left shared the last few sips of her bland soup. The girl to her right offered a piece of moldy bread. "Helen." She pointed to her chest. "Bertha." She pointed at her sister, who frowned and shot her sister an injured look. "Sorry, Berth, I meant the Queen of England." Helen gave Mary a rueful smile. "She's my sister. We'd never spent a day apart. I couldn't let them take her alone. She wouldn't survive here without me."

Mary nodded but didn't speak. What could she say to that? She never wanted to talk in this horrid place—ever.

Mary retched in the corner of the large room. Again. Some of the women launched dirty looks in her direction. She was disturbing their peace, if one could call it that. It was evening, and the inmates were supposed to be praying.

Mary prayed for death. She'd scarfed down the disgusting food like a ravenous wolf eating a rotten carcass in the forest. The butter on the bread had been rancid. Mary's stomach turned out the contents, meager as they were, with rapid and repeated force.

Dot took pity on her and brought a cloth to wipe her forehead. She held Mary's hair back with a mother's care and hummed a comforting melody. The kindness almost broke Mary's heart. *How can one survive in such a place?*

"Why are you here?" Dot asked, not unkindly.

Mary wiped her mouth with the back of her hand and looked at Dot in confusion.

"I mean, what's your story, doll?"

Mary didn't respond.

"You don't talk much, do you? Everyone has a story. Me, my old man sent me here. He feels guilty about what he done, so he bribes the warden to let me have my little corner over there." She tossed her glossy blond head in the direction of her oasis. "Makes him feel better, I guess." She paused a moment. When Mary didn't comment, she continued, "Yeah, he called the authorities and had me committed, he did."

Mary's eyes widened in shock. *Who would do such a thing?*

"Couldn't stand the sight of me, large belly full of another man's get. Had me sent away, easy as one, two, three." Dot followed Mary's gaze, aimed at her slim waist. "The baby? Oh, he's gone. I had him here. Well, not in this room, but over in Dandy Hall. It's the attic of the main hospital, where all the pregnant gals go. Never saw the little scamp. Woulda named him Clyde, I think."

Mary couldn't take it—not another word. She pushed away from Dot and ran from the room. She had to escape this madness, but she didn't get far. The night guard—the large redhead—was already positioned outside their dormitory, waiting for trespassers in the hallway. She sneered at Mary and threatened her with a baton, but Mary didn't need convincing. The last thing she wanted was a whack on the head. She hurried back into the room and found Nurse C cleaning up her mess with a mop and bucket. Mary wanted to stop the girl, but Dot touched her arm.

"Leave 'er. She's happy to do it."

Mary could hear Nurse C chatting away, laughing, and responding to the mop as if it had asked her a question.

"She's crazy. That's her name. Nurse C for crazy. C'mon, let's get you to bed."

Dot steered Mary to her cot, tucked her in like a child, and then retreated to her snug den in the corner. The redhead shut the light, and Mary lay in bed, looking at the ceiling. A bat circled high above—only fitting for such a place. She silently recited the words of Charlotte Bronte's *Jane Eyre*: "I am no bird, and no net ensnares me; I am a free human being with an independent will." Repeating this mantra would be the only way to survive this God-forsaken place. Mary begged God for the oblivion of sleep on this, the first night of the rest of her life.

And God was merciful.

Sometime in the middle of the night, Mary abandoned her deep sleep and lay in her cot, listening to the sounds in the room around her. The moaner and the mumbler had ceased their moaning and mumbling, thankfully. Someone cried in her pillow, and Mary could hear the pitter-patter of tiny mouse feet running around the edges of the dormitory. She lay stock still and took inventory of her hurts. Her scalp stung from the powder the nurse had dusted on her head, her chest was sore from sobbing and retching, and she had a pounding headache. But her heartache was worse than all of it put together.

*Why are you here?* She heard Dot's question and attempted to answer. She'd been delirious at the station house and couldn't remember much of the magistrate's questioning. Last she knew, she had been lying in the dirt by the river with her babies in her arms. She hadn't done anything wrong! She was protecting her children. Why had they taken her to the House of Correction? What was her crime?

*Think!*

If she could piece together the details, maybe she could speak with the warden and explain her situation. She was no more insane than Dot, sleeping away in her little castle in the corner. Locking her up here was an injustice of the highest order, and she must prove her innocence and sanity before she lost it.

*Think!*

Mollie and Sarah—Mary's heart squeezed at the thought of them—were standing behind her, holding onto each other. Mendel was in Rocco's arms. She grabbed for him and…then what? She'd spotted one of the cops by the water's edge, making his way forward to pounce on Rocco. In the kerfuffle, Mollie had screamed and then fainted. *Mollie!* And Mary had thrust Mendel into the cop's arms, with Rocco close on her heels.

And then, and then…

The policeman's eyes had gone wide as moons, his mouth forming into a shocked "O" as Rocco stabbed him with his knife before running down the beach. *Rocco stabbed the cop!* Mary could see it in her mind's eye. That was it, the piece of the puzzle she'd been missing. She knew the policeman had survived the injury—she'd seen him kneeling in the sand, holding Mendel safe in his arms before she fell and crawled over to Mollie. It must not have been a severe injury. Maybe the cop had deflected the blow? A miracle her baby survived. But to stab an officer—that was a punishable crime.

That was it! Maybe the police thought *she* had stabbed the copper. She'd simply explain to the warden…

They'd sent her to the House of Correction because they thought she'd committed a crime, but why did they let her go? Why send her to a madhouse? Unless…

Mary's thoughts stopped in their tracks, the truth hitting her like a ton of bricks.

They knew. The authorities already knew that Rocco had stabbed the policeman. They knew and hadn't done anything about it—couldn't do anything about it—because they were in with the Duke too.

The Duke's man had gotten away, and crazy Mary was the scapegoat.

# CHAPTER TWENTY-FIVE

*Baltimore*

*June 1897*
*Baltimore, MD*

The sunset glowed bright with orange, pink, and purple stripes above the tall buildings of Baltimore. Jakob leaned against the doorframe of his brother's brick walkup, waiting for the right moment to venture to the corner grocery. Kopel and his wife Rachel didn't smoke. That was the hardest part about staying on the lam with his relatives. That, and missing his wife and children. *Mary!* The thought of her fierce and wild eyes piercing his when she'd grabbed her rosary out of his hands made his heart wrench. *It's only temporary. I'll be home soon.*

The sun completed its last beautiful dance across the sky. Twilight. The time of shadows before the lamp lighters made their rounds. Time to go. Jakob pulled his derby down far over his brow, stuffed his hands into his pockets, and set out in search of cigarettes. Not too fast, not too slow. *Don't look suspicious.*

After obtaining his vice of choice, Jakob couldn't help but linger outside the shop to light up and take the first deep drag—a costly mistake.

A hit to the back of the head blindsided him. The gang had popped out from a side alley as if crouched on coiled springs, waiting in the shadows for their prey.

The Brooklyn boys beat Jakob within an inch of his life and left him in the gutter.

When he finally awoke, Jakob had only disjointed memories of that night—flashing images of being spotted by a street lamp lighter, carried to Kopel's apartment, and laid on a thick carpet before the fireplace. Kopel had called for a physician and cared for his younger brother with a surprising tenderness. Jakob had abandoned his family—he didn't deserve kindness. But Kopel was family too, and he wouldn't leave his brother.

The doctor prescribed pain medicine and ordered Jakob to rest in bed for at least six weeks. He had a broken femur, acquired while attempting to jump the alley fence to evade his attackers, as well as a severe concussion, a bruised liver, and a bloody ten-inch gash down his torso.

"You're a mess, Jakob." Kopel shook his head and tsk-tsked every time he looked at him, lying there like a pile of discarded clothes crumpled in a heap. Jakob didn't need the reminder. He knew Kopel was speaking literally—that his body was a mess of broken parts—but he was a mess on the inside too, and that kind of hurt was more challenging to face.

*How could I leave my family?*

To make matters worse, Kopel had married in the years since Jakob had last seen him, and his wife had a cousin living with them. A beautiful cousin. A beautiful, single cousin. Deborah was a flirt. She was also in charge of his care. Kopel was gone all day, working at the bank as a manager of acquisitions, whatever that meant. His lovely wife Rachel was forever chasing after their son David and visiting her aging mother down the street, leaving Debbie to nurse Jakob back to health. Jakob resisted at first—honestly, he did. He was too weak to act on impulse, anyway. But eventually, Jakob healed. And when he did, there was no denying the attraction between nurse and patient.

He was a terrible husband, a horrible father, and a wretched man. Jakob was disgusted with himself for having a secret affair with the cousin of his brother's wife, right under their noses and roof! Alcohol and pain pills created a perpetual haze in Jakob's brain. He could hardly remember his encounters with Debbie and wished she'd leave him alone. After a few dalliances, he managed to rebuff her advances, but he continued to heap guilt onto his shoulders in bucket loads. He was guilty of adultery and taking advantage of his brother's kindness. His femur wasn't healing well, and the medical bills were rising. He was a mess, indeed.

Kopel never pressed him about Mary and the children. He'd always been a private man and respected the privacy of others. Jakob figured his brother thought Mary had left him and returned with the kids to her Italian Catholic family in Southwark. Jakob let him believe it. The months went by. Deborah married a banker friend of Kopel's. She cried at her wedding, casting furtive glances over her shoulder at Jakob throughout the ceremony. What a mess. Did he ruin the life of every woman around him?

# CHAPTER TWENTY-SIX

## *At the Archives*

*August 2018*
*South Philadelphia*

Ensconced in the corner of the Philadelphia City Archives at Sixth and Spring Garden, Bella and Sophie hoped to find a record of Mary's arrest. They wanted information about her time in the House of Correction and the almshouse, as reported in the article. While they waited for an archivist to help them, Bella told Sophie about Tony.

Sophie's eyebrows shot up to her hairline. "Do you think your mom sent him over to the bar to meet you?" Under her breath, she whispered, "Smooth move. I'm impressed."

Bella chuckled. "Yeah, maybe. Ma's good like that. Probably bribed him with food. Anyway, he's really nice, but obviously, I'm in no place to start dating again. It's just nice to have someone to talk to—other than you, of course." Bella gifted Sophie with her full, dimpled smile.

"Is he cute?" Sophie batted her eyelashes.

"Well, yeah, he is. Actually, I think..."

The archivist approached their table. "I'm James. Who and what are we looking for today?"

James was an intelligent man with a sweet smile who acted as if it were his own relative they were searching for. After a detailed interview to determine what they needed, James went into the storage stacks with their notes to find evidence of Mary's arrest and incarceration.

Full of nervous energy, Bella walked around the room. The archive viewing room was well-lit, long, and narrow, with large yellow tables scattered in the center. On the outer wall, which was painted with a subway map, windows stretched high toward the ceiling. Bella could see the feet of pedestrians ambling along.

The inner wall boasted a hand-painted mural of historic city scenes with ladies and gentlemen dressed in period clothing, toiling at jobs that no longer existed. The milk and coal delivery men, the streetlamp lighters. Their sepia faces gazed out at Bella with challenging eyes. *What are you searching for?* They seemed to ask. *Why won't you let us rest in peace?* One woman, pictured with a brood of children in front of a water pump in a brick alley, looked over her shoulder with sharp eyes. *Mary isn't here. She's gone.*

A shiver ran along Bella's shoulders.

Sophie patted her arm. "Here, take my cardigan. You look cold." She draped her wool sweater on Bella's shoulders and steered her to the long table with their papers strewn about. Bella glanced back at the mural, but it shifted as the painted portion on the door moved. James came through from the bowels of the storage area, pushing a dolly stacked with dusty books of all sizes, wrapped in brown paper and tied with twine. Bella's nerves were on edge, and the mural creeped her out, but she was glad to see so many items for them to review.

"This is everything I could think of." James scratched his head. "Looks like you'll be here a while. I'm off to help the next patron, but I'll check on you later. Good luck." He returned to the reception area.

Sophie considered the large pile of books, about two dozen or so, and instructed Bella to lay them across the sizable yellow table. Then she chirped, "Well, let's dig in!"

Two hours later, with dust-covered hands and a dry mouth—drinks were forbidden in the archive viewing room—Bella uncovered something interesting. On the spine of the book were the dates *July 1897 – September 1897*, the time frame of Mary's arrest. She read the cover aloud, "This is the casebook of Dr. Ella M. Henderson, and private in nature. If found, please return to: Philadelphia Almshouse,

Insane Department, Women's Ward, Blockley Township, West Philadelphia."

Dr. Ella M. Henderson. A woman? *Huh, how interesting. I can't imagine there were too many female doctors back then.* The book was large, and the supple, brown leather cover so worn, it was as soft as silk. Dr. Henderson must have been one of the first female doctors of psychology in the city and must have needed to prove herself to the men in the field. Keeping copious records would have been an excellent way to provide solid evidence of her findings throughout her career.

Bella flipped through the pages to find that Dr. Henderson had organized her meticulous notes by date. The casebook was more of a diary than a medical journal. "Sophie," she whispered.

Sophie sat across the expansive table, thumbing through police reports.

"Didn't the article of Mary's arrest mention an almshouse?"

Sophie nodded.

Bella paged through the book with care, as the paper was razor thin, until she came to August 3, 1897, the day Mary would have been admitted to this doctor's care. There was nothing there—not one entry. Crestfallen, she almost closed the book, but something told her to flip one more page.

Not quite believing her eyes—or her luck—on the following page, she found an entry on August 5, 1897, which referenced the admission of an M. Lichtenbaum.

"Well, I'll be." Bella slammed her hand down on the table. "They sent her to a stinkin' *insane asylum!*"

"What?" Sophie came to see. "You've got to be kidding me."

"I can't believe it. Of all the ledgers and records and journals and whatnot in this archive, I found her, Sophie!" It was as if Mary had directed Bella to this book—to this page. Mary had led them on the journey to unlock the past and give her a voice—to give her *peace.*

Bella turned to the ghostly woman in the mural and gave her an insolent smile. "Evidently, you were wrong."

"Eh, what? Wrong about what?" Sophie asked.

"Nothing." Shaking her head in disbelief, Bella used her finger to follow the scripted text and began to read aloud.

*August 5, 1897*

M. Lichtenbaum

*Interesting new case today. Mary admitted yesterday with diagnosis of feeble-mindedness. Questioned by Magistrate Smith and transferred from House of Correction. SPCC charged neglect of children, ages 5, 3, and 1. Children starving. Mary refused food from non-kosher hands. Abuse. Children put in care of orphanage.*

*Mary won't speak. Physical exam determines exhaustion and undernourishment, dark circles under eyes. Otherwise, perfect health. Police report states she'd traveled with the children by foot for two days before they were found in distress by the Delaware River. Speculation of attempted murder by drowning.*

*I don't believe it. When I asked her to confirm or deny this string of events, Mary didn't answer. She stared at me with vacant black eyes. I conclude she's fully aware but unwilling to speak. On a whim, I gave Mary paper and a pencil and asked her to write her story for me. Will check in on her tomorrow.*

*August 6*

*No change in new patient. Nurse reports no problems. Patient refuses to speak. Whether she used the writing tools, I do not know.*

*August 15*

*Mary in acute distress and could harm herself. Placed in monitored cell with patient L.*

*August 22*

*Two weeks without speech. Released from monitored cell. I gave Mary more paper and pencils and asked her to draw herself. She drew a bird. Curious. Detailed and talented artwork. It is a black bird with beady eyes, spindly legs, and a long, thin bill. The bird is surrounded by marsh grass and shells. Mary wrote "oystercatcher" at the bottom of the page.*

*August 23*

*I asked Mary about the bird in her drawing. She didn't answer. I provided her with more paper and drawing pencils and have given permission for her to take an hour from chores every day for the exercise. Warden agreed to set her up in a corner spot with a privacy screen. I am hopeful that if she won't speak, she may at least draw or, perhaps, dare I hope, write.*

*August 29*

*Bout of fever throughout wards. Many women ill. No time for notations.*

*September 17*

*Women's ward has come through the fever. We lost three older women from 2nd Ward, suspected tuberculosis. Overcrowding makes confinement impossible. Back to usual rounds.*

*September 18*

*Checked on Mary today. I'm astonished. I thought, perhaps, she would draw the bird again, but no, she has made great use of the paper and pencils I gave her weeks ago, before the sickness took my attention away.*

*She has drawn dozens of scenes. Some landscapes—the moors of England, a ship at sea, a trestle bridge spanning a river, and tall brick buildings all in a row. But most are drawings of people. Fascinating people. A regal woman sitting with her feet up and smoking a cigar. A large, smiling giant behind a bar table. A bunch of children in a row at a church.*

*There is one face that Mary has rendered a dozen times—a handsome man with deep-knit dimples. Her husband? She gifted many drawings to her fellow patients. I see smiles throughout the ward, as if the*

## THE OYSTERCATCHER OF SOUTHWARK

*art has given my patients hope. I will find a way to plaster them on the walls, as we don't allow hooks in the dormitory.*

*September 22*
*Mary approached me in the hallway, surrounded by some other patients. They follow her around now as if she is a mother hen. Her "entourage," I named them. Her kindness in gifting the artwork has caused devotion among her ward. She still doesn't speak, but perhaps there is no need for words in this place? She handed me a bundle of letters. My interest is piqued. I must move on to 3$^{rd}$ Ward tomorrow—new women arrive in morning.*

*September 22, after hours*
*I am home, resting by the fire, with my dog at my feet. I have read Mary's letters. She wrote to her husband and to her child. Her words moved me to tears. No wonder she won't speak. She has suffered a great deal. Poor soul. It is against policy to allow patients to mail letters. I enclose them here, for safe keeping.*

A little bundle of letters bound with twine fell out of the casebook. Bella held them in her hands and glanced at Sophie, a look of wonder on her face. "Mary wrote these," Bella whispered. She tucked the stack under her folder of research documents, glancing around the archive viewing room. Instinct told her to take the letters, but it would be illegal and would disappoint their new friend, James, the jaunty archivist.

Sophie nodded at the papers. "Do it."

Without a second thought, Bella slid the packet into her messenger bag and zipped it up. James was still in the lobby, speaking with the receptionist about her weekend plans. Heart pounding, Bella whispered to Sophie, "We're going to *borrow* them, you understand? We'll return them tomorrow."

Sophie winked at her. "Whatever you say, boss." She tidied up the table, preparing for a quick exit.

# CHAPTER TWENTY-SEVEN

## *I Am No Bird*

*August 1897*
*Blockley Almshouse*

"Wake up, doll. Time to get moving." Dot nudged Mary's side with her knee, doing up the last buttons on her blouse while looking around the room at the women shuffling into line at the door. They'd miss a day's food ration if they were late for roll call. Disgusting as it was, it was still food.

"C'mon, Mary. We gotta get in line."

Mary whimpered at the intrusion into her blissful unawareness. She resisted waking.

"Aw, last chance, doll. I'm sorry, but I can't go without a meal again. Happened to me last week when they caught me flirting with the warden in the hallway. Old Redhead didn't like that one bit. Here she comes." With a final tap, Dot trotted off to join her compatriots at the end of the queue.

Mary awakened. She twisted on the cot to see the lunatics lined up in a row, in various states of alertness. The moaner and the mumbler stood side by side, always together, like Tweedledee and Tweedledum. Mary wondered if they could understand each other and imagined them reciting the characters' lines from *Alice in Wonderland*, "The oysters were curious too, weren't they? Aye, and you remember what happened to them. Poor things."

Oysters! Mary groaned and shook her head to clear her longing for home. Redhead was storming her way. *I am no bird, and no net ensnares me.* She repeated her mantra. *I am no bird.*

Within seconds, Redhead's face was close to hers. Her mouth contorted in a maniacal grimace, and when she spoke, spittle burst from her mouth and landed on Mary's cheek. "What do you think you're doing, lying about when it's time to get a move on?"

*I am no bird.* Mary sat up straight. She met Redhead's eyes, pushed past her as she stood, adjusted her shift—the same homespun garment with which Nurse C had adorned her the day before—and pulled on the leather slats. Redhead must have been shocked at Mary's pluck because she didn't move a muscle. She watched as Mary walked past her and joined the line of fellow miscreants. *I am no bird.*

Mary had read enough Brontë and Dickens to know how these fanatical overseers operated. She refused to crouch in fear before their cruelty. Redhead was probably abused as a child and had no outlet for her meanness, and Mary almost pitied her. Almost.

With a slight cough and a tightening of her hands on the baton, Redhead marched back to the doorway and led the women into the hallway. They obediently shambled behind her like a flock of sheep.

Once established between Helen and Her Majesty, Mary held her breath as someone placed breakfast under her nose. It was barely identifiable beefsteak, gray and slimy around the edges. She looked around at the other ladies tucking into the meal with alacrity.

"One gets used to it," Helen whispered.

"You must keep your strength up," Her Majesty added.

*Why bother?* Mary wondered. But she didn't say anything. No one spoke at mealtimes, and she had nothing to say anyway. She choked down two bites of meat and washed it down with water that smelled of garlic. She concentrated on keeping her meal down, not necessarily for the sustenance but to avoid the discomfort of retching again.

After the meal was over and the women started clearing their dishes, Mary spotted a tall, well-dressed woman with spectacles standing in the doorway with the warden. The warden was pointing to Mary and speaking with deference to the lady. She had an overcoat of peacock blue that dazzled Mary's eyes—too colorful for such a place.

The stranger nodded and approached Mary's table. "Mary Lichtenbaum?"

Mary nodded.

"You're to come with me. I am Dr. Henderson, and I'd like to examine you."

A female doctor! Mary felt a rush of pride in her sex. What an accomplishment! But her eyes did not relay her emotions. She kept them vacant and didn't speak. She couldn't show emotion—she didn't yet trust this person. To think she would be an ally was too much to hope for. Mary followed Dr. Henderson out of the cafeteria and into a small, bright office.

The room had three electric lights hanging from the ceiling—plenty to illuminate the small yet cozy and well-appointed space. Instruments for examination lay on a clean table in an organized row. A tidy desk sat in the corner, topped with a beautiful green blotter, a silver pen and ink set, and a large paperweight holding an open book. The page showed a drawing of a butterfly, dissected and with all of its parts neatly labeled.

But, most surprisingly, every inch of the walls displayed stunning artwork. Oil paintings, watercolors, charcoal sketches, pastels, and an impressive fresco. Despite her circumstances, the sight enchanted Mary. She pivoted on her heels, taking everything in. Each piece of art touched her heart and spoke to her soul differently. She hadn't expected to find beauty in such a place as Blockley, and the shock of it left her vulnerable. She closed her heart and dulled her senses. Until she knew this doctor's intentions, she could not reveal herself.

"Have a seat, Mary." Dr. Henderson pointed to the examination table. "Please remove your shift. This will only take a moment."

Mary watched as the doctor conducted a thorough examination. She peered into Mary's ears with a small instrument, looked into Mary's eyes with a little flashlight, and tickled her knees with a rubber hammer. Mary couldn't imagine what she was searching for, but eventually, Dr. Henderson must have found it because she nodded and sat at her desk, writing notes in a little leather-bound diary. "You may get dressed."

Mary recoiled at the thought of putting the wretched homespun dress over her head again, but she couldn't walk the halls naked. Once she'd again assumed the humiliating robe, she looked at Dr. Henderson and waited.

Dr. Henderson read from a paper with an official stamp on the top of the page. "It says here that you tried to drown your children in the Delaware River." She looked up with piercing blue eyes, the color of her outlandish peacock overcoat, which she had hung on the coat tree when they entered the room. "Is that correct?"

Panic rose in Mary's mind, and she almost burst into hysterics at such an accusation, but she kept her gaze steady and her face blank of all expression. She would give nothing to this woman until she knew she could trust her.

"You refused to feed them? Why?"

Again, Mary didn't respond.

Dr. Henderson made another notation in her journal, then closed it with a snap. With a feminine sigh, she removed her spectacles and said, "Well, I can't help you if I don't understand your circumstances."

Mary stared at her with owlish eyes, unblinking.

"You're dismissed, Mary. We'll meet again tomorrow."

Mary took a last wistful glance around the beautiful office, full of vibrant color and texture. Dr. Henderson must have noticed her interest. "Eh, Mary, would you perhaps write your story for me? If you're unwilling to speak, that is."

Mary peered at her, suspicious of her kindness and surprised by her sense of normalcy.

"Here, take this piece of paper and pencil." Dr. Henderson came around the desk and placed the items into Mary's open hand. "You may return them to me tomorrow. Now, please report to the kitchen. I believe you're on slops duty."

Mary reached out with shaking hands to accept the precious writing implements. She would write to someone straight away and beg them to pay the warden to release her from this cage. *I am no bird.* With a renewed purpose, Mary returned to the drudgery of the long, dark hallway.

# CHAPTER TWENTY-EIGHT

*Letters From the Loony Bin*

*August 2018*
*South Philadelphia*

Bella and Sophie hurried to their cars across the Target parking lot behind the archive building. The contraband documents in Bella's bag weighed a thousand pounds. She imagined James jogging after them. "Miss! There must be a mistake!" He'd flag them down, waving to get their attention. "You didn't mean to remove those historical documents from my archives, right? Not a nice lady like you?" He'd shake his head in disappointment. Bella's conscience was in turmoil. When had she become a thief?

Sophie didn't make it any easier. She giggled the entire time they hustled along. Bella shushed her, but then saw the laugh lines around Sophie's eyes and the spring in her step, and a reluctant smile broke out on Bella's face. Not for the first time, she marveled at her newfound cousin. At eighty-three years old, Sophie was fit as a fiddle, sharp as a tack, and twice as funny as any late night show host. Her zest for life and confident assurance told Bella everything would be okay.

The women slowed down as they approached their vehicles. "I'm sorry you can't stay with me this weekend, Sophie." Bella placed the messenger bag on the passenger seat of her VW, suppressing the urge to buckle the seatbelt, which would be ridiculous. "My ex is at the house moving his stuff out this week, and I'm staying with my college girlfriend in the suburbs. I know you're just as excited as I am to see these papers, and I'm sorry we can't be together to see them, but it's getting late, and I need to get out of the city before rush hour."

"Stop being such a nervous Nelly." Sophie leaned out of her rental car window. "I already told you I'm comfortable at the Hyatt, and I can wait until morning to see the papers. In fact, I believe you're meant to read them alone tonight." Sophie waved goodbye, and Bella watched her maneuver through the crowded parking lot like a rally car racer.

Unable to avoid traffic, it took Bella an hour to get to her friend's house. It was empty when she arrived, but the lights were on in the cozy yellow kitchen decorated with bright blue and white pottery. A note sat on the kitchen counter.

> At the grocery—lasagna for dinner. Nate stopped by. Told me to tell you, "Just sign the papers, Bells." Tried to be nice to him. Wine chilling in the fridge—figured you might need it. Be back soon.

Bella's good humor and excitement died away. Seeing her nickname written there—Bells—knowing *he* had spoken it—made her eyes water and her stomach lurch. *He has no right to call me Bells anymore. He gave that up months ago.*

She crumpled the paper and tossed it into the trash with more force than she intended, then poured herself a glass of pinot grigio and settled down to the task. Mary's letters were the most important documents in her life right now, not Nate's stinkin' divorce papers.

With awe, Bella pulled out the stack of papers from the messenger bag and untied the twine. She fanned them out on the table. There were three letters. Mary had written two to Jakob and one to Mollie. A ratty black-and-white photo of a somber woman lay between them.

"I've seen this face before." Bella's heart raced as she remembered the painting from her mom's attic. "Could it be?" She turned the photo over and read the writing on the back. *Second and Christian Street Station.* "Oh, my word, this is Mary's mugshot!"

She couldn't believe it. Immortalized in a mugshot from the

worst night of her life! "What a tragedy!" But, then again, there was something powerful about it. Mary had *survived*.

She opened the first aged page and was finally introduced to her great-great-grandmother.

*Mary Lichtenbaum*
*Philadelphia Almshouse*
*Insane Department*
*Blockley Township*
*West Philadelphia*

*August 5, 1897*

*Jacob Lichtenbaum*
*c/o Efraim Danzig*
*Market Street*
*Newark, New Jersey*

*Jakob,*

*Things did not go as well for us in Philadelphia as I had hoped. I will die here. They stole our little birds away and locked me into a cage. The children are gone—I don't know where. I'm bereft. If you hear of them, Jakob, you must send word to me! The address is above. Please plead my case to the warden. They must let me out so I can see the children! Surely, they have an ounce of mercy?*

*They will inform you that I am crazy—that I tried to drown the children. I did not! There is a kind doctor here, though I'm unsure if I can trust her. The doctor is a woman—can you imagine? She gave me this paper and pencil to write, as I refuse to speak in this dreadful place.*

*What happened is this: we were desperate at the river. Rocco found us. He pursued us. He caught up with us. In his jealousy and rage, he grabbed Mendel from me by force. He would have thrown him into the river, Jakob, I know it! The girls and I screamed. The police came. Then Officer McMurtrie came and brought us to the station, where I was separated from the children and questioned. When someone called McMurtrie away, two other men interrogated me for hours. One was the magistrate. I was distraught, exhausted, and hungry, and I couldn't answer the questions. They assumed I was insane. Insane! Me!*

*I laughed until I saw their faces. I vacillated between laughter and terrible tears, which made my position worse. The men spoke in hushed tones to each other, glancing over their shoulders at me. All the while, our babies were in the other room—alone?—or being fed who knows what by the matron of the station? My fingers itched to open the door that separated me from our little birds. I had to sit on my hands for fear I'd make a run for the door and cause my situation to be even worse.*

*All the while, the men continued to discuss me. To be taken as insane! To be unable to convince them otherwise—for everything you say can be twisted and turned until it is unreasonable and not what was intended. Then, Jakob, then, when you panic at not being believed, they point at you and say, "Aha! She's in hysterics. Consider her eyes—they are big as saucers. Her pulse is rapid, and her voice is trembling. She can't stop wailing. She is raving."*

*Questions crowded my mind. Where are the children? What will happen to them if we are separated? When I rocked forward and wrenched my hair—as you know I am prone to do when in great distress—the gavel came down and sealed my fate. "She must be insane. Put her away. The babes will go with the agency."*

*Jakob, there is no greater hell than this: When they condemned me to the asylum and took my children*

*and my freedom, they made me insane. Jakob, you did
this to us, and you are the one who should burn in hell.
I don't even know where you are or if the warden will
allow this letter to leave this wretched place.*

*I write this in sound mind,*
*Mary Lichtenbaum*

# CHAPTER TWENTY-NINE

### *The Madhouse*

*August 1897*
*Blockley Almshouse*

That night, in the darkness, Mary slipped the paper and pencil out from under her blanket. Dot had promised her a safe spot, a tiny candle stub, and a single match. Glancing over her shoulder to ensure Redhead was asleep in the corner—Mary could hear her rumbling snores from the middle of the room—she sneaked out of bed and joined Dot behind the screen. Dot was waiting for her. She placed the candle on the bedside table and ceremoniously handed Mary the matchbook, which Mary took with shaking hands.

She had a thousand words running through her mind and had to get them down on paper. At first, she thought she'd write her story for Dr. Henderson, imploring her to believe her innocence. The Duke and his cronies had accused her of abusing her children, framed her for the stabbing of a police officer, and tucked her away here. They wanted to silence her. She knew it was true. She'd beg Dr. Henderson to believe her. But when she placed her pencil on the paper to write the words, they would not come. The tale would sound crazy, and she would be handing them proof of her insanity—in writing.

She rubbed her hands over her face. She'd be blamed regardless of what she did.

Dot gave her an encouraging pat on the back, then settled in her bed, offering what privacy she could. Mary considered the page and started in. *Jakob, Things did not go as well for us in Philadelphia as I had hoped.* What a cathartic feeling to release the horrible story onto paper, to propel her accusations across the page, to give in to her anger, and to beg for mercy. When she finished, Mary folded the letter. She never wanted to reread it, but was relieved she'd birthed the words into the world. Someday, someone would read them and understand.

The next few weeks went by in a blur, every day the same. Wake with the sunlight, shake off the bedbugs, don the leather straps, and shuffle to the dining hall. Hold court with Helen and Her Majesty, choke down foul food scraps, labor at chores until her fingers were red and raw, and retire to her pallet in the ward, then fall asleep to the sounds of Tweedledee and Tweedledum moaning and mumbling. The drudgery would drive her mad. She was sure of it. *That's how this works. They drum up a reason to stuff you here and then make you insane to prove their diagnosis.*

She had to hold onto something, tether herself to sanity so she wouldn't go adrift like so many other women. Some may have genuinely been mad before coming to Blockley. Nurse C certainly seemed so. There she was now, speaking to the door as if it were an old friend. Maybe Her Majesty as well, but not her sister. Helen was as sane as Mary. She had thrown herself into this place, shackled herself to this fate, for the love of her twin. What heroism!

*I will survive this cage. I am no bird.*

But try as she might, Mary's mind began to slip as the weeks passed. Dot took special care of her, inviting Mary into her sanctum and brushing her hair at night with even strokes. The motion calmed Mary's frayed nerves and was a balm to her broken heart. The tears finally came during one such session. Mary had kept them at bay, fearing if she let loose her emotions, her mind would dissolve with her tears. Perhaps she was right. Dot sat beside her on the bed and patted her back, but Mary couldn't stop. The tears turned to sobs, and the sobs turned to moans. By morning, her throat was hoarse, and her eyes burned, but the moaning continued. Some other patients stopped by Dot's corner room, checking in to see what was amiss. The older ladies shook their heads with knowing eyes. They'd seen it all before. Perhaps they'd hoped Mary would be spared.

Dr. Henderson arrived by mid-morning, along with two strong men, to retrieve the broken Mary and escort her to a small room in a section of the almshouse she'd never seen before. It was a cell with a padded wall and two cots, one on each side. A tiny window let in light from high up in the thick wall. A large woman occupied the other cot, tied to the bed with some sort of muffler, her hands over her belly. Mary balked at such an apparatus and tried to shake herself into alertness. But she couldn't. She hardly cared what happened to her anymore. Her moans became sobs again, and the entire process threatened to start over.

Not unkindly, Dr. Henderson directed her to the empty cot and told her to rest. She left with the two strong men and locked the door behind her. At the sound of the key clicking in the lock, Mary fell into a daze and knew no more.

*Mary Lichtenbaum*
*Philadelphia Almshouse*
*Insane Department*
*Blockley Township*
*West Philadelphia*

*August 20, 1897*

*Jakob,*

*They had me in a room with another woman. She moaned every night. Then I realized she was me. I was the moaning woman. I wasn't well for some time. Dr. Henderson says it was a time of difficult transition for me. I am much better now because I understand why I am here. I have accepted my fate.*

*Blockley is my purgatory, and I am here for penance. I was never Jewish, Jakob. I'm sorry. I tried to transform myself for you, but I am a Catholic. I disowned Jesus and betrayed him and must pay for my sins. Having my children taken from me—isn't that payment enough?*

*I will die of sorrow, but Dr. Henderson is kind to me. She gives me paper and pencils to draw. She tells me I will one day go home. To heaven, I wonder? Where is my home? To keep myself occupied, I play the little rhyme game the girls used to play. Do you remember? "Polly want a cracker?" I ask the walls. The walls don't answer.*

*-Mary*

*Dr. Henderson says she will give my personal effects to you when I die, as you were are my husband. So, I assume you will see this letter. Jakob, I forgive you. Now let me rest in peace.*
*~Mary*

A curious sound came from the hallway. Four or five women from Mary's ward rushed to see what the commotion was about. Before them, Nurse C lay on the ground, convulsing and foaming at the mouth. Her eyes rolled back in her head, and her limbs jerked and contorted. Her abdomen was rigid in the air, as if an invisible string attached to her belly button pulled her to the ceiling. The *thump thump* of her arms and legs on the hard floor had drawn the spectators.

Mary and Dot pushed through the crowd and were at Nurse C's side as quickly as they could say jackrabbit. Mary had never seen anything like it before, but she and Dot took Nurse C's arms and held her tight. Mary looked around for a clue as to what might have happened. A bucket had tipped over, and murky water cascaded down the hallway as if searching for a crevice to escape this hellish place. Nurse C's favorite mop, which she'd recently called "Hector," lay broken in two beside her flailing body.

In her fit, Nurse C choked as if she couldn't get air. Instinct took over. Mary heaved Nurse C into a sitting position despite her rigid muscles that fought against it. Dot called to her roommates, barking directions for someone to find a leather strap to keep their friend from choking on her tongue, bring a damp cloth, and—for God's sake—fetch Dr. Henderson. The women scattered in different directions to do as commanded.

Mary looked over Nurse C's flopping body and made eye contact with Dot. *What do we do?* Her eyes asked.

Dot shrugged and held tight to their friend's arm. Mary prayed.

"She's gone." Dot returned to the dormitory, rumpled and disheveled. Dr. Henderson had arrived in time to prevent Nurse C from choking and instructed Dot to assist in lifting the patient and carrying her downstairs to the infirmary. Redhead had joined them, wordlessly lifting Nurse C's feet. The three women had held the convulsing girl in an awkward dance of jutting limbs and shaking bodies. Yet an hour later, Dot gave the distressing news.

Mary couldn't believe it. No one could. The entire ward was silent.

"Dr. Henderson said it was epilepsy. A shaking disease. Must have happened before 'cause it was in Nurse C's record, and the doc wasn't surprised it'd happened." Dot fought back a sob, her hand to her mouth. "Her name was Cecilia. The 'C' was for Cecilia, not 'Crazy.'" She raised her eyes and surveyed the room, challenging each woman to face the truth. "We're all gonna die here."

Mary went to her and wrapped her arms around Dot's shoulders, leading her to the little corner where she could have some privacy and rest. It would do no good to scare the others.

Throughout the night, many of the inmates came to Dot's space to check on her and receive comfort from Mary. They'd all loved Nurse C and mourned her death. Though Mary was still silent as the grave, she now possessed a calm presence that hadn't been there before. Since her heroic efforts to save Cecilia, Mary seemed at peace with her destiny at Blockley and even—could it be?—that she had a purpose here. One by one, the others drifted behind the screen, sat on the bed next to Mary, and basked in the peace and strength emanating from her. Sometimes, Mary held their hands or patted their backs. Other times, she made the sign of the cross and bowed her head in wordless prayer. No one ever asked her to speak. But from that night on, Mary became the mother hen of the women's ward.

As the weeks and months rolled by, Mary met with Dr. Henderson often. The two women had struck up an unlikely friendship, perhaps because of their shared love of art. One day, the doctor surprised Mary with a gift. "I have something for you," Dr. Henderson said as she reviewed Mary's recent drawings in her office. "These are beautiful, by the way. It's amazing what you can do with charcoals."

Mary looked up from the table in the corner, where Dr. Henderson had created a space for her to work. The doctor handed Mary a small package wrapped in brown paper. Joy tugged at Mary's heart. It was rare to receive a gift at Blockley. She gave her friend a tentative smile, then opened the wrapping. Inside was a gorgeous collection of colored pencils—an entire rainbow of colors!—and a stack of quality paper bound in twine. She looked at Dr. Henderson, her eyebrows raised. This was an extravagant offering.

Dr. Henderson leaned against the examination table and crossed her arms as if defending her position. "Mary, you've transformed the ward." She waved her arms as if taking in the cavernous space upstairs. "I've seen the drawings you've done for your roommates. I've seen the renderings of their loved ones—some in great detail, down to the scars and warts! I've enjoyed the landscapes with vast skies, sloping hills, and wide rivers. I know you draw every night after lights out. The warden knows about Dot's contraband candles." At Mary's look of alarm, the doctor chuckled. "Don't worry, at our monthly meeting, he declared, 'Watching that girl sketch is the only form of entertainment the lunatics at Blockley can expect in life.'"

Mary looked at her hands, a blush blooming on her neck. That the warden's words made her heart swell confused her. She should hate her jailor, but knowing he had offered praise made her feel proud.

The doctor continued, "Mary, you've given them something important. Something priceless from their life *before*. You've given these women hope." The doctor's eyes teared up, and she looked away. "I know you won't speak, Mary." She turned back to look Mary in the eye. "But you communicate your care and concern for your fellows through art. And that is an extraordinary gift."

Mary prized her colored pencils more than she'd coveted anything in her fancy apartment in Newark. They were proof that kindness still existed in the world. Her drawings covered every inch of the walls, and the women in the ward—especially Dot—took turns tackling Mary's evening chores so she could have time to draw before the sun went down. Mary found purpose in bestowing artwork to her ward-mates and solace in their company. But, best of all, when the room was quiet at night, and everyone was asleep, Mary often lit a candle in her corner oasis and drew Jakob. She'd finally captured his eyes like she never could do when they were young and in love in Southwark. She'd mastered his strong chin and his regal eyebrows. Despite herself, Mary still loved him, and somehow, over the next few years at Blockley, she found it in her heart to forgive.

*Mary Lichtenbaum*
*Philadelphia Almshouse*
*Insane Department*
*Blockley Township*
*West Philadelphia*

*November 18, 1897*

*Dear Mollie,*
*My darling daughter, I see you every day. You run and laugh and play with your sister and baby Mendel. I see you having a grand time and being well cared for. I must believe the images I see, or I won't make it through the day, the month, the year.*
*Dr. Henderson has been kind to me. She has given*

*me paper and beautiful colored pencils to draw with. I can't bring myself to speak here, and my mouth won't utter a word in front of another person in this dreadful place. I sometimes talk to the Lord at night. I pray often—and I draw.*

*I have drawn everything I can remember—my childhood home in Italy, the chickens pecking around the dirt courtyard. Mama, bending over the pot, stirring the oyster stew. Papa, sitting at the table, speaking with Giuseppe. I sketched a beautiful scene by the river—the gulls diving for fish. And I drew Jakob, your father, with his glorious dimples. I can't bear to draw your face or those of Sarah and Mendel. For me, the pain is too great. I see you in my heart and mind but can't capture your likeness on paper.*

*I've learned much about myself here at Old Blockley. In my life before, I had many nicknames. Folks always named me after a bird. Father called me his nightjar, a strange choice, but a bird he loved from our home in Italy. It's a funny-looking bird, reminiscent of an owl, and loves the dark. I remember learning of its unusual habit of abandoning its eggs on the ground without a nest to provide safety. Is that what I have done to you, dear one?*

*Some now call me a loon since I'm housed in a place full of loons.*

*My favorite name was given to me by Cenzo—do you know him? Cenzo nicknamed me oystercatcher. It was because I had the errand of purchasing the oysters and other fish for the grocery on Fridays, but the oystercatcher is my favorite bird. It is long and sleek with simple black wings. But when it flies—oh, when it flies, it reveals its secret! The white stripe across the wingspan can be seen from the ground. What a striking sight. It resembles the cross on Calvary. I'm sorry I never taught you of Jesus or his Mother.*

*And now, here I am—nightjar, oystercatcher, loon. I am caged and no longer able to fly. I transformed myself too often, dear daughter, and lost sight of my authentic self. The complications of my life crowded my mind, and I buried my identity deep inside.*

*I loved my family, and I worshiped Papa. I planned to care for the family using my knowledge and talents. I hoped to better our circumstances and get us out from under the Duke and his men. I feared Rocco.*

*I loved my books and wanted to live in all of the landscapes where I found my heroes and heroines—the haunting moors of England, the exciting ships at sea, the beautiful Arabian nights, the wild islands in the Caribbean where one must hunt and catch his food to survive. I was a dreamer, and part of my mind would get lost in such lands.*

*I loved your father, Jakob. He says he loved me from the moment he first saw me. He did, in his way, but he never understood me. He swept me away from my nest—my home, my kin. Somehow, I allowed myself to be beholden to him, like Papa with the Duke. I was never Jewish, my dear one. I tried with all my might to keep a kosher home for his sake. That's what he wanted. But, in my secret heart, I wasn't being genuine. I attempted to transform myself to keep Jakob, and I failed. My white wing stripe was always there, hidden, until I took flight.*

*And now, my body can no longer take flight. I am in a cage. But, dear Mollie, my mind, my soul—these inner parts of me can always take flight. See, I am free inside, which matters more than anything. The God of the Hebrews is the same God I love. I understand that now, and I trust His plans for man's salvation. I am at peace.*

*You have your whole life before you, my Mollie. Take flight! Take flight! Look after your sister and baby Mendel. Never look back.*

*With love forever and always,*
*Your Muter*

# CHAPTER THIRTY

*Lasagna Dinner*

*August 2018*
*Newtown Square, PA*

Bella dropped the last letter onto the coffee table, curled up into the corner of her friend's couch, draped a blanket over her legs, and let the tears come. She wept for Mary and her great trials. She mourned for Nana, who'd thought her mother would have drowned her. She cried for all the injustice in the world—for the hardship of women. She grieved for her failed marriage, her lost innocence, and dreams that would never come true. She mourned the loss of her baby and let go of the guilt that had burdened her for so long. It wasn't her fault. She hadn't killed her child. The thought had permeated her blood for the past few years and seeped into her being. But it was a lie. Bella accepted the truth and allowed it to wash over her with a gentle caress. She would have loved her child with a passion, and she would have been a wonderful mother, just like her nana—just like Mary.

One phrase from Mary's letters came to her mind.

*I lost sight of my authentic self. The complications of my life crowded my mind, and I buried my identity deep inside.*

"I buried my identity deep inside," Bella repeated. The statement resonated with such intensity that she laughed and shook her head in wonder. The words were exactly what she needed to hear. Mary's story was tragic but not wasted.

Bella sat up a little straighter and dried her eyes as realization slammed into her. *This* was the lesson she had needed all along. All this time, with all this research, she had thought she was finding Mary—to free her silenced voice from the confines of history, to give her freedom. But, sitting on her girlfriend's sofa, Bella realized Mary had been reaching for *her* all along. Mary had given her a gift—to learn from her trials and keep fighting for her identity.

Bella's heart filled with great peace and thankfulness to her ancestor. She placed the letters back into their sacred pile, tied them up with the fraying twine, and stored them in the messenger bag. Her cellphone buzzed, and she saw Tony's name on the screen. He was probably calling to check on her and hear about her research. They were talking daily now, and Bella experienced a fuzzy thrill whenever she listened to his voice. *Take it slow, Bells.* For now, she wanted to sit in the quiet of this cozy room, let Mary's words rest in her heart, and wait for her girlfriend to come home. A lasagna dinner with a good friend was the perfect way to end the evening.

# CHAPTER THIRTY-ONE

---
From the Desk of Elisabetta Paragano-Cassia
Norfolk, Virginia
---

January 2, 1966

Happy New Year. My year started with a memory from more than sixty-five years ago. Can it be true? It was autumn—I remember that—in the year 1900. I was a young lady, in love with my beau and planning our wedding. Mama and I were laboring to clean out the market that morning. The Paragano grocery had failed a few years before. Papa had returned to the street sweeper gang to keep us clothed and fed. That he had to work once again under such circumstances was too much for him to bear. He died of a heart attack in the street, alone. We mourned him. Of course we did. I wore black for a year, like Mama and my sisters. But I didn't cry. My tears had all been spent the night Mary and the children disappeared.

Manny, Michael, and I swore never to speak of what we saw at the river. It was too dangerous to implicate Rocco in a crime. My brothers seemed to forget over time. They were young, after all. But I didn't forget. I knew something terrible had happened to Mary, Mollie, Sarah, and Mendel, for I never saw them again. I believed Rocco must have killed them all right there at the river. I thought I alone could have saved them, but my silence had betrayed them. The sight of Rocco in the neighborhood, roaming around as if he had never done wrong, made my stomach twist and my blood boil. I was afraid of him, yes, but more enraged at his evil soul. After a few weeks, Rocco disappeared too—never to be seen in Southwark again. I often wonder what happened to him.

Anyway, as Mama and I were clearing out the detritus of the grocery, I found a box of old ledgers and documents with notes written in Papa's scrawling hand. There, under the stack of papers, I saw the newspaper article.

Mama observed my demeanor change from across the room. I had gone still as a stone. I stood, mesmerized—drawn to and repulsed by the newspaper. As Mama closed the distance between us, I read the headline in my mind.

"Her Pitiful Story. Homeless with Three Young Children. Picked up by Police...the Youngsters Provided for by the SPCC."

Before I could hide the paper away, Mama read the story over my shoulder. She collapsed against the counter, a hand to her heart. "Sebastian!" Mama raised her fist at Papa's ghost. "You should have told me! My girl. My Mary!" She slumped down onto the floor in sobs. I went numb with grief.

Papa *knew*. He knew what had happened to Mary and the children that night. Yet he did nothing, said nothing. I wasn't alone in my betrayal. Papa had done the same as me.

What could I do? My heart cried out to God. *Lord, have mercy! Forgive my silence.* If I'd told Mama what we'd seen that night, if I'd confronted Papa, perhaps he'd have done something to protect Mary and the children.

But it was too late. I sat on the floor next to Mama, and we cried and cried until our tears ran dry. But the Lord gave me strength as evening fell outside, and we grew calm. My destiny was laid out before me. I would petition the warden of the asylum for Mary's release and write Mary a letter every day. I'd find the children, bring them home, and raise them as my own. This would be my penance—the payment for my silence. I'd make this right. I'd spend my *whole life* making this right. I spoke these promises out loud, and Mama grew strong. We stood up, clinging to each other, determined to get started.

I grabbed a pen and paper and wrote a letter to Mary. After that day, I sent dozens of letters to Mary. For years, there was nothing but silence from Blockley until one day in 1902 when it was almost too late.

                    *Elisabetta Paragano*
                    *1144 S. 8th Street*
                    *Southwark, Phila*

*Mary Lichtenbaum*
*Philadelphia General Hospital*
*Insane Department*
*34th Street*
*Phila*

                    *December 16, 1902*

*Dearest Mary,*

    *You are not alone, my sister. You have not been forgotten. There has not been one day that has gone by these past five years that we have not thought of you, prayed for you, or fought for you. We didn't know where you were for three years, Mary. We found a newspaper article in Papa's belongings about the horrible events of that tragic night. We have been lobbying to get you out ever since.*

    *Your children are alive. Mama found them in an orphanage where they had lived all these years. We will get them, and—I swear to you—I will care for them until they are grown.*

    *Papa died of arrhythmia a few years ago. He fell while cleaning the streets, clutching his chest. Our market hadn't been faring well, and he had returned to Valero, begging for his old position. I don't know which was worse—that he died in such a public way or that he had gone back to the Duke to begin with.*

    *The doctor says you are dying. She contacted Mama this morning. The warden will allow a letter to get through to you. I have written you a weekly letter for the past two years since we learned of your plight. Blockley returned each one to me unopened. Mama found them once—a thick pile of envelopes under the dresser in our room. She cried, and then she burned them.*

*Now that you are departing this life, we can send you words of comfort. How alone you must be! Five years! But you were never alone. Jesus and his sweet Mother were with you always. They never left your side and will now attend to you on your journey to the heavenly kingdom.*

*Mary, there is something you should know. The warden has also contacted Jakob. He is alive and has lived in Maryland these past few years with his brother Kopel. He has agreed to retrieve little Mendel—to raise him as a father should. Mama and I attempted to find your husband for years but never could. For good or ill, Jakob will now return.*

*Let these earthly troubles go, dear Mary. The children will grow and prosper, and your memory will live in their hearts. The Lord will take you home to rest.*

> *Be at peace.*
> *Your loving sister,*
> *Lizzy*

# CHAPTER THIRTY-TWO

*The Return of the Father*

December 1902
Saint Vincent's Orphan Asylum
Tacony, Philadelphia

I'm here to retrieve my children. The name's Jakob Lichtenbaum."

The sister's eyes widened, and she bit her lower lip as Jakob thrust his booted foot into the door frame to prevent it from slamming in his face. Then she nodded and opened the door. Jakob wasn't sure a nun would do such a thing as slamming a door in someone's face, but he wasn't about to take any chances. Since the moment Efraim Danzig had opened the door to his apartment and laid eyes on Jakob with a look of such scorn that it took Jakob's breath away, he anticipated animosity from even the kindest of souls.

The nun escorted him into the hallway, then pointed to a regal mahogany chair and asked him to wait as she spoke with the prioress. Jakob took a moment alone to survey the entryway and take deep breaths to calm his nerves. An impressive three-storied brick building with a columned portico, Saint Vincent's Orphanage sat on a bucolic site next to the river, north of Philadelphia. The lawns behind the building sloped down to the river, offering plenty of room for children to play. His children.

A decorated Christmas tree stood in the corner, with shiny red ornaments, garland, and tinsel. Festive wreaths adorned every door down the hall. It was a jolly site, to be sure, but it reminded Jakob of the glaring religious difference between him and the institution. This Catholic orphanage was no place for his three Jewish children.

Before learning of their fate, he'd spent the last five years in a haze of guilt, melancholy, and whiskey. Jakob had left his family in the care of Efraim and Edna, assuming he'd return within a few days, or at worst, a few weeks. And now, here he was, five years later, hoping—praying—his children would recognize him, forgive him, love him.

A few months before, in the fall of 1902, while working as a teller in his brother's bank, Jakob had envisioned his wife walking through the front door, regal and strong, her black hair wild about her head and her dark eyes piercing his soul from across the room. He missed Mary. She'd been his first love—the only woman Jakob admired. He'd wanted to respect her mind and talents, the parts of her that first drew him to her, but he'd obsessed over how things looked to outsiders. He'd needed to fit in with the crowd in Newark. The fellas had wives who cooked, cleaned, and cared for the babies at home, kept a kosher kitchen, and knew their role in the family. There had been no room for Mary's novels and artwork in that environment. He'd worn her down bit by bit—and he'd done it intentionally.

Although he'd worried about her and the kids over the past five years, the truth was, Jakob knew deep in his soul that they were better off without him. And so, he'd let them go over time, along with his broken heart.

When Kopel approached him at the teller desk on that cold December day in 1902, Jakob knew his brother was the harbinger of terrible news. Jakob slowly lowered his pen and closed the ledger book in which he'd been recording figures, all the while keeping his eyes locked on Kopel's. Without a word, Kopel nodded toward the staff room. Jakob stood, pulled the shade down over his station window, and followed like an automaton. Once inside the private room, Kopel handed Jakob the letter. The address read *Blockley Almshouse, Insane Department, Philadelphia.*

Jakob looked at his brother, eyebrows raised.

"Read it," Kopel ordered. He walked to the sideboard and poured himself a glass of water.

Jakob had to read the words three times before they broke through the fog in his brain. Mary was dead. They'd confined her to an insane asylum for five and a half years—had committed her weeks after he'd left. "Argh!" A dagger of shame sliced through Jakob's heart. He snapped his head up, looking at his brother for the truth. "The children?"

"In an orphanage."

"Blazes! Mary!" Jakob stood up and grabbed his brother by the collar. "How long have you known?"

"Take it easy, brother. The letter arrived a few weeks ago. I suspected something bad like this when I saw the return address, and I wanted to protect you—cushion the blow—so I opened it. I made some inquiries about the children and found them."

"Tell me everything."

For the two days it took to get his affairs in order and make the travel arrangements—no small accomplishment with the holiday rush—Jakob could neither eat nor sleep. Not only was he grieving the death of his wife, but he had to dismiss the horrible images he'd conjured up regarding his children's welfare. He hopped on the *Marylander* train to Philadelphia's Thirtieth Street Station, where he would pick up a regional line to Tacony, just north of the city.

On the platform, Jakob offered a weak smile as he waved to Kopel. He battled nausea and resisted the urge to take a slug from his flask. By the time he reached Philadelphia, his nerves were raw. The journey had been a blur as the train rattled down the line, past scenic views and waterways, and finally along the Delaware River to its destination. He hopped off the regional train at Tacony Station and walked the few short blocks to Saint Vincent's. His mantra during the trip: *They are well, and I will get my act together. We'll never be parted again.*

Jakob wasn't sure what he expected when the nun opened the door. A slap on the face for abandoning his children? Surely not from a Catholic nun. A smile and instructions to remove the children from the property immediately so more orphans could take their place? Maybe. But nothing, *nothing* could have prepared him for the prioress's response.

When Jakob presented his credentials and asked to see his children, she simply said, "No."

"*No?* You must be joking." Jakob laughed and wiped his sweaty palms on his trousers. He looked around the hallway as the prioress escorted him to her office.

"It's not that simple. Please, have a seat." The sister spread her arms out in a benediction of sorts, pointing to the settee across from her desk.

Jakob sat in the oversized leather chair and surveyed her well-appointed office.

"I'm Sister Juliette, in charge of this orphanage. When the authorities brought your children here in August 1897, we baptized them within days of their arrival."

Jakob cleared his throat. "Baptized?" His voice sounded froggy, like he had something lodged in his windpipe. "What do you mean, baptized?"

"It's a religious rite, sir, claiming the soul for Christ through the waters of baptism."

"Well, I'll just claim them back then." Jakob fidgeted with his hat in his lap, twisting it in circles.

Sister Juliette smiled and laid her hands out on the table. *It's like she's showing her hand in a game of poker.* Jakob didn't know much about Catholicism and wasn't sure what the problem was.

"Mr. Lichtenbaum, we have cared for your children since they arrived. Of course, they have had religious education, and they have expressed their desire for Communion. Mollie will be old enough to partake next year. And Sarah has an interest in a religious vocation. She asks many heartfelt questions for one so young. So, you see, they love the Lord Jesus fiercely and wish to serve Him. Their Aunt, Elisabetta Paragano, has expressed a most fervent desire to raise the girls in the Catholic faith. She has delayed her marriage to do so properly.

Her letter arrived only last week. We have made arrangements for her to retrieve the girls this week."

Jakob looked at the woman as if she had three heads.

"Your son may return home with you, Mr. Lichtenbaum, as Mendel is too young to take Communion or to declare his own convictions about his faith. But I regret to inform you that your daughters may not leave with you. They are Catholics." She smiled. "Do you understand? I cannot release the girls to a Jew."

The force of her words hit Jakob like a blow to the head. "I am their father. How could you even say such a thing? Do you mean to say they will become nuns? I don't understand this arrangement." Jakob stood up, confusion and rage filling his chest. "I demand to see my children. Right *now*."

"Of course, but the sisters and I want to prepare the children first. They are not ready to see you unannounced after so much time has passed."

The rebuke punched Jakob in the chest and stole his breath. He'd abandoned his children. What kind of father would leave his children? Jakob repeated the mantra in his heart. *They are well, and I will get my act together. We'll never be parted again.*

"I'll be back first thing in the morning. I expect to see my children at that time."

"As you wish, Mr. Lichtenbaum. There is a respectable boardinghouse down the road by the train station. Look for the black wrought iron fence. If you let Mrs. Bohms know I sent you, she will accommodate you tonight." Sister Juliette stood and nodded a dismissal. Jakob hadn't noticed, but two large men had entered the room behind him and stood waiting by the door. They weren't wearing religious garments, so Jakob assumed they were security guards. He tipped his head to the nun in respect and let the guards escort him from the building.

*Jakob Lichtenbaum*
*Bohms Boardinghouse*
*Tacony, Phila, PA*

*December 23, 1902*


*Kopel Lichtenbaum*
*42 East Biddle Street*
*Baltimore, MD*

*Kopel,*
*I write with a cleaved heart—half devastated, and the other half exhilarated.*

*Five-year-old Mendel—my son!—is asleep on the bed in my room in this boardinghouse. I have been sitting here, watching him sleep, for an hour. He is beautiful. He looks like a prizefighter, with solid, chubby hands and a noble brow. Our parents would be proud to call him their own. Now, I finally know what you feel when admiring your son David. It's a peculiar feeling to have a piece of your heart walk the earth outside your body.*

*We leave on the morning train. Please extend the hospitality you have shown me to your nephew, at least while I save and look for suitable lodging. I want to live near you so our sons will grow up together and our family will be close. You and Rachel have been there for me. You never abandoned me, and I thank you for that.*

*I will endeavor to be a good father to Mendel. You are my role model, and I hope you don't mind, but I will look to you for guidance in the coming days. I haven't had a drink in two days, and though my hands are shaky, I feel good. Strong. I can do this. I will do this for my son.*

*You may wonder why I have not mentioned my daughters in this letter. Kopel, they are alive. I saw them with my own eyes today at the orphanage. They are divine little doves. My girls! Oh, fate has wrenched my heart from my chest! Mollie is all grown up—a lady of ten years. And Sarah, dear Sarah, right behind her. She looks to Mollie in all things. I fear she may not be as strong as her elder sister. She resembles Mary. And Mollie looks like me. She has my nose, of all things, can you imagine? The poor girl. But she is beautiful despite it, and I love her all the more for it.*

*They are not with me here and will not travel with us tomorrow. Yesterday, when I arrived at the orphanage, I presented myself, a bit forcefully perhaps, to the nuns and demanded they release my children to me at once. The head matron brought me into her office and told me the girls had already committed to their faith, and the order could not release them to a Hebrew. My skin itched, and I wanted to tear it off. I was beside myself with shock and anger. How could their Catholic God claim my daughters? Will they become nuns? I didn't quite understand. I wanted to scream. With great restraint, I allowed her strongmen to lead me away without much discussion, with the arrangement that I would see all three children first thing in the morning.*

*As you can imagine, I paced back and forth in this room all night. Weary and wary of the whole affair. With the dawn, I shaved and shook out my suit coat, shined my shoes, and combed my hair. I looked every bit like a respectable father when I rang the bell at their intimidating door for the second time. My heart fluttered like a bird trying to escape its cage. I was wild with anxiety over seeing my children.*

*I expected the nun to present the children to me upon entry to the hall, but no, they weren't there. Confused, I looked about when the great lady took my elbow and led me through the building. From the far end of the hall, she took me through a doorway onto a beautiful sloping lawn, which led to the river. The sun was high in the sky, and its light sparkled on the frost covering the ground. Chunks of ice floated along with the current of the mighty Delaware. It was a gorgeous sight. It looked as if angels were smiling down on the troupe of little ones playing under a tree. The orphans joined hands as they swung around in a circle, singing a morning song with smiles and giggles. It was an enchanting scene, full of peace and purity.*

*I spotted them then. My three little children—my Mollie, Sarah, and Mendel. I knew it was him because he was between the girls, and they were laughing and pulling him this way and that way in the circle, teasing as only siblings could. He loved their attention and threw his head back in laughter. The sister left me on the back stoop, staring at the charming sight like a nitwit. She approached the nun leading the whimsical group and whispered in her ear. The black-robed ladies both looked at me as they spoke. Their eyes showed compassion, not judgment, and my heart warmed. A large chunk of guilt fell from my shoulders. I hadn't realized how heavy it was. I stood straighter when it was gone and awaited my fate.*

*Presently, the prioress brought the children to me, hand in hand. I expected Mollie to run into my arms, but Kopel, she didn't seem to know me, and Sarah clung to her sister's skirts. My heart shattered into a thousand pieces. The girls refused to speak or even look at me. Is it possible to move forward from such grief? It is. Mendel put his chubby little hand out to shake mine. I removed my glove and grasped his hand, holding it like a lifeline.*

*Kopel, they are well, and I will get my act together. My son and I will never be parted again.*

*Your Bruder,*
*Jakob*

# CHAPTER THIRTY-THREE

*And in the End*

September 2018
Lansdowne, PA and Bristol, PA

Bella and Rosalie waited under a regal pine tree in All Saints Cemetery. It stood guard at the head of Mary Lichtenbaum's grave, where she was buried with her daughter Sarah, who had died at twenty. Bella fiddled with a pinecone in her hands, turning it around and around, thinking how this journey had come full circle. Bella and Rosalie watched as Sophie placed her hand on the cold stone, closed her eyes, and relayed a quiet message from Mary's son, her beloved cousin, Mendel. They couldn't hear much, but the intent was clear.

*You were never forgotten. I loved you my entire life. Be at peace.*

Bella had made the arrangements. Rosalie hadn't met Sophie until now. She had kept tabs on her daughter during this journey and cried when Bella revealed everything she and Sophie had learned about Nana's childhood. Mary's tragedy and the family's separation had broken Rosalie's heart.

Later, when her tears were dry, she'd said, "I need to meet Sophie."

So, there they were, quiet mourners huddled around the grave of Mary Paragano, whom they had never met but finally understood. After fifteen minutes or so, Sophie broke their reverie. "Okay, let's go eat. I'm starving."

Rosalie chuckled and turned to Bella. "Where is this place again?"

"We're driving up to Bristol in Bucks County. I made reservations for us at the King George Inn."

They lunched at a table facing the river at the inn, formerly known as Delaware House, where, for a short while, Mary had found peace and the possibility of a new life. She'd enjoyed a respectable vocation and a haven for her precious little ones here. Bella could picture Mary wiping the dark mahogany bar, straightening white tablecloths, and lighting little candles. What was it like for Mary to finally find a home, only to have her past hunt her down and drive her out? Bella could only hope she'd brought Mary some peace by finding the truth of her story and bringing it to light. She looked over the table at Sophie, her face animated as she talked about her beloved cousin Mendel, Nana's little brother.

"Mendel grew up in Chicago." Sophie pushed her empty plate aside and took a sip of cold water. "Jakob moved him there after living with Kopel in Baltimore for a few years. I think he was following a woman. Anyway, Jakob remarried in Chicago and started a new family. He became engrossed in the Socialist Labor Party and even ran for commissioner under the ticket one year in the 1920s. Mendel had no time for politics. He chose to become a prizefighter instead."

Bella laughed. "A prizefighter? Do you mean a *boxer*? You're joking."

"No, really. He went under the nickname Kid Menny and boxed in the heavyweight class from 1918 to 1920. Legend says one night, after stumbling home with a severe concussion and a massive shiner, his wife forbade him to ever step into the ring again. While wiping the blood from a gash at the corner of his eye, she announced she was pregnant. He never boxed again."

"Oh, that's so sweet," Rosalie chuckled. "What did he do with himself after that?"

"Well, he turned his attention to the art of selling furniture. During the next few decades, he became known as the King of the Bedroom—much to his wife's extreme embarrassment." Sophie winked while Bella and Rosalie laughed. "Although it wasn't for his prowess *in* the bedroom, but his ability to outsell the competition with sales *of* the bedroom. It was a luxury for families to have a bedroom set in those days. I found this article during my last foray into the archives." Sophie pulled a crisp newspaper copy out of a folder in her bag.

A handsome man in his eighties smiled out at them from the page. Bella raised her brow at Sophie and reached for the paper. "Sure, take a look. It's an interview upon Mendel's retirement in 1976."

Bella stared at the man in his dated seventies clothing, enormous eyeglasses, and pocket protector. He had an impish look, like he was hiding a secret or about to crack a joke. So much like Nana. Bella loved him immediately. In the article, the local journalist asked Mendel to name the key to his success at eighty years old. Mendel's answer confirmed Bella's suspicions about his sense of humor. "'I gave the customers a good performance when they walked into the ring.' He chuckled and corrected himself, 'I mean, when they walked into the *store*.'"

That Mendel had become a loving family man with a successful business didn't surprise Bella. After all, his sister Mollie's life had turned out the same way.

Bella sat back in her chair, enamored with Nana's brother Mendel. She listened as her mom told Sophie the details of her own life—growing up in a large Italian Catholic family, with Nana at the head. She'd brought photos to show their new-found cousin, and she handed one across the table while Bella cradled her cup of hot coffee. Nana, about sixty-five years old, dressed to the nines—complete with heels and pearls—stood at the kitchen counter, trussing a colossal turkey and winking for the camera.

Rosalie sighed. "I miss her. Without breaking a sweat, she could whip up a meal to feed a brood of six children and countless grandchildren. Mollie was generous and kind, sharp as a tack, and humorous too. She was the love of her husband's life, and we all adored her."

Bella wondered how these beautiful people—Mollie and Mendel—had survived such horrors as children yet blossomed into gracious, successful adults with so much love and laughter to share. She looked out at the river, the mighty Delaware. Those same waters had seen her great-great-grandmother struggling with three little children and a brutish man who would've drowned them all in his jealous rage. The men in Mary's life had failed her for sure. But looking across the table at her mom and Sophie, Bella knew in her heart that God had not forgotten Mary. He had been with her through it all and had protected her children.

Bella's heart swelled, and she felt the weight of tears behind her eyes. It was too much. To hide the emotion, she turned her face toward the window.

The waters of the river called to her.

Bella excused herself from her elders, who were laughing together, heads bent over a photo of a crazy family reunion thirty years ago at which an uncle had thrown Bella, fully clothed, into the pool. She hitched the messenger bag over her shoulder and left the restaurant, then wandered down the sloping lawn of the riverbank.

It was a beautiful day. Clouds across the sky hid the sun at intervals, casting dappled shadows over the water. As she walked to the river's edge, long, lush grass tickled Bella's ankles. She knelt and rummaged through her bag until she found what she was looking for. She extracted the divorce papers, grabbed a pen from the bottom of the bag, flattened the documents on her knee—and finally signed them.

It was done. A weight slid off her shoulders as the second piece of her new identity fell into place. *Click.*

As Bella placed the papers back into the folder, a melancholy settled over her heart. No husband, no baby. She was hopeful about Tony, but their relationship was still new and awkward. Apart from her mother and Sophie, she was alone. Tears pushed past her reserve and flowed down her cheeks onto the grass. Bella rummaged in her bag for a pack of tissues and spotted the ragged edge of a yellow-lined page peeking out from the back—Nana's letter. *My mother was going to drown us.*

Bella sat down on the grass and straightened the page before her on the ground. "It wasn't true, Nana," she whispered, reading the words on the page as she wiped the tears away. "Your mother didn't try to drown you." A sob wrenched from her chest. "We discovered the truth—Mendel's cousin Sophie and me. Your mother loved you, Nana, and would have died to protect you."

Bella took a ragged breath and considered the soothing water, flowing along as if nothing ever changed—or would ever change. And the peaceful reality hit home. "I think you knew that already, didn't you?" She looked up at heaven, smiling through tears. Was it possible that her baby knew the truth too? That she would never have hurt him and that she would love him forever? *Nana, please look after him. My baby!*

Bella kissed the paper with Nana's shaky handwriting scrawled across the page, crumbled it, stood, and threw it into the river. She watched it drift away down the Delaware. It got stuck momentarily, whirlpooling in an eddy as if deciding which way to go. Finally, it sailed downriver—toward Philadelphia, Southwark, and home.

# CHAPTER THIRTY-FOUR

*Vengeance is Mine*

*September 1897*
*Southwark, Philadelphia*

Rocco climbed the familiar stairs with nervous energy. The Duke never sent the Tucci brothers to get him in the middle of the night. Accepting orders from the brothers—who stood on either side of him now, escorting him up the narrow, dark-paneled staircase of Valero's downtown office—didn't come easy to Rocco. His blood boiled. Now, he was nervous *and* angry.

The Tucci brothers stopped at the top of the stairs, rapped on the massive oak door of the Duke's office, and then turned to him with smug smiles. Rocco wanted to wipe those smiles off their faces.

"We'll be waiting right here." Lorenzo Tucci snickered under his breath. His brother winked—winked!—at Rocco.

"Why, I oughta…" Rocco drew his arm back to pound the man's face in, but the brother restrained him.

A scuffle ensued until the door opened, and Bill Valero stood inside the door frame, scowling at the men like a stuffy schoolmarm. "Leave off and get in here, Rocco."

The Tucci brothers moved away from Rocco with obvious disappointment. Rocco heard Lorenzo tell his brother, "Don't worry, *Fratello*, we'll have our turn. This won't take long."

Rocco's shoulders tensed. *This won't take long? What the heck is going on here?*

The Duke had a chilly smile plastered on his face. He ushered Rocco into the elaborate office and offered him a seat in the gilded chair—the chair where recruits sat when given their initiation into the organization. Rocco hesitated. He sat down, sweat beading at his temples. *Why am I sitting here? This can't be good.*

Then Rocco spied a third man in the room. He was leaning against the enormous green marble fireplace with the antique clock on the mantle.

Officer Sullivan McMurtrie.

*What the devil is he doing here?*

McMurtrie grinned and gave Rocco a little bow.

Rocco's fists curled on the arms of the chair as silence filled the office.

Valero broke it by offering espresso and a cigar. Rocco shook his head, but Valero handed him the items anyway.

He downed the hot espresso in one gulp, burning his throat. He didn't care—pain kept his wits sharp, and he'd need his wits about him right now.

He put the cigar in the ashtray on the little table next to the chair, hoping there'd be time for it later.

"This is an unlikely alliance, Duke. What kind of business could you possibly have with a Democrat from the Fourth Ward?"

"Why, profitable business, of course. What other kind is there?" Valero took a puff of his cigar. He rounded his desk and sat in a leather chair, then put his feet on an ottoman. While he got comfortable, McMurtrie circled the room, appraising paintings on the wall, picking up objects from the bookshelf, turning them over in his hands, and nodding.

*This is the first time he's ever been in this room. What is that Irish git doing here?*

As if he read Rocco's mind, Valero said, "You may be wondering why Officer McMurtrie has joined us tonight." Valero took another pull on his stogie. He nodded for the policeman to finish the explanation.

Sullivan cleared his throat, rocked back on his heels, and announced the most surprising statement Rocco had ever heard. "Well, now, my boys and I managed to convince Bull McBride and our friends from the Fourth Ward to throw their votes behind your Duke here in the upcoming election for Congress."

Rocco coughed. "What?" He couldn't believe it. There was no way the Democratic Irish boss would back the Republican Italian Duke. *What was the price of that bargain?*

The Duke saw Rocco's expression of surprise. "It's true. Seems as though revenge against a certain someone in my ranks was worth the price of support."

"Revenge against a certain...someone...?" Rocco squirmed in the seat.

"Yeah, Sully here was upset about something that happened down by the river and figured he may want to see justice done."

"The river?" Rocco whispered.

"The very place. Seems you've been spending some time down by the water, Rocco. You must like it there."

Rocco's heart raced. "If this is about that *puttana* Mary, I'll..."

He never finished his threat. Lorenzo Tucci came from behind and gave Rocco a cuff to the side of the head. Rocco hadn't even heard the brothers enter the room. He shook his head to clear the ringing in his ears.

Sullivan advanced on Rocco, stopping inches from his face. "You stabbed one of my men. Thought you'd get away with it, didn't you?"

"You aren't gonna kill me, are you?" Rocco sank in the seat, fear settling in his bones.

"Kill you?" Valero placed his hand over his heart. "What kind of man do you take me for? No, I've got something better planned for you, Rocco." Valero took another pull of his stogie. "I'm sending you up the line. The boys will take you to Manhattan and see you're settled in with the gang up there."

Rocco let out a deep breath. He would keep his life. But leave Southwark? He'd have to start at the bottom! He'd be a peon—all his hard work to build himself for nothing!

"But...."

Valero yawned. "I'm tired, Rocco, and it's almost three in the morning, so I'd best be getting home before the missus starts to worry that I'm seeing some showgirl on the side." He stubbed his cigar in the ashtray and stretched his back, then came around the desk and made a show of choosing a hat and walking stick from the coat rack by the door.

The Duke laid his hand on Rocco's shoulder. "It's been a pleasure working with you, Rocco, truly it has, but business is business, you understand." Then he smiled a rueful smile. Rocco stood in protest, but the Tucci brothers pushed him back into the seat, hovering one on each side.

"McMurtrie and the boys will see you out."

With that, he tapped his stick on the floor, tipped his hat, and left Rocco to his fate.

# EPILOGUE

*Mollie*
*May 1977*
*Lansdowne, PA*

"Happy Mother's Day!" her family exclaimed as Mollie walked into the living room, drying her hands on the kitchen towel. Her old heart skipped a beat when she saw her adult children and their families hiding around the room, smiling like loons. Mollie had expected her son to come for lunch, but not her daughters and their families. She surveyed the scene, spotting at least five of her grown grandchildren and their little ones, her great-grandchildren. How wonderful!

Her husband Frank stood beaming beside the rickety piano as if he had conjured their offspring out of thin air. Mollie smiled at him, the warmth in her heart overflowing onto her face. Their daughter Julia pinned a corsage to her dress, winked, and returned to her seat.

The great-grandchildren danced about, excited to show her the next surprise. Their mothers shushed them. "Wait, wait!" Frank sat down at the piano to play. His clear tenor rang out true, singing, "Little Mother of Mine."

Tears streamed down Mollie's face. This was a day to bless mothers everywhere. She knew he serenaded both his momma—long dead now—and her, the mother of his beloved children.

> *Sometimes in the hush of the evening hour,*
> *When shadows creep from the west*

*I think of the twilight songs you sang*
*And the boy you lull'd to rest;*
*The wee little boy with tousled head,*
*That long, long ago was thine;*
*I wonder if sometimes you long for that boy,*
*O little mother of mine!*

Choking up at the piano, he played the melody on the keys as his voice grew silent.

*Oh, my dear husband. What a long and beautiful life we've shared.*

With a little flourish of his hands at the tune's end, Frank turned to the audience of his progeny crammed around the little parlor and bowed, tears in his eyes. Then he looked at his wife, leaning against the kitchen doorway with a dishcloth in her hands. His wrinkled eyes showed what was in his heart—*I love you* was written on his face. It was almost too much emotion for Mollie. Blushing, she turned her attention to the little ones.

They were hungry and ready for lunch. Mollie cleared her throat. "Well, my beloved ones, I hope you enjoy peanut butter and jam sandwiches because that's all we have to share with so many unexpected guests today."

The kids cheered at this news, but her granddaughter, Rosalie, playfully chastised her. "Now, Nana, would we have invited ourselves over on your special day without planning for a meal to feed a crowd? Salvatore's Seafood will deliver pasta, clams, and oysters at noon. Your favorite." She winked, a twinkle in her eye.

The children grew restless, clamoring for their sandwiches, as Frank and their youngest daughter, Penny, exchanged furtive glances and asked everyone to please sit down again for the presentation of a special gift. He reached behind the piano to pull out a large, framed picture wrapped in brown paper. Frank motioned Mollie to the davenport, where he presented the gift. Penny stood before her mother, rolling onto her tippy toes in her old childhood habit, too excited to stay still. Mollie gingerly slid her nail below the tape. A hush fell over the room. She nudged the thick brown paper away to reveal a portrait of a woman painted in deep blues.

She sucked in her breath and bit her lip to keep from crying out. Her mother gazed out of the frame through space and time. Her mother, Mary, whom she hadn't seen since she was five years old. Since that fateful night in the station house when she'd fallen asleep against the bench with her little brother and sister and woke to a sense of loss too significant to put into words. Her mother was right there, alive in the frame. She seemed solemn, strong, beautiful, and...at peace. Mollie was speechless, and the room fell quiet while she stared into her mother's eyes.

"Muter," she whispered in a small voice. She smiled at Penny. "How...?"

"Dad found the tattered photo the orphanage gave you. I'm glad you didn't notice its absence. I've had it for a few months," Penny admitted with a sheepish grin. "Anyway, I hope you like it?"

Before Mollie could answer, Frank stepped closer and whispered, "It was my idea. I wanted to give your mother dignity."

At that moment, the doorbell rang, breaking the spell cast over the family. The children ran to the door in a flurry of giggles and smiles, their parents following—old Salvatore himself was delivering the food for lunch. He had a habit of singing a song to the children in the old style of the fishmongers of Italy. At the song's end, he handed taffy to the children.

Frank kissed his wife on the forehead, then followed the children to settle accounts with Sal. Mollie ignored the exodus. Her mother's face enthralled her. Little Bella, the youngest of her great-grandchildren, stayed behind from the group and climbed up onto the sofa, sucking her thumb. They could hear Salvatore singing on the porch. "Leche Leche Ladi-a-La, Fresh-a Fish-a, Baccala."

Bella studied the portrait wide-eyed, then looked at her great-grandmother. In her precious two-year-old voice, she asked, "Nana, who is *dat*?"

Mollie propped the portrait against the coffee table at her feet and gathered the sweet girl into her arms, snuggling tight, her chin resting on the child's fluffy head. Together, they gazed at the portrait. After a moment, she answered. "That, my little oystercatcher, is your great-great-grandmother—*my* mother, Mary."

Bella considered her, head tilted to one side, as if Mollie had told her it was a painting of a fairy. Like most young children, it hadn't occurred to her yet that her Nana would've had a mother of her own.

"*Your* mama?" Bella asked skeptically.

"Yes, Bella." Mollie kissed her head. "Someday, when you are older, I will tell you all about her. I promise."

# A WORD FROM THE AUTHOR

This is a work of fiction, but much of the story is true. Mollie was my great-grandmother (Nana), and Mary was her mother. So, what's real and what's not?

My great-great-great-grandfather, Rafaele (the model for Sebastian), was a seminary student in Salerno, Italy when he spotted Filomena (Florentina), "the most beautiful girl in the world," and changed course to marry her. He immigrated to America before his family and settled in Southwark, where he worked as a street sweeper. History tells us the street sweepers of this period worked under the "Dukes of South Philly," a trio of Italian-American brothers who had significant influence in the city.

The *padrone* system and political machines were standard in America in the late nineteenth century, and one can assume Rafaele toiled under a "boss." Thankfully, Rocco is a purely fictional character. Rafaele eventually opened a corner grocery at the house on South Sixth Street, where his family joined him. The market failed, and Rafaele returned to work for the Duke, dying of "heart disease" while sweeping the streets of Southwark.

Mary was the third daughter of Rafaele and Filomena's thirteen children. She and her sisters worked in a Jewish Quarter sweatshop where Mary met Joseph (Jakob). Joseph had immigrated with his older brother from Warsaw in 1886, just as the Russian *pogroms* against the Jews were heating up. When Mary was sixteen, the couple eloped to Newark, where Mollie was born a few months later. The reason for the elopement is speculative. Was her father such a stern Catholic that he disowned Mary for becoming pregnant before marriage? Was it because she loved a Hebrew? Was there pressure from an outside force? Mary never used her maiden name; all historical documents—marriage certificate, her children's birth certificates—list her with a different last name of German or Polish origin. Was Mary hiding from someone? Or was she trying to put her painful past behind her and assume a new identity as the wife of a Jewish man?

Mary and Joseph's children, Mollie, Sara, and Morris, were raised in Newark in relative financial security until suddenly they were penniless. Family rumor has Joseph either owning a tavern or spending a significant amount of time in one. He may have been an unsuccessful businessman or a gambler. He was also heavily involved in the Socialist Party and ran for office in his later years.

For whatever reason, the young family's circumstances changed, and Joseph left. A few weeks later, the Southwark police found Mary in distress with her three young children. Family legend said Mary had tried to drown her children in the Delaware River before being committed to an asylum, but historical records do not mention the river. Mollie and Sara spent five years at Saint Vincent's orphanage. As a child growing up in the area, I was obsessed with the story. Their brother Morris (Mendel) was a mystery, and their parents even more so. The women in my family assumed Mary's husband was a scoundrel because he had abandoned his family.

The story died with Nana in 1988—she was ninety-six years old when she passed, and I was thirteen. She'd never spoken of her father, Joseph. He was a ghost. For me, however, Joseph wasn't the real scoundrel of the story. It was Mary. How could a mother plan to drown her children? Was she crazy? Was she evil? A shudder went up my spine at the thought of it whenever I passed the river where I imagined the desperate scene had taken place.

Years went by, and I became a mother myself. Love for my children is the driving force in my life. I wondered what desperation had driven Mary to the river, and I realized Mary had no voice in our family. She'd been silenced by shame and time, and I felt a deep calling to free her from the confines of history. As I experienced the ups and downs of my marriage, I thought perhaps, just perhaps, her husband wasn't a bad guy. Maybe it wasn't as simple as that. Maybe

Joseph was a complicated man. Perhaps he and Mary both struggled with mental illness, addiction, or depression. They were people, after all.

Then, in 2016, as I was taking my daily walk in the neighborhood, I heard a man's voice in my mind. He spoke to a buddy and said, "I'm gonna marry that girl." It was Joseph, and that was the beginning of this story. It took its time, and there was much to do, but eventually, the story began to emerge.

My mom, Anita, and I spent countless hours researching, studying, reading, and learning. We had help from many corners and discovered beautiful revelations along the way. The best surprise was Phylis, who found Mom on an online genealogy site. She was a descendant of Joseph and grew up knowing and loving Morris, my Nana's long-lost brother, whom Joseph had freed from the orphanage.

Mom and Phylis were a dream team. They met up, became friends, and fearlessly pursued history. We found a part of our lost family. Phylis reminded us of Nana—the resemblance was startling. Thank God Mom and Phylis found each other when they did because Phylis passed away from cancer in 2020, a heavy loss.

Three original documents are recorded word for word in the novel apart from name changes. Anita found Nana's letter in which Mollie claims her mother tried to drown her; Phylis found the newspaper article in the *Philadelphia Evening Item* at the national archives, which describes the police finding Mary and the kids on the streets of Southwark; and I found the SPCC's report that documents Mary's arrest. Mom and I found the Blockley ledger showing Mary's intake information at the Philadelphia City Archives.

It was real—it was all real.

> *An excerpt from Mollie's letter: "Mother eloped at age 16. The next I remember is where we lived in Newark was Polly want a cracker. Phila & my Mother was going to drown us. Police picked us up. 3 of us my Broter Morris my sister Sara and me."*

The research journey of Bella, Rosalie, and Sophie mirrors the actual events of my mom, Phylis, and me, but they are fabricated characters. Their personalities and life experiences capture the collective spirit, hopes, dreams, and struggles of the female population of my extended family.

Every family story and tidbit my memory holds is woven through this work. My Grandmom Edna's kitchen appears in the Newark apartment. My Pop Pop, Nana's husband, sang the fishmonger's song when he bounced his grandchildren on his knee. Their daughter painted the portrait of Mary, which hung above the mantle in the family home for generations. We have a vinyl recording of Pop Pop playing the piano and singing "Little Mother of Mine."

A few mysteries remain. Why did Mollie think Mary was going to drown her and her siblings? Had they spent time at the river in distress, and Mollie's five-year-old mind imagined such a thing? We'll never know, but I hope this novel provides a plausible reason for what she believed. Mom and I couldn't solve the mystery of where Morris lived before Joseph came to claim him. We know from the register of Blockley that Mary was sent there with baby Morris in her arms, but later, he disappears from the records. Was he moved to a children's ward? Was he transferred to the orphanage with his sisters? To avoid confusion and simplify the storyline, I have Mendel going with his sisters to the orphanage immediately.

The biggest mystery is how Mary and her three children traveled from Newark to South Philly. Did Mary spend her last pennies on train tickets for herself and the children? We have no record of her travels across those eighty-three miles. It's unimaginable that a distressed mother with three children under five could walk that far. They would have had to break up the journey. A stop over in Bristol, Pennsylvania, made sense.

The Delaware House stood proudly on the river in 1897, owned then by Mrs. Sophie Lincoln (Mrs. Oliver), who captivated my attention. Although she was an actual person, her personality, interests, illness, and everything else about her and her children in this novel are fictional. I imagine she was a force to be reckoned with, and Mary would have been drawn to her like a magnet.

Like the Delaware House, the Biddle family home, Andalusia—occupied at the time by Charles and Letitia Biddle—would have stood on Mary's path to Philadelphia. I've elaborated on Andalusia's gardens, adding the intricate hedges. Letitia was an avid gardener but did not start the garden club until 1904.

During our research, my mom found a long-lost cousin, Dennis, the grandson of Mary's sister Congetta (Elizabetta). Through Dennis, we learned that Congetta brought Mollie and her sister out of the orphanage and raised them as her own. Congetta went on to care for dozens of foster children with her husband over the decades. Mollie grew to be a beautiful and faith-filled person because of the love of her aunt.

Mollie and her husband Fred raised their children in the Catholic Church. No one in our family knew she was from a Jewish family until Mom met Phylis. It's a miracle that a child who suffered so much—who was separated from her parents and lost her siblings—could grow to be a great-hearted and forgiving woman. I believe this is the redemption God offers to all creation, whatever our expression of faith. This hope has been carried throughout history, and it can never be silenced.

# SPECIAL THANKS

Without the intense research efforts of my mother, this book would not exist. She is the keeper of family information, and I am forever grateful for the many questions she's answered over the years. Mom is my biggest fan and best promoter. My parents and brother—Richard, Anita, and Michael Colahan—are never surprised when I accomplish something new. "Of course, you did, Erica." Their unfailing belief in me built the foundation of my confidence.

I am eternally grateful to Phylis Banish, whom we lost too soon. She was immediately family to Mom and me due to her generous heart and larger-than-life personality. I wish we could have had more time. She is missed.

Thank you to Dennis Hartig, the grandson of Mary's sister Congetta, who brought a wealth of information about Congetta's role in raising Mollie and other orphans throughout her lifetime. Dennis put another piece of our family puzzle into place through his research efforts.

And to our cousin Jim Grueff, who spent countless hours editing my work. His eagle eyes and sharp mind helped to mold my first few drafts. Thank you, cousin Ken Maginnis, for the enhanced photos of Mary and for preserving your mother's painting of our ancestor.

A huge shout-out goes to my beta reader, Liz Colahan, the sharpest high school English teacher in New England, who made my day when she gave the final decree of, "It's gorgeous," after reading my first draft. I'm incredibly grateful for her time and enthusiasm. And thank you to Ken at the Philadelphia Archives—I'll never forget your joy when Mom and I found Mary in the Blockley ledger.

Thank you to Hope*Writers, WFWA, CWG, and the Scribes group at ACFW—especially Susan Sloan and Alyssa Schwarz—for teaching me the craft of writing. And to author Kimberly Duffy, who graciously took the time to review my work. Your insights and critiques have been priceless. Marsha Hicks, I'm so glad you recommended Hope*Writers to me! Leslie's Ladies—never forget, we can do hard things!

Writing a novel takes an enormous amount of effort (and coffee), and I couldn't have done it without the support of my family and friends. Thank you to my in-laws Bob, Maryann, and the Ruggieri clan; Chandler Colahan and my extended family—especially the Greg Colahans, Triss, and Kate and Mark Neustadter; and to Sarah and Jason—thanks for helping me get started!

To my church family at Ascension—your graceful compassion and unwavering faith have taught me, challenged me, and comforted me throughout my adult life.

Thank you to the friends who show up—Jenn and Jim Sawyer, Heather and Eric Keller, you've always had my back; my cousin Jenica—my sister—your wit and wisdom have gotten me through some tough days. I could not navigate this life without you, Jonathan, and your precious kids. To the local moms, Stefanie Garity, Lauren Borden, Pam Gifford, Melinda Moran, Jill Ross, and Jeanette Vergis; to Caroline Pauley, Jill Mowery Haywood, Jonel Thaller, Lorraine Sikora, Tammy McCauley, Sheri Girgenti, the SwanBio team, Doreen Bourbon, Allison Adamousky, Kim Conti, and Anne Chmielewski—you inspire me; and to Colleen Sutor, the best hairdresser (and confidant) this side of the Mississippi, who always said I should write a book.

To Melanie Qualls Wolfe, my best friend since the dawn of time, or pre-K, whichever came first. I'd been encouraging her to write for decades until I realized I was actually encouraging myself. She's my mirror, my greatest critic, and my number-one cheerleader. To quote our favorite SNL skit: "Go do it and be successful with it."

To my new friends at Chrism Press—Karen Ullo, Rhonda Ortiz, Marisa Stokley, Rebecca Martin, and David and Roseanna White—thank you for taking a chance on me. I am indebted to you, and I'm happy to be so. Karen and Rebecca, you are incredible editors, and this story has significantly benefited from your hard work. Roseanna, thank you for perfecting my vision of the cover. It's stunning!

And to my family. Tom: "Where there is love, there is no question" (Harbhajan Singh Yogi). Jr and Bella—you've brought joy to my life, and I have a mother's heart for you. And to the beautiful souls I am blessed to call my children: Earthly words don't exist to express my love for you. Jake, Ryan, TJ, James, and Sophie—you are my world.

And finally, to Mary—I pursued you through time, and you reached right back to touch my life during a difficult season. I wish you could have lived in a time of equality between men and women and in a society that smiled upon the marriage of a Catholic girl and a Jewish boy. The world is kinder now, but we still have much work to do. Some old wounds only God can heal. Thankfully, the Lord goes before us and prepares a way. He's the ultimate giver of hope and abundant life.

Made in the USA
Monee, IL
19 March 2025

14282675R00184